Basil Frederick Albert Copper was
Copper moved with his family to Kent, where he attended the local grammar school and developed an early taste for the works of M.R. James and Edgar Allan Poe. In his teens he began training as an apprentice journalist, but with the outbreak of the Second World War, he found himself put in charge of a local newspaper office while also serving in the Home Guard. He then joined the Royal Navy and served as a radio operator with a gunboat flotilla off the Normandy beaches during the D-Day operations.

After the war, Copper resumed his career in journalism. He made his fiction debut in *The Fifth Book of Pan Horror Stories* (1964) with "The Spider," for which he was paid £10. His first novel, a tongue-in-cheek crime story in the Dashiell Hammett/Raymond Chandler mode, *The Dark Mirror*, was turned down by 32 publishers because it was too long, before Robert Hale eventually published a cut-down version. Four years later, in 1970, Copper gave up journalism to write full-time.

Copper published some fifty novels featuring the Los Angeles private detective Mike Faraday and also wrote several horror and supernatural novels and a number of collections of macabre short stories. His horror fiction in particular has been receiving renewed attention recently with new editions from PS Publishing and Valancourt Books. Basil Copper died at age 89 in 2013 after suffering from Alzheimer's disease.

Basil Copper's *The Great White Space* (1974) is also available from Valancourt Books.

Stephen Jones is a prolific editor of horror anthologies, including PS Publishing's two-volume *Darkness, Mist & Shadow: The Collected Macabre Tales of Basil Copper* (2010), and the author of *Basil Copper: A Life in Books* (2008), which won the British Fantasy Award. His books have previously received the Hugo Award, several Bram Stoker Awards, and the World Fantasy Award.

NECROPOLIS
Basil Copper

illustrated by STEPHEN E. FABIAN
with a new introduction by STEPHEN JONES

VALANCOURT BOOKS
Richmond, Virginia   2013

Necropolis by Basil Copper
First published Sauk City, Wis.: Arkham House, 1980
First Valancourt Books edition 2013

Published by Valancourt Books, Richmond, Virginia
Publisher & Editor: James D. Jenkins
20th Century Series Editor: Simon Stern, University of Toronto
http://www.valancourtbooks.com

Library of Congress Cataloging-in-Publication Data

Copper, Basil.
Necropolis / by Basil Copper ; illustrated by Stephen E. Fabian ; with a
new introduction by Stephen Jones. – First Valancourt Books edition.
pages ; cm. – (20th century series)
ISBN 978-1-939140-50-0 (acid-free paper)
I. Fabian, Stephen E., 1930- II. Title.
PR6053.O658N43 2013
823'.914–dc23
2013016688

Cover art by Christopher Balaskas
Set in Dante MT 11/13.2

INTRODUCTION

ALTHOUGH best known as an author of macabre short stories and Lovecraftian novels, Basil Copper was also the author of two popular detective series, set almost half-a-century and two totally different genres apart.

Born in London on February 5, 1924, Basil Frederick Albert Copper soon moved with his family to Kent. "Little Willy", as he was affectionately known, attended The Tonbridge Senior Boys School, where he contributed early fiction to the school magazine, took part in the amateur dramatics, and was a member of The Leicester Football eleven.

When grammar school failed to satisfy his wide range of interests, Copper started haunting the local bookshops and libraries. A voracious reader, he soon discovered the works of Algernon Blackwood, M.R. James and Edgar Allan Poe, whose influence was to serve him well in later years.

While attending a local commercial college, he learned book-keeping, economics and the useful skills of shorthand and touch-typing, which proved invaluable when he began training as an apprentice journalist. With the outbreak of World War II seeing so many reporters conscripted, Copper soon found himself in charge of a county newspaper branch office at the age of seventeen, while also serving in the Home Guard.

He then joined the Royal Navy, in which he served for four years in Light Coastal Forces in Newhaven, Portsmouth and Portland. Having completed a course at the Glasgow Wireless College, he mostly served on gunboats and torpedo boats, and he was a radio operator on board a motor gunboat flotilla off the Normandy beaches during the D-Day operations. While escorting the first wave of landing craft ashore, Copper's flotilla lost half its six craft, mostly to acoustic mines.

After going on survivor's leave, he subsequently spent two years on radio stations in Egypt, Malta, and Gibraltar, before demobilization. Having contributed pieces to the London *Times* since the outbreak of the war, Copper resumed his career in the provincial press, working for the *Sevenoaks News* and the *Kent and Sussex Courier* before rising to editor of the Sevenoaks edition of the *Kent Messenger*. He also contributed to three national newspapers: the *London Evening Standard*, the *Evening News* and *The Star*.

Basil Copper made his debut as a fiction writer with "The Spider" in *The Fifth Book of Pan Horror Stories* (1964), for which he was paid the princely sum of £10 by the editor, Herbert van Thal. Around the same time, he began writing his first novel while working in the newspaper office. He set out to write a tongue-in-cheek crime story in the Dashiell Hammett/Raymond Chandler mode entitled *The Dark Mirror*. When it was completed, he sent it to thirty-two publishers, who all turned it down because it was too long. After he made four attempts to cut it down, Robert Hale eventually published the novel in 1966. His writing career took off, and four years later he gave up journalism to write full-time.

The Dark Mirror launched a series of hard-boiled thrillers featuring Los Angeles private investigator Mike Faraday, an obvious and acknowledged homage to Chandler's Philip Marlowe. Although critics admired the author's authentic descriptions of the City of Angels, Copper had in fact never been to California. All his knowledge was gleaned from watching old movies and referring to maps. The first book was popular enough to spawn a series and, over the next twenty-two years Copper produced fifty-two volumes, often at the rate of two or more books a year, until the series ended in 1988. Faraday's charm as a tough protagonist and poetry-quoting narrator, ably supported by his faithful secretary Stella, proved popular with readers in other countries as well, and the books were translated into numerous foreign-language editions.

American author August Derleth had begun writing his series of stories about consulting detective Solar Pons (whose name in Latin literally means "Bridge of Light") in the late 1920s after he received a letter from Sir Arthur Conan Doyle stating that there would be no further tales of Sherlock Holmes. Derleth's Pons was closely modelled on Doyle's character—he lived at 7B Praed Street, not far from Paddington Station; his own Watson was Dr. Lyndon Parker, and Mrs. Johnson was their long-suffering landlady. Eight volumes of these Holmes pastiches were published between 1945 and 1973 under Derleth's specialist Mycroft & Moran imprint.

Unfortunately, the author's research left much to be desired, and seven years after Derleth's death in 1973 Copper was controversially asked to revise and edit the entire series of seventy short stories and one novel. The task took almost eighteen months, and the result was published by Mycroft & Moran as *The Solar Pons Omnibus* in 1982. Copper was invited to continue the Pontine canon himself, and he produced seven collections of novellas and the novel *Solar Pons versus the Devil's Claw* (2004). Copper's Pons stories have been collected by various publishers, although the author has disowned some editions after unauthorized rewriting by in-house editors.

His macabre and supernatural novels (like the actor Boris Karloff, he disliked the term "horror") include the transgressive *The Great White Space* (1974), *Into the Silence* (1983), and *The Black Death* (1991), along with a trio of Gothics comprising *The Curse of the Fleers* (1976), *The House of the Wolf* (1983) and the volume you are holding in your hands.

Originally published in 1980 by August Derleth's legendary Arkham House imprint, *Necropolis* was one of the most successful books in the publisher's first forty-one year history, quickly selling out its 4,000-plus print run and becoming the first non-H.P. Lovecraft Arkham title to achieve a second printing.

A macabre mystery set in Victorian England, inspired by the work of such authors as Wilkie Collins and Sir Arthur Conan Doyle, it is very much in the 19th century literary tradition as "reserved" and "rugged" private detective Clyde Beatty, together with his trusty assistant Dotterell, investigates the suspicious circumstances surrounding the death of the father of a beautiful young woman.

It is interesting to note that much of the action is set in the atmospheric Brookwood Cemetery, just outside Woking, where the London Necropolis Railway really *did* run funereal trains on a branch line from Waterloo Station to the cemetery from 1854 until the end of World War II in response to the overcrowding in the city's existing graveyards and cemeteries.

As the author later recalled: "The idea of a funeral train carrying corpses and mourners of all denominations and nationalities

from the heart of London on a railway line to the specially constructed Brookwood Cemetery in Surrey, is something that could
probably have only evolved in Victorian England, where a great,
gloomy ritual surrounded the fact of death."

The novel appeared the following year in the UK as a mass-
market paperback from Sphere Books, and that was the last time it
appeared in print until this present edition, which happily includes
the original illustrations by Stephen E. Fabian that were featured
in the original Arkham House edition.

Two of Copper's early collections of short stories, *From Evil's
Pillow* (1973) and *And Afterward, the Dark: Seven Tales* (1977), were
also issued by Arkham, and his shorter work was also collected
in *Not After Nightfall: Stories of the Strange and the Terrible* (1967),
When Footsteps Echo: Tales of Terror and the Unknown (1975), *Here Be
Daemons: Tales of Horror and the Uneasy* (1978), *Voices of Doom: Tales
of Terror and the Uncanny* (1980), *Whispers in the Night: Stories of the
Mysterious and the Macabre* (1999), *Cold Hand on My Shoulder: Tales
of Terror & Suspense* (2002), and the self-published *Knife in the Back:
Tales of Twilight and Torment* (2005).

In recent years there has been a resurgence of interest in Copper's work, starting with my own British Fantasy Award-winning
bio/bibliography *Basil Copper: A Life in Books* (2008) from PS Publishing, who went on to collect all the author's macabre fiction in
the impressive two-volume set *Darkness, Mist & Shadow* (2010) and
reissue his 1976 novel *The Curse of the Fleers* in a restored version for
the first time in 2012.

Now Valancourt Books has published long-overdue reissues of
Necropolis and *The Great White Space*, and forthcoming from PS is a
complete collection of all the author's Solar Pons tales.

Copper's story "Camera Obscura" was dramatized on the TV
series *Rod Serling's Night Gallery* in 1971 starring René Auberjonois
and Ross Martin, while the author's *conte cruel* "The Recompens-
ing of Albano Pizar" was adapted as "Invitation to the Vaults" for
BBC Radio 4 in 1991.

A member of the Crime Writers' Association for more than
thirty years, serving as its Chairman from 1981-82 and on its com-
mittee for seven years, he was elected a Knight of Mark Twain in
1979 by the Mark Twain Society of America for his outstanding

"contribution to modern fiction", while the Praed Street Irregulars twice honoured him for his Solar Pons series. In 2010, the World Horror Convention presented him with its inaugural Lifetime Achievement Award.

Basil Copper died on April 3, 2013, aged 89. He had been suffering from Alzheimer's disease for a couple of years.

STEPHEN JONES

April 14, 2013

NECROPOLIS

I usually give up one day to pure amusement when I come to town, so I spent it at the Museum of the College of Surgeons.

JAMES MORTIMER, M.D.,
THE HOUND OF THE BASKERVILLES

CONTENTS

I — The Problem

II — The Crimes

III — The Solution

AUTHOR'S NOTE

THE London Necropolis and National Mausoleum Company is a real company. It still exists, as does Brookwood Cemetery in Surrey, once the largest in the world. The Ghost Train was a real funeral train which ran every day from Waterloo Station or Waterloo-road, as it was known in Victorian times, to Brookwood Cemetery, near Woking, discharging its melancholy load of coffins and mourners at the two stations within the cemetery walls.

This daily pilgrimage to the cemetery's four hundred and fifty acres—the total given over to burial from Brookwood's twenty-six hundred acres available—went on from the inauguration of Brookwood in 1854 until the outbreak of the Second World War in 1939 when it ceased, never to begin again.

These circumstances, bizarre and macabre in themselves, were ideal for the framework of the Gothic thriller and immediately suggested a number of possibilities for fictional purposes. I need hardly add that no reflection is intended on the integrity or activities of the London Necropolis Company, and that the locale is used merely as a background for entirely imaginary crime in Victorian times.

For plot purposes a number of changes have been made, notably relating to procedures at Brookwood and the layout of the cemetery; the walls in particular are nowhere near as high in reality as those depicted in the novel. Similarly the rolling, undulating countryside beyond Pirbright has been transferred to the locale of Brookwood for the purposes of the story.

While the period has been carefully evoked, there is no point in looking for exactitude of geographical detail or railway practices and time-tabling; these, together with locations and places, have been altered to suit the demands of the plot. But those seeking a genuinely romantic spot should visit Brookwood and its Glades of Remembrance, as I did. They will not be disappointed.

BASIL COPPER

The Problem

I

THE CLIENT

It was January, the very bleakest time of year, hoar-frost covering the railings in a film of silver, yellow fog rolling in from the river, and cab-horses slipping and slithering over the setts. It had been abominable weather for the past month and promised to last for a month more.

It was not yet midday, but the sky was so dark and the fog beneath pressing against window-panes and rolling sluggishly along alleys so dense and impenetrable, that it seemed like evening.

The shivering pedestrians drew their thick ulsters about them and hurried on as though the very density of the atmosphere had a corroding and baleful effect. A few cabs clopped their way along Holborn, but all the heart of the city seemed subdued and comatose beneath the iron grip of winter.

In a secluded office in one of the smallest courts off Holborn, two people were sitting. The room was a fairly large one, and all the exertions of a heaped coal fire which flickered in the grate were necessary to warm it. The fog crawled at the thick bull's-eye window-panes, and both the twin-branched gas-jets were lit, throwing a vibrating yellow light down on to the worn grey carpet and the broad battered desk.

The street lamps were lit also, and the yellow light gleaming through the glassed entrance door carried with it the image of the gilt-lettered inscription on the panel and impressed it on the opposite wall: CLYDE BEATTY. PRIVATE INVESTIGATIONS. Beatty himself sat at the desk and looked with some degree of bafflement at his visitor as he ruffled a sheaf of papers on the blotter in front of him.

He had a frank, open face and a strong jaw which bespoke a determined nature. His hair was black and curled and clung closely in a thick mat to his scalp, giving him a Roman aspect. He was clean-shaven but with long sideburns which stretched to the lobes of his ears.

His wide brown eyes were fixed questioningly on his visitor as he turned in the swivel chair, first one way, then the other. He wore a thick checked suit of fashionable cut, and his red silk tie was pulled in tightly beneath the striped collar of his shirt. He had no rings or personal jewellery, and his clothing was likewise devoid of ostentation. His only concession to fashion was the discreet red silk handkerchief, matching the tie, which peeped from the breast pocket of his jacket.

His square, capable hands with their blunt, well-manicured nails made small gestures in the air as he waved the papers. His voice had a faint Scottish accent that would not have been out of place in some Edinburgh lawyer's office. But there was nothing of the lawyer about his style and manner, as he exclaimed for the third time, "But madam, I have already told you there is nothing further to be done in the matter."

The woman sitting opposite him in the deep leather chair flushed with anger.

"I have asked you to do a perfectly simple thing, sir, and you seem quite incapable of grasping my purpose."

Beatty drummed with his fingers on the desk and threw the papers down in front of him with a barely suppressed exclamation.

"I can assure you, madam, that everything that can be done has been done. You have my report before you."

The woman rustled the sheet of paper she held in her hand.

"Yes," she replied. "And it tells me precisely nothing."

"Perhaps that is because there is nothing to tell," Beatty said levelly.

He was a man of about thirty-five and there was something appealing about him, despite his rising anger, that the woman evidently realised. She herself was a comely looking person in her late twenties or early thirties. She was well and expensively dressed, and the voluminous fur stole that she wore could not entirely disguise the voluptuousness of her figure.

Her hair was blonde and curled naturally beneath the wide, broad-brimmed hat she wore. Her blue eyes looked angrily at Beatty as she crackled the paper again with slim fingers. She moistened her full lips with a pink tongue and put on a more placatory expression.

"Do not misunderstand my motives," she said winningly. "It is just that this affair is so important."

Beatty crinkled up his brows and leaned back in his chair. A clock in a nearby church tower tolled the hour of twelve. The reverberations, muffled and distorted by the fog, seemed to take a long time to die away in trembling silence. The coals sputtered comfortably on the hearth, and the footfalls of passing pedestrians in the street beyond the windows came as though through cotton wool.

Beatty leaned forward and his eyes were now not at all soft or sympathetic. Rather they seemed focused to points that his fair visitor evidently found uncomfortable to face.

"I tell you, madam, that your husband is innocent," he said evenly. "It is there in plain black and white. Would you have me set a lie on paper?"

The woman bit her lip and started impulsively to her feet. The report fluttered unheeded to the carpet.

"Mr. Sherlock Holmes would have done it."

"Then had you not better apply to him?" said Beatty politely.

The woman stared at him incredulously for a moment. She looked like some beautiful but savage animal.

"Good day, sir," she said icily. "Forward your account and I will see that it is settled."

Beatty rose to his feet and bowed as she swept angrily from the room. She slammed the door so violently that the whole building shook, and billows of fog eddied and danced with the disturbance of her passage.

Beatty stared after her for a moment and then sat down again. He locked his hands behind his head and chuckled.

"By God," he said ruminatively. "There goes a firebrand for you, Dotterell. Did you get that down all right?"

"Just about, Mr. Beatty."

The tinny voice came from a point just behind Beatty and to the left of the fireplace, where the lighting left a patch of shadow. In the gloom, almost unnoticed, was a large cone which might have passed for that of a gramophone. It was made of some varnished wood, beautifully polished and of first-rate craftsmanship. In the centre of the cone was a large brass nozzle about six inches across.

In fact it was an ordinary voice-tube, ingeniously adapted to carry the voices of people sitting near it to another part of the building. Similarly, the cone acted as a sounding board for the voice of any person at the other end of the tube.

Beatty rose in leisurely fashion now and glanced out with distaste at the fog rolling beyond the windows. He crossed to the fireplace and spoke directly into the cone.

"We will charge the standard fee for this enquiry, Dotterell. Any excess to be returned."

"Just as you say, Mr. Beatty," the voice from the cone went on dubiously. There was a pregnant silence, before the unseen speaker continued dourly, "I would have my own ways of dealing with such a lady."

Beatty smiled.

"No doubt," he said crisply. "There is no need to transcribe the notes for the present. I fancy we will not be seeing our client again. What Mr. Holmes would make of her is beyond my understanding."

He laughed and stooped to the fireplace, warming his hands at the blaze.

"When you are ready, I have completed the modifications for which you asked," the voice from the cone went on.

Beatty nodded.

"I will be up in a little while," he said.

He lifted the brass stopper of the speaking tube and clamped it into the orifice before turning back to his desk. He was still sitting there, his pen scratching busily across the paper, when the vestibule bell again sounded for the second time within the hour.

It was another woman who nervously entered the investigator's office, but one in marked contrast to she who had just left in such a precipitate manner. She came hesitantly toward Beatty's desk at his loud invitation to come in, and the young man rose until he seemed to tower over her.

"Mr. Beatty," she said uncertainly. "Mr. Clyde Beatty?"

"The same," Beatty said, noting the girl's expensive clothing and well-bred manner. She was of average height and her dark hair shone sleekly with health beneath the glow of the gas-jets.

"I am in the most terrible trouble, Mr. Beatty," the girl said sombrely. "I really do not know where else to turn."

Beatty came round the desk to take the hand the young woman extended to him. Her clasp was warm and dry despite the coldness of the day.

"Pray take a seat, madam," he said. "And then we will endeavour to see what can be done. One finds that problems, when looked at in the light of logic, often have a habit of becoming resolved."

The girl sank gratefully into the depths of Beatty's capacious leather chair.

"Would it were so in this case," she said fervently. "Unfortunately, my father is already dead."

"I am indeed sorry to hear it," said Beatty, a serious expression on his face. He crossed back to seat himself behind the desk.

"And that is why you are here?"

The girl nodded. She leaned back in the chair and momentarily closed her eyes. Beatty studied her in silence, while the thunder of a dray passed beyond the entrance of the narrow court in front of the windows. The girl could have been no more than about twenty-five years of age.

She was well proportioned, her bust high and firm beneath the tight-fitting buttoned coat she wore. Her black calf knee-length boots with their cross-lacing were glistening with the dampness of the atmosphere; she was hatless and moisture sparkled on her carefully tended coiffure.

Her hands, now that she had removed her gloves, were pink and delicate, the fingers devoid of rings. She wore no jewellery save a small gold watch in a slim case which was pinned to the breast of her jacket.

Her eyes were blue but of a mild cornflower shade, in marked contrast to the woman who had quitted the same chair only twenty minutes before. The brow was broad and clear, the lashes long and silky over those blue eyes. The face was a frank and candid one, appealing to a young man of Beatty's stamp. Her full lips parted in a hesitant smile, revealing white and regular teeth.

"Will you not tell me something of your troubles?" he said haltingly, uncomfortably aware of the attractions of the young woman who sat so close to him in the warm room.

"Miss . . . ?"

The girl started, a flush suffusing her smooth cheeks.

"Oh, do forgive me, sir. I am quite forgetting my manners. You see, it has been such a trying time lately. I have a card here."

Beatty waited patiently, while she rummaged in her reticule. She found the card-case after a moment or two and passed the slip of pasteboard across the desk to Beatty. According to the gilt script she was a Miss Angela Meredith. The address was a good one, in St. John's Wood. Beatty put the card down on his blotter.

"I am all attention, madam," he said.

Miss Meredith fiddled with her card-case, keeping her eyes down on a corner of the desk. She seemed more relaxed than when she had entered the room, but there was still something of strain showing about the eyes. Beatty said nothing further, merely waited for her to go on, but he had drawn sheets of foolscap toward him and sat, pen poised to take notes.

"My father had settled an allowance on me," Miss Meredith began in a low voice. "Therefore, I follow no set occupation, but pursue my own interests and studies. I state this from the outset. You may therefore name your own fee for your services. Money is not a matter of any consequence to me."

Beatty held up his hand peremptorily; little spots of red were burning on his cheekbones.

"I had already marked you as a young lady of quality, Miss Meredith," he said stiffly. "But had you no means at your disposal it would not have influenced my decision to take your case. My fees are not excessive, I can assure you."

The girl looked at him, startled. She flushed and put up one hand to her mouth in a childlike gesture at once helpless and appealing.

"I beg your pardon, sir," she said, fixing him with her eyes. "I trust my innocent remark has not caused offence."

Beatty smiled and relaxed in his swivel chair.

"I am a proud man, Miss Meredith, and mayhap I spoke hastily. Please continue."

Miss Meredith slightly inclined her head and went on hesitantly.

"My father was Tredegar Meredith, the banker. He was a director of the City and Suburban Bank, one of the most highly respected private concerns in the City."

"It is not unknown to me," said Beatty drily. "Pray go on."

His eyes were very alert now and never left Miss Meredith's face. She, as though unconscious of his scrutiny, kept her own gaze on a corner of his desk and hurried on in low tones.

"My father had been a widower for many years, Mr. Beatty. We lived in comfortable, not to say affluent, circumstances at St. John's Wood. We have a housekeeper, three maids, and two gardeners."

Beatty nodded, his pen scratching over the paper, but he did not interrupt. It was very quiet in the office now, the fog having muffled all traces of the outside world.

"This was the situation which obtained until about two months ago," Miss Meredith went on. "My father then appeared worried and ill at ease. It was something to do with his business affairs, I think."

"You questioned him about this?" Beatty asked.

Miss Meredith nodded.

"On several occasions. We had been very close since mother died. He seemed embarrassed and tried to make light of the matter. But I knew there was something extremely wrong, Mr. Beatty."

The young investigator made another scribbled notation on the sheet in front of him.

"When was the last of these talks?"

"About three weeks ago," said the young woman. "Just a few days before he died."

She stopped as though overcome with emotion and fumbled in her bag for a wisp of linen which she held to her face. Beatty affected not to notice, merely dropped his eyes to his notes for a fraction and sat frowning.

"How did he die, Miss Meredith?"

"He was taken ill quite suddenly," the girl went on, stirring in the leather chair and seeming to collect herself. "It began with vomiting and night-sweats, followed by stomach cramps."

Beatty leaned forward, his brown eyes staring fixedly into her own.

"Just so," he said. "There has been a lot of illness in the capital of late. I read only yesterday of an epidemic."

The girl nodded affirmatively.

"Just the opinion of our doctor, Mr. Beatty. Only now I am

not so sure. The progress of the thing was so rapid, you see. And father had never been ill in his life."

"There must be something more, Miss Meredith," Beatty went on. "Or you would not have come to me."

"Supposition only," the girl said fiercely. "But only you can help me. I know of no other place to turn."

Beatty seemed surprised by the vehemence of his visitor's manner, but his face showed little of his thoughts.

"My father was ill for just three days," the girl went on. "At first he seemed to be getting better, then he would have a relapse. The doctor tried every remedy he could think of. But nothing was of any use and father died of convulsions."

Beatty's face had been getting sterner as Miss Meredith's narrative had continued.

Now he asked, "What was the cause of death, Miss Meredith?"
The girl shook her head.

"Pneumonia and heart failure, I believe. The doctor gave me the death certificate, but I could not bear to look at it. I believe the housekeeper handed it to the undertaker."

Beatty made another notation on his pad.

"It's no matter," he murmured, as though to himself. "It will be easy enough to check when the time comes."

He leaned forward to the girl.

"Miss Meredith, you have so far told me nothing out of the ordinary, tragic as the circumstances must be from your point of view. There is something else I take it?"

The girl looked startled. She pursed her lips as though about to say one thing, then apparently changed her mind. She sat in thought for a moment, looking fixedly at Beatty.

"It is my considered opinion my father was murdered," she said.

2

DEADLY POISON?

"Indeed," Beatty drawled.

He had drawn himself up in the swivel chair now and was looking at the girl with shining eyes. The deep silence was broken by a sharp explosion, followed by an equally violent cracking noise. Beatty sat without flinching, but the effect on the girl was electric. She jumped out of her chair and stood looking round her with a startled countenance.

"What on earth was that, Mr. Beatty?"

Beatty laughed at her expression.

"I must apologise, Miss Meredith. I forgot to warn you. That will be my assistant, Dotterell. He is quite an expert with a gun. I have no doubt he was merely testing one of our weapons. We have a small laboratory upstairs."

He smiled kindly at the girl, who sank back into the chair.

"You are used to violence then, Mr. Beatty?" she asked, giving him a sharp look.

Beatty inclined his head.

"Not exactly, Miss Meredith. But my life has led me into some pretty tough scrapes from time to time. And the muzzle of a blued-steel revolver is a powerful argument in a tight corner, wouldn't you agree?"

The girl put out her hand impulsively.

"I was sure I had come to the right place when I first set eyes on you. You will help me?"

Beatty smiled again.

"Not so fast, Miss Meredith. We are rather running ahead, are we not? I have heard nothing yet of the real reason which brought you here."

The girl relaxed into the depths of the chair. Her face was sad as she glanced across the big desk to where Beatty sat, his Roman head poised over the notepaper, the pen in his hand almost bristling with the impatience of the strong, capable fingers.

"I don't know what's behind it all, if that's what you mean. Money, probably. But I do know my father didn't die a natural death."

"These are serious matters," said Beatty. "And we must proceed carefully. There is nothing, I take it, in your father's will which would benefit any of your relatives, for example?"

The girl shook her head.

"I have no close relatives except for a maiden aunt. And my

father's estate falls to me as the next of kin. I have been to see the lawyers. All is in order and there are no problems, though my father's estate was smaller than I had been led to believe."

Beatty shot her an enigmatic glance and his pen raced across the paper again. He waited patiently for her to go on.

"A week after my father died, the house was burgled," the girl said. "My father's desk was broken open and certain papers taken."

Beatty put up his left hand and rubbed his chin.

"What papers, Miss Meredith?"

The girl shook her head.

"I have no idea. And the people at the Bank were unable to help."

"You reported it to the police, of course?"

"Certainly," Miss Meredith replied. "But there has been no result to date. Professionals, the Inspector thought. But why, Mr. Beatty?"

Beatty went on writing before he answered.

"Who knows? But you must have something more tangible than this."

For answer, the girl again rummaged in the reticule she had balanced on the edge of the desk. She had a strange look on her face as she brought out a plain foolscap envelope.

"Yesterday, Mr. Beatty," she said, "I was cleaning up the study. The parlour-maid was clearing the fireplace. It had not been touched since my father's death, you see. He was very particular about the study. The girl found a partly burnt letter in the back of the grate. It was in my father's handwriting."

"And this is it?" Beatty said.

Miss Meredith nodded.

"Fortunately, the girl was unable to decipher it and passed it to me. I spent a sleepless night on it, and seeing your announcement in the newspaper I decided to come round."

"You have done perfectly correctly," Beatty said. He took the envelope from the girl and held it under the light of the overhead lamp.

Beatty drew out the sheet of heavy blue notepaper and examined it carefully under a powerful lens he took from the drawer of the desk. It was, he now saw, not a full sheet but a half-sheet. The paper had been torn across for it was not burnt on that side. It looked like the draft of something which the writer had torn up.

The inked handwriting, done with a heavy pen and in an irregular hand, began in midsentence and ended in the middle of another. With difficulty, due to the scorching and buckling of the paper, Beatty made out the message. It read: "I must have the truth of this matter. Your threats do not . . ."

Beatty grunted and examined the sheet with barely concealed enthusiasm. Then he put the paper back into the envelope and straightened up.

"You did well to come to me, Miss Meredith," he said crisply. "This looks like a deep business. And something which the official police could not very well act upon. You have told no one of this?"

Miss Meredith shook her head; her cornflower blue eyes were shining as they looked at Beatty.

"No one, sir," she said decisively.

"And no one knows you have come to see me?" Beatty went on.

The answer was again in the negative.

"Very well," Beatty said. "It is late now and if you will permit me, I will take you to lunch. Over lunch we will decide on our plan of campaign. But this is a very tricky affair and we will have to proceed extremely carefully."

The girl put back her card-case into the reticule.

"Then you have formed an opinion?" she said.

"A fairly obvious one, perhaps," Beatty said. "But one is drawn to several inescapable conclusions. Your father evidently received threats against his life. The utterer of the threats was known to him or he would not have written to him. Of course, we do not know whether the letter was ever sent. This fragment may indicate that he destroyed it. But I myself consider that it was a draft that he burnt, or tried to burn, perhaps thinking better of its contents."

The girl was silent for a long time, and she made no movement except for the restless intertwining of her fingers.

"And the manner of my father's death?"

Beatty averted his eyes.

"You have carefully avoided that subject, Miss Meredith. It is obviously painful to you. Yet we must go into it. It is plain that you dislike and suspect the doctor. Is it not so?"

The girl flushed.

"I cannot really explain, Mr. Beatty. It is something only a woman would understand. But deep down inside me I am convinced he had a hand in father's death. He had nothing but a chill just before Dr. Couchman came to the house. And within a short while he was suffering convulsions."

Beatty was silent for a space.

"I appreciate and make allowances for your feelings of filial affection, Miss Meredith. But I fear we shall need just a little more to go on than your woman's intuition."

Miss Meredith looked at him impatiently.

"You have surely formed some opinion."

"I am keeping an open mind. But one is led inevitably to the subject of poison."

He held up his hand as the girl started to speak.

"Not a breath of this to anyone. We are dealing with the medical profession, and in that world we must tread very carefully indeed. And in a household such as yours anyone could have administered it. Then again, we have the matter of the burglary. It is all too close to be coincidence. We have a number of threads here, and it is no use theorising further without more solid data. We cannot obtain that except through thorough groundwork."

He sat pondering for a moment longer.

"The doctor?" he said at length. "The details so that we may eliminate him from our enquiries."

"He is an old friend of my father's," the girl said quickly. "He runs a private nursing home near Woking."

She stumbled in her speech at Beatty's interrogatory glance.

"We used to live in Surrey. That is where they met. Dr. Couchman was father's family doctor. So when he became a director of the Bank and moved to town, father kept on the connection."

"So Dr. Couchman came all the way from Surrey?" Beatty mused. "Would it not have been more convenient to call in a London man?"

"Dr. Couchman was already in London for a week or two on

business," the girl went on. "He was in town when father was taken ill, so naturally we called him in."

Beatty's brow cleared.

"I see," he said. "Pray give me this Dr. Couchman's address if he is still in town. A call would not come amiss."

"He has gone back to Woking," Miss Meredith went on. "Or rather, the nursing home is a few miles outside. It is called Brookfield. You will find Dr. Horace Couchman in the *Medical Directory*."

Beatty made another note.

"Well, no matter. I will make arrangements to see him in due course."

He stood up with a decisive gesture.

"And now, my dear Miss Meredith, we will go out into this freezing fog. And over a meal in a comfortable chophouse not more than three hundred yards from here, we will discuss this tragic business further."

3

PREPARATIONS

IT was not yet three when Beatty put his key in the office door and let himself into the vestibule. But so dark was the day and the rolling fog had grown so impenetrable that it might just as well have been midnight, and the feeble rays of the gas-lamps were powerless to penetrate the murk. Beatty shook the droplets of moisture from the cape of his thick check overcoat and stamped his feet on the rug.

He put the door on the latch and the catch of the bell in position before crossing to his desk. He silently turned up the gas-jets and ignited the pressure-lamp on his desk so that the whole room was a blaze of light. That done he poked the fire into a semblance of life and opened a door at the rear of the office, his mind full of his lunch-time conversation with Miss Angela Meredith.

He swiftly mounted a short staircase; when he was halfway up there was a loud cracking noise followed by a grunt. Beatty chuckled with satisfaction. He opened the small oval white-painted door at the top of the stairs and slightly stooped under the lintel. It was a strange apartment in which he found himself, but one which he had designed with enormous care to facilitate the sometimes bizarre requirements of his highly specialised business. Part laboratory, part workshop, it was a broad chamber which was fully forty feet long, with fireplaces at either end which now gave out a comfortable reddish glow. Gas-lamps with specially designed mirror reflectors threw back a warm, clear light on to the objects beneath. The walls were panelled in oak and with other accoutrements would have been handsome; but the chamber had been adapted for a different purpose and now rough wooden benches lined them.

There were heavy mahogany filing cabinets near the left-hand fireplace; a desk covered with a litter of equipment. A bunsen burner's bluish flame glowed dimly in the shadow at the far end of the workshop. On the opposite wall to the benches were glass cases in which could be glimpsed racks of weapons. A sword-stick with the blade exposed was leaning carelessly against the desk.

Its silver top contained a miniature whisky-flask. The opened bottle on the desk proclaimed that it had just been filled. Beatty smiled to himself and walked down the room toward the figure standing by the desk. He picked up a bullet-proof waistcoat on one of the benches as he passed. He examined it critically. Faint indentations in the padding showed where it had been subjected to the most rigorous testing.

On the left-hand side of the room, in a clear space and at floor-level, was a small fan-shaped window of heavy glass. Just below it, on the ceiling of Beatty's own office below and high up, where it could not be seen by clients, was a highly accurate mirror. Through this window Beatty's assistant could see the entire office area and everything that went on in the room below. It was an arrangement which had often proved highly beneficial in the past.

And Dotterell was able to gauge exactly when his master was within range of the voice-tube. The companion to the instrument below was screwed to the panelling above the small viewing window, and Beatty drummed on it affectionately with his fingers as he passed. The tall, cadaverous figure that awaited his approach gave no outward sign of his presence, but went on with his delicate adjustments with an admirable concentration.

With the magnifying lens glinting in his right eye and the thin screwdriver poised over the equipment in the vice in front of him, Dotterell looked like some ancient alchemist. Behind him, on a small folding card-table, lay plates bearing scattered crumbs and a soup bowl, denoting that he had spent his lunch-hour engaged on his self-imposed tasks.

Beatty waited patiently, idly picking up *The Times* which Dotterell had evidently been examining with his customary thoroughness. He smiled at two items in the Agony Column his assistant had ringed round and turned to the Home News page. He scanned the headlines briefly. He was about to pass on when his eyes narrowed and he drew in his breath.

A column, headed in heavy black type, was given over to an inexplicable robbery at the City branch of the Mercantile Bank twenty-four hours earlier. The thieves, after breaking their way into the strong-room, had escaped with a quarter of a million pounds' worth of gold bullion. Scotland Yard had not yet formulated a theory as to how the criminals had transported their booty.

"That's the sort of job we ought to be getting," Dotterell observed with a dry chuckle.

He made a last adjustment and looked at Beatty dourly from under shaggy eyebrows. Beatty tapped the item with a fingernail and put the newspaper back on the table. He studied his assistant warily.

"You're right enough," he grudgingly admitted. "I'd like to get my teeth into a case of that magnitude. But we can't expect to be called in on such affairs. The official force has far more facilities than we can muster."

Dotterell shot him a stabbing glance from his piercing blue eyes.

"True," he observed. "But we have a lot of advantages the Yard lacks. Technical expertise, for one."

Here he looked with pride round the jumbled benches of the workshop.

"And there's a second, more important thing."

Beatty turned carelessly and looked down through the mirror-window at the office below as though he were still envisaging the slender form of the girl who had sat there not so long ago.

"What might that be?" he queried.

Dotterell chuckled.

"We have it here," he said, tapping his forehead significantly.

Beatty smiled bitterly.

"A palpable point," he observed. "But one not yet recognised by the general public."

"It will come, Mr. Beatty, it will come," his assistant said earnestly, bending his cadaverous figure back over the vice. He straightened up and gave the private investigator his entire attention for the first time since he had entered the room.

"I wish I had your faith," Beatty said carelessly. "Have you done as I asked?"

Dotterell nodded with satisfaction.

"I have increased the muzzle velocity of the derringer to your specification."

He jerked his thumb toward the two-inch oak board set up against a rough frame filled with sandbags at one end of the bench. Beatty looked slightly incredulously at the neat hole drilled clean through the board. He took the small weapon Dotterell handed him and hefted it appraisingly.

"Best be careful with that, Mr. Beatty. It's a dangerous toy."

"Precisely my intention," Beatty said.

He checked that the weapon was loaded. Then he sheathed it carefully in a small leather holster strapped to the calf of his leg, beneath his check trousers. Dotterell sat down on the edge of the bench and watched him silently. Beatty took a turn or two about the desk. He was evidently satisfied with the weight and fitting of the weapon within the holster, for he made no further reference to the matter.

"That reminds me," he said. "I'd prefer some notice of your experiments when I'm interviewing clients. You almost frightened the lady out of her wits."

Dotterell smiled mockingly.

"Assuming Mrs. De Carton had any wits to frighten," he replied.

Beatty clicked his tongue impatiently.

"I am not referring to that lady," he said. "I speak of Miss Angela Meredith of St. John's Wood."

Dotterel's eyes lit up.

"Ah, then we have a client."

Beatty nodded. He sat down on a rough wooden chair at the other side of the desk.

"We have. And a nasty business it may turn out to be if my suspicions are justified."

Dotterell stood watching him, not saying anything further. He was a formidable figure in the light of the overhead lamp, and Beatty thought, not for the first time, that he could not have picked a better assistant or one more suited to the rough and dangerous adventures into which he so frequently plunged.

It was not only Dotterell's height and strength; he had once been a professional boxer, and his skill at fisticuffs and the brute courage which so often went with that occupation made him the ideal companion in a tight corner. More unusually, he had more than a smattering of education, which ran to Latin and mathematics; and he had great skill as an engineer and practical mechanic.

There was some mystery about Dotterell's background, but Beatty had never enquired too closely into it; it was not his way. He suspected that Dotterell was a well-educated man who hid his capabilities behind a rough exterior for purposes of his own; he was scrupulously honest and fair in all his dealings, but there might be some misdemeanour in his past which he was anxious to conceal.

Certainly Beatty respected his taciturnity regarding his own antecedents; he was content to leave things as they were and was only grateful that the brain within the massive cranium and the steel-like strength of those lean arms were his to command. He paid Dotterell exceptionally well, but then he received exceptional service in return. He looked at his assistant in silence for a moment longer.

"Listen carefully," he said at length. "There are some things I want you to do. We have to proceed cautiously in this business and nothing must go wrong."

"It sounds like a dark and sinister affair if your suppositions are correct," Dotterell observed.

His deep-set eyes were shining with enthusiasm. With his lean face, lank hair, bottle-green suit, and limp bow-tie, he looked like a successful undertaker. He took off his jacket as he spoke and tied a baize apron around his waist.

"Dark enough and sinister enough," Beatty replied sombrely. "I don't usually make up my mind at such short odds, but there was that in the young lady's manner which convinced me she was telling the truth. And the strange events surrounding her father's sudden and mysterious death cannot be coincidence."

Dotterell finished tying the apron.

"You suspect the doctor?"

"I suspect everybody and nobody," Beatty answered. "But a doctor would have many opportunities of administering poison if it suited his purpose. So I shall commence with him. If he passes my test, then we may eliminate him from our enquiries and proceed on systematic lines with the people in the house."

Dotterell nodded. He sat down at the desk and reached for a pen.

"You'll need to exhume the body to obtain proof one way or the other," he said, his eyes glinting with excitement. "That won't be easy if the doctor is involved."

"I have thought of that," said Beatty calmly. "Everything must be ready by tomorrow in time for my unexpected call on Dr. Horace Couchman of Brookfield Nursing Home, near Woking."

Dotterell put down the pen and rubbed his hands together.

"You would not be thinking of trying the medical method again?"

Beatty turned a smiling face to him.

"And why not? It is one of my most successful. I have found that there is nothing in life so easy of acceptance as imposing credentials. And when one makes an appeal to a colleague, nine times out of ten it is complied with without question."

Dotterell nodded. He had picked up his pen again and was writing rapidly, the nib squeaking over the paper.

"I have the address," he said. "What will be your alias?"

Beatty shifted in his chair and fixed his eyes on the beams of the ceiling from which various pieces of equipment were suspended.

"On this occasion I shall be Dr. Clyde Fitzgibbon, M.D."

Dotterell gave him a lopsided smile. He got up and went over to one of the big filing cabinets. He came back with a thick catalogue and ran through it with his forefinger. He slid it across the desk to his employer.

"If I might suggest the deckle-edge, with curlicue gilt script," he murmured. "That seems to go down very well."

Beatty ran down the examples of type-faces and concurred with Dotterell's choice. It was uncanny just how exactly his assistant had the correct solution to any given problem and how quickly he came up with the right choice of alternatives.

Dotterell had already turned on a pressure-lamp above the massive hand-press which stood shrouded in a corner. He took off the white dust-sheet with a flourish and folded it carefully.

"I should be able to run the cards off before the end of the afternoon," he told Beatty. "I have the correct grade of board in stock. I'll do a dozen to be on the safe side."

To Beatty's raised eyebrows he went on, "Just in case you want to call on anyone else in the Woking area."

Beatty smiled and got up. He looked down into the silent office below, empty beneath the glare of the lamps. The fog appeared to be writhing at the windows more thickly than ever.

Dotterell sat down at the desk again and made further entries on the document before him. Beatty knew he would be setting out case-notes in formal language and detailing the procedures used. Beatty was coming to find these more and more useful as time went by.

An empiricist by nature, he was polishing and refining his techniques as he went along. Beatty turned back to the desk. Dotterell finished his notations and leaned back in the chair. He was consulting other volumes on the desk surface in front of him.

"There is a train which leaves Waterloo-road just after midday," he said. "It is a stopping train which takes a little over the hour."

Beatty nodded.

"Normally, that would suit me nicely. I could then lunch at Woking and call on Dr. Couchman afterwards."

He paused and stared distantly at the ceiling.

"But on this occasion I prefer to get the ten o'clock from London Bridge."

"London Bridge?" said Dotterell. His mouth had dropped slightly open.

"London Bridge," Beatty repeated. "That will get me to Guild-ford with plenty of time to spare."

Dotterell stared at him in astonishment.

"Guildford? Why such a roundabout route to Woking?"

"I have my reasons," said Beatty enigmatically.

Dotterell was frowning over a gazetteer.

"From what you tell me, Mr. Beatty, this nursing home will be about two miles from a place called Send. Do you wish me to tele-graph ahead for a cab to meet you?"

Beatty shook his head.

"Thank you, no. I will make my own arrangements after I have lunched. I now want some suitable properties appropriate to a somewhat staid medical gentleman."

He had already crossed the room to a large wardrobe which was built into the panelling. He opened it up and rummaged among the contents. Each item of clothing hanging from the rails inside was fastidiously labelled in ink in Dotterell's careful hand.

Beatty selected a voluminous caped overcoat with large black buttons. He put it on and regarded himself critically in the full-length mirror mounted inside the cupboard. There were labelled hat-boxes in compartments set along the top of the interior and mahogany drawers containing such useful items as shirts, collars, and cravats.

Dotterell was rummaging in his turn. He produced an item with a grunt of triumph.

"Try this, Mr. Beatty. Just the thing under the circumstances."

Beatty took the small black holdall. He opened it; it contained a stethoscope and a brown leather instrument case. His mouth opened at least half an inch. Dotterell laughed at his expression.

"Railway Lost Property," he said. "I bought it cheaply through a friend in the trade a month ago, thinking it might be useful."

"Excellent," Beatty said drily. "This will be most impressive."

He had already selected a rusty black top-hat from one of the boxes. He adjusted it rakishly over his forehead. He could not for-bear a burst of laughter at his aspect in the glass.

"The Spirit of 1880," Dotterell said solemnly, handing his employer a pair of gold-rimmed pince-nez with a thin matching gold chain.

"I have fitted them with plain glass, Mr. Beatty, so as not to interfere with your eyesight."

Beatty put them on and hooked the chain through his waistcoat button-hole.

"Capital! Capital!" he said, laughing again and grimacing at his expression. "Even Miss Meredith would not know me."

He hunched his shoulders slightly, and the stoop, combined with the elements of the disguise, gave him an entirely different aspect. One would not have known that a young man stood there. Dotterell stood by rubbing his hands with satisfaction.

"Perhaps a moustache?" he suggested. "I have some excellent examples in the drawer there."

Beatty shook his head.

"There is a maxim of mine that I never transgress," he said sharply. "Never overdo things. If I were calling on Couchman at night under poor light, yes. Then I might risk it. But I shall be in Woking in broad day. I shall eat in a public restaurant, and I fear that even the dimmest-witted of waiters would realise there was something peculiar about my features. No, this is well enough; let us leave the broader aspects alone."

Dotterell looked disappointed.

"Just as you say, Mr. Beatty. But I've made up a new line with human hair, and I daresay even you could not tell the difference between that and the real thing."

"Some other time perhaps," Beatty said, closing the matter.

He swivelled again, surveying his image with satisfaction.

"Now, we both have much to do before tomorrow."

"You'll have a real medical man in reserve, of course?" said Dotterell, looking at him through narrowed eyes.

"Of course," said Beatty shortly. "I shall see about that this afternoon."

Dotterell's face fell slightly.

"You'll not be wanting the special kit on this occasion I'm thinking."

The young investigator shook his head. He was already divesting himself of his overcoat.

"Perhaps later," he said enigmatically. "I should overhaul it in readiness."

Dotterell sighed and went back to the desk.

"I envy you getting between the Surrey pines and breathing good country air."

Beatty regarded him with amusement.

"It will be London fog with birdsong if this goes on," he said crisply. "Just make sure you have everything in readiness. We will make a final check tomorrow morning."

"Everything will be in order, Mr. Beatty," said Dotterell imperturbably.

He turned back to his scribbling as Beatty went out and down the stair.

4

TO WOKING—VIA GUILDFORD

BEATTY adjusted the angle of his top-hat in the mirror and surveyed his image with satisfaction. Dotterell stood to one side and watched him silently. The case of medical instruments reposed ready packed on the chair; with it was the current number of a medical journal which the investigator thought would add credence to his appearance, and a copy of that morning's *Times*.

Beatty finally completed his examination. Dotterell picked up the bag and the journals and accompanied him down the stairs. A watery sun was already piercing through the foggy haze into the courts of Holborn, and the day promised well, though the iron frost continued.

"You have a good hour yet," said Dotterell, looking with distaste around the office which he would have to occupy for the remainder of the day in his master's absence. As Beatty well knew, he preferred his domain upstairs, except for when he was on more active assignments.

"Of course," he went on, catching Beatty's amused expression. "There is a distinct possibility that the doctor may not be at home. Have you thought of that?"

"I have indeed," Beatty replied innocuously. "I had Miss Meredith send a carefully worded telegram to the doctor last night. It concerned a gold-mounted walking stick which he had left at the lady's house. I received a message from Miss Meredith at my private address this morning. The doctor was at the nursing home. He said he would collect the stick when he was next in town, probably the week after next."

Dotterell smiled thinly. He shook his head.

"Is there no catching the man out?" he asked the silent office.

He turned back to the transformed figure of Beatty in the top-hat and voluminous overcoat.

"I will be available night and day if you need me, Mr. Beatty."

"I know that," said Beatty, looking at his assistant reflectively. "But I expect little from this opening gambit. I should be away two days at the outside."

He nodded and stepped out into the vestibule. A few seconds later the hazy mist of midmorning had swallowed him up. Dotterell stood looking after him for a moment and then walked slowly over toward the desk.

Beatty strode swiftly through into Holborn, the icy air cold and stinging against his face. The pavements were damp beneath, and the rawness of the day seemed to penetrate to the bone. He hailed a passing cab which clip-clopped from out the mist and settled back on to the damp leather cushions of the interior after giving the driver his destination.

Beatty was satisfied that his new persona would pass casual scrutiny. The cabby, a big man with sharp penetrating eyes, had sized him up swiftly and retorted, "Right away, doctor!"

Beatty smiled thinly to himself as the cab lurched over the cobbles, settling down to read the medical journal but finding it dull stuff indeed. He turned instead to *The Times,* only half-hearing the roar caused by the iron-rimmed wheels of brewers' drays. Once a horse-bus passed perilously close, and Beatty heard the cabman give the driver a string of obscenities as he hauled his horses' heads round.

The mist was thinning now as the cab eased its way down Cheapside toward Cannon Street. The sun broke out fully as the driver whipped up, and they made a spanking pace. As they turned on to London Bridge Beatty could see ice glinting on the surface of the sluggish Thames, and in places brown water swirled where the passage of barges had smashed a channel. There were few people about on the pavement and these were thickly clad and walking fast, beating their feet on the flagstones as an aid to circulation.

Beatty wondered idly why his cases always took him out of town at the most inclement times of the year; an excursion to Surrey would have been delightful in June or July. He shrugged and huddled deeper into the thick overcoat, the pince-nez sitting uneasily on the bridge of his broad nose. He hoped that no one would notice the lack of indentation marks, the infallible sign of one who had worn glasses for years.

There was a throng of traffic crossing the bridge, and Beatty could see St. Paul's lifting its dome briefly through the enveloping mist. A few minutes later the cab was clopping on to the south side of the river and up the incline past St. Thomas's Hospital. The flap lifted and the cabman's face appeared.

"Greenwich Railway offices, guv'nor?"

Beatty shook his head.

"A little farther down, if you please. This will be near enough."

They were in Tooley Street now and the cab pulled up in front of the Italianate façade of the station, where thick knots of human beings were surging to and fro through the arcades. Beatty descended and paid the cabman the statutory shilling, adding threepence for good measure. He nodded briefly and proceeded along the covered way set on iron columns, past the refreshment rooms and into the massive booking vestibule.

He had twenty minutes in hand, and he remembered in time not to bound along at his usual athletic gait but to walk sedately as befitted a staid medical man. He bought a first-class ticket for Woking from the wizened red-haired clerk behind the wicket, explaining his reasons for the roundabout journey.

"Change at Reigate Junction for the Reading branch, sir," the clerk reminded Beatty, who thanked him and walked on to the barrier, giving his ticket to the gold-braided official who stood imposingly guarding the portals.

The train was already in, and Beatty walked along under the vast eight-hundred-feet-long wood and glass-panelled roof through which the sun was struggling to penetrate the soot and to send its pallid fingers down to the platforms beneath.

Beatty entered his first-class compartment to find an elderly lady in black bombazine ensconced in one corner. He gave her a formal bow. Apparently reassured by his respectable bearing and by the medical journal he carried prominently displayed, she gave him a frozen smile and retired into the penultimate tome of the three-volume novel she was reading.

Whistles were shrilling beneath the grime-encrusted gloom of the girders, and the rumble of iron-shod wheels, the stamping and beating of horses' hooves as the cabs discharged their passengers in the far arcade, punctuated by the hiss of escaping steam, brought a gleam of excitement to the eyes of the young detective beneath the glinting surface of the plain glass of his pince-nez.

Beatty loosened the folds of his overcoat and settled back to the sober pages of *The Times* as the train drew out of the terminus with a grating shudder. Smoke billowed past the windows and was immediately torn to tatters as the carriages left the shelter of the great roof and were exposed to the cold embrace of the outer air.

He noticed that there were some more details regarding the bullion robbery at the Mercantile Bank and perused the report as the train cleared the suburbs. There did not seem to be anything new, but Beatty read it to the end as a matter of professional interest. Then he laid the paper aside. He drew out his railway lamp from a corner of the medical bag and checked it. He did not know exactly when he would be returning to London, and for numerous reasons, if it were after nightfall, he did not wish to travel in the dark.

Beatty glanced out of the window at the tall chimney of the London Armoury Company, and soon they had whirled through New Cross and the glittering mass of the Crystal Palace was rising from the mist. The train stopped at Norwood, and an elderly gentleman entered the carriage and sat down in the corner opposite to Beatty.

Beatty resumed his role as medical man under the eye of his new companion and read desultorily in his exceedingly boring journal until the train stopped at Croydon. They were in open country now and the sun, penetrating the mist, disclosed rolling hillsides and a charming rural scene, welcome after the smoking chimneys and serried brick boxes of London.

But the charm and richness of the Surrey landscape soon palled on Beatty's town-bred mind, and he turned his thoughts ever and again to the mystery surrounding his visitor of the morning before. There was something tragic and mysterious in Miss Meredith's eyes which overcame his natural caution and scepticism.

After all, her father might well have died of natural causes; there was much illness in the capital at the moment. And the burglary might have been sheer coincidence. Beatty would have relegated the matter but for the discovery of the burnt fragment of letter in Tredegar Meredith's study-grate.

That was the one incontrovertible factor in the whole business which reeked of intrigue; taken with the sudden illness of the father and the burglary immediately afterward, it had a sinister effect on Beatty's trained mind.

He drummed with strong fingers on the window-sill, conscious of the raw cold which had begun to penetrate the carriage. They were leaving Caterham Junction Station now and were already fourteen miles from London. As the mist streamed from off the landscape, Beatty saw a section of straight road beyond the railway and a pony and trap spanking briskly down it.

The driver was evidently hoping to race the train. Beatty smiled with admiration at the efforts of the trim athletic gentleman at the reins who was driving in great style. But slowly, inexorably, the snorting steam-engine gained on him until he and his gallant horse were hidden from the young investigator's sight by an intervening grove of trees.

The country was again changing in character, with steeply wooded hills and the characteristic darkness of pines. Then the daylight was abruptly cut off as the train entered a gloomy cutting, over a hundred feet deep in places, and the roar of its progress was buffeted back from the solid chalk and flint walls.

The darkness now became absolute as the train thundered into Merstham Tunnel, smoke and sparks billowing back from the engine. The old gentleman in the corner had lit a pipe, and the glow of the bowl, apparently suspended in midair, was the only illumination within the carriage, though Beatty could see the beams of a carriage lamp in a coach farther down reflected on the tunnel wall.

He got up, feeling cold and damp, and gathered his belongings as St. Catherine's Church at Merstham glided past to the right of the line. The old gentleman descended at Merstham, and Beatty sat down again to while away the few remaining minutes until Reigate Junction was reached.

He rapidly descended and crossed the platform, drying now in the sun, to where the chocolate-brown carriages waited to carry him on to Guildford. Beatty found another empty carriage on the train, which was smaller in length than the one he had left and which was now whirling the old lady on in the direction of Dover, and sat down.

The sun was casting quite a strong light, limning the range of chalk hills running from Farnham in the west toward Westerham to the east, and shimmering on the rails which beckoned onward down the Holmesdale Valley.

The agreeable brick residences of Reigate, dotted about the hillside, receded as the engine settled to its work along the incline, and Beatty could now make out that the splashes of yellow in the far distance were the workings of numerous sandpits.

Within a very few minutes, it seemed to Beatty, the train had roared its way through Box Hill Tunnel and rocked across the Mole on a tall viaduct some fifty feet above the river. Despite himself Beatty's senses were lulled by the agreeableness of the journey, and it was with something like regret that he saw the white tombstones of Dorking Cemetery whirling past the window.

Beatty left the train at Guildford. An hour later he returned to the station, the puzzled frown in his brow quite erased. He took a local train direct to Woking. It drew up in the neat confines of Woking Station and he descended, drawing his coat about him and clutching his medical bag. The spire of a big church pierced the misty sky as he hurried down the platform with a surprisingly large crowd of passengers.

After surrendering his ticket to the bearded giant at the barrier, he waved away an importunate cab-driver and walked toward the main street. It was market day apparently, and cattle, sheep, poultry, and produce were much in evidence, the former being driven and the latter displayed on carts.

It was just after half-past one, in a clear, sparkling world far removed from Holborn, when Clyde Beatty walked in through the portals of the town's best hostelry, the White Horse Hotel, and ordered his lunch.

5

TOBY STEVENS

BEATTY pushed back his second cup of coffee with a contented sigh and beckoned to the gaunt-looking waiter. It was just a quarter past two and he had much to do.

"I want to hire a cab this afternoon," he said crisply. "Who is the best person in the town?"

The waiter smiled, eyeing the coins held casually in Beatty's fingers.

"There's no question o' that, sir," he said. "You'll want Toby Stevens."

Beatty nodded. His eyes were surveying the comfortable oak-beamed dining room from behind the clear glass of the pince-nez. The medical bag stood on a chair at his side.

"Where can I find him?"

"He's usually on the stand outside the station, sir," said the waiter eagerly. "If you wish I can get the bootboy to run over and fetch him."

Beatty got up, dropping the coins into the waiter's receptive palm.

"Have him outside the hotel at two-thirty sharp," he said.

"He'll be there, sir," the waiter promised him.

He hurried off as Beatty went back into the main parlour of the inn. The landlord, a fat man with a red, jovial face and mutton-chop whiskers, had already been apprised of Beatty's arrival and now hurried forward.

"I've taken the liberty of having your bag sent up, doctor," he said. "Room seventeen. It's a nice one and I'll show you the way if you are ready."

"Lead on," said Beatty shortly, keeping to the role he had out-lined for himself.

"Will you be staying for long?" said the landlord, turning and pausing at the bend of the stair.

"Possibly two nights, possibly longer," said Beatty casually. "But two nights certainly."

"We don't get many medical gentlemen," said the landlord, throwing open the oak-panelled door of a very pleasant room, well up in the building and facing the High Street.

"I think you'll be comfortable enough here, doctor."

"I'm sure I shall," said Beatty.

He waited until the landlord's withdrawal and then disposed his few toilet articles and relocked his valise before placing it on a heavy oak rack at the foot of the brass bedstead. He washed his hands in the bowl on the solid dresser and glanced at his face in the hanging mirror. He looked the part perfectly; he could not detect any flaw in his appearance. Precisely at two-thirty he descended to the ground floor, hung his key on the hook designated, and made his way out into the main street.

A smart-looking cab with yellow door-panels was drawn up at the kerb. By its side, leaning casually against the shafts, was a tall, middle-aged man with an alert face and iron-grey hair, cut *en brosse*. He gave a smart salute as Beatty came up and looked at him shrewdly with piercing grey eyes.

"Toby Stevens at your service, doctor."

Beatty smiled inwardly. The waiter's messenger had evidently wasted no time in conveying the intended fare's degree and his generosity.

"Can I rely on your discretion, Stevens?"

The cabman put his finger to one side of his nose and looked at Beatty carefully.

"Try me, sir."

"Fair enough," Beatty replied. "I shall be in this town only a few days and I require someone who can carry messages if need be and generally assist me in my purposes."

Stevens grinned.

"I'm your man, sir. If you'd be good enough to step inside the cab, we can talk more easily and privately en route."

He pronounced the French phrase with the correct emphasis, and Beatty looked at him in surprise. However, he said nothing, but got into the cab and a few moments later they were lurching their way through the streets of the town and out into the rolling countryside beyond. Before they had cleared the town, Stevens had opened the communicating flap.

"I want to go to Brookfield Nursing Home," Beatty told him without any further preliminaries.

The young man could not see the driver's face, but there was something about the set of his back and the poise of the head which indicated that the information had not had a pleasing effect. The driver grunted. There was suspicion in his tones as he replied.

"Dr. Couchman's place?"

"Is there something wrong with it?"

Stevens shrugged.

"Then you don't know it, sir. Best stay clear is my advice. It's a strange sort of establishment and some queer sort of things go on there, from what I hear."

He turned to give Beatty the benefit of his honest features.

"Begging your pardon, sir. You aren't intending to take up a position on the staff by any chance?"

Beatty smiled. It might be out of character with his persona as Dr. Clyde Fitzgibbon, but he could not help it.

"Good heavens, no," he said. "I have some medical business with Dr. Couchman, that is all."

Stevens gave a sigh of relief, but Beatty's curiosity had been aroused.

"You said something about queer things. What sort of queer things?"

The cabman shook his head.

"I'd rather not say, sir. You'll find out in due course. But they have loonies up there and there's some shocking screaming from time to time."

Beatty put up his hand and adjusted his pince-nez which was in danger of quitting his nose with the lurching of the cab. They were clear of the town now and turning at a cross-roads. The countryside was open and rolling and probably would have been cheerful in summer, but now the haze was again obscuring the sun; the cold was advancing with the lateness of the day, and there was a melancholy engendered by the cabman's information which Beatty was finding hard to shake off.

They had gone some little distance along a winding rutted road before the young investigator spoke again, this time of more mundane matters.

"I will not question you further, Stevens. And after all, asylums do get strange reputations. What will be your fee for taking me there, waiting, and bringing me back?"

Stevens named his price. It seemed inordinately modest to Beatty.

"Does that include the waiting?" he asked.

Stevens smiled.

"All day if necessary," he said, cracking his whip over the fine-looking chestnut between the shafts.

"Very well," Beatty said. "My business today will not take long. I will add a guinea to your payment if you stand at my disposal."

Stevens smiled broadly this time, turning his strong face back over his shoulder to look at his passenger.

"For that, doctor, I will stand at your disposal all the while you are in Woking."

He closed the flap and left Beatty to his thoughts; the road had been rising for some time, and it was just half an hour later that they came to a signpost which indicated that the village of Send was only a few miles off. Stevens turned on to a rutted track which spiralled off in a south-easterly direction through heavy thickets of pine and spruce.

The road was still rising and the cold was beginning to penetrate the cab now, the hooves of the horse sending ringing echoes from the iron-hard ground. The jingle of the harness, the occasional crack of the driver's whip, and the distant lowing of cattle should have had a sprightly effect on Beatty's mind, but the young man's thoughts were beginning to be coloured more and more by the nature of his errand; by the talk about the doctor's nursing home for the insane; and by the wild and inhospitable nature of the landscape into which every beat of the horse's hooves was taking them.

The cab lurched and Beatty was flung from side to side, the

springs creaking, as the vehicle rumbled across the ruts; the windows were commencing to be rimed with frost and the cushions were ice-cold to the touch. The harsh cawing of rooks sounded from far off, and the shadows were long upon the ground.

Beatty scratched a patch of clear glass in the casement and looked across to where the trunks of the pines barred the sullen sky; in the valley beyond the belts of trees there was not a single cottage, not a wisp of smoke to denote any human habitation in all that bleak desolation. The young investigator realised with a wry astringency that he was a city man at heart; nature unadorned by man's handiwork had an uncompromising alien quality that was not at all to his taste.

The cab lurched again as they came to a place where the trees dropped away, and they were traversing an upland plain; the sun was sinking now, a red ball beyond the haze, and the long shadows on the ground seemed to fall with a leaden weight upon the heart. Thin curves of smoke were ascending from sweeping parkland below, and Beatty could see large iron gates.

Stevens reined in the cab and pointed with his whip at the massive grey stone building that lay athwart the distance.

"Brookfield Nursing Home," he said.

The cab turned in between the huge stone pillars and rumbled up the long driveway which ran straight as a rule between the fenced fields on either side. Once they had probably been lawns, judging by the remains of flower beds that Beatty could see, and by the occasional gracious sweep of an elm which threw heavy shadows across the grass.

But now the terrain was unkempt paddock, and rough-coated cattle grazed beneath the trees, pausing only to glance momentarily in the direction of the cab before turning back to their browsing. The driveway was longer than he had thought, and it was several minutes before Stevens at last turned the cab in a circular expanse of gravel, and the vehicle gritted beneath a stone portico into a gloomy courtyard which blocked out most of the light from the sky.

Beatty got down from the step, his breath smoking in the bitter air, and gazed up in distaste at the grey stone walls. The upper

storeys were stained with the light of the dying sur
casements were like so many black holes in the
hemmed him in on three sides. He clasped the mec
ging deeper into his overcoat, and slammed the dc

It made a sullen, echoing noise that reverberated round the courtyard and seemed to emphasise the doom-laden aspect of the place. God help any inmates here, Beatty said to himself; it was a strange-looking nursing home Dr. Couchman operated, and he began to see something of the background out of which Miss Meredith's suspicions had been formed.

He glanced up at the façade again, noting the damp patches where rain had penetrated from the roof; sickly coloured lichens grew on the walls, and there were ferns jutting from cracks in the dilapidated brickwork.

Stevens smiled at his expression.

"I'll be here, sir," he said reassuringly.

He drew a pipe from his pocket and began to fill it, apparently well at ease, though the horse snuffled nervously and pawed at the gravel. Beatty crossed over toward the immense Palladian porch which jutted from the centre wing. As he got close to the worn steps he could see the legend in faded gold script on the fanlight above the oak door: BROOKFIELD NURSING HOME. He turned to glance round once and saw that Stevens had stepped into the interior of the cab.

A few wisps of smoke from his pipe remained in the air, but already, in the brief seconds that had elapsed as Beatty crossed the courtyard, he had thrown a thick blanket over the horse. Beatty again had an impression of efficiency and kindliness; they were useful traits he might have need of.

He pulled the rusty iron bell-pull in the metal rose that was green with verdigris and heard the cracked echo of the bell resounding along the corridors. The brass handle gave easily to his touch, and Beatty stepped into a broad lobby with a dusty parquet floor. There was a second glass door within, and Beatty opened it to find himself in a long corridor painted a depressing shade of green.

There was a stone floor underfoot and a pervasive aroma of carbolic hanging in the air. Two gas-jets burned feebly in wall fittings, and there was a printed list of rules on the far wall which made equally depressing reading. Beatty walked a little way down the corridor and found two more passages which led at right angles. It was bitterly cold in here; almost more so than in the open air outside. To add to Beatty's disquiet there was the faint sound of someone sobbing, coming from the far distance.

He walked a little farther down, looking more at ease than he felt. A large door on the right bore the legend "Matron" in white lettering, and he was making for this when he heard the sharp, imperative footsteps of someone hurrying along one of the intersecting corridors. A small woman with iron-grey hair under her cap, and wearing a long belted smock of grey material, almost burst into view. She carried a large bunch of keys at her leather belt, and she gave off a harsh jangling noise with every step she took. Little grey eyes, red and inflamed, looked suspiciously at Beatty.

"No visitors allowed!" the apparition snapped. "Sundays and Thursdays only."

Beatty was on familiar ground now. He gave the woman an imperious glance and said in an offhand manner, "Pray tell Dr. Couchman that I wish to see him."

A startled expression passed across the woman's face, but she drew her narrow shoulders up in a manner which suggested astonishment at the visitor's impertinence.

"Dr. Couchman does not see visitors without prior appointment."

"He'll see me, I think," said Beatty easily.

He got out one of the cards and handed it to the woman.

"Just tell him Dr. Clyde Fitzgibbon is here to see him on an important matter."

The woman turned the card over as though she could not read. A red spot was burning on either cheekbone. She bit her lip and checked what she had been about to say.

"I beg your pardon, doctor. I am the Matron, Miss Price. Would you step into my office, please."

Beatty gave her a frosty bow and walked through the door the woman in the grey gown opened for him. It was a once handsome room, now dusty and neglected, lit only by a single gas-lamp in a white shade, and with a fire of small-coals glowing on the hearth. Beatty stepped toward it, putting down his bag on a plain deal table, extending his hands to the warmth.

"Brutal for the time of the year, do you not think, ma'am?" he said in his most pompous manner.

The Matron stood watching him, awkward but still vigilant, holding the card stiffly at her side.

"Indeed, sir," she said at last. "Some of our old people feel it so. We buried two only last week."

Beatty clicked his tongue.

"Ah, well, Matron, they will do it," he said, shaking his head. "They will do it."

The Matron was evidently confused by his enigmatic remark for she suddenly bobbed her head as though she had remembered an important duty.

"I will just tell Dr. Couchman you are here," she said.

She went out quickly and shut the door after her. Beatty crossed over to it and listened. He could hear the sharp rap of her feet in the distance. She was running. He was smiling to himself as he went back into the centre of the room. His practised eye was already raking shelves, tables, and desk in the semigloom, looking for details that would assist him in his present line of thought.

A bureau at the far side of the room, against the fireplace wall, attracted his attention. He went over, walking quietly on the worn carpet, his ears alert for any unusual sounds. He opened the desk and searched through it expertly. There were files there; he carried one over toward the light of the fire. They were in crabbed handwriting; mostly case-notes relating to patients, he guessed.

What he wanted was something on the girl's father; he would not find it here, in the Matron's office. Couchman would keep such files on private patients in his own office, unless he had a consulting room in Woking. Dotterell had already checked on the doctor's background; he would have put it on record had it been so. Beatty pushed the documents back in the bureau and closed it, convinced that the case-notes on Mr. Meredith would lie ready to the doctor's hand.

He was ostensibly admiring the cast of a particularly hideous bronze eagle that fluttered over the mantelpiece when the door was suddenly flung open. The Matron stood framed in the opening. Beatty smiled mockingly at her.

"I see you can walk quietly, Matron, when you have a mind to."

The woman flushed, anger in her eyes, but she controlled herself with an effort.

"If you will follow me, sir," she said smoothly. "Dr. Couchman will see you immediately."

6

BROOKFIELD NURSING HOME

BEATTY followed the woman in the grey uniform down a succession of gloomy corridors where flickering gas-jets cast a feeble light on discoloured walls and peeling paintwork. The linoleum underfoot was worn and cracked, and twice he almost stumbled. The place was a labyrinth of corridors, and once they passed a large oak-panelled hall in what was evidently a more opulent part of the house.

Beatty surmised that Brookfield was a private mansion that had seen better days and was now reduced to its present level through the enormous expense of its upkeep. The cold persisted through all the corridors, and the young investigator pitied the inmates with all his heart. From what he had seen he had already formed the opinion that cold and malnutrition were two of the major factors in the deaths of elderly patients.

They had twice passed small groups of inmates in the corridors; one composed entirely of women of shrunken and imbecilic countenance, whose vacant eyes and drooling lips bespoke minds that were already far beyond the confines of earth. The other was of men, mostly of the same type, but one was of imposing bearing and a cut above the others. His eyes had caught Beatty's and he had seemed about to open his mouth to utter some greeting, but a warning glance from a tall black-bearded fellow in a long smock, evidently one of the male attendants, had reduced him to mumbling silence.

As they passed the entrance of the panelled hall, a great bubbling cry as of some mortal at the very furthest extremity of terror had sounded and echoed along the corridors. Beatty had stopped suddenly with an involuntary constriction of the heart; the pain and sadness in the mindless howling had seemed to epitomise the hopelessness and utter helplessness of the inmates of this melancholy place.

Beatty glanced swiftly around him, but so complex was the maze of corridors it proved impossible to locate the direction from which the sounds were coming. The change of colour in his cheeks may have betrayed him, for the Matron gave him a sharp look and pursed her lips.

But all she said was, "Number 314. Mad Bess. Bread and water diet tonight. She has always been troublesome."

Beatty nodded, making some noncommittal remark to conceal the animosity he was beginning to feel for this woman. She had turned again now and was leading the way past the hall-entrance. They rounded another corner and were upon soft carpeting where cut-glass lamps glistened on gilt-framed oil-paintings that hung on the ornately panelled walls. The contrast was so great that Beatty blinked in astonishment.

The Matron rapped deferentially on a great oak door with highly polished brass fittings. She waited, her head bent against the panel before repeating the knock. A brass plate screwed to the door bore the incised inscription: SUPERINTENDENT. A gruff voice muttered something unintelligible from within.

The Matron opened the door and beckoned Beatty across the threshold.

"This is Dr. Fitzgibbon, doctor," she said in a markedly different voice to that she had used to Beatty. She actually simpered as she held the door open.

"You may leave us, Miss Price."

The Matron's eyes flickered as Beatty strode past her into the room, and he heard the door close softly behind him. He walked across as a tall, cadaverous-looking man in a rusty black frock-coat rose forbiddingly from behind a desk near the fireplace. The apartment was a handsome one with an elaborately painted ceiling, picked out in gilt and chocolate-brown. It had evidently once been the drawing room of the house but was now given over to more mundane processes.

Hundreds of sombrely bound books containing medical texts, Beatty guessed, were encased in stout wooden bookcases along two sides. The other sides were taken up respectively with long French windows looking on to the courtyard outside; and the fireplace wall, which had faded tapestry hangings on either side of the mantel.

A handsome fire roared in the marble fireplace, and the room, despite the lofty height of the ceiling, had a pleasing warmth that denoted the fire was kept going night and day in the winter-time. Beatty noticed one other curious thing in his brief walk toward Dr. Horace Couchman, who stood severely awaiting his approach.

All the bookcases were encased in stout wire-mesh grilles and, judging by the padlocks on them, were kept securely locked. Beatty skirted an insolent-looking lap-dog which sneered to itself upon a cushion set in the middle of the carpet.

"Your servant, sir," said Dr. Couchman in a metallic-sounding voice. "Though I should have preferred your writing. I never see visitors without an appointment."

"Then I am indeed honoured," said Beatty, coming to a halt and giving the other a slight bow. "You have made an exception in my case."

Dr. Couchman did not advance his hand, neither did Beatty extend his own. The two men stood looking at one another in silence for a moment. Beatty got the impression of a formidable intellect. Then Dr. Couchman turned away, inclining his slim hand toward a big leather-backed chair which stood at the fireplace side of the desk.

"Now that you are here," he said ungraciously, "pray take a seat. But be quick about your business. My time is precious."

He was about sixty years of age and of great height, though a premature stoop made him look shorter. He had a narrow, gaunt face, with deep lines running from the corners of his mouth which made the flesh look as though it were carved from some yellowish substance. The ears were large, the thinning hair still black and plastered down close to the skull. He had a large bony nose and the green-tinted spectacles he wore gave him a sinister appearance; he looked like some ungainly bird of prey in his severe black stock, white shirt, and the rusty black frock-coat.

Beatty, as he lowered himself into the chair, thought that he had seldom seen a more repellent-looking human being. He wondered why Meredith had such an ill-favoured personal physician. The girl had told him how they had come to meet, but it did not entirely explain the father's choice. He saw now that Couchman had reseated himself behind the desk and was regarding him with ill-disguised animosity.

"I'll not beat about the bush, Dr. Couchman," said Beatty in measured tones. "I'm here on disagreeable business."

He was not prepared for the doctor's violent start. He felt rather than saw the piercing glance the doctor's hidden eyes were giving him from behind the spectacles.

"How so, Dr. Fitzgibbon," he mumbled. "How so, sir?"

"We have a mutual acquaintance, I believe," said Beatty.

He opened his medical bag at this point and rummaged around importantly in its contents. He came up with a sheaf of papers and pretended to consult them. He looked at Couchman disarmingly through the clear glass of his pince-nez.

"Miss Angela Meredith."

This time the doctor's bony fingers on the desk in front of him twitched almost imperceptibly. Beatty could see a slight shudder pass through his frame. It was like a wind blowing through dead grass in a churchyard. Beatty chuckled quietly within himself at the simile. It was an extremely apt one for Dr. Couchman. The gaunt doctor inclined his head toward his guest.

"I know the lady," he said grudgingly. "Her late father, Mr. Tredegar Meredith, was a personal friend and a patient of mine. A dreadful tragedy."

He bowed his head toward the desk as though the memory of Meredith's demise was almost too much for him. He reached in his trouser pocket and produced a none-too-clean handkerchief and blew his nose noisily upon it. Beatty waited until the small pantomime was over.

"Miss Meredith is not ill herself, I hope," Couchman went on, looking at him over the green spectacles. His eye-sockets were so deep they looked like holes in his face. He smiled thinly.

"But you are, of course, a physician yourself, are you not?"

He frowned and drummed with his fingers on the desk surface.

"I have never heard Meredith mention you."

"I am more in the way of being a friend of his daughter's," Beatty said.

Couchman sat back in his chair and regarded his visitor steadily for several seconds. The only sound in the big room was the fierce crackling of the fire. The warmth flowed out from the fireplace and lapped the two men.

"I see, Dr. Fitzgibbon. But what I do not see is why you should waste my time on such a busy afternoon."

"If you will hear me out, doctor, you will understand," Beatty said, a little more sharply than he had intended.

From the other's stiff attitude and tense position he knew he momentarily had the advantage; he followed it up swiftly.

"What was the cause of Mr. Meredith's death?" he said softly.

The green spectacles swivelled slowly to hold his own eyes. The voice was calm and icy.

"Are you not aware, doctor? Miss Meredith had the death certificate."

"I have not seen it," Beatty said.

He was watching Couchman carefully and he was satisfied with his own tactics so far. He would spring his surprises at the correct psychological moment. He had nothing but suspicion to work upon. Couchman said nothing, then bent swiftly and unlocked a drawer of his desk. He took out a green-backed file and put it down with much rustling and crackling.

"I have a copy here if you would care to see it."

He stopped as though a sudden thought had occurred to him. He glanced swiftly at Beatty's card in front of him.

"It occurs to me, Dr. Fitzgibbon, that I am expected to take a great deal on trust. . . ."

Beatty smiled.

"Oh, if that is what is concerning you, doctor, I have a letter of authorisation from Miss Meredith here."

He detached the letter the girl had written at his dictation and passed it over to the thin man. Couchman scanned it with rapidly rising anger. He was controlling himself with difficulty as he looked up.

"All seems in order."

He consulted the certificate.

"As Miss Meredith knows, her father died of a heart condition, accelerated by pneumonia, or in medical terms . . ."

"I understood he had a number of vomiting attacks," Beatty interrupted.

He studied the annoyance on Couchman's face. The doctor put the tips of his lean fingers together on the desk in front of him and regarded his interrupter balefully through the green spectacles.

"Meredith was a chronic dyspeptic," he said stiffly. "There has been much fever and sickness in town of late, as you must know, if you practise there."

He waited for Beatty to say something, but the young investigator merely inclined his head and the doctor went on.

"He had some sickness and vomiting, yes, in the earlier stages. Also acute diarrhoea and tenesmus. He went out without a coat, I understand, and caught a severe chill. That was no light matter for a man with angina. The pneumonia was the end of it."

He passed the certificate over to Beatty and regarded him grimly as his visitor studied the document in silence. Beatty looked up, the paper rustling in his hand.

"I have heard it said that the authorities are currently worried about cholera," he said mildly. "I practise in Wiltshire so I do not know if that be true of London or not."

"The idea is ridiculous to anyone with the slightest smattering of medical knowledge, in Mr. Meredith's case," Couchman sneered.

His eyes were very bright and glowing as he stared at Beatty.

"No doubt," returned Beatty. "But just to put the matter beyond question Miss Meredith has decided to have the body exhumed and an autopsy performed."

There was a silence so thunderous that it seemed like a physical presence within the room. Couchman turned an incredulous face toward Beatty. He opened his mouth once or twice, but only a faint choking noise came out his thin lips.

"I thought it only ethical to inform you in order that you may be represented," Beatty went on. "I shall be serving the papers later today and the examination will be carried out tomorrow afternoon."

Couchman had a face like death as he clutched at his throat and took a half-step toward the young investigator. Too late, he realised he was faced with a *fait accompli*. With an enormous effort of will he forced himself into calmness. He shrugged and crossed to the desk.

"An extraordinary idea," he said. "And had I been present I would naturally have disabused Miss Meredith of it. Frankly, I am surprised at your condoning Miss Meredith's actions, Dr. Fitz-gibbon."

Beatty put the death certificate back on the desk.

"But you were not there, Dr. Couchman," he said. "Miss Meredith was alarmed at the possibility. Naturally, there would be certain dangers to the household if her supposition were correct."

Couchman sat down suddenly like a puppet whose strings had been severed.

"A preposterous supposition," he said harshly. "I do not know how she could have reached such a conclusion. In cases of cholera the patient has great thirst . . ."

"You and I know differently, doctor," said Beatty sympathetically. "But there was a case of cholera confirmed in Paddington only yesterday. Should we not defer to the lady's wishes?"

Couchman stirred uneasily in his chair. Thus appealed to he was quite evidently at a loss.

"Mr. Meredith was buried at Brookwood," he said. "This is very short notice. The Superintendent will hardly be pleased . . ."

"I intend to visit him just as soon as I leave here," said Beatty coldly. "The cemetery has attendants enough, I understand. It should not take more than an hour or two to exhume the remains."

Couchman took another tack. He drummed with his thin fingers on the desk.

"I will go over and see the Superintendent myself," he said harshly.

"Very well." Beatty bowed. "Just as you wish. You will be present yourself?"

"Naturally," said Couchman, turning the green spectacles menacingly toward his visitor.

"Shall we say three o'clock, then?"

"If you say so," said Couchman.

He stood up, outwardly calm; he seemed to have recovered himself by now.

"You will be performing the autopsy yourself?"

Beatty shook his head.

"I am merely an interested observer. I have an eminent authority coming down from London in the morning. No, doctor, I really cannot take up any more time of such a busy man. Good afternoon."

Beatty broke off abruptly and got up from the chair. He affected to overlook Couchman's outstretched hand.

"I can find my own way out, thank you."

He was chuckling to himself as he strode down the corridor, Miss Price pattering ineffectually at his heels. He went through the glass lobby into the bitter outer air of the courtyard. The lamps of Stevens's cab glimmered through the darkness. The pipe-smoking form of its owner ejected itself from the interior.

"At your service, doctor. Where to now?"

"Back to Woking," said Beatty, stepping up into the vehicle. "I want to send a telegraph message at the station and then to see if the hotel dinner is as good as the lunch."

Stevens chuckled. A shower of sparks came from his pipe and formed a dancing chain in the air as he ascended to the box. He cracked his whip over the horse, removing the blanket with his disengaged hand almost in the same movement.

"You won't be disappointed, sir."

He was already turning the cab down the long entrance drive, the wheels rumbling over the rutted ground. They had hardly gone a few hundred yards before there was a thunder of hooves behind them. A gig with bright sidelights bounced and hurtled alongside and was then lost in the gloom ahead. But not before Beatty had seen the lean figure of Dr. Horace Couchman standing up on the seat and lashing the horse like a madman.

Stevens opened the hatch and glanced downward at his passenger.

"It's not only the inmates as is mad," he observed sagely, his eyes still fixed on the careering figure of the asylum-master in the dusk ahead.

The carriage rumbled through the entrance gates of Brookfield and proceeded back in the direction of Woking at a more sedate pace.

7

INSPECTOR MUNSON

BEATTY examined Dotterell's telegraphed message for the third time and put the crumpled form back into his overcoat pocket. He beat his feet on the station platform and crossed over to the waiting room. There were few people about this afternoon, and despite the lingering effects of his postlunch brandy at the White Horse, the rawness of the day was getting to him.

He smiled vaguely at the two ladies huddled on the oak bench of the waiting room and bent toward the small-coal fire which burnt in the grate. The sunshine of the previous day had gone and a thin mist was rising. He hoped Rossington's train would not be delayed because of the weather conditions; it was almost ten minutes to two and it would throw out the schedule he had planned.

He looked up as a low thunder made the floor tremble; steam swirled across the frosted window-panes as the train pulled in. Beatty hurried out and went anxiously down the platform, scanning the passengers as they descended quickly from the carriages. Doors slammed and the station-master went by, a self-important figure in gold braid.

A young man of athletic appearance, dressed in a stove-pipe hat and wearing a heavy plaid cloak, was just lifting two cases down on to the platform as Beatty approached him. White teeth showed beneath his thick beard as he burst out laughing on catching sight of Beatty.

"My God, Clyde," he said, taking a small cigar out of his mouth and pumping the investigator by the hand. "What are you meant to be? I did not know that Woking was noted for its fancy dress parades."

Beatty looked round cautiously, bending to lift one of his friend's cases.

"I thought Dotterell had apprised you of the importance of the occasion," he said drily.

Rossington shoved his hat back on his head and slammed the carriage door with a muscular elbow.

"And so he did," he said calmly, puffing furiously at his cigar. "But he didn't prepare me for this."

They were walking down the platform now, making for the station exit, following the groups of passengers. Rossington was looking keenly about him.

"I really appreciate this, John," said Beatty. "I cannot do without expert medical advice. The doctor in the case has all the appearances of a scoundrel."

Rossington shot his friend a shrewd glance from his steady grey eyes.

"I will reserve judgement until later," he said. "In the meantime this will cost you a decent dinner and a bottle of wine."

"No fear of that," said Beatty, laughing in his turn. "In fact I have booked you a room next to mine at the White Horse. It's an excellent establishment and should furnish all your requirements."

"As long as the barmaids are up to standard," said Rossington approvingly.

He was about thirty-five years of age and his robust build bespoke the man of action.

"You had best make your own arrangements over that," said Beatty, smiling.

"I can spare only two days," warned Rossington as they came to the station entrance.

"The business will not take that long," Beatty told him. "And don't forget I am Dr. Clyde Fitzgibbon down here."

"I won't forget," Rossington replied, giving up his ticket at the barrier.

The two men walked across to where the lamps of Stevens's cab shimmered through the encroaching mist. Rossington pulled his cloak round him more closely and puffed fragrant blue smoke from his cigar.

"You've got all the equipment, I take it?" Beatty asked.

The doctor nodded.

"Everything we're likely to need," he said shortly. "I have the exhumation order here."

He tapped his chest with a prodigious forefinger.

"A magistrate friend of mine. I won't bore you with the trouble I had getting it. It will cost you a glass of brandy tonight."

"It's worth a bottle," Beatty assured him.

He was scanning the passers-by as they crossed to the carriage. Stevens got down from the driving seat and handed in the doctor's two cases.

"This is Dr. Rossington," Beatty told Stevens. "He will be staying at the White Horse tonight. I wish you to extend to him the same service as you would to me."

Stevens straightened up and gave the young doctor a salute.

"I'm your man, sir."

He saw his fares in and slammed the door behind them. He got back up in the driving seat and opened the flap.

"Where to, gentlemen?"

"Brookwood Cemetery," said Beatty crisply.

It was quite dark inside the cab, but Beatty noted a strange expression pass over the driver's face. But he said nothing further, merely slammed the hatch shut and whipped up the horse. The hoof-beats made a melancholy sound in the clammy envelope of the mist which was rapidly increasing as they turned in the roadway and set off for their sombre destination.

"What did you think about my poison theory?" said Beatty.

The two men sat opposite each other in the cab and stared grimly at one another. Rossington shook his head.

"It's difficult to tell," he said cautiously. "From the young lady's description his death could be entirely natural. On the other hand . . ."

He let the sentence hang unfinished in the air. The mist was thicker now and penetrated clammily into the cab, but the horse, sure-footed on its own local roads, proceeded at a smart trot as though confident of its destination.

"Exactly," said Beatty.

"Anyway, I've come well prepared," Rossington assured him. "I presume you wished me to test for arsenical poisoning. And I shall naturally look for other poisons. This Dr. Couchman will not be too pleased. What was his reaction to all this?"

"Baffled rage, followed by wild alarm," Beatty grinned. "I have told him the young lady suspects cholera."

"Preposterous!" exclaimed the young doctor, slapping his hands together sharply either in expostulation or to restore the circulation.

"Almost exactly Couchman's words," his friend went on.

He looked shrewdly at the other.

"However, that does pose a problem. As soon as he sees you with all your apparatus he will know what poisons you are testing for."

"I can't help that," Rossington exclaimed. "I'm here to conduct a post-mortem examination. As the physician who signed the death certificate, Couchman has a perfect right to be present."

Beatty stroked his chin in silence for a moment.

"Then I must find some way of drawing him off," he said.

"That's as may be," Rossington rejoined, sinking back gloomily on to the cushions. "I shall be glad to get through to this evening and that dinner you promised me. I had a most sketchy early lunch."

Beatty chuckled.

"The fast will do you good, John. You've put on weight since last I saw you."

Rossington's eyes sparkled with humour. Then a frown crossed his bearded features.

"I hope all arrangements have been made for the exhumation. Because otherwise we shall have a devil of a wait. The ground's as hard as iron at the moment. It will mean pick-axe work."

"I don't think you need worry about that," Beatty countered. "The last time I saw Dr. Couchman, he was riding like a demon to warn the Superintendent."

"No matter, then," said Rossington. "I thought it advisable to ask. It wouldn't be the first time I've arrived at a cemetery to find no arrangements made and no one aware of my coming."

"They order things better in Surrey," said Beatty, smiling again.

The cab lurched just then and they appeared to be turning. Beatty got up to look out the window. He saw they had come to a cross-roads. Through the mist appeared a plain van with a fine pair of horses in the shafts. As they came closer Beatty could see that the vehicle wore the cipher of the Surrey County Force emblazoned on its side. Beatty got down as Stevens reined in his horse.

A small, alert-looking man, clean-shaven except for long side-whiskers, jumped down from the box and came to meet him. He had a flapped cap jammed on his head and a flowing brown cloak. His bronzed frank face wore a welcoming smile.

"Dr. Fitzgibbon?"

Beatty bowed and shook his hand.

"I'm Inspector Munson of the Surrey Constabulary," said the short man. "I got your message. Exceedingly civil, if I may say so."

"I thought it as well under the circumstances."

Munson gave him a sharp look from deep, thoughtful eyes.

"I wish I could say the same for everyone who comes into our territory," he said crisply. "Only a month ago I learned of a similar exhumation through reading one of our local journals. That one reached as far as Scotland Yard."

He smiled reminiscently.

"Will you ride with us or do you prefer your own conveyance?" said Beatty.

The Inspector ordered his driver to follow on behind and sprang up into the interior of the cab, Rossington moving his cases and making room on the seat.

"This is Dr. Rossington, who will be performing the post-mortem," said Beatty, making the introductions.

The police officer shook hands with him effusively.

"We have met before, doctor," he said jovially. "Of Charing Cross Hospital, are you not?"

Rossington looked startled.

"I'm afraid I cannot recall . . ." he began.

"You are becoming famous," said Beatty maliciously.

The Inspector chuckled.

"You met a mixed Surrey team at rugby last year," he said. "I've seldom seen a more aggressive three-quarter. I bear the marks of your tackling on my nose still."

And he stroked that appendage tenderly while R
into peals of laughter. He pumped Munson's hand

"A new breed of police officer, by George," he
man after my own heart . . ."

"What do you expect to find, gentlemen?" said Munson
shrewdly, settling himself back and producing a pipe which he proceeded to fill.

"I'd rather leave that open for the moment," said Beatty. "The
dead man's daughter has expressed herself not quite satisfied with
the manner of her father's death. There's no more to it than that."

Munson nodded, his square face a carmine mask as he puffed to
get the pipe going.

"You have the necessary authorisation, of course?"

For answer Rossington produced the exhumation order and
other documents while Beatty passed over Miss Meredith's letter.
The County detective studied them in silence before passing them
back.

"Very well, gentlemen. Routine. But Dr. Couchman won't be
pleased."

"You know him, then?" said Beatty shrewdly.

Munson nodded, his face impassive in the glow of the pipe. It
was darker in the cab now with the thickening of the mist.

"I know him all right," he said significantly. "But I know nothing
against him. There's a deal of difference, gentlemen."

And with that somewhat enigmatic pronouncement he ventured nothing further until they had reached the end of their
journey.

8

POST-MORTEM

It was just ten to three when the cab lurched and rumbled on to
a rutted lane in which the pools of frozen water reflected back
the misty sky like diamonds. It was, if anything, even colder than
before, and Stevens's face above his pipe looked pinched and
shrunken as he drew the horse back to a slow walk. The mist had

.nomentarily thinned, and the occupants of the cab could see that they were running alongside a high stone wall.

In response to Beatty's querying look, Munson, with a careless glance through the window, said briskly, "We've arrived, gentlemen. I've no doubt the Superintendent will be using one of the small chapels. They tend to be discreet about these affairs."

The cab was turning again and came to a halt in front of an iron gate. Rossington and Beatty descended, each carrying one of the doctor's bags. They looked curiously about them, but Munson went on puffing unconcernedly at his pipe. Another closed carriage was standing just inside the gates, the tall gaunt form of Dr. Couchman standing sourly beside it. He gave a start as the three men came toward him.

"I did not realise, Dr. Fitzgibbon, that this was to be a public performance," he said in sneering tones.

"Hardly public, doctor," Beatty replied imperturbably. "May I introduce you to my colleague, Dr. John Rossington of Charing Cross Hospital. He will be making the examination."

"Indeed," said Couchman with a stiff bow. "This is an honour, Dr. Rossington. Your reputation—and your scientific papers—are not unknown, even in this backward corner of Surrey."

Rossington took the gaunt man's hand with ill-concealed distaste. An instinctive dislike of this tall figure with the green-tinted spectacles was welling up in his mind, despite his private resolution to maintain a professional impartiality. A grey-smocked attendant was already closing and locking the cemetery gates behind them. Beatty noted that Stevens had got down resignedly from his seat and had disappeared into the cab. It was likely to be a long wait this afternoon.

"And this is Inspector Munson of the County Constabulary," Beatty said, as the little officer came forward with a smile.

Couchman recoiled as though something had stung him. He took the official's hand gingerly and relinquished it as soon as possible.

"The police," he hissed between his teeth. "I did not understand that the police were to be present."

"It has no significance," said Beatty impatiently, the clanking of the chains of the cemetery gate sounding unnaturally loud in the bitter air. "It is required by law."

"Of course, of course."

Couchman drew back, a little mollified' suspiciously at the three men.

"Nothing to worry about, doctor," said Mu. "Just routine."

"Had we not better get on," said Beatty, impatience ᴄ the edges of his voice. "Dr. Rossington is an extremely busy n.

"Quite, quite," said Couchman, motioning with his hand. "It is only a short distance."

He led the way down the path which wound among great green banks of rhododendron, flowerless and forbidding now, back-grounded by heavy groves of birch trees. Their feet made brittle scraping noises in the dead leaves which carpeted the path and which were thickly bonded by the frost. A brisk walk of a hundred yards, round the shallow curves of the path, brought them within sight of their destination.

To the right was a green canvas shelter, and two men in thick grey uniforms were stacking tools; just beyond them could be seen the gaping hole in the loam which had contained the mortal remains of the late Mr. Meredith. At that melancholy sight Beatty, hardened as he was to death and the violent events of his chosen profession, could not repress a faint flicker of foreboding.

The mist was curling damply through the trees and the coffin evidently had only just been removed, as two more attendants came back from the small stone chapel in the distance, wiping their hands.

The canvas was pulled back round the grave, hiding the heaped earth and the blank pit. The men blew on their fingers and stamped their feet; their large red faces were turned incuriously in their direction as the small procession went past.

Beatty had noted a metal marker which carried the painted number 2334 set into the turf at the side of the grave before the canvas was pulled across, hiding it from view.

"A fine job they had of it," said Couchman. "Two hours, most of it pick-axe work."

He led the way on to a secondary path which led directly to the chapel. Near the entrance they were met by a burly man with an ash-grey beard who was wheeling a heavy wooden trolley. He gave

.tty a curious look and pushed the vehicle up against one of the
.ittress walls of the building.

The Superintendent, a middle-aged man with a heavy black
beard and piercing eyes, was waiting in the chapel annexe, suitably solemn and with a large register in his hand. Couchman made
brief introductions. The Superintendent, whose name was Bateman, nodded distantly.

"I must apologise for the short notice," Beatty said affably. The
Superintendent smiled, showing white teeth beneath the red, full
lips.

"It happens, gentlemen," he said in a voice which had a strong
Scots accent. "In any event we're used to the unusual here, if I may
say so."

He ushered the party through into a bare stone chapel with
a tiled floor and locked the door behind them. The coffin stood
on trestles at one side, near the windows. Its occupant had been
removed and lay now on the plain stone altar, wrapped in canvas.
Oil lamps shone a mellow light on to the bleak scene. It was bitterly cold in the chapel. Their feet echoed hollowly over the flags
as they went forward.

"Members of my staff are ready to assist, doctor, if you wish,"
said Bateman, looking from Rossington to Beatty and then back
again. Munson, who was known to him, stood against the wall of
the chapel, his hat in his hand, and gazed in a bored manner at the
proceedings.

"It's very cold in here," Beatty said.

The Superintendent and the two doctors looked at him in surprise and Beatty realised he had made a cardinal error.

"So I should think, doctor, for an autopsy, eh?" said Bateman
jocularly.

"It can't be too cold for me," said Rossington crisply, taking off
his cloak and throwing it carelessly over the back of one of the
pews. He shot a warning glance at Beatty.

"We'll just get rid of the formalities first," said the Superintendent. He consulted the register, holding it to the light of the
lamps and in a position where the three doctors could see it. None
of them seemed interested, so he lowered his glance again and ran
his thick finger along the columns.

"Here we are: Tredegar Meredith. Number 2334. You have the necessary documents?"

They were produced and he studied them in silence, the breath smoking out of his mouth, so cold was the chapel.

"All appears to be in order, gentlemen."

He pointed across at an oak door.

"And now, if you'll step over yonder to the private room you'll find a fire. You'll want to warm yourself before you start work, doctor. And I've an excellent cordial for the inner man."

"That sounds a good idea," said Rossington, his eyes lighting up, and even the acidulous Couchman relaxed the severity of his features.

"You have somewhere for me to wash, I take it?" Rossington went on.

The Superintendent's smile gleamed briefly in his beard.

"Certainly, doctor. We have every facility at Brookwood. Now, if you'll follow me."

He led the way through the far door and the party filed in, leaving the chapel to the silent occupant beneath the grey canvas shroud.

The case of instruments winked in the lamplight as Rossington put it down on the trestle table which had been pushed forward into a position near the altar. His strong, capable hands moved to the shroud, drawing back the thick canvas. Despite the coldness of the chapel he had removed his jacket and stood now in embroidered waistcoat and rolled-up sleeves. He rummaged in his bag and produced a white apron which he tied round himself without looking at the others.

Beatty, watching him from near the window, realised that this was a different Rossington from the man he knew; he was the absolute professional, completely absorbed in his task, oblivious of anything or anyone else. He shifted his gaze across to Munson who stood smoking, one leg crossed over the other, his bored glance in reality missing very little.

Dr. Couchman sat on a high stool near to where Rossington was placed, so that he could see every movement that his colleague made. Despite the warmth of the punch he had just drunk, the chill of this place was beginning to penetrate the bones. Mr. Bateman, the Superintendent, his register and other papers under his arm, stood stiffly midway between the tableau formed by the corpse and Munson; he was so erect he looked as though he were at a military parade.

An addition to the scene, the burly man with the ash-grey beard, who had been wheeling the trolley as they arrived at the chapel, stood somewhat nervously near the Superintendent, so as to be on call. Bateman had insisted on his presence; he was the Foreman-gardener at Brookwood and would no doubt act as a witness for his superior if anything untoward occurred today.

Beatty shot him a glance from time to time; there was something curious about the man's manner, he felt, which did not stem only from the sombre nature of the occasion. Dr. Couchman evidently thought so too, because he got down from his stool and went over and spoke to the man in low earnest tones. Beatty looked up to find Munson's gaze fixed upon him in an ironic manner.

He eased himself away from the wall and went over to stand near the little detective. The pipe smoke was not unwelcome in the charnel atmosphere of the place. Dusk had fallen outside now, and the light of the lamps shone on the white luminescence of the mist which wreathed damply about the window-panes.

Rossington had pulled back the canvas and was examining the corpse with deft, practised movements. Beatty thought he saw Couchman start as the bulk of a large fat man slid into view. The body was of lardlike consistency and sagging, but the extreme coldness of the weather had acted as a preservative and none of the usual processes of decay appeared to have taken place.

But the deadly sponge of putrefaction had already settled over the obese, heavy features, with their handlebar moustache, and the outlines of the visage, never firm in life, had begun to blur. Beatty was not squeamish, but there was something obscene about the figure on the altar slab; the young investigator was the last person to expect nobility in death, but this was something else again. Strange to realise that so gross an envelope was the source for such a beautiful woman as his client.

Rossington had seized a scalpel and was beginning his initial cut, a long furrow of concentration on his face. Beatty turned back to the figure of the County detective, who gave him a wry smile, noting his expression.

"Pathology is not my forte," said Beatty hastily, conscious that he might be cutting a rather odd figure as a medical man. "And these surroundings . . ."

Munson nodded sympathetically.

"I entirely agree, doctor. I feel we'd be better occupied in the Superintendent's parlour, yonder."

Beatty concurred. A germ of an idea was in his mind. He crossed over to Couchman who was about to resume his stool. The cadaverous doctor stiffened as Beatty touched his arm.

"This may take some time," Beatty whispered. "Our friend here has suggested we would be more comfortable in the Superintendent's room. Would you care to join us?"

Couchman hesitated, his skull-like face turned over his shoulder to where Rossington bent forward in the lamplight.

"We are supposed to be observers," he muttered.

"Quite so," said Beatty swiftly. "But Dr. Rossington is an impeccable and impartial authority in these matters. And we have two witnesses in the Superintendent and his man there."

Munson grinned.

"I have a flask of whisky in my hip pocket, gentlemen," he added. "Just the thing for a cold day."

Dr. Couchman's eyes brightened.

"I am agreeable, if we both withdraw," he said softly. "As a matter of fact there are a number of things I wanted to ask you, Dr. Fitzgibbon. I will just have a word with the Superintendent."

He crossed over to that official while Beatty took the opportunity to move toward Rossington, averting his gaze from the thing on the table. He noticed a U-shaped glass tube with a nozzle inside the doctor's half-open bag.

"We're going inside," he said, so softly that the Foreman, only three yards away, heard nothing. Rossington nodded curtly.

"Give me half an hour," he said.

Beatty withdrew as Couchman came toward him. Munson had joined them. The doctor's green spectacles glinted in the lamplight.

"The Superintendent is agreeable," Couchman said crisply. "Shall we adjourn to a more salubrious atmosphere?"

9

BEATTY IS DISAPPOINTED

"Completely negative, you say!"

Dr. Couchman's face was alive with triumphant malice. He turned toward Beatty in the dimness of the chapel.

"I told you there was absolutely no need for this, Dr. Fitzgibbon."

"Nevertheless, I was obliged to carry out Miss Meredith's wishes," said Beatty stonily.

"My findings generally corroborate your stated cause of death," said Rossington. "I shall be sending you my formal report, of course. There are slight discrepancies, but that is natural, as some conditions are not verifiable without an autopsy, as you are well aware."

"Certainly," said Couchman smugly.

Beatty turned abruptly away and looked toward the group round the altar where the remains of the late Mr. Meredith were being none too reverently lifted back into the coffin by the cemetery attendants. The Superintendent, his face wearing its official expression, hovered massively to one side, an occasional sharp word keeping his workers briskly to heel.

Munson, his face wreathed in pipe-fumes, stood a short way off and watched the proceedings, his hands thrust into his overcoat pockets. He had not said anything when Rossington's findings were announced. It was quite dark outside now, and lanterns had been lit in the chapel porch. It was, if anything, even colder than when they had first arrived, and the attendants looked blue and pinched.

Beatty, his disappointment at Rossington's verdict covered by outward indifference, lounged over toward the Superintendent and aimlessly watched the proceedings. The sharp smell of carbolic came to his nostrils; the men were scrubbing the altar and the surround with hot water and soap.

Beyond the group was another, struggling to lift the coffin back on to the trolley. The young investigator again noticed the Foreman, the burly grey-bearded man, who was screwing the coffin lid back in place now that the casket was secured. His face was as grey as his beard in the light of the lamps, and twice the screwdriver slipped, gouging the woodwork of the casket, so that the Superintendent was obliged to remonstrate sharply.

He turned haggard eyes toward Beatty and then bent to his task again. The young man was aware that Rossington was back at his elbow, buttoning his coat, his frank open face looking quizzically at his friend.

"I'm to partake of the Superintendent's hospitality if you'll forgive me," he said jocularly, putting his hand on Beatty's arm. "I was working, you may remember, while you were sitting in comfort."

Beatty smiled, turning his eyes from the group by the coffin.

"Wait," called the Superintendent sharply to his men, coming back toward Rossington.

"Well, doctor," he said keenly. "You've had a cold afternoon of it. But if you'll step inside we'll endeavour to make up for that."

"You have been most kind," said Rossington, preparing to follow him. "I'll not be long," he added over his shoulder to Beatty.

The young man nodded and went to join Munson. The thin form of Couchman had already disappeared through the main entrance of the chapel, doubtless on some errand of his own. The Surrey detective was silent for a moment. Then he took the pipe from his mouth. A thin chain of red sparks danced to the floor, like fireflies in the gloom.

"You seem surprised, doctor."

He chuckled, the sound seeming incongruous in that place of death.

"And in fact, at the risk of causing offence, I would say that you were disappointed at the outcome."

He looked sharply at Beatty as he put the pipe back in his mouth.

"I thought the profession stood together."

Beatty turned away, confused. He would have liked to confide in the efficient, engaging Surrey man, but the bitterness of failure was still heavy in his throat. And yet he had a sense of relief at the back of his mind; that the suspicions of his client were unfounded.

At least that would help to relieve her distress. And once again, as earlier in the afternoon, the image of Angela Meredith came unbidden to his consciousness.

"You don't answer, doctor," Munson persisted, walking into the centre of the floor and staring at the workmen, who were just finishing securing the coffin lid. Beatty followed automatically, his footsteps echoing in the darkness of the bare vaulted ceiling.

"This is hardly the place," he said shortly.

Munson clapped his hat back on his head; the little sharp noise the palm of his hand made on the hard brim caused one of the men around the coffin to start. Once again Beatty caught the quick, almost furtive look of the Foreman.

"Meaning that you might discuss it elsewhere?" said Munson keenly. "At the White Horse, perhaps?"

"Possibly," Beatty said cautiously.

He had to move carefully in his simulated role, and he had already made two mistakes today; he was half-aware that the sharp little Surrey detective suspected that he was not a genuine medical man. Much as he would have liked to confide in him he could hardly do so without giving away his alias. Besides, what was the point now, he thought to himself. He had been infected by Miss Meredith's suspicions, and before he had ever left London he was convinced there was something sinister in Meredith's death; now that theory lay in ruins and he had instigated an expensive postmortem enquiry to no avail.

Something of his chagrin must have showed on his face because Munson, glancing shrewdly at him, was about to make some other remark when the door opened again to admit the emaciated figure of Couchman. Munson melted away in the gloom of the chapel as the doctor advanced toward them, his feet striking sharp echoes from the flagstones.

"Come along, doctor," Couchman said, with a return to his old manner. "We must see Mr. Meredith safely under ground again."

Beatty ignored the implied criticism in the man's tone and waited stonily as the attendants latched back the doors of the chapel, letting in gusts of raw foggy air. The Superintendent's door

opened at that point, and Rossington and Bateman came out with
satisfied faces and humour dancing on their lips.

One glance at the small procession drawn up, and Bateman
had resumed the sombre persona of Superintendent. He carried a
small prayer-book under his arm.

"This will only take a moment, gentlemen," he said quickly. "I
expect you'll be wanting to get back to town."

He walked briskly to the head of the coffin, the trolley squeaked
and rumbled as it was eased over the door-sill and on to the flags of
the porch. Beatty followed the others out, and the great portals of
the chapel slammed to behind them.

The cab rattled and scrabbled over the ruts with a grinding vibration as Toby Stevens put the horse into a smart trot. Beatty smiled
to himself in the semidarkness of the cab. The sidelights, throwing
yellow illumination through the frosted windows, made dancing
bars of shadow on the faces of Rossington and Munson on the seat
facing him. Apart from that and the occasional red glow from the
little detective's pipe, there was nothing else to relieve the darkness
which pressed in on them.

They were right out in the country, and not even the light of a
solitary cottage pierced the impenetrable curtain of mist. Munson
leaned forward and looked at Beatty intently for a moment, before
relaxing once again on to the cushions.

"You are smiling, Dr. Fitzgibbon," he said. "A curious conceit on
such a day as we have had, if you'll allow me to say so."

Beatty came out of his brown study with a jerk.

"I am sorry," he told his companions. "I was just thinking of
Stevens, our driver. He would rather risk a tumble in the dark than
wait a moment longer for the warmth and liquid refreshment
awaiting him in Woking."

"I daresay you would be the same in his place," said Rossington
carelessly. "May I speak in front of Mr. Munson here?"

"As doctor to doctor," said Beatty cautiously.

The Inspector looked curiously from one to the other and then
drew on his pipe with an ugly sucking noise.

"So you did have some preconceived ideas about this afternoon's proceedings," he said smugly.

"There was a suspicion only," said Beatty quickly. "There has been a deal of sickness in London of late. The symptoms are very similar to those of arsenical poisoning."

"I see."

Munson drew in his breath with a slight catch. His eyes shone brightly in the rays of the sidelamps.

"And you obviously found nothing, doctor?" he added, turning to Rossington. The doctor's beard shone golden in the flare of his match as he lit a cigar. He puffed out fragrant smoke into the damp interior of the cab before replying.

"I found only what any practitioner would expect to find under circumstances where a doctor had recorded a natural death on the certificate," he said slowly. "I must confess I had been led to believe by friend Clyde here that things might be otherwise."

The cab lurched again as he spoke, and Rossington and Munson were momentarily thrown together. When Stevens had reined in the horse a little and their progress was less wild, Rossington looked expectantly at Beatty.

"I hope this will be the last trip I have to make to Woking on your behalf," he said pointedly.

Beatty smiled.

"It was no more pleasant for me than for you," he reminded his friend. "And now that you have seen Miss Meredith you will surely understand the reasons. You carried out the Marsh Test, of course?"

"Of course," said Rossington shortly. "There was not a trace of arsenic. But what I did find bore out Miss Meredith's description of her father's death."

Beatty clapped one hand against the other with such violence that the contact made a sharp cracking noise. Munson looked at him quickly.

"I felt certain that there was something here," Beatty said. There was a savage edge to his voice, Rossington noted with surprise.

"It was nothing solid, of course. But one gets these feelings."

"I know what you mean, doctor," Munson said. "I get them in my profession. But they are apt to lead one astray unless kept on a tight rein."

He gazed at Beatty in silence for a long moment. A gloom

seemed to have descended on the carriage beyond that engendered by the natural coldness and dampness of the day and by the darkness that pressed rawly in on the windows of the vehicle.

"I had hoped for something else," said Beatty. "Beyond that I cannot commit myself."

If he looked for answers from his companions he looked in vain. Lights were twinkling in the darkness now, and Beatty rubbed his hands together.

"We seem to be approaching the outskirts of Woking," he observed. "Are you engaged for this evening, Mr. Munson?"

The little detective went on drawing at his pipe for a moment or two longer. Rossington sat stolidly, his head thrown back, the sidelights glowing on his light beard, puffing furiously at his cigar. The interior of the cab was beginning to fill with smoke now, but the three men did not find it at all oppressive. Munson leaned forward at last and knocked his pipe gently against the framework of the carriage door.

"I have a little paperwork," he said carelessly. "But then there is always that."

"But nothing that cannot wait until tomorrow?" persisted Beatty.

Munson shook his head smilingly.

"I only wondered if you would care to join Dr. Rossington and myself for dinner at the White Horse. As my guest, of course."

It may have been a trick of the light, for they were now rapidly approaching the centre of Woking, but Beatty thought he saw the Inspector flush slightly.

"That is extremely kind, doctor," he said. "Such an invitation would be difficult to refuse."

"We can rely on you, then," said Beatty, putting back his glasses and resuming his identity as a rather stuffy medical man. He was aware, uneasily, that he had dropped his guard on several occasions this afternoon. It did not matter among friends, but it might have been important in the presence of men like Munson if things had turned out differently. Beatty felt a slight edge of annoyance growing within himself; his own standards of professional behaviour were being compromised.

He put it down to the strange atmosphere of these frozen Surrey uplands and the weird background of Dr. Couchman's nursing home. His expectations had led him on to conceive of some bizarre and extraordinary adventure when instead there was nothing but the squalid fact of natural death. John Rossington had once observed, when they were at college together, that he had all the makings of a Renaissance man. He may well have been right.

"It will be a rare occasion," said Rossington smilingly, turning to glance at his companion on the seat beside him. "Friend Clyde here has promised me one of the finest bottles from the White Horse cellars. And no doubt he will be equally lavish on your behalf."

He roared with laughter at Beatty's expression, then turned again to Munson.

"And we shall be able to discuss rugby tactics over the coffee, eh, Inspector?"

The cab shuddered as Stevens turned, and Beatty saw with a sigh of relief that they were passing the gaslit façade of Woking Station. A moment or two more and the horse had drawn up outside the imposing bulk of the White Horse, where welcoming red gleams of light shone from beneath the thick curtains. Beatty got down stiffly, his sense of disappointment heavy within him. He wondered what he would say to Miss Meredith on the morrow. Dotterell too would express his own disappointment in a very practical manner.

"I hope you had a successful day, gentlemen," said Stevens, clambering down heavily from the box.

"I shall probably be returning to London tomorrow," said Beatty shortly.

He handed Stevens the fare and added a generous tip to compensate for the cabman's long and tedious wait. Stevens put his hand to his hat in salute.

"Thank you kindly, Dr. Fitzgibbon. I'm sorry to hear you'll be leaving us. And not only on account of your generosity. I had some hopes today that justice would be done."

Beatty looked at the man sharply. Rossington and Munson had gone into the hotel by now, and he lingered here in the cold and mist, the second case of Rossington's instruments weighing him down heavily. He put the bag on the ground. Stevens's face was in shadow and it was difficult to make out his expression.

"You must have some reason for such a curious remark?"

Stevens shifted uncomfortably.

"It's something we might have a drink about one evening, doctor," he said. "If you could spare the time. Perhaps you'll be in Woking again. It concerns my late wife, you see, and it's a story that's too long for a cold street corner on a night like this."

Beatty nodded, his interest aroused by the cabman's enigmatic manner.

"It touches on Dr. Couchman, of course?"

Stevens looked round sharply in the gloom and put his hand up to his nose to indicate caution.

"It does, doctor. But I have to be careful in a small place like Woking."

"Of course," Beatty reassured him. "Perhaps if you'd care to give me your private address I could get in touch with you if ever I am again in the town."

Stevens brightened. He gave the details, which Beatty took down in a small leather notebook he always carried in his overcoat pocket.

"I may see you tomorrow before we depart," he said. "If not I will certainly be in touch."

The man brushed his hat again.

"Always at your service, doctor," he said affably. "And if I'm not at home you'll most likely find me outside the station, unless I'm called away."

"I'll remember," Beatty said.

He strode off up the steps and vanished into the inn. Stevens stood looking thoughtfully after him. Then he clambered up on the box. A few moments later his thin tuneless whistling died in the enveloping mist.

10

THE WRONG MAN

THE sun was sparkling cheerfully on the hoar-frost gilding the railings of the houses as Beatty paid off the cabman and descended.

The house in St. John's Wood was a tall mansion of imposing dimensions which stood by itself in a large wooded garden on a corner situation. Beatty, sans his disguise as Dr. Clyde Fitzgibbon, was in less dejected mood than the day before, but his heart was still heavy as he pushed open the big iron gate and followed the gravel drive which wound between the trees.

There was a dog-cart standing in front of the main entrance of the neo-Georgian building, and Beatty cast it a curious glance as he bounded up the steps. A motherly looking woman with grey hair and a cheerful smile opened the hall-door to the young investigator's tattoo. She ushered him into a large panelled hall, tastefully furnished with period furniture and lit by a crystal chandelier.

"Miss Meredith is in the drawing room to the right," she said, closing the door. "The other gentleman has already arrived."

"The other gentleman?" Beatty said, momentarily startled.

"Dr. Rossington I believe," the housekeeper said quizzically. Her steady grey eyes had a sparkle of amusement in them. Beatty smiled, handing her his cape and hat. He looked at himself in the hall mirror, not dissatisfied with his appearance.

"Oh, I see," he said. "He did not waste much time."

"I beg your pardon," the housekeeper said, hanging up Beatty's things on a massive mahogany coatstand.

"No matter," said Beatty. "I'll announce myself if I may."

He walked across the hall to the door with the gilded handle and white and gold panelling, knocked quickly, and then went in on the murmured command to enter. It was a tall, elegant room he saw, with long French doors adjoining the grounds. Miss Angela Meredith sat with Rossington in the middle of a deep bay which faced a roaring fire in the Adam fireplace.

She was in the act of pouring tea from a silver pot and rose in a rather agitated and flushed manner on his entrance, Beatty thought. She came forward, putting both warm hands on Beatty's to draw him forward to a chair near the low table. Rossington's bearded face looked with grim amusement at his friend.

"I do think you might have waited," Beatty said, somewhat shortly, after he had finished greeting his hostess.

"The tea, you mean?" Rossington said with a grin. "You were rather late, so we made shift to begin . . ."

"You know very well what I mean," said Beatty, looking from Angela Meredith to the young doctor. Miss Meredith cast Beatty an agitated glance and resumed pouring the tea into porcelain cups.

"Oh, that," said Rossington carelessly. "The young lady was rather curious, naturally, but I felt it best to wait until your arrival. It is your affair, after all."

The girl looked from one to the other with mounting bewilderment.

"I am not quite sure that I understand . . ." she began hesitantly.

"I must apologise to you both," Beatty said firmly. "I thought Dr. Rossington had already informed you of the result of our mission to Woking."

The girl shook her head.

"I can assure you, sir, it was our intention to await your arrival. But I see from your expression that the news is bad."

"You put me in some small difficulty, Miss Meredith," began Beatty awkwardly, looking to Rossington for support. The doctor merely took the proffered cup and stirred it, his brow knitted with thought. Miss Meredith herself sat with one slim hand on the handle of her cup and waited for him to go on.

"As a professional investigator I had hoped to be of some service to you," Beatty plunged on. "Your story about your unfortunate father, the manner of his death, and the mysterious circumstances that followed . . ."

He broke off again and took a tentative sip of his tea.

"You're not being very tactful, Clyde," said Rossington shortly.

Beatty shot the doctor a quick glance of annoyance which was not lost on the girl. She wore a dark blue dress today, with a gold brooch at the throat, and Beatty thought she looked even more attractive than when she had first appeared in his office. The girl laid a hand on his arm.

"I quite understand," she said softly. "You were intrigued. You hoped for an interesting case. I hoped for justice in a dark and unfathomable business."

Beatty again regarded Rossington reprovingly as the doctor opened his mouth. He shut it with a snap and leaned forward with a smile to accept the biscuit his hostess was offering him. Beatty turned back to the girl.

"I was about to say, Miss Meredith, that the story of your father led me to fear the worst. I went to Woking with preconceived ideas, partly influenced by your own conversation and suspicions, partly by my own. In fact, I now feel I believe what I wanted to believe."

"What he is trying to tell you, Miss Meredith," Rossington broke in rudely, "is that your suspicions regarding your father's death were unfounded. I carried out the examination for which you asked and found absolutely nothing abnormal. I have my report here, should you desire to see it."

He rummaged in the breast pocket of his coat and produced a long envelope. A startling change had passed across the girl's face. She looked at Beatty helplessly for a moment.

"It's perfectly true," said Beatty. "Though I cannot see how the fact squares with the fragment of letter you found or the burglary of this house."

"Coincidence, perhaps," interjected Rossington unhelpfully.

"It was no coincidence, I swear, Mr. Beatty," the girl said fiercely.

She put one hand against the breast of her blue dress.

"I feel it here, sir. And so far, short though my life has been, my instinct has not led me wrong."

Beatty was silent for a moment. Rossington's report lay on the table, unopened. He picked it up.

"I must confess I was not impressed with Dr. Couchman or his establishment," he said diffidently. "But suspicions and mere theorising are not enough. We must have absolute proof of foul play. And Dr. Rossington's examination rules that out completely. He is an authority in his own particular field."

The girl looked agitatedly from one young man to the other.

"I beg your pardon, gentlemen, I did not mean to cast any doubt on the professional standing of either."

"That was perfectly understood, Miss Meredith," Rossington said gently. "And it was not taken so, I can assure you."

He looked at the envelope in Beatty's hand.

"If you would just glance at the report."

The girl shook her head.

"I could not bear to, gentlemen. What you are now telling me is that we can go no further in the matter?"

Beatty half rose from his chair and then sank down again as

the girl made as though to get up in her agitation. The young investigator looked at Rossington, but he kept his eyes on his plate as he nibbled at his biscuit.

"If you could indicate to me a direction in which to proceed . . ." Beatty began. "I should be happy to act for you. I could, of course, begin at the other end. From the burglary, I mean. But if the official police were unable to help . . ."

He broke off and a heavy silence descended on the room, interrupted only by the faint crackling of the fire and the far-off cawing of rooks in the leafless trees of the grounds outside the windows. The impasse was ended by a deferential tapping at the door. The housekeeper appeared, and the girl got up and went forward to meet her.

"I am sorry to trouble you, Miss Meredith," said she, "but I would be grateful if you could just step out for a moment."

"Oh, yes," said the girl, with a sudden toss of her head. "I had quite forgotten, Mrs. Throgmorton. Excuse me, gentlemen."

She hurried off, to the obvious relief of the two young men, and as the door closed behind her Rossington leaned over and poured them both more tea.

"Well, doctor?" said Rossington satirically. "What now?"

"A good question," Beatty drawled, sitting back in his chair and crossing one leg comfortably over the other. He looked approvingly at the luxurious furnishings of the room.

"A persistent lady, our Miss Meredith."

Rossington glanced at him shrewdly, his head on one side, the teacup looking frail and insubstantial in his massive hand.

"Your Miss Meredith," he said pointedly. "Not mine. You forget I am engaged to be married."

"I thought it was you who had forgotten that," said Beatty mildly. "Especially with your talk of barmaids at Woking."

Rossington grinned crookedly at him and raised the cup to his lips.

"All the same, it's a setback that can't be got round," said Beatty, getting up and wandering about the room. He paused by the fireplace, looking aimlessly at the photographs and other bric-à-brac on the mantel. Then he went to stand facing out across the grounds. Rossington had picked up *The Times* from a side-table and was perusing it, a biscuit in his right hand, which he munched from time to time. He looked as though he were at home in his own consulting room.

"You are on the wrong side of the business, Clyde," he said, tapping a column of heavy type with his thick index finger.

"How do you mean?" said Beatty, coming forward.

"Why, this series of bullion robberies," Rossington continued. "I see there was another last night, while we were wasting our time at Woking."

Beatty only half looked at the item. He noticed that a fourth City bank had been burglarised. The method appeared to be the same as in the earlier robbery. A sum of about £100,000 was involved in bar-gold, but the total had not yet been worked out. As in the previous crime there had been no trace of the thieves and nothing untoward had been observed.

"Nobody about in the City at night," said Rossington, noisily swilling the remainder of his tea. He put the paper down again and looked at his watch.

"I must be going soon, anyway. My leave expires at seven o'clock this evening, and I want to see Rosalind before I get back to Charing Cross."

Beatty nodded, his mind far away. Something only half-formulated was stirring in his consciousness, and Rossington's prattle was tending to drive it out altogether. He held up his hand for silence. It was just at that moment Miss Meredith chose to put in her reappearance, and the slam of the door quite interrupted Beatty's train of thought. He concealed his annoyance as best he could and resumed his seat opposite Rossington.

"Please forgive my absence, gentlemen," said Miss Meredith, reseating herself at the table. "I hope that you have had enough tea?"

"Quite, thank you," said Rossington affably.

"If you require any more toasted crumpets, I can ring for them," the girl went on.

Beatty shook his head, smiling.

"This is quite sufficient, thank you. And we have yet to map out our future course."

The girl's cornflower blue eyes were candid and appealing as she stared at Beatty. The lights of the chandelier gleamed and shone on her black hair, and her breasts rose and fell with her agitated breathing. It was obvious that her sorrow over her father would never leave her until she had some clear-cut proof that would set her mind at rest over his death. And yet what could be more clear-cut than Rossington's report which Beatty now again held in his hand.

Miss Meredith's full lips opened in a hesitant smile, revealing her white and regular teeth. Closer today and in broad daylight she looked even more disturbing to Beatty. There was something about her frank and candid features that dissolved his doubts. If Rossington had not been present he would have made light of the doctor's report. But he did not see how he could take the matter any further. More for something to do than for any valid reason, he held up the envelope.

"You had better keep this in a safe place, Miss Meredith, even if you do not desire to know its contents."

The girl nodded.

"As you will, Mr. Beatty. Perhaps later, I will look at it. If you would be good enough to leave it on the mantel yonder. I will have Mrs. Throgmorton put it with Daddy's effects."

Beatty rose from the table and crossed to the fireplace. He put the envelope down and stood frowning at a photograph in a silver frame which stood there. It depicted the girl and an elderly gentleman in a frock-coat. Its impact still did not register.

Something about his immobility drew Rossington's eyes to his in sudden surprise. The girl glanced from one to the other and got up quickly. She came forward to Beatty, saw the object of his gaze.

"That was one of Daddy's favourite studies," she said. "It was taken in the garden here last year."

Beatty frowned, turning back to the girl.

"And who is the gentleman?"

The girl looked surprised.

"Why, my father, of course."

Beatty gazed incredulously at the photograph.

"This is impossible," he stammered.

Then, to the absolute astonishment of Rossington and the

young lady, he started a mad sort of half-dance, half-pirouette on the carpet. The girl stared at him in amazement, while Rossington got up.

"Have you taken leave of your senses, Clyde?" he said irritably.

"On the contrary, John, I have just come to them," Beatty almost shouted.

He picked up the photograph and waved it wildly in front of Rossington's face.

"Don't you see, John, this gentleman is Miss Meredith's father."

Rossington's face had a blank, wary look.

"Well, obviously, Clyde. Has she not already said so?"

Beatty's eyes were shining and there was a fevered flush in his cheeks.

"Look, man, look," he said, pressing the photograph under the young doctor's nose.

"Miss Meredith's father was an elderly gentleman, thin and clean-shaven. You performed an autopsy on a large fat man with a heavy moustache!"

He strode about the room with long nervous steps.

"Don't you see, Rossington, it was the wrong body! Somebody had substituted another. That was why you found nothing wrong."

Miss Meredith looked just as bewildered as Rossington. Beatty ran across the drawing room and looked round for his hat and cape before remembering he had left them in the hall.

"I must see Dotterell," said Beatty, completely ignoring the other two people in the room. "I am for Woking at once. There is black work here, just as Miss Meredith supposed."

Rossington put the picture back on the mantel with a barely suppressed groan.

"So I must go through all this again?" he said.

"I am afraid so, friend John," said Beatty crisply. "There is not a moment to be lost or vital evidence may be destroyed. You had best get further leave from Charing Cross."

Beatty smiled as Rossington went on muttering to himself.

"There is a train at seven o'clock tonight, I believe," he added, as his friend rushed out, without even saying good-bye to Miss Meredith. "We'll meet beforehand at my office."

He turned to the girl, found her hands clasped in his. Her eyes were suddenly brimming with tears.

"I do not pretend to understand the implications of everything you have said, Mr. Beatty, but you will have my everlasting gratitude if you can bring this affair to a successful conclusion."

Beatty carried her fingers to his lips in an instinctive gesture which he was too late to correct. The girl's features flushed and she drew back suddenly, confusion in her eyes.

"Forgive me my hasty departure, Miss Meredith," Beatty said, taking the opportunity to make his way to the door where the housekeeper had appeared with his hat and cape.

"I have much to do before this evening. This is a sombre business, but rest assured that we shall see it through."

II

EXHUMATION

LONG plumes of steam were hissing in the bitter air as Beatty and Rossington strode on to the forecourt at Woking Station. Stevens had been alerted by telegraph and now came toward them, a welcoming smile on his broad good-humoured face. He took the two heavy cases and threw them up on to his box with contemptuous ease.

"Glad to see you back, gentlemen. A cold night. The White Horse again?"

Beatty shook his head.

"Later. We have booked rooms there, but first I want to see the Superintendent. Do you know where he lives?"

Stevens looked startled, and there was a curious expression in his grey eyes. He opened the yellow door of the cab and ushered the two men in. He lingered at the window, putting it half-open on the strap, so that he could talk through.

"Mr. Bateman. The Superintendent of Brookwood? He lives about a mile from the cemetery."

He looked dubious.

"It's almost ten already. He won't be too pleased."

"That is hardly your business," Beatty said crisply.

He had resumed the persona of Dr. Clyde Fitzgibbon again and evaded Rossington's amused gaze. Stevens appeared confused.

"I'm sorry, gentlemen. No offence, I'm sure. It's just that I didn't want you to have a wasted journey."

"That's all right," Beatty replied, modifying his manner. "It is a matter of the greatest urgency. Just get us there as quickly as possible."

"Brookwood House," said Stevens, jumping up on to the box with alacrity. He pulled his heavy cloak more closely around him and whipped up the horse, turning the cab smartly in the gaslit forecourt. They clopped forward through Woking, the lights of the houses dropping gradually away behind them.

"We're taking a risk in this business," said Rossington sombrely.

He leaned forward on the seat opposite, one big hand resting on the bag beside him, and fixed his friend with worried eyes.

"I don't see how," Beatty said, the image of Miss Meredith before him. He could still feel the warmth of her hand against his lips. His brown eyes stared steadily back at his friend as he shifted on the seat, the light of the sidelamps falling on his strong Roman face and close-curled black hair.

"We still have the original exhumation order. It relates to the body of Meredith. You have examined the body of someone else. Hence the original order is perfectly valid."

Rossington smiled.

"I am not bothered about that," he said shortly. "It is this fellow Couchman. Meredith was his patient. It's a little unethical doing the examination in his absence."

"Exactly," Beatty chuckled. "And no doubt if he knew we were coming he would find some excuse to delay the proceedings."

Rossington nodded gloomily.

"Even so, the Superintendent is not going to like it. Supposing he himself is involved?"

Beatty tapped the front of his cape significantly.

"I have the best persuader in the world here," he said.

The doctor's eyes widened.

"I always knew you were a little wild, Clyde, but this beats all.

If there is any trouble we'll be outside the law. To say nothing of Inspector Munson's attitude when he finds out."

Beatty shook his head.

"Just leave this to me, John. This isn't your forte, but it's meat and drink to me. I have a feeling about the matter. If there is any trouble I shan't involve you, rest assured."

"I hope you're right," said Rossington, but he still looked dubious.

The cab was now grating up a gravel drive, and the two men became aware of large stone pillars swinging by on either side. Lights glowed ahead, and the flap above them opened to frame Stevens's animated features.

"Brookwood House, gentlemen."

It was more than a minute before Beatty's knocking was answered. The large panelled door with its florid stained-glass swung back to reveal the ascetic features of an elderly man-servant. He looked at the two men hesitantly.

"We wish to see Mr. Bateman," Beatty said quickly. "On a matter of the utmost urgency."

The thin man looked discomposed.

"I do not know whether I can disturb him, sir. I believe the master is still at dinner."

"He'll see us," said Beatty confidently. "Just tell him Dr. Fitzgibbon and Dr. Rossington."

The servant drew the door back, eyes wide in his bony face.

"If you'll just wait a moment, sir."

He left them in the draughty hall while he hurried through the heavy portières which separated it from the main house. Beatty and Rossington stood in silence for a few moments until the heavy footsteps of Bateman were heard across the parquet. The Superintendent's bearded face was flushed and his eyes glittered angrily.

"What's this, what's this?" he said in a harsh voice, pushing the servant aside. Then his face cleared as he caught sight of the two men.

"Ah, doctor. A strange time to call."

The servant behind Bateman hesitated until dismissed by the bearded man. Beatty waited until his footsteps had died out along the corridor.

"I must apologise for this intrusion, Superintendent, but we come on a matter of the utmost gravity."

A cautious expression passed across Bateman's face. He put out his hand to indicate a door opposite to that from which he had just emerged.

"We have dinner guests. We had best go into my study."

He led the way into a small apartment lit only by the embers from a dying fire. The two men waited while he struck a match to light the gas. The yellow light from the globe above the mantel threw the hollows under his eyes into high relief. He lit the second jet on the corresponding bracket at the other side of the fireplace.

"Will you sit down, gentlemen? A glass of wine perhaps?"

Beatty shook his head.

"Thank you, no. We have no time to waste. I am afraid we are here regarding another exhumation. Or rather, that of the right person on this occasion."

Bateman seated himself behind a small walnut desk and looked with glittering eyes at his visitors.

"I still do not understand, Dr. Fitzgibbon."

Beatty and Rossington sat down in the chairs indicated by Bateman, but before Beatty could go on, his companion interrupted.

"Not to put too fine a point on it, Superintendent Bateman, I performed my autopsy on the wrong body. According to your registers it should have been that of Mr. Tredegar Meredith. As you will recall the corpse was that of a fat gentleman with a thick moustache. Miss Meredith informs us that her father was a very thin man and clean-shaven to boot. The implication does not escape you, I am sure. Either someone has substituted the remains for those of another; the grave numbers have been changed; or there has been a genuine error. It is important to find out, as I'm sure you'll agree."

A shocking change had taken place in the Superintendent's face; he stared at the two men incredulously. There was no sound in the room but the ticking of a clock and the low crackling of the fire.

"You are surely not implying, gentlemen, that I . . ." he began in a faltering voice.

Beatty shook his head.

"We are implying nothing, Mr. Bateman. But I am sure you will see that we must put the matter right and without delay."

Bateman got out a silk handkerchief and passed it across his forehead.

"Of course, of course. Fortunately, I have the register here. I sometimes bring it home in the evenings."

He opened the desk-top and took out the heavy volume. He ran his finger down the entries while the two men waited.

"There is only one possibility to my mind; that somehow the grave markers have been transposed."

He looked up, his face suddenly hard.

"I can assure you, Dr. Rossington, that there will be the fullest investigation of this matter."

"I would prefer for the moment that there be utter discretion," said Beatty softly. "That is absolutely vital."

Bateman looked at him in bewilderment.

"I do not quite see the implication," he said.

There was a decanter of port and a tray of glasses at the side of the desk. Bateman poured himself a glass of the ruby liquid. Beatty noticed the faint tremor in his fingers. He let Rossington reply.

"I will put the matter in the subtlest way I can," the doctor said. He leaned forward in his chair, fixing the Superintendent with his eyes.

"It might have been to someone's advantage to change the grave markers. To avoid the findings I might have made had I performed the autopsy on Mr. Meredith's remains. Therefore, we must exhume the correct body with all despatch. In short, I intend to carry out my examination tonight."

Bateman looked as though Rossington had struck him a physical blow. He hurriedly swallowed the contents of his glass and poured another.

"We regret the disruption of your domestic life this evening and the trouble this may entail," went on Beatty quickly. "But I am sure you will see that it is in the interest of us all. And you may rest assured of our support if it comes to any enquiry."

He saw that his words had not been lost on the Superintendent. His eyes no longer had their worried look, and he gave him a grateful glance.

"Since you put it like that, gentlemen, nothing could be simpler.

We could use the chapel, and I have a night staff available."

He paused, pursing his lips.

"Should we not inform Dr. Couchman? And there is the problem of Inspector Munson."

"Leave that to us," Beatty said authoritatively. "If all is well there may be no need to let anyone know of this unfortunate error."

He was conscious of the Superintendent's second grateful glance in as many minutes and went on, overriding any possible objections on that official's part.

"On the other hand, if my colleague's findings are of a certain nature, then the police may have to be called. Either way we avoid much unpleasantness by being discreet. How long would it take you to exhume Mr. Meredith's body, presuming you can now locate it?"

Bateman flushed and shifted in his chair.

"I have already consulted the register," he said in a hurt voice. "I can see what has happened. There are two graves close together. Number 2333 is, I should imagine, the one we want. It is only a few yards from Number 2334, which we have already exhumed. That body should be that of Mr. Lewis Archer, a retired silk merchant which was consigned to Number 2333 according to my register. The funerals took place on consecutive days."

Beatty exchanged a long glance with Rossington.

"The Superintendent's explanation is obviously the right one. Someone has transposed the markers."

"Or a genuine error has been made on the part of my staff," Bateman put in anxiously.

"We shall see," Rossington told him with a grim expression.

The Superintendent got up briskly and put the register back in his desk. His face was regaining its normal colour now.

"You have some means of identification on this occasion?" he said.

Rossington nodded.

"I have a photograph supplied by the dead man's daughter. I have brought all my apparatus. If you would provide identical facilities as on the previous occasion, I should like to start work within the hour."

The Superintendent looked at his watch.

"I will just let my wife and guests know I have been called away. I agree that the sooner this matter is disposed of, the better. I will get some extra men to work."

He smiled thinly.

"Shall we say forty minutes?"

The sound of pick-axes breaking the icy ground fell heavily on Beatty's heart. He stood now, his heavy cape pulled closely about him, looking down into the open grave. It was a lurid scene, lit by the glare of naphtha flares by whose flickering light four brawny workmen toiled to reach the level of the coffin. Heavy canvas tarpaulins were drawn round the grave to screen their activities, though in truth there was no one to see them in that remote place at that late time of night.

Rossington's strong bearded face seemed to shift and waver in the shimmering glow of the flares as he smoked a cigar and stood impassively watching. The Superintendent, a troubled expression on his face, his register under his arm, stood as one carved in stone. Sweat glistened on the workmen's faces, despite the bitter coldness of the air. The only sounds, apart from the occasional call of a night bird, were the whistling breath of the labourers, the metallic crunching as the picks bit into the frozen ground, and the intermittent grunts from Bateman as he directed the operations.

The Foreman, whose name Beatty had ascertained was Varley, stood at the edge of the group round the graveside, saying nothing; he seemed afraid to assert his authority when the Superintendent was present, though ever and again he leaped forward with a spade and shovelled back frozen clods of earth which were in danger of falling back into the gaping rawness of the open hole.

Beatty had kept a careful eye on Varley and more than once had again caught the troubled expression which had first drawn the man to his attention on his initial visit; tonight he seemed more agitated than before, and his glance caught first Bateman and was then, it seemed to Beatty, reluctantly drawn to himself. Each time he started and looked hurriedly away when he felt Beatty's eye on him.

The investigator had made a mental note to seek out the burly Foreman on a more propitious occasion and put some seemingly innocuous questions to him; perhaps he frequented one of the local hostelries. Beatty could draw his address from Bateman, and a few discreet enquiries among the locals would do the rest. Varley had sprung forward again now and stared down into the grave as the hollow clatter of wood on wood came to the ears of the watchers.

His face was the colour of parchment under the flickering light of the flares; his mouth made a black O in his face, but no sound came forth. Beatty glanced at Rossington, but his friend stood carelessly belching out blue smoke, apparently absorbed in his own thoughts. Beatty got out his watch; the Superintendent had been as good as his word. Only thirty minutes had passed since the interview in his study, and yet the men were already easing the coffin to the surface, placing boards beneath it.

Things were already prepared within the chapel; Beatty had arranged with Bateman that the workmen engaged would be kept within the chapel building itself while the autopsy was performed. The door would be locked, ostensibly to prevent outside interference; in reality to prevent anyone on the cemetery staff from leaving. Beatty did not want anyone warning Couchman of what was afoot. He smiled quietly to himself as he thought of the angular doctor's possible reaction.

Of course, he might be premature; this second test might also prove negative. But Beatty, all his investigative instincts attuned to fine degrees, felt within himself that there was something black and horrifying behind Meredith's death; he recalled again the girl's anguished face and her utter conviction of foul play. Beatty looked quickly around; the coffin, encrusted with frozen earth and glistening in the light of the flares, was already being eased on to the big wooden trolley Varley held rigid to receive it.

There were only the five cemetery attendants and Bateman beside himself and Rossington who knew about the second exhumation tonight. They had merely to keep the affair and its results secret for a few hours; then, if necessary, Beatty would await daylight and seek out Munson for a warrant. He had his plans laid carefully. Beatty moved over, heavy with thought, and followed Rossington and the Superintendent as the small procession made its way with its melancholy burden back toward the chapel.

The wicks of the lanterns carried by Bateman and Varley flared and fluttered in the cold air, sending fantastic shadows dancing over the heavy foliage which hemmed them in as they followed the winding path which led them to their destination. The yellow light, striking upwards on to the face of Varley, revealed to the trained gaze of Beatty an expression at once troubled and conscience-stricken. At one moment the trolley juddered on the stony ground; the coffin lurched sideways and slid on the bier, the heavy rasping sound bringing a muffled exclamation from the Foreman.

His face was sick with fear as he righted it with a trembling hand, preventing it from sliding over the edge; an exhortation from Bateman and the other men had shouldered it back in position. Beatty felt he would never forget the haunted look in Varley's eyes as the cortège came in sight of the chapel and slowly filed into the interior.

12

THE MARSH TEST

IT was nearly two A.M. Rossington adjusted his apparatus, his face heavy with thought. He glanced at Beatty, noting with cynical amusement the dark stains of fatigue under his friend's eyes.

"I thought it best to be thorough on this occasion," he said drily. Beatty nodded.

"Bearing in mind also that I do not wish any of these men to leave here before dawn."

He was whispering now, glancing across at the huddled forms of the five cemetery attendants, sleeping figures under the blankets on the canvas stretchers set about the walls. Rossington chuckled softly.

"I can hold the body here as long as you wish," he added. "Within limits, you understand. But it must remain so until I have completed my tests."

Beatty nodded. The lamplight in the chapel shone on the thin ascetic features of the dead man on the altar slab, the canvas cover mercifully concealing the sutured wound where his companion had carried out his investigations. He inhaled Rossington's cigar smoke gratefully, turning his gaze from that of the corpse to Rossington's steady eyes. There was no doubt that the body on the slab before them was that of the late Mr. Meredith; a comparison with the photograph they had brought with them made identification certain.

"If you will bring that case with you, we will continue this in the other room," Rossington whispered. "We shall be more comfortable."

Beatty lifted the doctor's bag, and the two men, walking quietly across the flagstones, entered the private apartment they had left only twenty-four hours earlier. A bright fire burned in the grate, and by the light of the oil lanterns the sleeping figure of the Superintendent, his head buried on his arms, shifted uneasily in his cramped posture at the round table.

Rossington went quickly over to the sink in the corner and scrubbed his hands in a carbolic solution, taking the brass kettle from the trivet at the fire. Beatty took the case to the bench near the sink and left it, returning for one of the oil lamps which he put down to give Rossington maximum light. The doctor was already shrugging on his coat. He looked significantly at the port decanter at Bateman's elbow.

"I think, friend Clyde, a small libation before we commence the next stage," he said with a thin smile.

Without a word Beatty got two glasses from the sideboard near the fireplace and rinsed them under the tap. He filled them from the decanter, and the two men silently toasted each other. Beatty went over to the fireplace, holding out his hands to the blaze. He was aware that Rossington had followed him. Both men looked silently at the sleeping form of the Superintendent.

"What will you do if my test proves positive?" said Rossington, turning penetrating eyes on his companion.

"We shall commence with Couchman, of course," said Beatty shortly. "He was the physician in charge of the case."

"You misunderstand me deliberately, Clyde," said Rossington irritably. "What is behind all this? Certainly not money, according to Miss Meredith."

"That is an entirely different matter," said Beatty maddeningly. "I have already given that a deal of thought."

And he would say no more on the subject. Rossington put down his glass on the mantel and went over to the bench at the far side of the room without another word. Beatty finished his own glass at a more leisurely rate and poured another. Rossington was unpacking his equipment and Beatty went to stand beside him, the liquid in the glass in his hand shining amber in the lamplight.

Rossington cast another glance at the sleeping figure of Bateman and then bent to his apparatus. Beatty noted that he had a U-shaped glass tube held in a wooden stand; one end of the tube was open, the other terminated in a nozzle which tapered to a point.

"You are familiar with the outlines of the Marsh Test, I take it?" said Rossington mockingly.

Beatty shook his head. He carried a chair over from the table and set it down near the bench. Then he mounted on to the seat and sat on the strong wooden back so that he could more clearly see what the doctor was doing.

"I have here a measure of sulphuric acid," Rossington went on, busying himself with his materials. "Hydrogen is produced when the acid is mixed with a fluid containing arsenic, and zinc is added. The result is arsine. Do you follow me?"

"Vaguely," said Beatty dubiously, looking curiously at the doctor's preparations. He ignored the heavy sigh with which Rossington gave expression to his feelings.

"The reaction between the acid and the zinc produces hydrogen. And the hydrogen reacts with the arsenic to produce arsine in the form of a gas. Now look closely at this."

Rossington deftly suspended a small plate of zinc on a wire in the nozzle of the tube. A glass jar contained material he had extracted from the corpse's stomach. Beatty tried not to look at what Rossington was doing, but he felt compelled to do so. He saw that the doctor was suspending a pipette of another fluid over the stomach contents; he assumed that this was the sulphuric acid Rossington had spoken of.

Now he was carefully pouring the solution into the open end of the U-tube. Beatty watched fascinated as it trickled slowly through. Rossington had taken a spill from the fire. He gave a slight exclamation as a small bluish flame erupted from the nozzle.

Beatty glanced at him, but his bearded face told him nothing; only the eyes were glittering with the light of fascinated interest.

It was deathly quiet in the room, and Beatty saw something infinitely sinister in the minute flame which burned like a will-o'-the-wisp and might be the sure sign of murder. Rossington was holding a white porcelain bowl against the flame, rotating it slowly, making tiny grunting noises between his teeth. Beatty could see that a black deposit was forming on the inner surface of the bowl.

Beatty turned to make some comment to his friend, but one glance at the set, determined expression on Rossington's face prevented him. Instead, he turned quickly to look over his shoulder, but the thick, heavy breathing of Bateman told him that the Superintendent was sound asleep. Indeed, Beatty's own eyelids were heavy, but he was buoyed up by the hope of bringing the affair to a conclusion.

To achieve that he was prepared to stay up all night if necessary, for several nights on end, and in fact had done so on other previous cases, as Dotterell could attest. Beatty wondered vaguely what his indefatigable assistant might be doing at this moment. If he had any sense he would be sound asleep in bed, but he had told Beatty before his second visit to Surrey that he intended to sleep in the office and that receipt of a telegraph from Beatty would bring him hot-foot to Woking if required.

Beatty smiled grimly and watched the blue cigar smoke ascending in slow streamers to the ceiling of the small room. He noted that the bottom of the bowl was black with the deposit. Rossington's teeth were clenched tight, and there was an expression in his narrowed eyes which his friend had not seen before. The tiny flame of the gas faded and then died. Rossington gave a long sigh and carefully put down the porcelain bowl on the bench. His face was grim as he looked at Beatty.

"Well, friend Clyde, your instincts have not led you wrong," he said quietly. "There was enough arsenic in that specimen to poison the whole of Woking."

Beatty stared at him for a long moment without speaking. Then he got down from the chair.

"You are quite certain?" he said, aware even before the words were out that the question was an absurdity. Rossington held the bowl up with a brusque movement.

"See for yourself," he said curtly. "This precipitate is metallic arsenic. And, I may say, one of the most lethal concentrations I have ever seen in such a sample."

Beatty raised his head, trying to shake off his weariness.

"There is no possibility that the arsenic could have come from the soil?" he began.

Rossington shook his head violently.

"A ridiculous supposition, even for a layman, Clyde. The body has been buried only a short while. And there is no moisture in the ground, which is bonded hard with frost . . ."

He broke off as a shadow crossed the room. They found the Superintendent at their side. He looked at them with bleary eyes.

"You have your results, doctor?"

"You will be informed in due course," said Rossington crisply. "That is all I am prepared to say at this stage."

It was dawn. Beatty unlocked the chapel door, giving a sidelong glance to the attendants round the coffin. He stretched his aching limbs in the harsh light, thinking regretfully of the warm bed which had been awaiting him at the White Horse. But it had been a good night's work. He had much to engage his attention, but his brain would not function without breakfast and hot coffee.

First there remained a few more tasks. He looked up as Rossington came through the door.

"I quite forgot Stevens," the latter said.

Beatty screwed up his eyes against the growing light.

"I sent him back to Woking by relaying a message through the Superintendent. Just as soon as I realised it would be an all-night affair. And, incidentally, I have saved us some money. That is worth a breakfast, surely."

Rossington smiled.

"I'm obliged, Clyde. I hope he is returning this morning."

Rossington belched out blue cigar smoke, stepping aside as the trolley emerged from the chapel door behind him. The two men paused as Bateman's party wheeled the coffin back down the path toward the open grave which awaited it.

"He will be here at seven," said Beatty, consulting his timepiece. "Or in exactly half an hour."

Rossington put down his case in the porch and followed the coffin-party, which had disappeared in a cold and clammy mist which enveloped the graveyard. Beatty waited until he was out of sight and then turned back. But instead of going into the chapel, he took the gravelled path which ran alongside it. It led onward, through ornamental tombstones and a forest of white marble crosses.

Beatty pulled his cape more tightly about him. His footsteps grated raspingly on the ice-bound gravel, and visibility was limited to only a few yards. His eyes were noting many things which a casual observer would have missed. Indentations of feet in the grass at the side of the path; an inscription on a faded bunch of flowers at the foot of a grave; the Latin message on a grandiose mausoleum.

After a few hundred yards he came to a place where the path bifurcated; the left-hand branch led round the chapel and then broadened out, evidently giving on to another part of the cemetery. The smaller path went straight on. Beatty took it, stepping carefully on the rough surface. It led downhill, the air becoming colder, and Beatty could suddenly see the cemetery wall looming through the mist high above him. This was evidently a disused part of the graveyard; a jumble of sheds was composing itself from out the mist before him.

Beatty stood stock-still for a moment, the whiteness of the vapour lapping pallidly about him. He was conscious of the burning cold which seemed to sear his cheeks and eyelids. The breath smoked from his nostrils, but his head was clearing from the oppression of the night. An overriding sadness, engendered by this charnel place, was slowly lifting from the young investigator's soul.

There was no sound except for the faint far-off grate of wheels and the clop of hooves which came from somewhere over the cemetery wall, probably from the road beyond, Beatty supposed. It might even be Stevens returning with their conveyance back to town. He stood a moment longer and then walked forward.

The huddle of huts and sheds was set up quite near the graveyard wall. Tools leaned against the sagging boards of the structures, and there were heavy iron bars securing the largest of the doors in front of him.

Two wooden wheelbarrows stood to one side, their handles glittering with frost like the icing on a cake. There was a rough barricade of planking across the path at this point, linking up with a fence which formed a barrier round the hutments. Beatty stood for a minute longer, taking in the details of the scene, his logical mind working again. He put out his hand to rattle the barrier, when footsteps suddenly pattered across the rough grass and a burly form was at his side.

The deathly bearded face of Varley the Foreman appeared from the mist. The trembling lips opened, stumbling with the words.

"I'm sorry, sir, but it's dangerous through there. Repairs going on, you see."

"I beg your pardon," said Beatty deliberately, giving the Foreman a searching look. "Idle curiosity, merely."

Varley bent swiftly to see that the barricade was still secure.

"There should be a notice here, doctor," he went on quickly. "But the public are forbidden entry in any case."

Beatty stared at him mildly and turned away. The big cemetery attendant fell into step with him, keeping deferentially a pace or two behind.

"I quite forgot, sir," he went on. "Dr. Rossington, your friend, is ready to leave. He said the cab would be here in a few minutes."

"Thank you," Beatty replied casually. "I should just like to ask you a few questions, if you can spare a moment."

A startled expression passed across Varley's grizzled features. He shook his head.

"Not now, sir, I'm afraid. I have to be back at the graveside. The Superintendent is not in a very good mood this morning."

He saluted by bringing the flat of his hand up to the side of his forehead and had then broken into a shambling run, swiftly disappearing between the gravestones. Beatty, some ideas half-formulated in his mind, went back to join Rossington. His face wore a faintly mocking expression and he muttered to himself from time to time. Rossington wisely kept his own counsel.

13

THE DOCTOR IS ELUSIVE

THE dining room of the White Horse was half-filled with garrulous breakfasters. Blue smoke curled lazily to the beamed ceiling. A big fire was blazing in the hearth, and Beatty, the fatigue of the night quite erased from his features, sat on an oak settle in a nook facing the fire and frowned at his companions across the gleaming white cloth.

Rossington leaned back with his inevitable cigar and looked with half-closed eyes toward the fire. Munson, dressed in a thick salt and pepper suit, twisted a fork on the table before him and waited for Beatty to go on.

"So what you are telling me is that you are not, in fact, a doctor?" he said at last, fixing Beatty with his steady grey eyes. "Somewhat irregular but hardly a criminal matter, eh, doctor," he said, turning to smile at Rossington. He looked from one to the other.

"I take it there is no doubt that Dr. Rossington is a genuine medical practitioner?"

He paused as the waiter laid steaming platters of fish before them. His eyes twinkled shrewdly at Beatty.

"I had my doubts, Mr. Fitzgibbon, once or twice there in the chapel."

"Beatty," the other corrected him quietly. "My name is Clyde Beatty. I am a private investigator from London."

Munson's eyes were puzzled. He shook a liberal sprinkling of pepper over his plate and leaned forward to take a slice of bread from the dish in the centre of the table.

"Masquerading under a false name," he said in a bantering tone. "Well, we might make something of that if we worked at it. Normally the Surrey police don't take too kindly to gentlemen of your profession, but I must admit to being impressed with your style. You're on to something?"

Beatty nodded.

"A very serious matter. We may need a warrant."

The Surrey man put a forkful of fish into his mouth. His face was expressionless.

"On what charge?"

"Murder," said Beatty quietly.

Munson gave a visible start, but he went on chewing his mouthful of fish. Rossington had crushed out the butt of his cigar in the tray on the table and was making notable inroads into his breakfast. He picked up the big earthenware pot and poured black coffee for the three men without interrupting. Munson put down his fork and gave a heavy sigh. He looked reproachfully from Rossington to Beatty.

"What have you two gentlemen been up to?"

"On my return to London I found that the examination Dr. Rossington here had carried out was on the wrong body," said Beatty quickly. "Either there had been a substitution or a genuine mistake had been made. We had to make sure. We returned last night and the doctor carried out a post-mortem on the remains of the real Mr. Meredith."

Munson had a slightly shocked look on his face now.

"This is highly irregular . . ." he began.

"That is what we told Superintendent Bateman," Beatty went on doggedly. "Tell the Inspector your findings, John."

"The late Mr. Meredith had enough arsenic in his body to poison the population of Woking," Rossington told the police officer stolidly. He reached for his coffee cup again.

"Which leaves Dr. Couchman in a very awkward position," Beatty concluded. "It is my intention to interview him this morning, but I thought it only correct to inform you of the facts."

Munson snorted. His face was grim as he stared at Beatty.

"Not only correct, Mr. Beatty, but your duty. If I had found out after . . ."

"But there was no need for you to find out after," Rossington broke in urbanely. "It was our intention to keep you informed at all stages, Inspector. As indeed we did when we first arrived at Woking. We thought last night that there had been a simple administrative failure and as we had the original exhumation order . . ."

"Yes, yes, gentlemen," said Munson in more mollified tones. "Forgive me for perhaps being a little hasty."

He smiled at them both.

"And most particularly as you have invited me to breakfast . . . But as you say, this is a serious business. We shall have to go carefully."

"I thought if we merely interviewed Dr. Couchman initially . . ." Beatty interjected. "His explanation of his part in the affair may be perfectly satisfactory. Then, if we need a warrant . . ."

Munson masticated a morsel of fish slowly and reached for his coffee cup. He shook his head, little sparks of humour dancing in his eyes.

"Satisfactory explanation! If Dr. Rossington's findings are correct—and we shall obviously want corroboration from our own police surgeon—then Dr. Couchman is in trouble."

A silence fell among the three of them, broken by the landlord coming to the table to enquire whether the service was satisfactory. He smiled reassuringly at Beatty's eulogy, looking with curiosity at the three men.

"I had wondered, gentlemen, whether anything was amiss. And when you did not return last night . . ."

"Everything is in order," Beatty reassured him. "Dr. Rossington and I were out all night on an urgent call. Inspector Munson here is an old friend from rugby days."

The landlord smiled again.

"Ah, I see. Then you may be wanting to retain your rooms?"

"I shall be returning to London today," said Rossington, briefly lifting his face from his coffee cup. He did not look at Beatty, who still retained the pince-nez and the formal attire of his persona as doctoral colleague. Beatty knew that he found this amusing and hoped that his friend would not give him away before he left.

"I may stay on for another two days or so," Beatty continued. "I have some unfinished business in the neighbourhood."

When the landlord had moved out of earshot, Beatty turned to Rossington.

"I will write you a note for my assistant, Dotterell, which I would be grateful if you would despatch by special messenger on your return to London. I may have need of his services and equipment which I can't get in the neighbourhood."

He felt Munson's eyes on him as he again gave his attention to the meal.

"You have formed some opinion, then, as to what lies behind this business?" said Munson casually, signalling to the waiter to come forward to remove his first dish.

"Not really."

Beatty sounded more offhand than he felt. "You are referring to Couchman's motive, of course? If indeed he is guilty."

The detective studied his face and waited for him to go on. Rossington was already pouring himself a second cup of coffee, his eyes on the attractive blonde woman with high-buttoned bustline who was sitting with an elderly gentleman three tables from them.

"No, I have no real inkling at the moment. Money is not involved. I have ascertained that much from Miss Meredith herself. But the London house was burgled soon after her father's death. There may be darker strands here than we imagine, with the threads reaching back to London."

Inspector Munson's tense attitude revealed to Beatty that he had the officer's full attention.

"For example, John, you have not yet offered any opinion on the method of administering the poison. As I understand it, arsenic floats on the surface of liquids."

"It is usually administered in such foodstuffs as porridge," said Rossington drily, looking pointedly at Munson's bowl. The little detective smiled wryly as he poured cream and eased his spoon into the mixture before him.

"I hardly think the White Horse's kitchen would go that far, even if the Surrey Constabulary are not always popular with the local publicans," he replied lightly. "And in any event we shall have to await our interview with Dr. Couchman before we can proceed further."

"I will have a formal post-mortem report for you before I catch my train," Rossington went on. "I have all the necessary documents with me."

He smiled across at Beatty.

"For now, I feel we can leave this matter temporarily, and do full justice to the excellent breakfast before us."

And he reached out vigorously for another slice of toast.

The horse's hooves rung iron-sharp on the icy ground. Toby Stevens grunted as he cracked the whip in the air, and the cab bowled smartly across the uplands. Sunlight sparkled on the frost that dusted the grass-blades and glittered on the icicles in the hedgerow. The sun hung in the sky as bright and large as an orange and cast the gaunt shadows of the trees in long swathes across the ground.

Beatty was silent for a moment, his strong face clear-minted as a coin, absorbed in the scene outside the window as the cab advanced swiftly across the ground. Inspector Munson, his face wreathed in blue smoke from his pipe, kept his own counsel and surveyed the toes of his stout boots as though the solution to the problems that absorbed them both was to be found in the stitching of his toe-caps.

"But why, Mr. Beatty?" he said for the third or fourth time since the drive had begun. "What is the point of a man like Dr. Couchman poisoning one of his own healthy patients?"

"If we knew that we should know the answer to a lot of things," said Beatty enigmatically.

He took his gaze off the window and stared frankly at the Surrey detective. He still retained his personation as Dr. Fitzgibbon for the benefit of Stevens but had taken off the pince-nez and hat, so that he presented his normal alert appearance. The change had not passed unnoticed by the Inspector, who was regarding him keenly through the writhing veils of pipe smoke.

"There is something very odd going on at the cemetery," Beatty observed. "I commend it to your attention."

The Inspector smiled slowly. He took the pipe out of his mouth. "Ah," he began. "You noticed it too."

He was interrupted by a startled exclamation from his companion. The cab had now gained the height of the hills, and in a few more minutes they would be looking down on the grim bulk of the doctor's nursing home. The road they were on had wound among thick groves of birch and pine, denuded now of their summer covering. But there was a gap in the trees, and below them another road wound across open ground before disappearing in a fold of the hillside.

Following Beatty's pointing finger Munson observed that a fly drawn by a black horse was being driven at a furious pace on the lower road, in the opposite direction to their own. Beatty gave him an ironic smile. He was already rummaging in a small black bag on the seat beside him. He clapped the powerful spy-glass to his eye and rotated the lens with an intense concentration. He swore and passed the glass to the Inspector.

"There, unless I am much mistaken, is the man we seek."

Munson adjusted the glass; the image leaped out pin-sharp against the blur of trees. He had just time to make out the cadaverous form of Dr. Horace Couchman standing up in the driving seat of the fly, as he urged the horse to greater efforts. There was no mistaking the gaunt features and the green-tinted spectacles. Then man, horse, and vehicle were cut off by the farther edge of the trees.

Beatty was standing up, rapping on the hatch of the cab. Stevens's startled face appeared in the opening as he reined in the horse.

"Back to Woking!" Beatty snapped. "As fast as you dare."

Stevens nodded, the trap flap snicked to, and then the cab was rumbling and lurching back the way it had come. The two men were silent for a moment.

"Where does that lower road lead to?" Beatty asked.

"Back to the town," the Surrey detective answered. "But there are a number of turns off which connect with local villages."

Beatty's face had turned dark with suppressed anger and disappointment. He looked so formidable that Inspector Munson ventured no further remarks but sat enveloped in blue smoke and holding on to the corner-strap until, in an astonishingly short time it seemed, they were once more threading the streets of Woking. Stevens was turning the cab into the station forecourt, even before Beatty's injunction, but the two occupants of the vehicle saw that they were already too late.

The smart-looking fly, drawn by the black horse which was in a lather of sweat, was being led off by an ostler to the local livery stables while a dark plume of smoke half a mile down the line showed that the train had left. Beatty struck his hand on the edge of the window with a barely suppressed cry of anger.

"The London train?" he asked.

Munson nodded. He looked sympathetically at the young investigator.

"Direct to town," he said. "Or he may have another destination. But let us just make sure he was on the train."

"There is no doubt in my mind of that," said Beatty gloomily, but he followed his colleague into the booking office where the local Inspector speedily elicited the information that Dr. Couchman had indeed caught the train by the very narrowest of margins.

The two men walked back into the sunshine of the forecourt where Stevens was obediently awaiting their instructions.

"I shouldn't be so downcast, Mr. Beatty," said Munson sympathetically. "It is only an interview deferred, after all. Dr. Couchman will probably be back tonight or tomorrow. And I shall be on the lookout for him."

"Who knows what he may be up to in the metropolis," said Beatty darkly. "I had hoped we would resolve one or two questions this morning. As it is I find I must return to London as soon as may be."

The two men had now turned toward the hospitable portals of the White Horse.

"The utmost discretion, of course," said Beatty, seizing the detective officer's wrist with a strength that astonished him. "No one knows the true import of the autopsy apart from ourselves and Rossington. No one must know until we have had a chance to interview Couchman."

"Naturally," said Munson a little shortly. He bore a piqued expression, and Beatty at once hastened to repair the damage his remark may have inflicted.

"There are certain things connected with this matter which may have far more serious implications than either of us imagines," he told Munson. "As for myself, I am not yet certain whether the ends lie in London or Surrey. For the moment I must return to town to make my arrangements. It may be someone has told Couchman of the second post-mortem."

"I will telegraph you just as soon as I have any news of him," said Munson. "And I will delay contacting him until you have a chance to be present."

The two men turned to look back toward the station, as if moved by a common impulse. The faint plumes of smoke from the train were still hovering in the far distance. Then they were dispersed in the blue haze of the hills.

14

A MESSAGE FROM MUNSON

DOTTERELL leaned forward, his eyes glittering with suppressed excitement, his lank black hair falling over his forehead and making him look more like an undertaker than ever. His pen raced over the paper as Beatty went on speaking. He put up his hand once, and Beatty paused while his assistant changed over notebooks. The two men were sitting in Beatty's Holborn office, the fog writhing thickly at the windows.

It was early afternoon, and only the footfall of an occasional pedestrian sounded from the courtyard outside. Beatty got up from behind the desk and went over to the fireplace. He frowned at the right-hand gas-jet and turned it up a little. He went back to his place with a grunt of satisfaction. Dotterell was silent for a long while as Beatty finished.

His piercing blue eyes had a strange expression as he gazed unseeingly out at the grey sea of fog which eddied sluggishly beyond the windows. He opened his mouth as if to say something, then closed it as the thunder of a passing dray echoed under the courtyard arch outside. He waited until its iron-bound wheels had passed down Holborn.

"And you have heard nothing today, Mr. Beatty?"

He glanced down at his notes. Beatty shook his head. He fidgeted with a silver paper-knife on the blotter in front of him.

"I should have heard from Inspector Munson if there were anything."

Dotterell turned over the pages of his notebook. He sat to one side of Beatty's desk, his lean body half-turned to the well-banked fire.

"This Dr. Couchman sounds a most damnable villain," he said.

Beatty smiled grimly.

"I should greatly appreciate the opportunity of clapping the cuffs upon him," he admitted. "But that is a pleasure I fear reserved for the good Inspector."

Dotterell glanced toward the door and then quickly back to his employer.

"And Miss Meredith? Does she yet know about this?"

Beatty shook his head.

"I am to call on her later this afternoon. But this will only confirm what that young lady has long suspected."

Dotterell had turned to the notebooks again; he ruffled the pages disconsolately. He looked shrewdly at Beatty from beneath lowered brows.

"There is a great deal more to this than meets the eye, Mr. Beatty."

"You think so too," said the young investigator, stretching himself in his leather chair. He focused his eyes up on to the ceiling, his fingers still playing with the paper-knife.

"The case has a number of promising features. For example, why should an obviously prosperous doctor suddenly poison a client who was also a personal friend? He stood to gain nothing financially."

Dotterell sat looking at him with glittering eyes without saying anything, so Beatty went on with his apparently disjointed musings.

"To say nothing of risking a nursing home which is housed in one of the largest private mansions I have ever seen."

He looked interrogatively at his assistant without, however, drawing him. Disappointed at Dotterell's immobile silence, Beatty turned in his chair and went on, as though to himself.

"But there are some interesting indications. Assuming that Dr. Couchman is the culprit. And there is no doubt at all in my mind that he is the guilty party. He would need some assistance in the matter of altering the grave markers, for example. . . ."

Dotterell leaned forward.

"We must not forget the matter of the burglary at Miss Meredith's home and the fragment of letter in the fireplace."

"Precisely," said Beatty calmly. "The indications are that Mr. Tredegar Meredith may have been killed to prevent him from doing something. Or because his actions—or contemplated actions—were endangering others."

"This cemetery seems a strange place, from what you say," said Dotterell in his abrupt fashion.

Beatty smiled thinly.

"Excellent. I was certain that would not have escaped your attention. I have given a lot of thought to that aspect of the matter. To return to my earlier remarks on the grave markers. The doctor, perhaps, returned to change them over after dark."

Dotterell's eyes sparkled.

"But the gates would be locked, and you say there is a day and night staff on duty."

"Exactly," Beatty said. "So I think we may safely assume some degree of collusion on the part of the staff. There is a Foreman there called Varley, who has been acting in a most peculiar manner . . ."

He broke off as the outer bell jangled, and an elderly man in the thick, rough uniform of a messenger entered the office, blinking in the radiance of the gas-jets.

"Telegraph for Mr. Beatty, sir?"

"I am he," said Beatty, stretching out his hand for the buff envelope.

Dotterell signed for it and gave the man a coin as Beatty impatiently tore open the flap. His eyes widened in surprise, and he glanced at his assistant with barely suppressed excitement. He rubbed his hands together and waited until the messenger had left the building. He flung the form across to Dotterell, his body stiff in the chair. Dotterell perused the enigmatic message in silence: BROOKWOOD FOREMAN VARLEY DIED A.M. LONDON 25 ELGIN TERRACE AWAITING COUCHMAN RETURN ADVISE MUNSON.

"I'm not sure I quite understand, Mr. Beatty," he said. "What does it mean?"

"I may be wrong," said Beatty, getting to his feet. "But if it means what I think it means, we have two murders for the price of one."

And he took down his coat, clapped on his hat, and rushed out.

Miss Angela Meredith stared at Beatty with wide blue eyes, but said nothing. The two sat now in a small drawing room of the St. John's Wood house. Silver tea-things were on the table between them. The fog outside had cleared a little, and the jingle and staccato rhythm of a hansom cab passing beyond the grounds sounded sharp and clear through the biting air.

"I am indeed sorry to have brought you such sombre news, Miss Meredith," said Beatty at length, picking up his cup and draining its contents. "But at least we now know your suspicions were justified."

The girl's eyes never left Beatty's face. Only her hands, twining restlessly in her lap, betrayed her inner tension.

"But what does it all mean, Mr. Beatty?" she burst out at length, no longer able to contain herself. Beatty shook his head and held out his cup to the proffered silver pot.

"I fear this is a complicated business and there are no easy answers. I may know more before the day is out."

The girl's eyes widened.

"You have learned something further?"

Beatty leaned forward and cupped strong fingers round his knee.

"I received a telegraph from the Surrey police officer I mentioned, not an hour since. I have already sent him a reply."

He paused, shaking his head as Miss Meredith offered him another sandwich. He selected one of the small pastries instead. The girl moved in her seat and her eyes searched his face. There was no sound in the room apart from the low crackling of the fire.

Beatty thought for a moment of the contrast between Miss Meredith's comfortable, well-ordered world and that of the bleak one he was presently inhabiting; particularly that of the milieu in Surrey where he seemed to have spent most of his time lately in the charnel atmosphere of the cemetery chapel. Then he looked at his client's troubled face and his glance softened.

"Can you tell me no more?" Angela Meredith entreated him. "Everything seems so black and dark."

She looked round the room, clenching her hands together on her lap. Beatty wiped his fingers on his handkerchief and moved closer to her in the warm dusk of the shaded lamp. The orderly sounds of the household came from a distance. The soft tread of servants' feet, the silvery chime of a clock marking the quarter hour.

"There is little to tell, unfortunately, Miss Meredith. Until we can interview or apprehend Dr. Couchman, we are unable to take matters further. It seems obvious that someone moved the markers on the graves in order to cover up a crime. Dr. Rossington's report showed a great deal of arsenic present . . ."

He broke off. The girl bowed her head. She was weeping silently. Beatty glanced round awkwardly, then moved closer as though by instinct. The girl came into his arms; Beatty felt the soft pressure of her breast against him, the warm perfume of her hair in his nostrils. His hands brushed her shoulders as he whispered calming words, conscious of the grief that was eating at the heart of this attractive young woman.

He let her cry until at last she lay limp and exhausted in his arms; he could feel her warm tears against his face. Despite his reserved, rugged nature, Beatty had a passionate heart, and the presence of this enchanting woman whose body was pressed so close to him came near to making him lose the self-control on which he prided himself. He was conscious too of the absurd picture they must present if one of the servants came suddenly into the room.

The girl seemed to recollect herself; she stirred and gave a startled little cry. Beatty's lips brushed her forehead fleetingly as she drew back. Miss Meredith trembled, her face flushed and agitated. She dabbed at her eyes with a scrap of lace and pushed gently away from his restraining arms. Her breast rose and fell with the intensity of her emotions.

"Forgive me, sir," she said in a trembling voice. "I cannot understand what came over me."

"It is nothing to be ashamed of," Beatty said in a low voice.

He remained close to her, and his hands found hers and held them. She made no move to relinquish his clasp, and they sat thus for some minutes in a soothing silence. When Beatty judged her emotions had subsided, he moved gently away and resumed his own side of the table. The girl patted her hair absently and cast him a grateful glance. She moved mechanically over and poured him another cup of tea.

"What we must do now, Miss Meredith," Beatty went on as though the preceding scene had not passed between them, "is to establish some sort of link between your father and Dr. Couchman. Something that would account for the black business we are engaged upon."

He avoided the girl's eye, but she noted with all her woman's shrewdness the slight trembling of his own voice.

"The Bank would probably know," she continued. She had somewhat regained her composure and took a small tortoise-shell hand-mirror from a drawer in the table and repaired the ravages to her face.

"How do you mean?"

"He was the Bank's doctor, I believe," the girl replied. "I understand he treated members of the board for various ailments from time to time. And he kept up a connection there through my father."

"Indeed," said Beatty.

There was intense interest on his face, and he leaned back in his chair and put the tips of his fingers together as he stared at the girl.

"Is that of importance?" Angela Meredith asked.

Beatty nodded.

"It might be," he said. "Frankly, it was not something which had occurred to me. We must investigate further your father's business activities. I am convinced there is a link somewhere there."

He took out his watch and glanced at it.

"I must be leaving shortly. The message I received today concerned the Foreman at the cemetery where your father was interred. Though apparently in perfect health yesterday, he died this morning. Mr. Munson feels this is something which should be investigated further. Or at least that is how I read it. I agree with him."

The girl had risen to her feet with an agitated expression. Beatty silenced her.

"No more questions. And I must ask you to regard what I have just told you as confidential. I may be able to throw more light on this by tomorrow."

The girl came toward him. Her eyes searched his face carefully.

"Please take care, Mr. Beatty. There are depths here which are beyond me. I pray that you will not take undue risks for my sake."

Her lips were warm on Beatty's cheek, and then she had run to the door. The housekeeper appeared in the opening as her footsteps echoed down the hallway. Beatty was smiling, the imprint of the kiss still warm on his cheek, as he strode out into the icy air.

15

MCMURDO'S

ELGIN TERRACE was a crescent of yellow-brick houses in a mean area of the East End. Beatty had some trouble in finding it after quitting the horse-bus at the end of the line. Thin mist was descending again as he picked his way across the greasy setts, moisture settling cold and dank on the folds of his cape. He had abandoned his Surrey impersonation, and his strong face was firm in the gaslight as he passed down the street, pausing to search for the numbers.

It was almost eight o'clock in the evening, and he had found a tavern of a better sort where he had eaten a sandwich and taken a glass of rum. Now, fortified by this, he was prepared to tackle the problems involved by Munson's enigmatic telegraph. One of the facets whirling about in his mind concerned the London address; he could not imagine what connection that could have with a man who would surely live in Surrey near to his place of work.

He had asked for further details in his reply to the Detective Inspector, but nothing had come through from Dotterell so Munson may have been away. Beatty did not like to proceed on such vague information, but he had little choice at the moment. And Munson would not have sent him the message had it not been urgent—and important.

He pulled the crumpled form out of his pocket and studied it once again under the light of the nearest lamp. Then he strode on, his keen eyes searching the numbers of the houses. Many of them had been converted into warehouses and small manufacturies, and faint yellow light still glowed from some of the windows.

Horses snorted and stamped on cold flagstones as he crossed

the entrance to a stable yard; horse-buses were being shunted round, the beasts' hooves sliding on the icy cobbles. Beatty pulled the thick cape about him; he could feel the derringer in its special holster against his shin. He had another pistol in a specially tailored pocket beneath his left armpit; and what was ostensibly a folding fruit-knife in a leather case in his trouser pocket completed a formidable trio of weapons.

But he did not anticipate any problems this evening, and he hurried on across the stable entrance, ducking round behind the bulk of a slowly moving tram-car to regain the high pavement. Number 25 was only a few yards farther on, a narrow-chested yellow-brick building. It was a blaze of light, and the investigator soon saw why. As he got closer he could see unmistakable signs of the premises' function displayed in the bow-windows.

Above the façade he made out the faded legend in gilt lettering: McMurdo and Company. Funeral Furnishings. Beatty smiled grimly. Whichever way he turned in the case he was confronted by indications of mortality. He had his cue now. He rapidly made up his mind. He set his shoulders and thrust open the front door. He was met with a fresh smell of new pine, hot varnish, and wax polish. A bell jangled rustily in the rear.

Beatty closed the door behind him. He looked keenly at the oaken coffins set behind the railings of the bow-windows, noting their ornate brass handles and purple silk linings. Footsteps sounded in the shadowy interior of the premises, and somewhere far off he could hear a woman sobbing. A mahogany door at the end of the office opened abruptly, and a balding middle-aged man with stoop shoulders came with mincing step toward him. He had a quill pen behind his ear, and the ink-stains on his fingers proclaimed his calling.

"Mr. Varley," said Beatty in a curt voice.

The little man recoiled and looked at him closely. He pointed with his thumb to another door, opposite that by which Beatty had entered.

"Mrs. Varley is in there," he said. "It's been a trying afternoon, Mr. . . ."

"I am a solicitor representing the family," said Beatty boldly.

The little man's face cleared.

"Ah, sir, never more welcome," he said. "You will no doubt know what to do in the way of comforting Mrs. Varley."

"She must be got home as soon as may be," said Beatty decisively.

He glanced round the shadowy interior of the office. The gasjets were set to illuminate the windows and their melancholy display, leaving the rear of the premises in shadow.

"Sudden, was it?"

The clerk nodded.

"Convulsions," he said. "Shocking business. He died within the hour."

He lowered his voice to a whisper, looking back over his shoulder to the room he had just quitted.

"On these very premises."

"Indeed," said Beatty.

He stared reflectively round the room, his eyes noting each small detail that might assist his present purpose.

"You have the certificate?" he asked.

The little man nodded again.

"It was given to the lady on her arrival this afternoon. She came up by the first available train. It was fortunate we had a doctor on the premises."

Beatty gave an audible intake of breath, but he said nothing, merely gazed stolidly in front of him.

"Fortunate indeed," he drawled. "I had better see the lady now."

He followed the clerk over to the far door and waited while the little man tapped deferentially. He stood aside for Beatty to enter.

"Here's a gentleman who's come to see you safely home, ma'am," he said sympathetically.

The middle-aged woman with a black scarf round her throat and wild signs of mourning on her face rose awkwardly to her feet and stared at Beatty with red-rimmed eyes. She had been half-sitting, half-lying on a rough wooden bench at the foot of a plain elm coffin which stood on trestles in the silent room, and Beatty motioned her to reseat herself. This she did immediately, giving him a look in which curiosity was mingled with grief. The fire of small-coals in the room had burned low and it was cold in the chamber, which was evidently used as a chapel.

There were few furnishings apart from two candlesticks which guttered in tall iron candle-holders at either side of the coffin; the bench, a solitary chair, and a brass crucifix on the white-washed wall. Beatty went to sit in the chair opposite the grey-haired woman and spoke in kindly tones.

"I have come to offer what help I can, Mrs. Varley."

The woman put forward a trembling hand and caught his fingers.

"Ah, sir, if only you could!" she burst out and then subsided in a paroxysm of tears. Beatty waited for the storm to pass; if she had been here some hours already it could not last. And so it proved, for Mrs. Varley soon recovered herself again. She went on in a toneless voice, keeping her eyes fixed unwaveringly on the candle-flames.

"Such a terrible day I cannot remember, and that is the plain truth."

"You were informed by telegraph?" Beatty asked.

The woman shook her head.

"The police came to fetch me this morning. I live in the village of Send, you see, sir, and they kindly gave me transport into Woking. But you said you were here to help me, sir. Who might you be, and may I know your name?"

"I am a colleague of Inspector Munson's," said Beatty, glancing round the shadowy room. "My name does not matter for the moment. I had a message from the Inspector to come here."

The woman's face cleared.

"Ah, that explains it, sir. I chanced across the Inspector this morning, when I was waiting for a train at Woking Station. He was deeply sorry to hear about Varley. He had never been ill in his life."

"So I understand," said Beatty. "Which makes the circumstance even more curious. But we cannot talk here. You need food and warm drink to sustain you."

He rose to his feet as he spoke, drawing the woman up by the arm.

"We can do no further good here, ma'am. I will find somewhere for you to eat and rest and see you on your way this evening."

"You are very kind, sir," said Mrs. Varley, giving a last glance at the coffin.

Its heavy shadow flickered on the wall in the insubstantial light of the candles. The two walked across to the door and passed out of the chamber of death, leaving it to silence and the night.

Beatty sat opposite his companion in the dining alcove in the chop-house and looked curiously at her as she finished her meal. He signalled to the waiter who came forward with another pot of coffee. Mrs. Varley was making a remarkable recovery of appetite. Beatty guessed she had not eaten since the previous evening.

"It is a strange business, this of your husband," he ventured, when the waiter had once again withdrawn.

"You may well say so, sir," said the woman, turning her pale face to his. "For months past Varley had not been himself."

Beatty gave her a sharp glance. He leaned forward across the table.

"How do you mean?"

The woman shrugged.

"Little things, such as a woman notices. About his work mostly."

"At the cemetery?"

Beatty could not keep the note of rising excitement out of his voice.

"I have often spoken of it," Mrs. Varley went on. "But he would never say what it meant. And then only yesterday he had this message to come to London."

"That was unusual, was it?"

The woman nodded vehemently. She put her yellow-skinned fingers round the rim of her coffee cup for warmth.

"I have never known it to happen, sir. The message seemed to upset Varley a great deal, for he turned quite white. He told the messenger there was no reply."

"What messenger?" Beatty said.

"Oh, some rough-looking man. I've seen him hanging about Woking Station sometimes. He runs errands in the locality."

Beatty nodded. He drummed with strong fingers on the oak table in front of him, his Roman head sharp-etched in the lamplight.

"Did you ask him about it?"

Mrs. Varley put down the coffee cup and stared at the table surface.

"He would not say anything. He was always a close one, was Varley. And I knew it was no use to ask further."

"You said something about him not being himself. Can you be more specific? For example, had something happened at the cemetery? Trouble with Superintendent Bateman, for instance?"

The woman screwed up her eyes as though she were trying to remember something that might be vitally important.

"Not the Superintendent, sir. It was something else."

She looked Beatty straight in the eye. There was a furtive aspect about the look that Beatty found out of character.

"May I speak openly with you, sir?"

"I would prefer you to do so. I am a lawyer and used to keeping confidences."

The woman nodded once or twice as she took in the import of what he was saying.

"I wouldn't want to get into any trouble. And I need the money more than ever."

"Go on," Beatty said.

"When I heard the terrible news this morning," Mrs. Varley continued, "I went to a place in our house where we keep our few valuables and trinkets safe. I needed something, you see, for the fare and the expenses."

Beatty waited without saying anything. Encouraged by his look Mrs. Varley went on.

"There was a small wooden box tucked away in a corner, sir. I found there was well over a hundred golden guineas inside it."

Her red-rimmed eyes looked frightened as she stared at Beatty.

"Now I ask you, sir, where would a man like Varley, a Foreman at the cemetery, get money like that?"

There was a long silence between them. The murmuring of the everyday life of the chophouse went on, ignored by both. Beatty had sunk his head on to his breast in order to hide the expression of his eyes. Now he looked up at his companion.

"You have done well to confide in me thus, Mrs. Varley. You will not be the loser, rest assured. You may rely on my confidence. But we have a strange business here. I must think more about it."

The pair prepared to rise as the waiter came forward with the bill. Beatty paid it and left something on the table. He waited for Mrs. Varley to gather up her belongings.

"The clerk said something about a doctor being present, Mrs. Varley."

"That's correct, sir. What good fortune. A most excellent man and a wonderful doctor. Strange that he should come from the same district of Surrey."

Once again Beatty's breath was drawn in. He looked at Mrs. Varley keenly.

"You have the death certificate?"

The woman fumbled in her bag, handed him the crumpled document.

"Signed by that excellent gentleman himself."

The lighting was poor and the handwriting crabbed, but there was no mistaking the signature of Dr. Horace Couchman. The effect on Beatty was startling. He clapped on his hat and seized Mrs. Varley by the arm, hurrying her into the street.

"I will put you into a cab for the station, madam. You will hear further from me. I find I have some urgent uncompleted business at McMurdo's establishment."

16

DEATH ON THE BRIDGE

IT was nine o'clock. The neighbouring clock on a church tower had just tolled the hour. Beatty felt cramped and stiff from his position deep in the shadowy doorway of a provision shop. The establishment had closed only a short while earlier, and he had taken up his stance here from a less sheltered one in a carter's yard, which was dark and unlit. By now his feet were extremely cold but he dare not stamp them, which would have immediately drawn attention to his presence in the doorway.

The lights were still burning in the premises of McMurdo and

Company. He was almost opposite and could see the clerk he had spoken to earlier. The man was working at a tall desk, seated on a high stool and occasionally consulting a massive ledger. Several people had been in and out during the past hour, mostly humble folk, dressed in black; obviously bereaved relatives making funeral arrangements, for the clerk had been busy consulting catalogues and offering advice on the various types of coffin.

Beatty had seen no other members of the staff since he took up his vigil. Occasionally he had moved off a few yards as a patrolling policeman came round, but he returned within minutes; the inner doors of the funeral office had remained shut as on the occasion of his visit. But the investigator had noted that there were lights burning behind the window shades over the premises, which indicated offices above. One thing had left a doubt in his mind. Though a black-plumed hearse drawn by two coal-black horses had set off from in front of the building half an hour before, there did not appear to be any yard or manufactury attached to the premises. It would seem that the establishment acted as an office for booking funerals, with a chapel for lying-in, and that the mortuary and coffin side of the business was carried on elsewhere.

A thin mist was rising now, and Beatty blew on his half-frozen hands, glancing again at his watch. He would give it another hour. His idea, at first seized on with such enthusiasm, was losing strength with each minute that passed. Yet Couchman had been at the establishment earlier today. Might it not be that he could be there still, perhaps in the premises above?

Certainly he had not been at Woking that day, and Munson had not seen him since he drove away from the nursing home, or he would have reported it. The sinister doctor had almost certainly spent the intervening time in London. Beatty wondered again if the unfortunate Varley's London appointment had been with Couchman. In which case the doctor would be aware of the second post-mortem at Brookwood.

Neither Rossington nor Beatty had breathed a word of the results to Superintendent Bateman, but Couchman would surely know by now that he was seriously implicated in a crime. So he would not be returning to Woking if he had any sense. Varley was to be buried at Brookwood the day after tomorrow, according to his widow; Beatty would have to telegraph Munson that night. A police surgeon must perform an autopsy on the corpse of Varley before the interment took place.

All this would take time, and Beatty hoped to avoid any further distress to the widow. The complexities of the case were gathering, and Beatty could see no way clear in the tangle which surrounded him. He drew his cape around him and looked sharply about as a quick footfall came to his ear. A man was walking rapidly along the opposite pavement toward McMurdo's premises. Though the encroaching mist made things difficult, Beatty could see he was tall and garbed in black.

The investigator swiftly withdrew into the doorway and waited. A small pulse beat somewhere in his throat. From far away the drawn-out siren of a ship sounded from the river, now bound solidly in a casing of ice. The footsteps were clear and sharp; the figure had disappeared behind a dray which stood at the edge of the kerb a little farther down, and then they ceased.

Beatty waited, hope contesting with disappointment within him. If the pedestrian had gone into a house hidden behind the vehicle, then there was an end of the matter. He stood, stiff and cold, hunched in the doorway, his ears strained to catch any resumption of the footsteps. Then they resumed, and a moment later Beatty saw a tall cadaverous form step out briskly toward the doorway of McMurdo's.

There was a gas-lamp a few yards from the door, and the man in the top-hat and long ulster, carrying a small black bag, paused and looked keenly about him before trying the handle. There was something so furtive and predatory about the movement that Beatty hardly needed the skull-like face and green-tinted spectacles to identify his man. Then the door-bell jangled and Dr. Horace Couchman had disappeared into the interior.

Beatty had not long to wait. Barely a quarter of an hour had passed before his quarry reemerged. The clerk accompanied him to the door, and they stood chatting for a few moments until the doctor again regained the pavement, while the little man bolted the door behind him. Then, without looking right or left, Couchman strode out along the street.

Beatty was already on the move, walking casually on the opposite pavement, treading lightly and avoiding the more well-lit places. He saw that Couchman had turned at right angles across a small square, and he followed, keeping in the shadow of the high railings. It was half-past nine now, and there were few people about, though the rumble of wheeled traffic sounded from the more populous highway which bounded this area of back streets.

When he gained the corner, Beatty paused and waited for a moment. Then he casually rounded the edge of the square; his quarry was a hundred yards away, the gaunt, angular figure of the doctor monstrous and elongated on the façade of the buildings opposite, as he passed in front of a gas-lamp. His footsteps, magnified and brittle in the wide spaces of the square, sounded sharp and clear as Beatty casually moved after him.

The doctor had gone into an alley approached by a high flight of steps, he saw a moment or two later. Beatty walked farther along, the mist swirling about him, and then came back quickly. He ran lightly up the steps, making no noise, and almost cannoned into a burly figure emerging from between the iron bollards at the top of the entry.

Beatty smelled the sharp, rank odour of beer on the fellow's breath; the big carter with the broad greasy face lurched and almost slipped on the setts. He mumbled obscenities as Beatty hurried on, guided by the sharp, regular footsteps of the doctor ahead of him.

He was only thirty yards behind when he heard Couchman's muffled shout through the mist; there was the clatter of hooves and the rumble of wheels over the icy thoroughfare. As Beatty gained the high road he saw the cab already stationary, the doctor climbing aboard. The vehicle turned and came back. It was abreast of the alley as Beatty ran swiftly and clambered on to the step.

Then he had opened the door and tumbled inside. The lean, startled face of Dr. Couchman was thrust into his own. The young investigator felt the man's breath on his cheek as he hissed in surprise.

"What the devil do you mean by this intrusion, sir?" he rasped. "Can you not see this cab is already taken?"

Beatty sat calmly down on the seat opposite the doctor, who

rapped peremptorily with his knuckles on the hatch above his head. It slid back swiftly to disclose the hard bearded face of the driver.

"I beg your pardon, sir," said Beatty politely. "But I had thought the cab unoccupied. As I was in a hurry to keep an appointment near Charing Cross and as the vehicle was going in the same direction . . ."

Beatty paused and the cabman's puzzled expression changed to one of benevolence.

"No harm done, guv'nor, so long as you don't mind sharing," he said cheerfully. "And you did ask for the Embankment, sir."

"Admirable," said Beatty. "And naturally we would share the expenses also."

Couchman's eyes were invisible behind the green-tinted glasses, but the corners of his mouth were drawn down in the semblance of a scowl. Now, however, he made an evident effort to appear more amiable. He nodded briefly up at the driver.

"Very well, very well," he said harshly. "As you are already here, sir. But I cannot help regarding it as an infernal impertinence."

"Look on it as providence, sir," said Beatty earnestly. "And you have saved fifty per cent of your outlay."

The cabman gave his two fares a crooked grin and slammed the hatch shut. He whipped up the horse, and they were soon bowling rapidly through the thinning mist, leaving the meaner streets behind and coming to the broader, more prosperous thoroughfares of the approaches to the City. Beatty was silent in his corner, studying the frigid figure of his companion.

"Perhaps we might introduce ourselves, sir," he said after a minute or two. "Seeing that we are fellow-travellers."

"I see no reason, sir," said Couchman stiffly. "But if you insist, you may as well begin."

"My name is Beatty," said the young investigator, studying the pale oval of the doctor's face. "I am a student of human nature."

Couchman sniffed and shifted on his seat. The lights from a shop beat garishly into the closed cab at that moment and made a gaudy mask of his face.

"Bergson," he said shortly. "My business is of a private nature."

Beatty leaned forward, examining the doctor's features.

"You might say that of mine," he said softly. "Yes, you might well say that."

He appeared unaware of the other's sharp intake of breath. Instead, he turned and looked casually out through the misty window, rubbing the pane to give himself a clearer view. They had been travelling steadily for some minutes, and now the reassuring façades of the City were about them; opulent, prosperous, and well-ordered.

They were in a wide thoroughfare, choked with horse-buses and thundering drays. The cab was turning, the horse's head fighting to get into a narrower lane that led down toward the river. Conversation was impossible for the moment, the iron-shod wheels making a deafening din between the high walls of the entries. Beatty felt Couchman's eyes upon him behind the green glasses. He sensed the man's puzzlement, mingled with suspicion and veiled hostility.

The young investigator glimpsed the gilded sign of the Mercantile Bank; it reminded him of something, he could not quite tell what. Then the cab was clear of the jumble, and they were proceeding at a smart trot through the rapidly thinning mist to where beams of lamplight gilded the gaunt trees of the Embankment.

The cab turned again and they were alongside the river, the chains of lamps burnishing the sheets of ice which lay like a thick cloak over the water. Barges lay crookedly, their sterns and upperworks frosted with ice like the filigree-work on an ornamental cake. Beatty drew his cape about him in the dampness of the cab interior. Seldom had he seen the Thames look more bleak; the gaslight seemed only to emphasise the bitter coldness of the water beneath.

They were coming up to Blackfriars Bridge when Couchman suddenly rapped on the hatch communicating with the driver.

"I will get down here," he snapped as the man's head appeared in the opening.

"I will descend too," Beatty told him.

The cabman's eyes were puzzled.

"We're a long way off Charing Cross, guv'nor," he expostulated.

"The walk will do me good and it wants some while to my appointment," Beatty said cheerfully.

Couchman's face was turned toward the floor of the cab as he groped for his bag, but he made a sharp movement with his shoulders which was not lost on Beatty. He was already down and the two men settled their dues with the cabman. The tall, lean figure of the doctor was striding across the road, and Beatty hastened to join him. The doctor turned as Beatty came up.

"Good night, sir," he said sarcastically.

"Oh, come, Dr. Couchman," said Beatty affably. "Our business is not yet concluded."

There was a long silence, broken only by the noise of the cab turning in the misty night. Even the river was silent, the low creaking of the ice betraying its presence from time to time. Couchman put his hand to the front of his ulster with a convulsive movement, as though he had suffered a heart attack. His right hand, the one holding the bag, clasped it fiercely, as if he purposed using it as a weapon.

The gaunt head, the green glasses looking like blank eye-sockets, turned toward Beatty, and the blue tongue licked the thin lips.

"Who are you, sir?" he whispered in so faint a voice that Beatty had to lean forward to make out the words.

"I know you not and yet you know me."

"Oh, yes, I know you, Dr. Couchman," Beatty said slowly. "Well enough to realise that you are not Mr. Bergson."

He was relishing the moment. The doctor had stopped in his stride when his pursuer had spoken, but now he resumed his walk toward the bridge. Beatty fell into step beside him and the conversation was continued jerkily, with short pauses between.

"We met in London or out of town?"

Beatty shook his head.

"Somewhere much more prosaic, Dr. Couchman. At your nursing home in Woking, to be precise."

Couchman did not stop his measured tread, but he momentarily faltered in midstride, as though a tremor ran through his body. They were turning on to the bridge now, the piles held captive by the jumbled fretwork of the ice, an occasional glimmer of lamplight on black water showing where the Thames had momentarily broken through.

"And yet I know no one of the name of Beatty."

The doctor's voice was thick and muffled. They were on the bridge; the wind, gusting down river, caught at them and plucked at the skirts of the doctor's coat. He walked on the outside, Beatty warily at the pavement edge. A few closed cabs edged on to the bridge from time to time, the horses quickening their pace, as though anxious to be out of the wind.

"My name is Clyde Beatty," the investigator said in level tones. "I am a private enquiry agent. You knew me as Dr. Clyde Fitzgibbon."

Couchman made a strangled noise and stopped in his tracks. He half fell against the balustrade of the bridge. His glasses were lowered now, his eye-sockets looking black against the whiteness of his face. He plucked at his collar, staring at Beatty the while, but said nothing.

"Miss Meredith was dissatisfied, as you know, with the circumstances surrounding her father's death," said Beatty.

The doctor recommenced walking, and the young man kept pace with him. He glanced at his companion; he was wiping the corners of his mouth with a none-too-clean handkerchief.

"Dr. Rossington recently carried out a second post-mortem. This time on the correct body. The grave markers had been changed over. But you know that too, do you not?"

Couchman's face was dark and heavy, set like stone. He uttered not a word, so Beatty went on doggedly.

"Dr. Rossington found enough arsenic in the unfortunate Mr. Meredith's body to destroy half the inhabitants of Surrey. Inspector Munson holds a blank warrant. It will be the work of a moment to insert your name in the appropriate space. But this is stale information also, as you undoubtedly left Woking to prevent that eventuality. And now we find you at McMurdo's establishment, where the Foreman of Brookwood, James Varley, died in convulsions only today. When you were conveniently on the premises. Too extraordinary to be coincidence, wouldn't you say?"

Couchman's only reaction was a muffled snarl. Beatty's face wore a set smile. He hunched his muscular shoulders and glanced at his silent companion.

"Now, as to motive . . ." he began, when his discourse was suddenly broken. Too late, he tried to sidestep. The heavy medical bag Couchman was carrying came round in the gloom with tremendous force. There must have been enormous strength in that emaciated figure. The bag, full of instruments, caught Beatty on the side of the head and dropped him, half-stunned, to the pavement. As he groped to his feet he heard the swiftly running footsteps of his adversary and saw him far out on the bridge.

But Beatty was young and fit. His head was clearing rapidly as he tucked in his elbows and ran with enormous speed down the paving. The thin figure of the doctor was a hundred yards before him, a rectangular strip of shadow beneath the faint luminescence of the gas-lamps that spanned the river on iron standards atop the bridge. A cab was clattering along the roadway at the far end. Beatty guessed Couchman's purpose and redoubled his efforts.

He fairly flew down the pavement in his efforts to overtake the doctor. The moon, breaking momentarily from behind dark clouds, sent a wavering light through the mist at this moment. Beatty was closing with Couchman; something glittered in the doctor's hand. The young investigator dropped to one knee as a streak of silver glanced against one of the uprights of the bridge. The knife clattered harmlessly to the paving.

The barrel of the revolver pointed steadily in the doctor's direction as Beatty got to his feet. His head was throbbing from the blow now, and his eyes, stinging from the wind and filled with tears, momentarily saw two gaunt figures by the parapet. The noise of the cab grew in the middle distance.

"The jig is up, doctor," Beatty said steadily. "Don't be a fool."

He was only yards from his quarry. The gaunt man gave a wolfish grin. He put his top-hat down on the parapet near him. Then he threw the medical bag at Beatty's head. Beatty stepped back and put one shot into the air. It slapped echoes from the windy roadway, and scarlet flame lit the night.

Couchman smiled a crooked smile at Beatty.

"There's only one way of it," he muttered.

He put the palm of his right hand on the parapet and vaulted over. Beatty, running forward, was in time to feel the thick material of the doctor's clothing rush through his powerless hands.

The cracking noise of Couchman's impact with the ice was drowned by the thunder of the cab. Beatty put his hands on the parapet, searching the jumbled mass of ice below. Now, there was nothing but the swirl of broken water. The babble of voices was about him as the cab disgorged its passengers. As one they rushed to the parapet. Beatty turned away, suddenly feeling tired and old.

17

COUNCIL OF WAR

"So the case is finished?" Angela Meredith said.

She sat in Beatty's office, in the big leather-backed chair, and looked tremulously from Beatty to Dotterell and then back again. Rossington sat equidistant between her and the desk, saying nothing, but keenly watching the scene. Beatty shook his head. He eased himself in the chair and smiled grimly.

"Hardly, Miss Meredith. There is something monstrous afoot here. Something so dark and sinister that I cannot for the moment see my way. . . ."

His body was tense with excitement and for a short space nobody spoke. Thin sunshine was picking out the railings of the courtyard beyond the office windows. It was only nine-thirty A.M., but the coffee cups and the debris on the desk gave witness to the fact that the occupants of the room had already been there for some time.

Miss Meredith looked thoughtfully at Beatty. She had thrown her mantle over the back of her chair, and her bust rose and fell gently beneath the tight-fitting grey tailored suit she wore. The gold watch in its oyster case was pinned to the breast of the jacket, and she sat nervously kneading her fingers as she waited for the investigator to go on.

Dotterell turned back the pages of his notebook and scribbled something in the margin with a flourish. His piercing blue eyes looked all sorts of questions at Beatty, but still nothing came from his dour lips. It was Rossington who finally broke the silence.

"But why attend Varley's funeral today?" he exploded impatiently. "You've made two visits to Brookwood already. What else can you expect to find?"

"I have found out more about Brookwood through last night's research in London than ever I did by going there," Beatty said enigmatically. "You forget we still do not know how Varley died. It is mere supposition."

"The police surgeon will not take an hour to clear that point," Rossington said. "Unless you want me to go down there yet again?"

His expression looked so disgusted that Beatty burst out laughing.

"No, John. I will not inflict that on you. Munson has everything in hand. But just look at the facts."

He glanced round at the faces of his listeners. Satisfied that he had their full attention, he went on.

"Mr. Tredegar Meredith was poisoned. We know that for an incontrovertible fact. Dr. Couchman, his physician, was the only one with the knowledge and opportunity to do so. Mr. Meredith is buried at Brookwood Cemetery. Dr. Couchman has his nursing home nearby. Do you follow me?"

Rossington shrugged impatiently. His cigar smoke went up in a still blue column in the warmth of the office.

"There is little to follow so far," he said testily.

"Patience, friend John," Beatty countered. "The Foreman at Brookwood, Varley, was alarmed at our second visit. Conclusion: that he knew the grave markers had been changed. He is therefore implicated. I have not yet made up my mind about Superintendent Bateman."

He drummed impatiently on the desk with his broad spatulate fingers.

"Later, Varley himself dies suddenly, with symptoms which strongly suggest arsenical poisoning, after being hurriedly summoned to London. Through the medium of a roughly dressed man who delivered him a note."

Miss Meredith's cornflower blue eyes had not left Beatty's face all the while.

"From Dr. Couchman?"

"That is the supposition," Beatty continued. "Now, if this be correct, why should Couchman first summon Varley and then poison him? To silence him, of course."

"But why?" Rossington burst out again. "What is the motive for all this?"

"That is the most interesting thing about it so far," said Beatty, rubbing his hands. "Something so big, so monstrous, that two men, so disparate in class, age, and station, must be murdered to ensure their silence. The only link in both cases being Brookwood Cemetery."

Rossington made an impatient, half-suppressed exclamation. He leaned forward and knocked his cigar-ash off into a bowl on Beatty's desk. Dotterell's pen went on scratching industriously across the paper. Beatty continued as though Rossington had not interrupted.

"Why should a humble employee at Brookwood Cemetery have upwards of a hundred gold guineas hidden in a box at his home?"

Dotterell gave a sharp intake of breath and stopped writing. He looked at Beatty keenly. Rossington's mouth was open, the cigar sagging from the corner of it.

"I thought that would interest you," said Beatty. "I had the information from Varley's widow. That is one of the reasons I shall be attending the funeral this morning. The other is, of course, why an apparently respectable physician like Couchman should commit two murders and then kill himself when discovered."

"That would be surely natural?" Rossington began.

Beatty shook his head violently.

"Entirely unnatural," he said in ringing tones. "Consider the circumstances and you will see that I am right. There are a number of other matters too peculiar to need stressing. But there is one recurring factor, one so obvious that it escaped me, even though, as friend John observes, I have twice visited the place. Brookwood Cemetery, at once the key and the enigma."

His brown eyes gazed keenly around, lighting on each of his three companions in turn, before becoming focused somewhere on the rapidly strengthening sunlight outside the windows.

"Brookwood," he almost whispered. "One of the most extraordinary places in the world."

He looked at Miss Meredith with sympathy.

"What I am going to say now may cause some distress in view of the circumstances. If you would care to withdraw . . ."

The girl shook her head. Little spots of colour were burning on her cheeks.

"I've set my hand to this, Mr. Beatty. I'll not turn back. My suspicions regarding Dr. Couchman were well-founded."

There was a brief silence broken by Rossington's drawl.

"I should imagine Scotland Yard would not have been too pleased at the incident on Blackfriars Bridge."

Beatty smiled grimly.

"I did not tell them I had fired a pistol in a public place, if that is what you mean," he said quietly. "I merely reported the suicide of a man wanted for questioning by the Surrey police. Inspector Munson will do the rest. Now, if you will pay attention . . ."

Rossington bowed ironically, cigar smoke billowing about him.

"I made a great many enquiries last night," Beatty went on. "As you can imagine I have given this case a deal of thought. I may be wrong, but the kernel of the matter appears to me to lie in Surrey. I was astonished at some of the findings. Dotterell and I have been all yesterday at the headquarters of the railway company."

Rossington narrowed his eyes and stared keenly at his friend through the smoke.

"Brookwood Cemetery was established in 1852 by a group of businessmen here in London," Beatty began.

He was reading from notes written out by Dotterell, and he consulted the paper on the desk in front of him, occasionally adding pencilled notations of his own.

"This was because graveyards in the capital were becoming overcrowded. The London Necropolis and National Mausoleum Company offered burial at Brookwood Cemetery at between five pounds and twenty pounds a grave originally. It is now, I believe, the largest cemetery in the world, with up to ten thousand bodies a year being interred there."

Rossington moved impatiently, a frown passing across his bearded face. His strong teeth gleamed in the beard as he removed the cigar from his mouth.

"I find that difficult to believe," he said. "I saw only a small country cemetery."

Beatty inclined his head, stopping his friend's flow of words.

"This misled me also," he said. "But consider the circumstances.

We arrived at night, under misty conditions. We were received at a secluded entrance in a section with its own chapel. We had no reason to believe the place anything but an ordinary cemetery."

Miss Meredith looked bewildered.

"But why should it be anything else?" she said.

"Yes," said Rossington belligerently. "Do you suspect Bateman of some underhand dealing?"

"There are many possibilities," Beatty went on imperturbably. "I am merely sifting through ideas for the moment. Brookwood is a strange place. Since last night I have come to realise I have not yet visited it at all. Which is why I propose to travel on the funeral train this morning."

He glanced quickly at his watch.

"Funeral train?" Rossington repeated.

Beatty smiled thinly.

"It certainly engaged my attention also. Brookwood, with its Glades of Remembrance, runs to more than twenty-five hundred acres of land. A stupefying total, is it not? Of this it is proposed to use some fifteen hundred acres for cemetery purposes. At the moment four hundred and fifty acres have been laid out for burial."

He glanced round the intent group surrounding the desk, seeing by their expressions that they were following every word.

"I thought you'd find it interesting," he went on drily. "So large is Brookwood that the London Necropolis Company operate their own private railway to and from the cemetery, with two stations within the walls."

Rossington blinked and his cigar made an agitated movement, sending sparks dancing to the carpet.

"Every day a special funeral train leaves the Waterloo-road Station in London from its own platform for Brookwood, carrying coffins and mourners together with clergy and priests. It travels nonstop to Woking, taking the different denominations to one of the two stations within the walls."

Dotterell smiled ironically.

"I saw it at Waterloo-road last night," he said. "It is painted white. A wag on the platform told me it is popularly called 'The Ghost Train.'"

Miss Meredith shivered suddenly and Beatty shot her a quick glance.

"Remarkably apt," said Rossington slowly. He had his eyes fixed on the carpet and his thoughts were evidently far away.

"A journey with a one-way ticket," he added.

"Precisely," Beatty snapped. "Which gives rise to some interesting possibilities."

He got up in an agitated manner and started to pace about the office, as though unconscious of his audience.

"Here we have a vast organisation, the London Necropolis Company and its melancholy activities, which embrace, as we have seen, a private railway company. Somehow connected with this company or cemetery is a proven murderer. An employee of the cemetery—a suspected victim of murder—a question which will be resolved by this evening, is in possession of a remarkable sum of money for a man in such a lowly station."

Beatty stopped pacing and came back to sit at the desk. Strange lights were dancing in his eyes.

"You surely do not suspect the company of complicity in these events?" said Rossington. "I confess that I am completely baffled as to motive here."

Beatty shook his head.

"But such a company could be used as a cloak for other things," he said quietly. "I must confess I have not been so intrigued by a problem for a long time. Whichever way one looks, the sequence of events appears to be pointless. Because we have as yet no motive. We will not find it by sitting still in London. Brookwood has not yet given up its secrets. Therefore, I travel by Ghost Train this morning."

He put the tips of his fingers together and stared sombrely at them.

"Superintendent Bateman is a powerful man," he said irrelevantly. "My enquiries have revealed that he has no less than sixty gardeners under his direction."

Rossington opened his mouth as if to say something, then changed his mind.

"Naturally, I shall be eagerly awaiting your report," Angela Meredith said softly. "I trust there is no danger."

Beatty and Dotterell exchanged glances.

"We have taken certain precautions," Beatty said. "Inspector Munson will be at Brookwood to meet me today. And Dotterell will be making his own way to the area with his special equipment. I think we have done all that may be for the moment. And I must insist that not a word of what we have discussed here today shall go outside these walls."

He smiled sympathetically at the girl.

"Be assured, Miss Meredith, that we shall not rest until we have got to the bottom of this business."

18

THE GHOST TRAIN

IT wanted twenty minutes to eleven when Beatty arrived at the Waterloo-road Station and paid off his cab. He wore discreet black this morning, and a holdall he carried contained a less sombre change of clothing and some specialised equipment he might need. Dotterell would be leaving for Woking that afternoon by the normal railway service.

In the meantime Beatty had done everything that reason and prudence might suggest. All that remained was to keep strict vigilance on the journey, which he would also occupy by examining the various factors of the case. The slight pressure of the derringer against his sock and of the pistol in his inside jacket pocket reminded him of the realities that lay behind the baffling façade of the Brookwood affair.

The hiss of steam, the swirl of vapour, and the babble of voices as people milled about the interior, rose up to greet him as he entered the terminus. He had already secured his ticket in order to avoid the long queues which jostled slowly toward the gaslit cubicles that housed the ticket offices. Now he walked under the vast soot-encrusted glass roof toward the bookstall, where he purchased a copy of the *Mercury*.

He tucked the journal behind the straps which secured his holdall. In his other hand he carried his railway lamp, a small metal portable affair weighing only ten ounces. Sold by Tucker and Son of The Strand, it was the best one Beatty had discovered during his travels and he always carried it when travelling by rail at night. It would come in doubly useful for the purposes Beatty envisaged during this latest visit to Woking—his third since he had commenced the case.

He smiled wryly at the thought and eased between the milling crowds of people: the young ladies, fashionably attired and with lace at their throats; the third-class passengers roughly dressed, many carrying boxes, hampers, crates, and parcels. Two solid-looking police constables, both with thick black beards, patrolled the platforms at this point.

The noise of all these myriads of human beings echoed and reechoed under the roof of the terminus, like that of a choir beneath a cathedral dome, chanting a litany in some obscure language that Beatty was unable to decipher. A group of nuns passed him, their pale faces white and spiritual beneath the upswept wings of their headdresses, their robes black and sombre in contrast.

The young investigator skirted round a huddled mass of people gathered at the entrances of the refreshment rooms; the smell of hot pies and strong sauces came rank and acrid to his nostrils in the cold morning air. A single ray of sunlight, penetrating the dirt-encrusted roof, gilded the tops of coaches and lent escaping steam the aspect of fire, as he hurried forward to his destination.

It was a quiet, hushed platform to which his footsteps led him. In the roadway beyond, black-caparisoned horses snorted and pawed the ground; caskets were being unloaded from hearses and brought down the concourse; black-garbed undertakers' mutes were huddled like flies round their charges. A pall of gloom almost visibly descended on Beatty as he tendered his ticket to the downcast attendant at the gate which separated this platform from the seething life of one of London's greatest termini.

The man merely glanced at Beatty's dark clothing, mumbled something inaudible, and eased the metal gate backward, ushering him through. There were a great many clergymen about, Beatty noticed; conversing in groups or ministering to their charges. The coffins were being loaded now, into the rear compartments of the train which was drawn up to his right. The undertakers, obviously

the heads of their establishments, were supervising the arrangements in low muffled voices.

Powerful, prosperous-looking men in top-hats and frock-coats,
against which gold watch-chains twinkled dully, they performed
their mournful offices with precision and despatch. On the
journey they and their men would be accommodated in special
compartments immediately forward of the carriages containing
the biers.

The station-master himself stood halfway down the platform,
a tall, elegant man with a wisp of black crêpe round his top-hat.
His keen eyes darted about the station, noting the position of
guards, engine-driver, fireman, porters, and other attendants, missing nothing. Beatty put his ticket back into his coat pocket and
stepped out down the platform. There was still some twelve minutes before the eleven A.M. Waterloo-road-Woking special set out
on its journey across the Styx.

The Ghost Train was an extraordinary sight. Dotterell had not
exaggerated, he mused. Both the engine and all the carriages were
painted a dull white; this, combined with the sunshine struggling
in through the roof overhead, gave it a blanched look. It was well-
named. It had an ethereal, insubstantial atmosphere about it. In the
winter-time, in deep countryside and with mist curling round, it
would look as phantomlike as any imagining of a Gothick novella.

Next to the station-master stood another official, almost as
imposing: a regal brown-bearded man with sad eyes, who personally welcomed each abject group of black-clad mourners,
headed by its priest or minister. Beatty paused by an iron colon-
nade and studied the scene. He guessed that the man next the
station-master was a representative of the London Necropolis
Company. He weighed in his mind whether to engage this gentleman in conversation en route; then decided against.

On such a difficult mission it would not do to be precipitate.
Besides, if there were anyone on the train on the lookout for a
person like Beatty, it would make the investigator too conspicu-
ous. No, Beatty concluded, turning away, there would be time to
question the official later if such a course were indicated.

He walked farther down the platform, searching the sad,
despairing faces about him, his mind retaining fragmentary

impressions; analysing and sorting the information he was ingest-
ing and storing. He hunched his shoulders, cast his features in a
sombre mould, mingling unobtrusively with the other mourners,
merging into his background. Beatty was good at that. Paradoxi-
cally, it was one of the things which had made him outstanding in
his profession.

Carriage doors were closing; it wanted but a few minutes of
departure. Beatty squeezed past a group of women in heavy
mourning, their faces half-hidden behind thick veils. Muffled sobbing filled the air. A priest had his arm round an elderly woman's
shoulders. He was halfway down the train now, searching the
compartments for an empty carriage. People wanted to be alone
in their grief; it was a natural sentiment.

He found a carriage in which there was one empty section; he
got in thankfully, hoping that no one else would come. He closed
the door behind him and put his bag on the seat. He sat down, pressing his head forward on his hands, as though consumed with grief.

Footsteps were hurrying down the platform; the door opened
and several people got in. Beatty swore mentally. He risked a glance
through his fingers. A heavily bearded clergyman; a young woman
in deep mourning; and two pale young men. Well, he would have
to put a good face on it. This meant forgoing smoking and reading
his newspaper. The four newcomers arranged themselves at the
far side of the carriage.

Beatty took his hands away from his eyes and relaxed his features into a suitably solemn cast. Whistles were blowing now and
hurrying footsteps were quickening along the platform. Carriage
doors slammed. Beatty saw the important figure of the station-
master shaking hands with the brown-bearded man. Then the
train gave a long-drawn-out sigh, there was a shudder along the
carriages, and a doleful whistle under the high roof.

Scalding steam hissed and spluttered as the pistons started
turning; porters and station staff stood rigidly to attention as the
carriages were set in motion. The station-master had his top-hat
off and stood erect, his head bowed in salute. It was a strange and
impressive ceremony, this leave-taking of souls, as the coffins of
these departed Londoners set out on their last journey from the
city they had known so well, Beatty thought.

His companions were silent, each occupied with his own thoughts as the all-white train gathered speed, snaking in a long curve out of Waterloo-road terminus. A ragged plume of steam, a final despairing whistle under the high-arched roof, and then they were in the cold sunlight of the open air. Once again the Ghost Train was Woking-bound.

The priest was reading from a prayer-book in low monotonous tones. Beatty eased his cramped position in the corner seat and risked a glance at the party opposite. The young lady's face was set like white marble. She stared unseeingly before her over the heads of the two young men at the opposite side of the carriage and said nothing.

Beatty pulled his bag round; the paper beneath its straps was right-side up. If he slid it toward him just a little more he would be able to read part of the *Mercury* front page, which at least would while away the journey. The City had been left far behind, and the train, as befitted its cargo, was making a sedate but steady pace. Its journey was specially routed and there would be no stops or changes.

It would proceed direct from Waterloo-road to its final desti- nation at the stations within Brookwood Cemetery walls. Beatty stopped his manoeuvres with the bag and looked back out of the window. Shreds of steam were being ripped apart by the train's quickening progress, and the wintry sun was striking facets of light from the frost which bound field and hedgerow. It was one of the few clear days they had had this January; ideal weather for Beatty's projected operations.

He caught the clergyman's eye, read the sympathy in it, and bowed slightly in the man's direction before lowering his glance. He saw that there had been another Anarchist outrage in Paris; a headless body had been discovered in a trunk at Penge; a Question had been asked in the House of Commons about the gold robber- ies which had been plaguing City banks of late.

Beatty felt his spirits begin to revive. Crime was on the increase; and where crime was, so were specialists such as himself. As crime flourished so the upholder of the law, the practitioner in his own field, flourished also. He settled himself to read such portions as were visible of the three articles which most interested him.

He was fortunate; the Anarchist outrage and the article on the House of Commons questions were complete; he was disappointed to discover that the report of the Penge murder, which promised to be a sensational affair, was cut off by the fold. He looked up, wondering whether he might slip the paper out of the straps. He saw that the clergyman had his eyes closed for the moment; bars of sunlight were momentarily striping the carriage.

Beatty slid the paper round. He found a whole new area of reading interest spread before him. He looked up again, this time at the advertisements in the spaces on the carriage wall opposite. They were all concerned with the activities of stone-masons, undertakers, and casket-makers. Beatty realised that there would be little point and some impropriety in advertising more frivolous activities on such a train.

The engine was slowing a little now; they were passing through a large station. The station-master in top-hat and tail-coat was drawn up in salute, his staff standing to attention in a long file along the platform. The white-painted train, the engine with its tall smoke-stack whistling a low chord, rumbled steadily through, the bearded faces of the station personnel lowered toward the ground.

Beatty wondered again at the enormous respect his countrymen had for death; this must be a daily ritual observed at all major stations the train passed. It would make an interesting thesis. They were in open countryside again, the engine picking up speed. Beatty noticed a group of old farm workers at a level-crossing; they had their hats off and were standing stiff and frozen, like some rustic frieze. Then wisps of steam cut them off, and he surreptitiously resumed the perusal of his paper.

Beatty finished the article on the Penge murder. The affair was as bizarre and absorbing as it had promised to be. He felt regret for a moment that he was not engaged on such a case; yet was not the present problem every bit as sensational on analysis? There had to be a key which, once turned, would make everything clear; where it was at present dark. Yet the solution continued to elude him. He raised his eyes from his case and saw that the young widow opposite was studying him intently. Their eyes met in mutual sympathy, then turned away.

The investigator felt a sudden stab of shame and remorse; he was here under false pretences, intruding on the grief of strangers. Yet his mission was of great importance; already two lives had been taken in the affair, and he might, with luck and judgement, help to prevent the taking of others. He drummed with his strong fingers on the top of the case, concealing his impatience.

The sky seemed darker now; there was snow there somewhere. They had just passed a largish station; they could not be far from the end of their journey. The train had plunged into a deep cutting, the light fading rapidly from the sky. Beatty looked up; the sides were so steep he could not see the top.

A few moments later, with a hissing of steam and a shuddering of brakes, they were running alongside a high wall. Great banks of evergreens and bare trees were about them. There was a blur of faces on the platform; so dark was it now that gas-lamps were lit beneath the station canopy. Beatty saw the large notice in gold lettering, CHURCH OF ENGLAND, slide past the window. The Ghost Train had arrived at its destination.

19

STRANGE ENCOUNTER

HE got down into the freezing air. To his surprise, he saw that his companions were remaining on the train. Railway officials were saluting, and the noise of slamming carriage doors sounded loudly down the platform. Coffins were already being unloaded from one of the rear compartments with smooth efficiency. Beatty transferred his carriage lamp to the hand holding his bag and looked about him.

The strong face of Munson materialised from among the swarms of black-clad figures. The little Surrey detective gave a smile of welcome as he pumped Beatty's hand. The expression seemed incongruous at that time and place.

"Everything is arranged," he said in a low voice. "I have seen

Mrs. Varley. The service will be held and all will appear as normal. But afterwards the coffin will be taken to one of the stone-masons' shops where our own surgeon will carry out the examination."

Beatty nodded. Munson wore a dark plaid overcoat and a derby hat. He looked a purposeful, efficient figure among these hordes of stricken people. He touched Beatty on the elbow.

"Come on," he said. "We'd best get something to warm us."

Beatty followed him as he strode down the platform, brushing past railway-men and black-garbed ministers. To the investigator's astonishment the Inspector pushed open a glass-panelled door. The murmur of voices came out to meet them. Beatty blinked in the warm gaslight, looking incredulously at the long buffet counter, the shelves full of bottles, the fire blazing cheerfully in the enamelled grate. A warm, cherry-coloured carpet stretched out underfoot.

"It's early in the day, but you'll not say no to a whisky," Munson said.

He pushed his way up to the bar, chuckling at Beatty's expression.

"Oh, the Necropolis Company thought of everything," he said. "They've not forgotten the comfort of the living. There's a buffet on each station at Brookwood. That's the best thing about it."

He toasted Beatty over the rim of the glass and paid the discreetly dressed blonde girl behind the counter. The place was half-full of people, some in mourning, others in ordinary clothes. The buzz of conversation was about them; it was as it should be in such a place. Brisk, cheerful even, but respectful.

Beatty turned, glass in hand, as the thunder of the engine sounded; the rumble of wheels followed, and steam obscured the buffet windows. The blanched length of the Ghost Train passed out of sight. Beatty looked enquiringly at Munson.

"They've unhooked the coaches containing the coffins for the Church of England ceremonies," the Inspector explained. "The train is now going on to the second station. That's for Roman Catholics, Parsees, and Muslims. They've even got a mosque here."

He lowered his voice.

"Death was supposed to be the great leveller. They still keep rank and protocol at Brookwood."

He smiled cheerfully as Beatty lifted his glass.

"Well, this is a strange business, Mr. Beatty."

The investigator nodded. The chill was going from his bones. He put his bag down in a corner and leaned on the counter, the gaslight shining on his strong Roman face.

"Strange enough," he said. "Dr. Rossington sends his regards and begs you to excuse him on this occasion."

The Surrey detective put his two hands together on the top of the counter and looked at Beatty sombrely.

"Dr. Couchman, now. The London Police will be sending me their report, of course. I'd be glad of your own account."

Beatty told him, in short, low sentences, while the conversation in the buffet went on about them. The Inspector listened sympathetically, his face flushing with excitement as his companion described the final encounter on Blackfriars Bridge.

"You have nothing to reproach yourself for, Mr. Beatty," he said as the recital finished. "I do not see what else you could have done. I shall say so in my own official account, if it is of any use to you."

Beatty thanked him, his mind already busy on other matters.

"I do not see where else we are to turn now," said Munson, his expression changing into one of the deepest gloom. "With Couchman dead a promising line of enquiry dies with him. I take it the River Police have not yet turned up the body?"

Beatty shook his head.

"The Thames is frozen solid. I had heard nothing at the time I came away. And they had promised that Dotterell or myself should be informed."

Munson nodded. His grey eyes were full of thought as he looked about the buffet.

"I shall be staying in Woking for a day or two," said Beatty casually. "We could talk further at your office tomorrow. It will be more convenient there."

"As you wish, Mr. Beatty."

Munson drained his glass with a sigh of satisfaction. He looked shrewdly at his companion.

"What do you intend to do in the meantime? Shall you attend the autopsy?"

Beatty shook his head grimly.

"I think I have had enough of such matters for one case. I have come to no definite conclusions. I thought I might spend some time exploring Brookwood in daylight. I have heard much of its glories since I was last here."

Munson chuckled and his eyes searched Beatty's face.

"Just as you say. You will be staying at the same place?"

Beatty nodded.

"Dotterell is coming down this afternoon."

Again the piercing look from the shrewd grey eyes.

"Then you have a line to work on?"

Beatty shook his head.

"Nothing but a supposition that some of the strands of this tangled affair lie in this area. I might have need of Dotterell. He is a mighty useful fellow. Had he been with me on Blackfriars Bridge, Couchman would not have escaped us. What news of the nursing home?"

Munson pulled down the corners of his mouth.

"I got a warrant, and my men and I searched his office, of course. We found nothing out of the ordinary. At least, nothing that would account for this business."

"You have not moved against Bateman, I hope," said Beatty.

There was a sharp tone in his voice and Munson looked at him quickly.

"I have known him for years. I would swear for him as I would myself. But I have not ruled him out. I watch and wait. In the meantime I maintain discretion."

And he smiled and laid his finger along the side of his nose. Beatty smiled too. He put down his glass and offered another to the Inspector, who declined. Beatty held out his hand.

"Well, good day then, Inspector. We shall meet again tomorrow. In the meantime a stroll among the refreshing atmosphere of your Surrey pines is indicated."

And he opened the door of the buffet and strode out down the platform.

It was a strange and sombre world which Beatty now entered. Quitting the platform through a sort of glassed-in conservatory, he found himself on a broad gravelled walk which debouched into subsidiary ways leading in many directions. Coffins were still being unloaded into hearses drawn by black-plumed horses; and broughams and barouches belonging to the various undertaking establishments were clip-clopping smartly along the paths, conveying the mourners to the various chapels.

Despite the darkness of the day, shafts of cold sunlight, occasionally glancing through the clouds, struck sparks of gold and silver from the hoar-frost which held the grass in bond.

Beatty followed the path, which led to a large chapel and then struck out to the side; rounding a clump of evergreens he found himself in a more secluded area, the busy scenes at the private station seeming far away.

He wandered on past a grove of silver birches, their branches making a delicate lacework against the now sullen sky which penned them in. The ground stretched away like a park with thick clumps of rhododendrons and azaleas, flourishing in the gravelly soil, and interspersed with pine and larch. Rooks cawed harshly from the leafless trees, and a thin mist was blurring the far distance as Beatty hurried down the pathway.

A sea of gravestones was composing itself from the distant landscape, and Beatty was startled to see Californian redwoods rising monstrously from the less pretentious native trees. He was beginning to get some intimation of the huge scale of Brookwood.

He had a definite destination this afternoon, and he wanted to reach it and return before darkness fell. He had noted the direction of the area which he and Rossington had originally visited, and he made for it, keeping observation from the sun, which now and again pierced the dark clouds to touch with fleeting gilt the melancholy scene about him.

White marble crosses mingled with more humble gravestones; weathered mausoleums competed with structures which seemed more like Eastern minarets; and once Beatty skirted a strange group of bronze statues whose sad, reproachful faces seemed to follow the young investigator with their eyes. Acre upon interminable acre spread before him as he walked; it was like a great city of the dead in which he, the solitary living thing apart from the birds, had his being.

Beatty stopped momentarily, adjusting the hook of his lamp round the handle of his bag. Its contents were light, but it was beginning to weigh heavily with the distance he was traversing.

He was out from among the gravestones now, and the land-scape was becoming more familiar to him. He unerringly chose the second of three gravelled paths which presented themselves, his footsteps echoing unnaturally loud in the frosty silence.

A chill wind blew, carrying with it a coldness and a dampness which would intensify at nightfall. Beatty shrugged deeper into his thick coat and looked keenly about him.

He gained the chapel where Rossington had carried out his autopsy and turned left along the path. He followed the cemetery wall, trying to remember exactly the route. It was not far from here. Beatty stopped suddenly, as though some thought had struck him.

For some minutes he had been aware of a faint vibration among the tombstones which were thickly sown in this portion of the cemetery; the masons specialised in white marble angels here, and more than once Beatty fancied he had seen the faintest shadow at the corner of his eye, flitting from stone to stone.

He had put it down to imagination; this was an extraordinary place and one would have to have been made of marble oneself not to have indulged in the occasional flight of fancy. But Beatty had heard a faint sound, like the echo of his own footsteps, as he gained the chapel path. He turned off the gravel quickly and walked on the frosty grass; he moved behind a mausoleum, ostensibly to examine an inscription, in reality to study the terrain behind him. The pistol made a comforting pressure against his chest muscles as he moved.

The footsteps which had been following stopped. Beatty was aware that his unseen follower might have exactly copied his own actions, by stepping on to the grass. Beatty stood stock-still for over a minute, his ears straining to catch any unusual sound. He smiled grimly and relaxed. He was not afraid of anything which walked in shoe-leather. He stepped boldly on to the path and resumed his way, pausing only when he had gained the group of huts which was his destination. He hurried downhill, keeping the cemetery wall to his right. Here were the wooden wheelbarrows and the rough barricade of planking across the path.

Beatty pulled at the planks; the woodwork was rotten and the structure was secured by only one nail at this point. It gave without any trouble, and he stepped across the lower bar and into the enclosure formed by the barrier and the metal fence. He walked toward the largest of the sheds, that secured by an iron-barred door. He was about three yards from it when it suddenly opened and a tall, bearded man in rough working clothes appeared in the aperture.

He had a long scar running down the side of his forehead, and his twitching features bespoke great inner agitation. But his voice was firm enough as he faced up to Beatty and said in a withered North Country accent, "This is private property, sir. No visitors are allowed."

Beatty looked him coolly up and down before replying. His eyes were searching the surroundings, noting and evaluating. He saw a wisp of smoke from the chimney of a big house beyond the cemetery wall; the flight of rooks; picks and shovels near the sheds; piles of earth; a stack of what looked like pit-props.

"I beg your pardon," he said mildly. "I lost my way and thought I might take a short cut."

The bearded man shook his head.

"Back up the path is thy best way," he answered dourly.

"You hold an official position here?" said Beatty crisply.

The workman hesitated. Something in the powerful young man's stance and the steady gaze of the wide brown eyes warned him to be careful. He adopted a more placatory attitude.

"Abraham Beardsley at your service, sir," he said thickly. "Under-Foreman at Brookwood."

"I see," said Beatty coolly. He glanced casually at the man's boots, noted his hurried breathing.

"I should imagine you have had quite a run in order to get here before me."

He walked away, leaving the big man dumbfounded, his jaw hanging slackly. Beatty got through the fence, adjusted the planking, and dusted his hands. He looked back. The Under-Foreman was still standing there. It was impossible to read the expression on his face at that distance.

Beatty walked back up the path with a springy tread. He was smiling as he hurried back in the direction of the cemetery entrance. His whistle was a jaunty intrusion in that place of the dead.

20

ENTER DOTTERELL

Dusk was falling. Dotterell slid his watch from his waistcoat pocket and studied it carefully before pushing it back. He sat in the parlour of a small refreshment room in a side-street of Woking and moodily studied the passers-by. The gas-lamps were already lit, and they only emphasised the wintry bleakness of the scene outside the window. Within, a cheerful coal fire burned with a warm glow and threw fluttering shadows across the red-brick floor.

Oil lamps hanging from the beams cast a mellow sheen over the old timbers and sparked points of light from china, copper, and pewter. There were a fair number of people taking tea, and an animated buzz of conversation arose above the clink of plates and knives. Dotterell's piercing blue eyes were turned back to the windows now, and a smile briefly illuminated his gaunt features as he sighted a familiar figure making its way briskly down the street in the direction of the refreshment room.

"We will take tea now," he told the old dame who had been hovering anxiously at his elbow for the past quarter of an hour. Dotterell rose and moved his overcoat from the adjoining chair as Beatty entered the tea-shop and joined him at the table. The two men's eyes met, the one querying, the other expressing satisfaction.

Beatty crossed to the fire and held out his hands briefly to the blaze before rejoining his companion. He took off his coat and sat down opposite his assistant as the old lady came back with a laden tray. When the buttered muffins, mountains of toast, and the large stone pot of tea had been set before them, Beatty let out a low sigh. Dotterell's eyes studied him across the table, but it was not until they were well into the meal before they spoke.

"You are settled in at our quarters?"

Dotterell nodded. He pointed to a large black bag which he had put down beside his chair.

"I brought all the equipment you ordered. Enough for any eventuality."

Beatty smiled and turned to pour another cup of tea for himself and his companion. He looked round the comfortable room with satisfaction.

"Apart from my brief sojourn at the White Horse, this is the first time I have felt really comfortable in Woking. All this graveyard work is a far cry from the metropolis."

Dotterell's thin face quickened with interest.

"You are on to something, then?"

"A number of things," Beatty said briefly.

He waited until the old lady had returned with hot water before he spoke again.

"I have seen Inspector Munson today. He was at the station to meet me. The autopsy on Varley should have taken place by now. We shall know for certain whether we have two murders or one by tomorrow. But there is no doubt in my mind."

"What is my part in all this?" Dotterell asked.

"A big one," Beatty said crisply. "I have been badly in need of your assistance and expertise since this case began. Having you here on the ground with me will be invaluable."

He told his assistant briefly of the events of the afternoon. Dotterell put down his cup. His eyes looked bright, his face quite transformed.

"What do you make of this cemetery business?"

Beatty chuckled. He kept his voice down as he replied.

"I see you have not missed the salient points. Item: Varley was extremely anxious to keep me away from a railed-in section of Brookwood Cemetery. Why?"

He looked moodily at the people passing in the narrow street outside the tea-shop windows.

"It is ridiculous to talk of repairs to a cemetery. This afternoon Varley's assistant, Abraham Beardsley, appeared extremely agitated at my interest in that portion of the cemetery. In fact he ran a considerable distance in order to arrive there before me to warn me off."

"What is there, then?" Dotterell asked.

Beatty shook his head.

"Nothing, ostensibly. Nothing but a few wretched huts and sheds and some gardening equipment; wheelbarrows and such-like."

He was silent for so long that Dotterell feared he would not speak of the matter again.

"We must find out what lies behind that barrier," Beatty said. "It must be something extremely important. Two men have already lost their lives. The answer may not be at Brookwood. The end of the skein may yet lie in London, but I am convinced the key is here."

He clenched and unclenched his strong hands on the table-top, then turned to gaze fiercely at his assistant.

"Listen carefully, because everything must go well this evening. Firstly, we must make sure we can get back into the hotel, whatever the hour of night."

"I already have a key," Dotterell assured him with a thin smile. "I have made friends with the domestic staff."

Beatty nodded approval.

"Good. I have given the matter some thought. From Bateman's answers to my questions on my previous visit, I know that the cemetery is completely surrounded by high walls and locked securely every night. There are, in addition, certain gardeners who remain on duty all night. This is in addition to a number of occupied cottages which are scattered about the extensive grounds."

"A curious circumstance," interrupted Dotterell. "You do not think Superintendent Bateman . . ."

"I think nothing," Beatty said, his eyes flashing. "This does not concern the Superintendent. It is common practice at all urban and rural cemeteries which have high walls and gates. There are many valuable building materials and equipment in the workshops which might attract the attention of thieves. To say nothing of religious fanatics who might desecrate graves if the place were open to all comers."

Dotterell nodded. He reached out for another slice of toast.

"What about the railway cutting? There must be access there."

Beatty smiled.

"I see you've been studying maps. There's nothing, as you would realise if you had been over the ground. The cemetery is approached by the railway line, it is true. But the cutting is too steep to descend into without considerable trouble. It is over a mile long. I had thought of walking it, but there is the danger of meeting parties of railway workers, who carry out maintenance on the line at night. There is a manned halt just before the cutting in any case. In addition, at night there is a heavy metal gate across the railway track at the point where it joins the cemetery grounds."

He shook his head with a wry smile.

"No, Dotterell, it will be more convenient to go over the wall, at a lonely place of our own choosing, where we shall be unobserved. It will mean walking out there, of course. I cannot risk taking a cab."

"A fine brisk night for a walk," Dotterell said sombrely. His eyes were afire with enthusiasm.

"You brought the grapnel?" Beatty asked. "And are you sure it will work?"

"It will work," said Dotterell confidently.

He kicked the bag with his foot.

"It has been tested over and over again."

"Very well, then," said Beatty. "I have to make a call at the local library and then we must pass the time with what patience we can muster. A drink at the hotel, perhaps, until we can safely set forth before nine o'clock. I want to start work not later than ten."

Dotterell grunted, drinking the last of his tea.

"Then perhaps we shall be at the end of this black business."

Beatty straightened up. Strange lights were dancing in his eyes.

"Not so, Dotterell. On the contrary, the case is just beginning."

The Crimes

21

OVER THE WALL

THEY had been walking just under an hour, and the lights of Woking had long faded behind them. It was a fine clear moonlight night, and the glow stamped their shadows on the ground before them. Beatty had brought a large-scale map with him and he checked it by the light of the moon from time to time, but there were no difficulties, except when they had taken a cut across woodland in order to avoid a long traverse.

He was pleased to see now they were nearing their destination that the moon was becoming obscured by thick cloud; moonlight provided the wrong conditions for an operation such as that upon which they were engaged. Dotterell had said hardly a word since they had quitted the streets of Woking; he walked with brisk, powerful strides at a pace he could keep up for hours, and he carried the heavy bag containing the special equipment as though it were a pillow-case.

Beatty had registered at the hotel under his own name, and his new—or rather real—persona had not attracted any attention. So well had he changed his identity on the previous occasion that no one connected the young, energetic man with the austere, ageing doctor of a few days earlier. As Beatty had so often opined, a mere change of clothing and the minimum of disguise could completely alter an individual's personality.

He and Dotterell had sat in the comfort of the smoking room for an hour or so, sipping their wine and looking silently into the fire. But even in that seemingly somnolent period, the investigator's agile brain had been searching and redigesting every factor of the bizarre affair in which he found himself involved. Earlier in the evening Dotterell had checked and double-checked the equipment they would be using. There was nothing else for them to do until they set out at eight forty-five P.M.

Most of the more prosperous citizens appeared to be at dinner;

Dotterell had avoided the station area where Stevens had his cab. It would not do to involve that kindly individual in their nefarious activities this night, especially when it might involve breaking the law. Beatty never hesitated to break the spirit of the law when it concerned a matter of justice; he was prepared to do so again this evening.

He glanced at Dotterell now in the waning moonlight, but the man's dour face told him nothing; it was bitingly cold and their breath smoked out of their mouths, their boots scraping echoes from the iron-bound roadway. Between the trees Beatty could see the faint outline of the cemetery walls looming up before them. As though by instinct the two men stepped off the road on to the grass verge as they got closer.

The moon was down now and the gloom was welcome after the brightness of the earlier evening. Beatty felt naked and exposed on the road. He was glad when they moved off it; it would not do for any farmer paying a visit in his trap, or any late-working carter, to come across two strangers here in such an odd place.

Lights pricked the darkness ahead of them and the two men altered course, which took them across a broad area of rough grass and into the deep shadow of woodland. There was a muffled snort ahead of them and both men froze immobile; the startled sheep bounded away, crackling twigs and branches attesting its passage, until all was silent again.

Dotterell and Beatty exchanged a long glance; there was grim amusement in Dotterell's piercing blue eyes. His floppy bow-tie was hidden this evening beneath a thick scarf wound round his neck beneath the overcoat. He wore a hard brown hat that was jammed down on his head. Altogether he looked a rakish and dangerous figure; Beatty asked for no better companion on such an adventure as this evening's.

The two men followed the path taken by the sheep, skirting the wood, still in deep shadow. The lights of the large house which had prompted their change of course were far to the right of them and hidden by the angle of the cemetery wall. Beatty now saw that they were opposite the small gate which led to the chapel he had twice visited in company with Rossington.

He had studied the cemetery plan and had pin-pointed the locations of the various inhabited lodges of the estate workers; but the plan was several years old and he had to make sure they would be able to work undisturbed. He waited while Dotterell put down the bag; there was the faint clink of metal as he took something out of it.

They were hidden from the cemetery area by the vast trunk of an old tree. The moon was quite gone and there was deep shadow all about them. Dotterell was assembling a telescopic metal tube; he secured it with an iron pin and started to screw a second section on. Short pegs protruded from either side. Extended, it made a small but effective portable ladder.

Dotterell shrewdly estimated the distance of the lowest branch of the tree from the ground and added another section. Assembly had taken less than a minute. Beatty glanced at his watch. It still wanted five minutes of ten. The eyes of Miss Angela Meredith floated in front of him. They were a deep cornflower blue and her lips were opened provocatively. Beatty came to himself with a start, aware that Dotterell was looking at him interrogatively.

He bit back a remark and took the glasses out of their case. Beatty went forward to the metal ladder, which Dotterell held firm against the trunk. The gaunt man looked at him sharply.

"Best let me go, Mr. Beatty," he whispered. "This is more in my line."

Beatty nodded and relinquished the glasses. He knew Dotterell was right, and there was no point in arguing about it. Instead, he leaned forward and took two of the ladder rungs, holding the extension firmly. It was so cold that the metal seemed to sear his bare hands, despite the fact that the ladder had been exposed to the air only a few minutes. Beatty smiled wryly. It was unlikely that they would be disturbed tonight under such bleak conditions.

The wind was rising, and he drew in closer to the trunk. Dotterell was ascending the ladder now, the rungs vibrating beneath his weight. Beatty shifted his grip as he approached the spot he was holding and then steadied the thing behind him. In a very few seconds Dotterell had gained the first fork of the great tree and swung himself up. He disappeared from view, the vibration of the ladder ceasing.

Beatty put his hands in his pockets and looked sharply round, standing a little away from the tree. Dotterell could not be seen from any angle. He worked his way all round and then came back. He secured the ladder at Dotterell's whisper. The tall man climbed down with considerable agility. He handed the glasses back to his employer and started unscrewing the ladder with the dexterity of long practice. He had, in fact, designed it himself, like much of the specialist equipment they used.

"Not a glim anywhere," he said briefly.

Beatty nodded. Such reticence stood for a long report in Dotterell's book. It meant he had kept meticulous watch for ten minutes and had seen nothing that would indicate a lighted residence anywhere in the area where they would be working. The ladder was stowed away in the bag. Beatty was kneeling, checking over the contents. He worked by feel mostly; he instinctively knew what should be there.

He was fully armed, but in addition to that there was a special kit which Dotterell had developed. It was a curious leather belt with canvas pouches, designed to be worn over the clothing. Within it, secured in leather loops, were all the instruments of the housebreaking trade and some special items which existed nowhere else, all products of Dotterell's fertile brain.

His assistant ticked them off, before strapping the belt round Beatty's waist. It was extremely light and the weight was distributed evenly.

"Picklock and skeleton keys mostly," Dotterell whispered. "But there's enough material there to cover pretty well all eventualities. Shall you take the railway lamp?"

Beatty shook his head.

"I shall be working mostly in the open. I only want to see what is inside those sheds. There will be enough light for my purpose."

The two men now rose. With Dotterell taking the bag containing the remaining equipment, they slowly worked their way toward the cemetery wall. Nothing moved in all the stillness of the night, though faint and far away the harsh, hoarse call of a barn-owl sounded. The melancholy noise was three times repeated, the ghostly echo seeming to Beatty to epitomise the lost souls of the countless thousands buried within the walls of Brookwood Cemetery.

Beatty straightened his shoulders, throwing off such thoughts. His face was impassive as he glanced at Dotterell. The two were close in to the wall, shielded by the bushes. It loomed before them, seemingly of tremendous height. Beatty tested it with his finger. There was a thin coating of ice on the brickwork which made it extremely slippery and dangerous.

"Grapnel, I think," said Dotterell drily. "I have already noted the group of trees."

"Do you think it will work?" said Beatty dubiously.

There came a sound suspiciously like a snort from Dotterell.

"I have carried out field trials for more than three months, under varying conditions. It works perfectly. The special powder I have developed for the rocket burns without spark or flame. I call it black light."

He chuckled throatily.

"But what about the match?" Beatty said irritably. "We cannot risk a flame in this open place."

Dotterell made an impatient movement of his head.

"I have thought of that too. The fuse is ignited by means of a clockwork mechanism. The flints actuate the charge within the casing. Hence no external lighting. I could, at a pinch, throw the grapnel over the wall, but I am anxious to test the equipment under actual working conditions."

"Very well," said Beatty. He knew it was no use arguing with Dotterell over his technical matters. "I should be no longer than an hour."

He looked with curiosity at the apparatus his assistant was erect-ing. Dotterell adjusted the tripod-stand and went back from the wall to see that he had the right range and trajectory. When he was satisfied he came back and made some screw adjustments to the tripod. Then he put the blunt container in the cradle designed for it. It looked more like a shell than a rocket, but Beatty knew that the streamlined nose was the head of the grapnel whose spring-actuated claws would extend in flight at the end of its trajectory, in order firmly to engage the branches of the receiving tree.

Behind it would be trailed yards of silken lightweight cord, culminating in the special woven rope ladder Beatty would use to scale the wall. It was still only five minutes past ten and their preparations were ready. Dotterell now took the tripod out from the wall and lined it up, checking visually once again. Then he manually actuated the plunger in the base of the shell.

Beatty heard a faint hissing noise and saw the flicker of something passing across the night sky at tremendous speed; there was no flash or flame, as Dotterell had predicted, and the crackling noise of branches in the distance showed that the grapnel had reached its destination. Beatty realised that the flickering motion had been the ladder trailing behind the rope.

Dotterell was already back beside him, his face alight with enthusiasm. He gently pulled on the rungs of the ladder, which now hung vertically from the top of the wall. The ladder gave and then caught again. Dotterell climbed on to the lowest rung, a foot from the ground, and exerted all his strength. The ladder remained immovable. He said nothing but looked expectantly at his employer.

"Congratulations," Beatty said crisply.

"You may have to cut the grapnel free for your return," Dotterell whispered. "You will find a second cord depending from the main line. If you pull that, it will actuate a self-cutting device on the shank of the grapnel."

"I'll do my best to retrieve it," Beatty told him, all thoughts of the coldness of the night banished from his mind. "On my way back in an hour."

Then he was gripping the ladder and climbing up the wall into the icy darkness.

He paused astride the wall, a chill wind plucking at the skirts of his coat. Dotterell looked more gaunt than ever at the foot of the ladder below him. Not a glimmer of light penetrated the darkness; thick banks of rhododendrons and other evergreen plants blocked the immediate foreground. Beatty nodded to his assistant and then slid across the wall, carefully feeling for the ladder-rungs on the other side.

The ladder lay out at right angles from the wall. Somewhere, the far end of it was attached to the cord secured to the tree. He reached out with his hands and swung himself away from the wall, descending it hand over hand. After a few feet it sagged quickly to the ground, and Beatty dropped on to frozen grass.

He went back to the wall and quickly whispered to Dotterell that all was well. He then went across, tracing the line with his hand, until he could see where it ascended into the clump of trees they had marked. The moon was breaking briefly through the clouds, and Beatty was able to see the cord of which Dotterell had spoken and which would sever the grapnel if it became necessary.

He tied the end of it to a convenient twig and then picked up a dead branch which was lying beneath the tree. He carried this at right angles to the tree and walked for a hundred yards until he came out on a gravel path. Beatty put the branch down in the rough grass at the side of the path, pointing in the general direction of the tree. He went down the path a way, making sure he could pick it out. When he was satisfied that he could find his way back to the ladder under the darkest conditions, he set out through the blanched gravestones to his destination.

It would have been an eerie experience for anyone of less steady nerves than Beatty, but to one who had once passed a night in a sewer to apprehend a gang of coiners, and kept a similar vigil in a suburban mortuary in order to entrap a murderer returning to destroy evidence left on his victim, it was a routine part of his assignment.

Even so, the peculiar character of the cemetery with its weird groups of allegorical figures, bronze angels, and other statuary had an unsettling effect on the nerves; the stone and metal effigies assuming strange and menacing shapes that seemed about to spring out at the young detective as he passed. Twice he crouched with heightened nerves, thinking the guardians of the cemetery must be aware of his presence, only to discover some innocuous reason for his alarm.

Then he was out near the familiar chapel and hurrying on down, in the shadow of the far wall this time. He passed a stout wooden gate set in an oval lintel which he did not know existed in this section of Brookwood. He stood for some moments examining the ground at this point; satisfied, he passed on and presently ducked under the rough plank barrier blocking access to the group of tumbledown buildings that crouched in the lee of the cemetery wall.

Beatty waited to make sure everything was still; there was no sound but the sighing of the wind in the branches and the faint, far cry of the owl. Then he had crossed the open space and was immediately in front of the huts. A damp, mouldy smell immediately assailed his nostrils. Beatty smothered an exclamation and unbuckled the belt from his waist. The moon was dying, hidden behind the clouds, and he knew he could not be seen from the path behind him. Nevertheless, his nerves tuned to a high pitch, he kept a very careful watch as he selected those instruments which would be of greatest use.

He went quickly along the group of sheds, noting that the large building to the right was more strongly constructed than the others. It was fronted by an extremely thick nail-studded door. Beatty knelt and examined it minutely. He gave a faint exclamation at the discovery that it was secured with a set of three padlocks. Using the thick leather belt as a kneeling-pad, he set to work.

He found that none of his skeleton keys would open the locks. This indicated that they had been made to special order. Beatty rose and methodically replaced the keys in the special pouch on the belt. He felt a slight quickening of his pulse rate. He looked carefully, but there was nothing unusual in the bleached images of the tombstones; nothing moving in the stippled shadow.

The moon was again down. He looked at his watch. Already, almost half an hour had passed. He knelt again with the immensely strong picklock Dotterell had developed; he grunted slightly as he put the full force of his sinewy wrist into the effort. There was an audible click as the padlock gave. Beatty had a slight smile of satisfaction on his face as he removed the lock and undid the hasp.

Now that he knew the action, the other two padlocks did not take long; they were of the same design as the first. Only five minutes more had passed before he had the door open. Beatty refastened the belt round his waist, leaving out only those few things he would still need. A strange foetid smell of damp earth and something else came out to meet him as he opened the door.

It was pitch-black inside the shed, and Beatty realised for the first time that it had no windows. The heavy door rolled silently back on well-oiled hinges. Beatty took the three padlocks in with him. This would avoid the danger of anyone's discovering his presence and securing the door behind him. Beatty stood quite still, taking in the smell of earth and decay.

He found a hasp on the leaf of the door and secured it on the inside. When he was quite sure that nothing could be seen from outside, he moved cautiously away from the door. He had put the padlocks in his pocket, and he carried the other things in his right hand. Most important among them was the tiny dark-lantern Dotterell had developed.

It was a japanned metal miniature of the large ones in use, but instead of oil it utilised a candle, cut down to half-size, its power amplified by a system of mirrors behind and to the sides of it. Even with the dark-slide open, the rays were focused through a narrow slit with a metal guard and mirror above it, so that a thin, strong beam of light was directed downward. It was one of Dotterell's happiest inspirations and Beatty had already found it invaluable.

Now he took out his box of matches and lit it quickly, extinguishing the match almost as soon as the candle had caught. He opened the slide and waited until the light was bright and steady enough for his purpose. He had already noticed that there were rough wooden benches in the shed; baulks of timber; racks of tools against the walls. Beatty's initial feeling was one of disappointment. What if the place were merely an innocuous carpenter's shop?

Then he remembered the notices outside; the barrier of planks; the two warnings by the cemetery employees; and the elaborate locks on the doors. There had to be something else behind all these precautions to keep people away. That was his purpose here this evening. He moved on down the shed, wood-shavings rustling beneath his feet in an unnerving fashion.

Once something scampered across the floor, casting an enormous shadow which fled down the wall in the light of the lantern. Beatty had the revolver halfway out of its holster before he realised that he had disturbed a rat. Nevertheless, his heart was pumping uncomfortably, and he could feel perspiration beading his forehead, despite the coldness of the night.

Beatty completed his examination and moved on. He was in a passageway now, the walls of the shed funnelling to make a narrow entry. This was barred, he saw, by a thick wooden door, secured by a simple wooden latch.

Beatty stood by the door for a long moment. A faint and nauseous stench had been growing for the last minute. It was composed of damp earth and foul air; but there was something less tangible, more elusive. It seemed to billow across the floor and with it came a charnel breath, sickly and offensive to the nostrils.

Beatty swore. He turned and went rapidly back to the outer door. He gently opened it and surveyed the cemetery outside. The moon had just broken through the clouds, and all the stretch of the graveyard looked as white and silent as eternity.

He put the catch down behind him and went back down the workshop again. He bound a handkerchief across his mouth and opened the door. It came on creaking hinges. There was a length of tunnel before him; the earth was rough and dank; there were fragments of wood sticking from it.

By the dim light of the lantern, Beatty saw the sides of the tunnel were secured by stout pieces of timber. He could see only a yard or two before him as he advanced step by step. His senses revolted at the stench which was all about him; Beatty was reminded of gangrenous flesh and the putrescence of a hospital surgical ward. He felt perspiration running into his eyes.

He stumbled and put out his hand to the side wall as the door-hinges grated behind him. Something fell from the ceiling of the passage, casting a great shadow before it. Beatty looked up. He gave an involuntary cry as the leathery corpse-face, green and putrescent, pressed against his own.

22

SIR INIGO IS WORRIED

SIR INIGO WALTON frowned. He had much on his mind these days. He walked up the short flight of steps toward the imposing entrance of the City and Suburban Bank. The rumble of horse-drawn traffic was about him, and the thunder of iron-wheeled brewers' drays made an incessant din, but he was oblivious of the noise. He pushed his way in through the swing doors, a top-hatted messenger hurrying to meet him, raising fingers to his forehead deferentially.

He advanced over the marble-floored entrance and past the polished oak counters, thronged with customers, and waited while the messenger opened the private door of the Counting House for him. He went on through, acknowledging curtly the murmured greeting from the black-coated clerks busy on their high stools.

Sir Inigo was an imposing figure. Of more than average height, he was broad-shouldered and deep-chested. His complexion was brick-red, and his hard eyes beneath grizzled brows and his fierce-looking grey moustache, the ends turned up in military fashion, gave him an alarming aspect.

He took off his top-hat now, and his iron-grey hair, cut short, looked like wheat-stubble after burning. He must have been more than sixty years of age, yet he strode out across the floor so fast that employees were often hard put to keep up with him. His appearance did not bely his nature. Short-tempered and impulsive, his rages were impressive, but quick to die away, and he could be generous and fair-minded when his judgement was not clouded by choler.

He wore a heavy plaid jacket with a fur collar against the biting cold of the day. He unbuttoned it as he mounted the oak staircase to the first floor of the Bank, revealing an impeccably cut pearl-grey frock-coat. His grey silk stock was held in under his bat-wing collar by a pearl and gold tie-pin. He flicked his gloves into his top-hat as he bounded up the stairs. His patent leather boots were brilliant and caught the cold winter sunlight as he gained the landing.

Muirhead, one of his partners, smiled grimly as they met in the corridor which led to the directors' private offices.

"'Morning, Inigo. Too damn severe for huntin' again."

Sir Inigo gave him a frosty glance.

"I have other matters occupying my attention at this moment," he said drily. "I take it you have directed your efforts toward the problem of security. We want everyone's opinion."

He drew out an exquisitely chased gold hunter from his waist-coat and glanced at it.

"I hope you have not forgotten the meeting at midday. I shall expect your report then."

Muirhead, a plump-faced individual with glossy black hair, looked discomfited.

"Certainly, Inigo, certainly," he mumbled.

He hurried off down the corridor in the direction of his own office. It was impossible to make small talk with Inigo, he told himself; he had forgotten the report, it was true. There would just be time for him to write down his thoughts on the matter and have copies made before the meeting.

Sir Inigo snorted deep in his throat and strode on, his mind busy with other matters. He heard but did not note the many muted sounds of commerce about him: the droning of voices behind closed doors; the hurrying of footsteps along distant corridors; the metallic rumble of presses being used; even the sharp, brittle scratching of pens through a half-open doorway.

He walked through into a small oak-panelled lobby; as the managing director of the City and Suburban Bank his quarters were appropriately imposing. A thick carpet yielded at his feet; the sun sparkled through white-painted oriel windows, throwing a pleasing pattern of lines and circles across the floor. He hung up his coat on the mahogany hanger provided; it had his initials painted on it in gold lettering.

He looped the hook over the top of the oak coatrack and put his hat and gloves down on a shelf by the umbrella-stand. That contained no less than three umbrellas and four walking sticks, which he used according to season and climatic conditions. Sir Inigo paused to admire the oil-painting of himself which hung in a position of honour in a massive gilt frame. Unconsciously, he adjusted the stock at his neck.

He was crossing to his own door when it suddenly opened, and a flushed young man with dark hair came abruptly out.

"I thought I heard you, Sir Inigo," he stammered. "Miss Angela Meredith is here to see you."

Sir Inigo stroked his chin with a big hand. The expression in his eyes was serious as he faced his private secretary.

"The poor girl," he said softly. "I am afraid I have neglected her since the funeral."

He made as though to pass into the room but paused again.

"It may be as well, Penrose, if you were to work out here for half an hour."

He indicated a desk in the corner of the lobby.

"This might be a somewhat delicate interview. I am sure you understand."

"Certainly, Sir Inigo," Penrose said.

He had a relieved expression on his face.

"If you will just allow me to collect my papers . . . I will tell Miss Meredith you are here."

The Bank director waited outside the door, humming quietly to himself. He heard the murmur of voices from inside the room, and then Penrose reappeared with a bundle of papers in his hands.

Miss Angela Meredith rose from her leather chair in front of Sir Inigo's desk and awaited his approach. It was a long handsome room, which paid tribute to the Bank director's importance and worth. It was lit by two large circular windows which overlooked the plane trees and grass of a small square, bisected by a quiet street serving mostly private houses.

Oak-panelled like the annexe, it bore the coat of arms of the Bank on a handsome shield set between the two windows. It was also used for board meetings, so a long polished table flanked by leather chairs stood facing the windows. The apartment was no less than forty feet wide at this point, but it tapered in a curious manner so that it was only half the width in the portion reserved by Sir Inigo as his private office.

Apart from a large and massive desk, which befitted a man of his importance, there was a smaller desk to one side which accommodated Penrose; an Adam fireplace in which a cheerful coal fire burned; an oil-painting attributed to Canaletto on the fireplace wall; a globe of the world; and a brass speaking tube on a stand at a corner of the desk, which communicated with another office immediately above and which was occupied by the Bank's senior director and Sir Inigo's next in rank, Connors.

A soft carpet muffled his footsteps as he approached the desk with a smile for the girl, who moved forward impulsively to shake his hand. He waved her into her chair and went round to take his own seat, his back to the fire.

"I trust you'll forgive this intrusion at such an early hour," the girl said.

"I am always delighted to see you, Miss Angela," Walton said warmly. "I fear my duties here have made me neglectful of your interests of late."

The girl's eyes softened.

"I should never accuse you of that, Sir Inigo. You have been kindness itself. Especially during that dreadful time . . ."

She faltered for a moment, unable to go on. Sir Inigo looked down at his blotter and waited until she had control of herself again.

"It was the least I could do," he said gently. "Your father was a most respected colleague. Everyone here at the Bank, from the humblest employee to director level, admired and looked up to him. His passing was a great blow to us. Please feel free to call upon me at any time."

He smiled at the young girl across his desk; she seemed almost lost in the vastness of the leather chair, which had been designed more with captains of industry and merchant adventurers in mind. She looked vulnerable and appealing, he thought, as he studied her. Today she wore a dark green costume which set off her figure in a way which the Bank director found a little disconcerting.

Her black hair was drawn back in a chignon, and her frank cornflower blue eyes were clouded with worry. With her broad brow and clear complexion; the full lips, drawn partly open to reveal the regular teeth; the candid expression; and her general air of breeding and assured comfort; she looked so appealing that Sir Walton, at his age even more susceptible to women's charms, wondered not for the first time why she had never married.

But he merely cleared his throat and looked benevolently at his welcome visitor, noting her elegance, from the tips of her patent-leather shoes to the crown of her well-groomed head. As always, she wore a gold watch in an oyster case pinned to the breast of her costume.

"I appreciate your kindness, Sir Inigo," the girl said in a low, well-modulated voice. "Therefore I took the liberty of calling upon you. I wanted to ask you something."

Sir Inigo folded his thick hands on the desk in front of him and shifted his bulk in the chair. The heat of the fire made a comfortable radiance at the back of his neck, and its glow threw a golden sheen on the surface of his desk.

"About your father?"

His voice had dropped to a low and serious tone. Miss Meredith nodded.

"I wondered if you could remember anything in particular. I have never spoken of this to you before. But I felt that father was worried just before his death. Business matters, perhaps."

Sir Inigo half closed his eyes and leaned back. He spoke without opening his lids or looking at his young visitor.

"I hardly follow you, Miss Angela. A large concern like this generates worries, of course. Your father was a senior director. A great merchant bank has many problems, many vexations, in the course of its daily business. Your father suffered the normal tensions to which we are all subject."

He sighed heavily.

"Just at the moment, a series of bullion robberies is plaguing the City. It is serious, most serious. I have someone coming from Scotland Yard only this morning to see me about our security arrangements."

The girl's blue eyes were fixed upon his face. She moistened her lips once or twice as though half-afraid to go on. He noticed a small lace-handkerchief clutched in one of her delicate hands. He went on kindly, before she could speak.

"Your father was a very close man, Miss Angela. He did not confide in his fellow-directors, least of all me. If something was worrying him, he did not speak of it; at least so far as I am concerned. We noticed nothing different about him, if that is what you are asking. If you could be more specific, Miss Angela . . ."

The girl half rose from her seat, with an agitated movement.

"It is nothing really, Sir Inigo. But I thought there might have been something troubling him. I felt I had to ask."

Sir Inigo rose and went round the desk. He put his hand affectionately on the girl's shoulder.

"I quite understand," he said gently. "This business has been a shock. Let me ring for some tea, and we will partake of it together as we did when you first visited here as a child."

The girl smiled up at him. The shadows were lifting from her eyes.

Sir Inigo's hand reached out toward the bell.

The banker put the silver spoon on the edge of his saucer and drew his cup toward him with an anticipatory smile. He frowned as their tête-à-tête was interrupted by a timid rapping at the door. Penrose appeared in the opening. He seemed ill at ease and licked his lips as he glanced worriedly at his employer.

"I regret disturbing you, Sir Inigo, but Inspector Bull of Scotland Yard is here to see you."

The baronet's face cleared. He rose to his feet.

"Ah, yes, we did have an appointment. Give me a minute and then show him in. And come in yourself. I shall need you to take notes."

He waited until the door had closed behind his secretary and then shook his finger as the girl made as though to depart.

"There is no need to break up our little assignation, Miss Angela."

He smiled conspiratorially, amused at the flush which sprang to her cheeks.

"If we merely remove the tea-things to my secretary's desk you may remain, and we will continue our talk after the Inspector's departure. I have no secrets from my former partner's daughter."

And he carried the silver tray over to the side of the big room and made the girl comfortable in a chair next the secretary's desk. He carried his own cup and saucer back to his own desk and had scarcely seated himself when Penrose entered again to announce the Inspector. Sir Inigo came down the room to greet him and briefly introduced him to the girl.

"Tell Mrs. Cleek to bring some more cups," he ordered Penrose.

The detective officer seated himself in the leather chair recently vacated by Miss Meredith and looked curiously about him. The two men waited until the secretary had returned, accompanied by a taciturn woman in black bombazine. She poured tea for the Inspector and the secretary and, after curtseying, went swiftly out in silence. Penrose went over to his own desk, smiled sympathetically at Miss Meredith, collected his notebook, and then sat down to one side of Sir Inigo's desk, ready to begin work.

Inspector Bull was a gruff, red-faced man with smart sideburns and a hard weather-beaten face. He had a thin pencil moustache but was otherwise clean-shaven. He had a strong blue chin, thin sandy hair, and sandy eyebrows; and deep green eyes that had a steady, penetrating look.

He was smartly dressed in a thick overcoat over a discreet check suit, and he set down his bowler hat and his gloves on a corner of the desk in a decisive manner which showed that he was used to dealing with wealthy and important people. He had a battered black briefcase which he kept on his lap throughout the interview. After the brief formalities were over and the three men around the desk had sipped their tea for a polite interval, the Scotland Yard man came quickly to the point.

"You know why I'm here, Sir Inigo. I've been detailed by the authorities to take charge of security arrangements for both private and public banks in the metropolis. We are taking exceptional measures, and I would be grateful for any cooperation you are able to extend."

Penrose's pen had already begun to race across the paper, but Bull ignored him and sat staring at Sir Inigo from beneath half-closed lids. The banker sipped his tea carefully and put his cup down with the agreeable clinking noise that fine china always gives out.

"Naturally, we will do whatever we can," he began cautiously. "We are always anxious to assist Scotland Yard."

Bull pursed his lips and looked across at the calm figure of the girl who was sipping her tea and eating her biscuits as though there was no one else in the room. He noted her beauty as he would have approved a well-secured bank vault or a cunningly argued case in court and then passed on to more pertinent matters.

"I need hardly beat about the bush, Sir Inigo. The police authorities are worried, extremely worried, at this current spate of bullion robberies. I cannot, for obvious reasons, go into the details."

He gave a discreet little cough at this point.

"I realise merchant banks are understandably cautious about their holdings, and they do not circulate details to their rivals. But to be quite blunt, what we have found in some of the recent cases—where extremely large sums of money were involved—has appalled us. It does seem to us at Scotland Yard that bankers can do a great deal to assist the police by overhauling and, where necessary, tightening up their present security arrangements."

He paused and Sir Inigo shifted uneasily in his chair. His red face had assumed an even deeper shade of crimson, and Penrose looked at him anxiously, as though fearing a choleric outburst. But his voice was surprisingly bland as he replied.

"I believe our security is as good as can be found in the light of present knowledge, Inspector. But we do not have closed minds at the City and Suburban. If there are things which need doing, then we are open to suggestions and are willing to act upon them."

He paused and added ironically.

"Providing, that is, that they are practical and do not incur an unrealistic amount of money in these days of ever-rising costs."

Inspector Bull stirred in his chair.

"I am glad to hear you say so, Sir Inigo," he said.

He rummaged in his briefcase and pulled out a sheaf of papers.

"We have produced a document, 'Notes to Bankers,' a copy of which I will leave with you. And I should naturally like to personally inspect your premises with a view to preparing a report and making further suggestions."

He drew out a printed sheet and passed it over to Sir Inigo, who glanced at it briefly, before again raising his eyes to the detective officer. He studied the Scotland Yard man's face in silence for a moment.

"And have you no line on these cunning rascals? This business is causing some concern in the City."

Bull turned a blank face to the banker.

"I would prefer to say nothing of the progress of our investigations at this stage, Sir Inigo. We are dealing with some very clever rogues."

Sir Inigo nodded. He drummed with strong, capable fingers on the desk in front of him.

"I understand, Inspector. Now, if you would wish to tour our premises, there is no time like the present. Penrose here will introduce you to our Heads of Department and accompany you to the strong-rooms."

He rose from the desk abruptly and the Scotland Yard man rose also.

"I myself will join you just as soon as I have concluded my business with Miss Meredith."

He smiled benevolently at the girl. He shook hands with Inspector Bull, who took his briefcase and hat, bowed silently to Angela Meredith, and followed Penrose out. The girl was already on her feet as the door closed behind them.

"I've already taken up too much of your time, Sir Inigo."

The baronet's face was rosily affable.

"Not at all, Miss Angela, not at all. If there's anything I can do . . ."

The girl hesitated. Her eyes searched his face.

"There is something, Sir Inigo. I have a friend, a Mr. Clyde Beatty."

Sir Inigo bowed gallantly.

"I'm sure you have many friends, Miss Angela," he murmured.

The girl smiled. There was a dancing look in her blue eyes which the banker recognised all too well.

"You misunderstand me, Sir Inigo. He is a well-known private investigator. He is also a gentleman and a person who is in the top rank of his profession."

They were standing by the door now, and Angela Meredith studied Sir Inigo's face, which had assumed its normal bored appearance.

"I could not help overhearing your conversation regarding the internal security of the Bank. I am sure Mr. Beatty would be pleased to advise you. He is extremely experienced in these matters."

The bored look had passed from Sir Inigo's face now. He had assumed an alert expression and he glanced at the girl shrewdly.

"An admirable suggestion, Miss Angela. Why not indeed? We are not so overprotected here that we cannot do without further advice. Ask your friend to send me his card and I will grant him an interview."

Angela Meredith turned a dazzling smile on Sir Inigo. He lifted her hand to his lips and kissed it warmly.

"Thank you, Sir Inigo."

"Thank you, my dear," he said gravely. "I hope to call on you at St. John's Wood soon."

The girl ran lightly down the stairs and out into the cold air of the City. She hardly noticed the ride back in the cab, the biting wind, or the scurry of passing vehicles. The rest of the day passed like a dream. Her mind was full of Beatty and his doings at Brookwood on her behalf. Dusk fell and she went in to dinner still preoccupied. She was so absorbed that twice she found herself using the wrong spoons for the courses.

The maid smiled and giggled with the housekeeper, Mrs. Throgmorton, until she was gently reprimanded by the latter. Angela Meredith said good night at length and ascended to her own room. She undressed by the light of a solitary lamp and crossed to the window. It was bitterly cold still, and there was frost on the pane. The night was cloudy, but occasionally the moon broke through.

Angela Meredith looked out at the night for a moment, her heart and mind far away in Surrey. Then she shivered and sought her bed. She put out her lamp, but it was a long time before sleep found her.

23

THE TUNNEL

BEATTY stooped to find the matches. His heart was beating irregularly and with heavy strokes in his throat. His hands were trembling very slightly as he relit the lantern with some difficulty. Light and sanity struggled back into the dark earthy tunnel. He lifted the lantern cautiously and stood back.

The yellow beams picked out the broken earth walls, the tumbled figure at his feet. He reached for a baulk of timber and turned it over with some difficulty. The corpse was a very old one but had apparently been preserved by the nature of the soil. Beatty ignored the rictus of the dead smile.

He bent to examine the harness of wire which was fastened round the remains. The trace from it went up somewhere in the ceiling. The thing was triggered by a small wooden peg in the centre of the passage which loosened a prop, causing the remains to drop downward. Beatty was smiling grimly now. He put the lantern aside and searched round for the equipment he had been using and which had dropped when the lantern fell.

He set the light on the ground and went over the earth floor carefully. He retrieved the picklock and put it in the pocket of his overcoat. He loosened the handkerchief from over his mouth and mopped the perspiration from his forehead. He fastened it back across his face, blotting out the nauseous, sickly smell that caught at the throat. He picked up the lantern and looked at the obscene thing in front of him. Then he stepped over it carefully and went on down the passage.

His senses were unusually alert. He looked searchingly at the walls of the passage, noting their condition and structure. The passage went gradually downward. He stooped and examined the floor carefully. There were boot marks in the compressed soil which composed the footing of the corridor, but the earth was impacted so hard here that it was difficult to make out any detail.

Beatty got out his watch and checked the time. It was almost an hour since he had gone over the cemetery wall. He dare not delay too long. His ears were straining to hear any unusual sounds, but everything was unnaturally quiet down here. Beatty smiled again. He had been going to equate the conditions with the quietness of the grave, but the simile was unnecessary.

He was still shocked from the incident in the passage and he could feel his limbs slightly trembling. The passage went on for quite a long way, and he stopped again. He listened, stand-ing upright, one hand on the timbered structure of the wall. He remained motionless for almost a minute, but not a sound broke the heavy silence.

Then he made up his mind. He removed the revolver from his pocket, checked it, and took off the safety-catch before replacing it. The derringer made a comforting pressure against his ankle as he picked up the lantern and moved on down the passage. Once again the image of Miss Angela Meredith flickered into his con-sciousness. The girl was leaning forward, one hand raised toward him, her mouth smiling appealingly.

Almost angrily Beatty forced the impression from his con-sciousness. This was no time or place to indulge in such dangerous fantasies. But there was no doubt that Miss Meredith and her problems occupied an inordinate amount of his attention during his waking hours. Beatty closed his fingers over the wrist holding the lantern and pinched the skin viciously. The pain momentarily made his eyes water, but he had achieved his purpose.

Every nerve was alert, his mind cool and evaluating data normally, as he trod cautiously down the passage, the tiny rays of the lantern stabbing now at the floor, now at the walls, now at the mass of earth pressing heavily above his head. He saw that the ceiling was well shored and realised the significance of the pit-props he had seen stacked outside the group of cemetery sheds. In a few seconds more he came to a heavy oak door bound with iron and studded with massive iron nails.

Beatty frowned. He held the lantern high and set its yellow beams dancing about the passage. He found a place where the prop alongside the door had split. In the ragged notch formed he set the hook of the lantern. By its light he could now see clearly to work on the lock. Despite its size and heavy-duty appearance, it was a comparatively straightforward pattern, unlike the padlocks securing the outer door.

But after a few tentative efforts with the picklock, Beatty realised he would need something more substantial. Kneeling, he felt among the contents of the pouches on the belt around his waist. He selected the biggest of the instruments and went to work again. He found himself perspiring as the pick slipped for the third time.

Then the lock gave a satisfying click, and he felt the door give significantly. Beatty was nothing if not methodical, and he did not immediately press on as most people in his circumstances would. He knew that the way before him was now clear. But that was no reason to neglect precautions. He put those tools he would not need back into their respective receptacles in the waist-belt.

Then he took the lantern along the passage to the far door leading to the workshops. All was as it should be. He stepped over the thing in the corridor, the lantern beam dancing over the walls, casting alternate bars of black and gold. His face was an impassive mask as he fetched up against the big iron-bound door again. Only the eyes were glittering with excitement in the strong Roman face.

He lifted the heavy iron handle and pushed at the door gently. It gave before the pressure of his fingertips. Unlike the other doors it had not been oiled, and the hinges started up a prodigious creaking that set the young investigator's teeth on edge. He noted, as it came back, that the door was some four inches thick. That was significant in itself.

The lantern beam showed an ever-widening band of blackness as he forced the door back. Somewhere, from far off, came a familiar sound; it was the sharp, insistent dripping of a tap. The falling water made a mournful fretting in the darkness of that underground tunnel, and Beatty felt a melancholy steal around his heart.

But he braced himself and pushed the door back another foot. He stopped then. The breath was pumping in his chest, and the faint trembling of his fingers showed how much his normal balance had been upset. Beatty paused for a moment longer, giving his nerves time to settle. He thought of Dotterell waiting in the bitter cold at the other side of the wall. He hesitated again; perhaps he should just go back and let his assistant know that all was well?

He quickly dismissed the matter from his mind. There was not time, and now that he was here he might just as well bring the business to a swift conclusion. And at least he would be a little nearer discovering the truth about the bizarre occurrences at Brookwood Cemetery. Beatty replaced the picklock in his overcoat pocket.

He took one step forward into the darkness alongside the massive door. The lantern beam went momentarily down toward the floor. Beatty reached inside the special pocket, his fingers encountering the smooth resistance of the gun butt. He half drew it from his breast when a slithering noise arrested his attention.

There was a faint vibration against the woodwork of the door, and something stirred in the shadow. The darkness changed to all the colours of the rainbow, and then consciousness left him and Beatty slumped downward into a far deeper blackness.

24

SAVED

BEATTY was dying. His body burned like fire. He choked, and water ran out his mouth. A face was beginning to come into focus.

It receded and then steadied. It was an anxious face. Beatty made out the features of Dotterell. He tried to struggle up, was gently pushed back by a giant hand.

"You'll feel better in a minute, Mr. Beatty."

The voice was concerned and considerate. Beatty had never heard Dotterell speak in such a manner before. He coughed violently and turned aside. He retched again and began to feel better. He sat up, Dotterell's hand supporting his back.

"Best drink this, Mr. Beatty."

The neck of a small silver flask was thrust into his mouth. Beatty gagged as the raw spirit ran down his throat. A warmth started coursing through, down to his stomach. He began to realise that he was bitterly cold. His clothes were soaked with water and a freezing wind blew.

He opened his eyes again, felt ice crack beneath his boot. Then Dotterell had lifted him effortlessly and set him against a tree. A dry overcoat was placed over him. Dotterell was massaging his face now with warm, capable hands.

Beatty saw the leather belt which Dotterell had unbuckled from his waist; the bag; the dark-lantern. His bewilderment grew. By the straggling light of the moon which filtered through the branches he could see that he was lying on the shore of a large lake. The surface was covered with ice, which glistened under the pallid moonlight. Near the edge was a dark, disturbed area of water with fragments of ice floating in it. He could see the marks of his heels on the ice near the margin where Dotterell had dragged him ashore.

"What has happened?" he said weakly, aware that he owed his assistant an immense debt of gratitude. Dotterell's cadaverous face with the lank hair falling over the eyes had never looked grimmer as he bent over Beatty, adjusting the overcoat round him; watching for the signs of returning circulation as the whisky did its work. His piercing blue eyes looked anxiously at Beatty.

"Four men," he hissed between strong teeth. "Four men I'd like to meet again. One of them had a limp."

Beatty was feeling stronger now; something of the deadly cold was beginning to leave his bones. He looked uncomprehendingly at the shoreline of the lake.

"I entered the sheds," he said haltingly. "I found a tunnel and locked doors. There was a corpse there, rigged with wires so that it would fall forward on to an intruder. Obviously meant to frighten away trespassers."

He chuckled grimly, easing himself against the trunk of the tree. Dotterell hurriedly packed the scattered equipment into the bags they had brought with them. His eyes never left Beatty's face.

"I opened a second door, thick and secured with iron bands," Beatty went on. "Someone must have hit me. That is all I remember."

Dotterell nodded dourly, kneeling in front of the sprawled figure of his employer.

"I waited an hour," he said simply. "I was getting damned cold. So I used the ladder and went over the wall. I knew the direction of the chapel. Before I'd gone more than a few yards I heard the sound of a horse and vehicle from the road outside the cemetery wall. It stopped and then moved off again. I found a small side-gate open. I got out on to the road again and followed the closed carriage. After about a mile it stopped by this lake."

Dotterell paused and looked at Beatty with a softening of his expression. The young investigator realised that this was the longest speech he had ever heard his assistant make.

"I kept in the shadows and got closer," Dotterell said. "No one saw me. They were too occupied with what they were doing. There were four men, including the driver and the limping man. They carried an unconscious figure to the shore and slid it out on to the ice with a long pole."

Beatty swallowed another sip of whisky thoughtfully.

"So that the warmth of my body would melt the ice," he said slowly. "And I would have drowned without regaining consciousness. Very ingenious. You didn't get to see their faces?"

Dotterell shook his head.

"They had their backs turned, and in any case they were too far away. I knew it was you as soon as they brought your case out and put it on the ice."

He shivered suddenly and looked round the bleak spot.

"Afterwards they went straight on, following the road. They will be miles away by now. Naturally, I hurried to get you out of there as soon as possible. Unfortunately, the ice broke with our combined weights. I am sorry to have endangered you in such a manner."

Beatty stared at Dotterell. His assistant was quite serious.

"My dear fellow," he said gently. "I am more grateful than I can ever convey."

He started to get up, but Dotterell pushed him back. There was a strange expression in the lean man's eyes.

"Say no more, Mr. Beatty. The old firm stands together. But I must say we've not seen a tighter spot than tonight."

He licked his lips, getting to his feet, recorking the flask.

"We have no time to lose. We must get you to bed as soon as possible. I'm afraid of pneumonia. And I have still to recover the ladder from the cemetery wall. Do you feel fit to stand?"

Beatty was already up. He tottered and put out his hand to steady himself against the trunk of the tree. He looked disbelievingly at the icy surface of the lake, deceptively innocent in the moonlight. The jagged expanse of broken water and ice made a dark star near the edge. He put out his hand and clasped Dotterell's.

"I'll take the bags," Dotterell said. "We must just foot it back to the White Horse and hope we are unobserved. It is after midnight now and I should not think it likely."

Beatty swayed and his legs started trembling. He braced himself, drawing in his breath. He was incredibly cold, and his clothes stuck to his skin in the freezing wind. He realised the deadly danger now that the effect of the whisky was wearing off. He stamped his feet upon the ground and moved away from the tree, his assistant's hand under his elbow.

Then he was walking easily, thrusting his hands deep into the pockets of Dotterell's thick coat. Dotterell fell in alongside him, carrying the two cases effortlessly. The road stretched before them bland in the moonlight.

"Now, Mr. Beatty," said Dotterell grimly, settling to the pace. "Walk for your life."

Beatty eased himself upon the pillow. His room at the White Horse seemed full of people and tobacco smoke. Munson smiled at him encouragingly. The police surgeon, a tall man with a heavy black moustache, whose name was Sanders, put on his most professional look.

"A nasty business," he said. "But no harm done. A mild concussion only. You should be up tomorrow, none the worse."

Twenty-four hours had gone by since Dotterell and Beatty had arrived back at the inn at dead of night. Dotterell had the key and they had gained Beatty's room unobserved. Beatty had slept fairly solidly since and now felt decidedly better, though still weak; this was the first opportunity he had had to discuss the situation, and a bedside conference had been convened. Munson had been apprised of the general situation but did not know the details. Now he shifted the pipe in the corner of his mouth and looked encouragingly at Beatty.

"I suppose I should be angry at such antics in my district," he said. But there was a twinkle in his eye which belied the severity of his voice. "Your assistant here has told me we almost had another murder on our hands. I hope you now see the folly of acting on your own."

Dotterell stirred from his position by the fireside and joined the small group round the bed. The police surgeon Sanders, a grave, discreet man, was party to their discussion; as well as being a bachelor he was as close-mouthed as a priest where confidences were concerned.

"My dear Inspector, if I had not gone over that cemetery wall we should be no further forward," Beatty said warmly. "I admit I have tipped my hand to our enemies, whoever they may be. But we are a good way along in our enquiries, and at least we know in what direction to pursue them."

Munson scratched his head and looked wryly from the man in the bed to Sanders and then to Dotterell.

"You may be the wiser, Mr. Beatty," he grunted, "but the business looks darker than ever to me."

"Draw up some chairs," Beatty suggested. "Then we can begin."

Munson carried his basket-chair to the bedside, observing, "Before I start I may as well tell you that Dr. Sanders's report on Varley was positive."

Beatty's eyes sparkled as the three men settled themselves round his bedside. He still felt weak, but his spirits revived as he looked at their alert faces. Sanders nodded.

"Enough arsenic for ten men," he said. "Almost identical to the case of Mr. Meredith."

"Capital," said Beatty, his face lit with enthusiasm. He took his hands from under the sheets and rubbed them together with a gesture that the Surrey detective remembered from the occasion of their first meeting. The three men waited while Beatty stared unseeingly at the flickering of the large coal fire which burned in the bedroom grate.

It was another example of the landlord's solicitude. Now he looked with knotted brows at the querying expressions of the men in front of him.

"We are faced with the traces of a diabolical conspiracy. Exactly what that conspiracy is has yet to be unravelled. The ends are here in Surrey, though the solution may lie elsewhere."

Munson screwed up his mouth around the stem of his pipe and sent clouds of smoke toward the ceiling. The doctor fidgeted as though he were out of his depth. Dotterell's eyes never left Beatty's face. He went on talking, relating the events of their night at Brookwood, leaving nothing out. Munson sucked in his breath once or twice at various points in the narrative but said nothing until Beatty had finished.

Then he took the pipe out of his mouth and scratched reflectively at the corner of his lower lip. Little sparks of excitement were dancing in his eyes.

"Well, this beats everything. We must get a thorough search made of that cemetery. And Superintendent Bateman . . ."

He stopped at the expression in Beatty's eyes. The young investigator made an explosive noise and leaned forward in the bed. He seized the Surrey Inspector's hand with a grip that made him wince.

"That is exactly what we must not do, Inspector!" he said impulsively. "It will ruin all. Everything depends on the secret of Brookwood being kept for the time being. The people behind this think I am dead. We must allow them to continue to do so."

Munson's face had clouded, and he sat puffing out streamers of smoke furiously.

"Two murders, one attempted, and a suicide, and you say we must do nothing," he muttered disgustedly. "Just who is in charge of police activities in this corner of Surrey?"

Beatty could not forbear a smile.

"You are right, of course, Inspector," he hastened to add. "But can you not see the virtue of keeping silence for the moment? If Superintendent Bateman is involved and he knows that his plan has miscarried, he would immediately take steps to cover himself. There is nothing to connect him directly with the passage in the cemetery grounds. Or with the people who left me in the lake. We do not even know what the passage is for. And there has been ample time to clear things up this past two days."

He glared fiercely at the three men sitting round the bed.

"What are we to do, then?" Munson asked sharply.

"Nothing for the moment," said Beatty. "That is our greatest strength. Superintendent Bateman may be entirely innocent in this affair. After all, he has more than sixty people on the staff at Brookwood. It would not be difficult to arrange things so that the head knew nothing of what was going on. On the other hand, if some other parties are involved and they think I am out of the way, why then they will carry on with their enterprise and we may trap them."

"There may be something in what you say," observed Munson.

"I do not see how we are to proceed otherwise," Beatty said.

Sanders stirred on his chair.

"You have a plan?" he began diffidently.

"An idea," said Beatty, leaning forward. "Which I propose to carry out with the approval of you gentlemen. It has a certain element of risk. An anonymous letter with a summons to London."

Dotterell gave a grim smile.

"The same ruse that drew Varley to his death," he observed.

"Exactly," Beatty retorted. "You have forgotten, gentlemen, the assistant foreman who has apparently stepped into the late lamented Varley's shoes. He has revealed the same anxiety under stress and the same desire to keep me from the private section of the cemetery. If he is involved he dare not ignore the message."

The basket-chair creaked as Inspector Munson shifted his weight.

"Abraham Beardsley. It might work. But I do not see how you are to summon him without revealing your identity."

Beatty smiled.

"There is a way. It will involve an anonymous note, whose meaning is unmistakably clear, suggesting a rendezvous."

Dotterell smiled also.

"Delivered by a rough-looking man who hangs about outside Woking Station," he said triumphantly.

"Just so," said Beatty. "You are excelling yourself, Dotterell. For that we shall need the services of our friend Toby Stevens."

"You cannot suggest your own office or that will give away your identity," Munson pointed out.

Beatty stroked his chin.

"It will have to be London, of course, Inspector. But I will keep you fully posted. What about the Shot Tower?"

"The Shot Tower!" said Munson in a bemused voice.

"An admirable spot," said Beatty. "An easily recognisable landmark on the South Bank of the Thames. Even a Surrey rustic could not miss it, begging your pardon, Inspector. And it has the advantage that I can conceal myself and spy out the ground beforehand."

He smiled round at them in turn. No one said anything.

"And now, gentlemen," said Beatty, reaching for a writing pad on the bedside table, "I must bait the trap. If you would be so good, Dotterell, as to ring that bell, I think we could all do with some tea."

25

A COMMISSION FOR STEVENS

DOTTERELL paused in oiling the revolver on the table in front of him and looked at Beatty sympathetically. The latter sat in his dressing gown by the substantial fire provided by the landlord of the White Horse and studied the pencilled notes on his lap with a frown. He had almost completely recovered from the ordeal of three days earlier, though he was still a little weak. He and Dotterell were returning to London on the late afternoon train.

It was midmorning, but the mist had only just cleared and the sun was beginning to break through and gild the frosted window-panes with pale yellow. Dotterell cleared his throat, put down the revolver on the clean rag, and gave a grunt of satisfaction.

"That's the last, Mr. Beatty. All the equipment is now in first-class order."

He gave his employer an interrogatory look.

"What puzzles me is why they should have been so careful. Even the lantern had been placed on the ice together with your bag."

Beatty nodded. A deep furrow of concentration had opened up across his brow.

"It was obvious they wanted everything out of the workings. But if I were found drowned, then no one could say that theft was the motive. A senseless accident, most likely, and the strange items found with me would have been something for the coroner to puzzle over."

Dotterell ran his eyes across the crowded table-top with satisfaction.

"Nevertheless, I was glad to see the dark-lantern again," he said. "I took a lot of trouble over that."

"You always take a lot of trouble over everything," Beatty replied.

He drew the dressing gown more tightly about him and looked again at the flickering light of the fire. He could see darker shadows amid the flames, and he knew just how much he owed to his strange gaunt assistant. But the two men had not returned to the subject; it was not their way, and Beatty realised that another twenty years could pass and Dotterell would never again refer of his own volition to the fact that he had saved his employer's life.

"Lunch in your room, Mr. Beatty?" Dotterell queried, rising from the table.

"It would be better so," Beatty said. "The fewer people in Woking who realise I am still walking about in good health, the better. And a crowded dining room would only serve to advertise my presence. Better to have Stevens bring the cab to the door this afternoon in order to avoid walking through the streets."

Dotterell nodded. He cleared his throat again. Beatty looked at him quickly.

"One strange aspect is the man with one leg shorter than the other," his assistant began. "That was the most distinctive thing about the four men I saw—and the only clue."

Beatty shrugged.

"It is curious, certainly. I did not expect anything to come of Munson's investigations regarding the vehicle you saw driving away. It would not be likely to leave traces upon the road. And it leads to a village and a cross-roads only four miles farther on."

He paused a moment and resumed his study of the dancing firelight.

"But it does not appear as though our limping friend is local. He would surely be known in Woking, otherwise. And I understand the Inspector has had his men enquire about the neighbouring villages."

A discreet tapping at the door interrupted the two men's reflections.

"That will be Toby Stevens," Beatty said, his eyes alert now, every line of his body indicating energy and determination.

"Show him in, please. I will see him alone. You might as well withdraw to the hotel bar just as soon as you have given my lunch order."

Dotterell nodded with an ironic smile. He gathered up the things from the table and put them down in a gladstone bag by the fireplace before crossing to open the door.

Toby Stevens came slowly forward and looked curiously at the figure of Beatty sitting by the fire. He was obviously intrigued by the summons to a guest's room, but he had trained himself not to appear surprised by anything. And he was noted in Woking for his discretion.

So he held his hat in his right hand and waited deferentially until Beatty should take notice of him. With his alert face and iron-grey hair he looked more like a personal valet than a cab-driver. Today he wore a large tweed cape over a smart snuff-coloured cutaway coat. His boots were impeccably polished as befitted a widower who took great personal pride in his appearance.

"I'm glad to see you again, Stevens," Beatty greeted him. "I have a small commission for you. And this afternoon I should like you to drive myself and my colleague to the next station down the line where we shall take train for London."

An odd expression passed over Stevens's face.

"Not Woking Station, sir?" he enquired delicately.

"I have my reasons," Beatty said curtly. "You will be able to manage that? I shall require you to be outside the inn at three."

"Oh, certainly, sir," Stevens hastened to assure him. "There will be no difficulty about it." He paused. "I should know you, sir," he said with a puzzled air. "It is Dr. Fitzgibbon, is it not? But you look somehow different, sir."

Beatty smiled but offered no explanation for the moment. Stevens hesitated before going on.

"Regarding the other commission, Dr. Fitzgibbon . . ."

"Ah, there I am afraid I have deceived you, Stevens," Beatty remarked, getting to his feet. "My real name is Clyde Beatty."

He fixed the cabman with a piercing eye.

"I am telling you this, Stevens, in absolute confidence, and I shall expect you to treat the information with the utmost discretion."

There was a sharp, excited look on Stevens's face now. He brought his hand up to the bridge of his nose in the familiar salute.

"You have my word, sir," he said quietly.

Beatty nodded.

"Excellent."

He sat down again.

"You may have wondered exactly what my actions in the Woking area have entailed, as they have not entirely escaped your notice. I am not at liberty to tell you my reasons, though I may do so one day. They are important reasons, however, and I can assure you that you will not go unrewarded."

Stevens shuffled his feet awkwardly.

"I do my duty, sir, as an honest man should. I ask no more."

"It does you credit, Stevens," Beatty rejoined, with an approving nod. "Now, I want you to do one more small service. I have a note here."

He glanced at the table which Dotterell had just quitted, and following his glance the cabman made out a small blue envelope with an inked inscription in block capitals.

"There is a rather untidy character, I understand, who hangs about Woking Station and runs messages and suchlike," Beatty began.

Stevens smiled.

"You mean Cronk, sir. He would run a message to hell and back for the price of a bottle of stout."

Beatty joined in the other's smile.

"I daresay. However, my commission will not tax him that far. But he must on no account know who has given you this message, you understand."

"You have my word, Mr. Beatty."

"Good."

Beatty was silent for a moment. Then he began again.

"Tell me something, Stevens. How does this man Cronk operate? For example, if I myself wished to know the source of any particular message that passed through Cronk, would I be able to find out?"

Stevens scratched his ear as he reflected.

"Begging your pardon, sir, there's no way of knowing. Folk who wanted to keep their business secret would do as you do. And then again, he has an arrangement with the booking clerk. Letters and the payment for their delivery are left at the booking office."

Stevens's eyes twinkled.

"The clerk takes a commission, of course, though the station-master knows nothing about it. So anyone could have a note delivered and no one the wiser about the sender. I could tell you some stories about Cronk if I had the time."

Beatty looked at him sharply.

"Talking of stories and the time to retail them, you once mentioned something about a conversation we might have if ever I found myself back in Woking."

A shadow seemed to pass across the cabman's face.

"Oh, about Dr. Couchman, sir. I recall it well enough. It was a cold night, outside this very inn."

"Well, it would seem that the time has come for us to have that conversation," Beatty went on. "It concerned your wife, I believe."

Stevens's eyes were hard as he faced the man in the easy-chair.

"I understand Dr. Couchman has left his nursing home, Mr. Beatty. There is some talk in the town."

"No doubt," Beatty murmured, "but we were discussing your wife."

Stevens drew a blue tongue across his lips.

"It's an old story, sir," he said heavily. "The wife had been ill for some time, on and off. Dr. Couchman, who has a surgery in Woking, had been treating her for stomach upsets. But none of it did any good."

He looked at Beatty with burning eyes.

"One night my wife was taken worse than usual. I went out myself to the nursing home, but they swore Couchman was away. It's my belief he wouldn't come. Her agony went on for three days. During all that time I couldn't get any medical help."

He looked at Beatty sombrely.

"It's my belief that Couchman had been drinking. He had fits of that sort every now and again. He made an appearance in the end, and the wife was admitted to hospital. She died of a burst appendix. He swore that nothing could have saved her."

The black anger in his heart showed on his face as he clenched his hands at his side and looked fixedly at the young investigator.

"As true as I'm standing here, he killed her."

There was a heavy silence in the room, broken first by Beatty.

"You need not worry about Dr. Couchman any more," he said gently. "He will not be troubling Woking further."

Stevens stared at him in disbelief.

"I will say nothing, sir. He is dead?"

Beatty nodded. Stevens's lip trembled.

"I hope he died badly," he said in a low voice.

"He did," Beatty told him simply.

He looked up. Stevens had a strange exultant smile on his face. Beatty shivered suddenly and turned his gaze back to the flickering of the fire.

26

AT CHEYNE WALKE

THE mist crept forward, trembling as the light wind ruffled it. It obscured the Thames completely now, and as Beatty watched, the outlines of the roadway shimmered, wavered, and disappeared, only the pin-pricks of light from the side lanterns of the cabs and other vehicles which passed and repassed, and the sharp resonance of horses' hooves striking the flinty roadway, affirming that the outside world so much as existed.

A few moments later the first tendrils of vapour were at the panes, and the entire world seemed transformed into a shapeless opaque mass. But the commerce of London still rattled on, existing only as a muffled clamour beneath a woolly blanket that concealed everything in the bleak January afternoon.

Beatty stood at the window of his Cheyne Walk house immobile, not seeing the mist or listening to the noise of traffic, but turning over the events of the past three days in his mind. Tomorrow was the day he had appointed for the assignation at the Shot Tower. He wondered if the man Beardsley would come. Beatty was convinced that he would, but some of Munson's scepticism at his proposed scheme had stuck in his mind.

Yet it was difficult to see how they could make their way forward in the affair unless the interview took place; to contemplate the Surrey detective's alternative would throw all in jeopardy. It would reveal their hand prematurely and might mean that the secrets behind the events at Brookwood Cemetery would never be unravelled.

The ache in Beatty's head had quite disappeared and the investigator felt his usual vigorous self; but instead of pacing about or using up excess energy in his normal manner, he continued to stand by the window, his broad shoulders hunched, his mind preoccupied and oppressed by the thoughts that shuffled and rearranged themselves in his brain, much as the mist eddied and swirled outside the casement.

Dotterell was back at the office in Holborn, picking up the threads of the practice; Beatty himself had been there that morning, dealing with the more urgent business. They had Toby Stevens drive them from the White Horse. Beatty had a scarf wound tightly round his face as they emerged from the inn; he had given out that he was suffering from toothache.

So they had departed from Woking, almost furtively; but such precautions were well justified, Beatty felt. They were up against cunning and cruel adversaries, and it was obvious from the events of the past few days that Couchman's death had not curtailed the sinister activities of desperate men on those remote Surrey uplands.

Beatty was convinced that they had not been seen; indeed, if any among the hurrying passers-by in the busy town of Woking knew anything of the nefarious activities at Brookwood, he would assume Beatty dead, his body long drowned and hidden beneath the ice of the lake. Why should he look for him in the streets of Woking?

This was the major card in Beatty's hand; he was determined to play it to the full. He had taken similar precautions at the London end. Now, he had only to wait until the next day; Munson had made arrangements with Scotland Yard without going into the details of their plans. Beatty would have to reveal himself to Beardsley, of course; he hoped to strike such fear into the man that they would learn a great deal more of what was going on behind the respectable façade of Brookwood.

If necessary he could call on Scotland Yard; Beardsley would be held in custody so that he would be unable to warn his confederates that Beatty was still in the game. The young man moved away from the window, his mind still preoccupied with these and other thoughts, when there came a sharp rapping at the door. Mrs. Grice, his housekeeper, stood in the opening. An apple-cheeked, motherly looking woman in her late forties, she ran his household with gentle but formidable efficiency. Now she smiled as she looked searchingly at her employer.

"Miss Meredith is here to see you, Mr. Beatty."

Her voice had a pronounced Scottish accent.

"Will I show her up, or would you prefer to receive her on the ground floor?"

Beatty had an inward flash of amusement. He knew that Mrs. Grice, for all her forward-looking nature, did not always approve of his unorthodox way of life. Her Puritan scruples led her to see faintly immoral connotations in his receiving clients, particularly young ladies, on the upper floor of the house. But Beatty had his study here; it was a large, elegant room, well fitted with books and other intellectual ornaments suited to a bachelor with a wide and ranging mind.

Besides, when the fog held off, it had a fine view of the Thames which the ground floor lacked. So Beatty merely returned Mrs. Grice's smile and said urbanely, "Show her up, please, Mrs. Grice. We will have tea in a quarter of an hour."

Mrs. Grice gave a slight bow as she prepared to withdraw.

"Very well, Mr. Beatty. You have some lint on your collar. You'll no want the young lady to think you suffer from dandruff."

"That is the least of my troubles," said Beatty absently. "But thank you for the observation."

The housekeeper swiftly crossed the parquet and removed the offending fragment. Beatty chuckled as he gazed affectionately after her. He glanced quickly in the small ornamental mirror set between the windows and was reassured at his appearance. Apart from being slightly pale he looked his normal self. He went toward the door as Mrs. Grice announced the girl.

Flushed from the open air she had never looked more attractive, Beatty thought. Today she wore a pale green travelling outfit with a small cape which seemed to emphasise and set off the suppleness of her figure. She looked keenly at Beatty and came quickly forward, clasping his hands warmly in her own.

"Come over to the fire, Miss Meredith," Beatty said, drawing her forward. "A beastly day, don't you agree? We will be having tea in a few minutes."

As always, the girl was hatless, and Beatty was again struck by the deep bluish sheen of her hair. She looked curiously about the room and with such obvious pleasure and interest that he again felt a sudden sensation that had been with him more than once of late.

"You will forgive me, Mr. Beatty," the girl said shyly. "You have a beautiful house. I wondered . . ."

Beatty laughed. He and the girl were standing in front of the elaborate marble fireplace, the latter holding out her hands to the blaze.

"You are quite correct, Miss Meredith. My house is not compatible with my profession. My activities as an investigator could not support such a house. There is only one man, to my knowledge, who is able to make a comfortable living so: Mr. Holmes. I have a private income of my own, left me by my parents. They were drowned in a shipping accident some years back."

Miss Meredith gave Beatty a long glance in which sympathy was blended with something else.

"I am sorry," she said simply.

Beatty moved awkwardly away from the fire.

"It was a long time ago," he said. "Won't you sit near the fireplace? I will bring the small table over."

They were ensconced comfortably around the hearth when Mrs. Grice returned with the tea-things. She retired tactfully after a modest exchange of pleasantries with the girl, leaving Miss Meredith to pour the tea.

"I like it strong," Beatty said, looking thoughtfully out at the fog. "I hope my message didn't startle you."

The girl shook her head. She passed him the cup.

"I was intrigued," she said. "I hardly expected you back quite so soon."

"There was an interruption to my plans," Beatty said grimly. "To make no bones about it, there was an attempt on my life."

A sudden rattle of crockery broke the silence, and Beatty was startled to see the agitation on Angela Meredith's face. She put the cup down with an abrupt movement and stared at him with white features. He was by her side in an instant, taking her small hands between his strong fingers.

"Don't be alarmed," he said gently. "I didn't mean to upset you."

The girl shook her head angrily. He was amazed to see that her eyes were brimming with tears.

"I did not mean to appear so foolish. Please forgive me."

Beatty smiled.

"There is nothing to forgive," he said.

He let go her hands suddenly and resumed his seat. He stirred his tea to hide the furious agitation within him. The girl studied him from beneath lowered lids.

"Have some toast, Miss Meredith," he said.

She raised her head. The colour was coming back into her cheeks.

"I think you might call me by my Christian name," she said hesitantly. "After all, it is as though we have known one another some time. And if we are to continue to be involved in this terrible affair . . ."

She broke off and reached out for the toast-stand. Beatty studied her face as he drank his tea.

"Very well, Angela," he resumed. "But remember, the danger is over now. I have no wish to tell you of the Brookwood business if it will upset you so."

The girl shook her head and looked at him with very bright eyes.

"It was foolish of me," she repeated. "It will not happen again."

She listened intently as Beatty gave her a full but tactful résumé of the events at Woking, emphasising Dotterell's part in the affair and minimising his own. Miss Meredith listened with evidently rising agitation but kept her feelings well under control, though her fingers trembled on the handle of her cup as he reached the climax of the story. She stared at him blankly as he concluded.

"It appears that we owe a great deal to Dotterell. But the affair is darker than ever."

"On the contrary," Beatty assured her. "It is growing lighter. A pattern commences to emerge. I cannot for the moment pretend to see the business in its entirety. But it will come, Angela, it will come."

He half rose from his seat with the vehemence of his thoughts and then sat down again. He was pleased to see that the girl was smiling and that some of the shadow had lifted from her brow. He got up and gallantly turned the cake-stand to allow her to select a pastry.

"We seem to spend most of our time drinking tea in elegant surroundings and talking about the most terrifying horrors, Clyde," she observed. Beatty laughed, partly to cover the strange impact the girl's sentence had upon him. It was the first time she had used his Christian name.

"It is the elegant surroundings and the tea that help to preserve one's sanity in this business," he said.

"Can you tell me no more?" Angela asked, cutting into her pastry with a tiny silver knife.

"I have half formulated some theories," Beatty said. "But nothing quite fits. I have laid out some bait and with that we must be content for the moment. I shall know more tomorrow. Rest assured, you shall be the first to know if there is a break in the clouds."

Beatty looked at her quizzically. It was quiet in the room now, the only sound the faint crackling of the fire. The fog pressed at the windows in a grey shapeless mass. Beatty went over and drew the heavy curtains at both windows facing the Thames. The girl watched him with an air of quiet expectancy.

"I have some news for you myself," she said.

Beatty went to reseat himself at the opposite side of the fireplace. She poured another cup of tea for herself from the intricately chased silver pot that Beatty's mother had inherited from her mother, and motioned him to pass his own cup. Beatty stirred the sugar in his tea and waited for her to continue.

"I have not been idle while you were in Surrey," Angela Meredith observed. "I went to see my father's old partner, Sir Inigo Walton."

Beatty looked at her sharply. All his professional instincts were at work now, and he had changed in some subtle way from the bantering young man who had been exchanging pleasantries with a very attractive woman a few minutes before.

"The managing director of the City and Suburban Bank? I hope you were discreet."

The girl shifted on her chair and put down her cup with a sharp, brittle sound in the silence.

"Of course," she said reproachfully. "I remembered what you had told me."

Beatty put the tips of his fingers together and studied her face.

"Excellent," he said. "As I remarked earlier, that is an aspect of this business we must not neglect. I should have called at the Bank before now had not more pressing matters in Surrey engaged my attention."

The girl nodded. "I have arranged that," she said. "But firstly, I made some tactful queries about father. About his business, any possible worries, matters of that sort."

"And what were Sir Inigo's conclusions?"

The girl shook her head.

"Negative, I am afraid. Father had never discussed his private affairs with his fellow-directors. I was not very helpful there."

"No matter," Beatty said. "Negative results are just as useful as positive on some occasions. From what you have learned we are able to draw certain conclusions. You did not mention Dr. Couchman, of course?"

The girl drew herself up.

"Naturally, I would not wish to prejudice your enquiries. I kept off the subject of Dr. Couchman."

"Good."

Beatty was silent for a long moment. He waited for the girl to go on.

"However, Sir Inigo was extremely worried about the recent bank robberies in the City and the problems of internal security," she continued. "He had a visit from an expert, an Inspector Bull of Scotland Yard, while I was there."

Beatty's eyes were beginning to sparkle.

"I know him. A first-class man."

Angela Meredith smiled.

"I suggested Sir Inigo might like to engage your services as an expert, and that you might care to advise him on the Bank's security arrangements."

Beatty stroked his chin with the edge of his thumbnail.

"Excellent, Angela," he observed. "It will give me a number of opportunities, among them the occasion to introduce Dr. Couchman's name while conversing with the staff."

"I told Sir Inigo you would be in touch with him," Angela Meredith continued. "He will then make the necessary arrangements."

Beatty nodded. With his alert expression and his black hair curled closely to his scalp, he looked more Roman than ever as he stared at the girl at the other side of the fireplace. She lowered her eyes slightly, and unspoken thoughts were heavy between them. She was the first to break the silence.

"When do you think you could find time to see Sir Inigo?"

"Within the next two days," Beatty said, uncoiling himself from his chair. His sensitive ear had already caught the faint tread of Mrs. Grice on the landing beyond.

"I have an extremely urgent appointment tomorrow. Everything else must take second place to that."

Angela Meredith put up her hand to her hair with a hesitant gesture.

"I understand," she said. "I may leave everything to you, then?"

"Certainly," Beatty said. "And thank you again."

The couple at the fireplace turned at the housekeeper's discreet tap on the door.

"I just wondered whether there was anything else you required?" she said blandly.

Beatty turned enquiringly to the girl. She shook her head.

"That was absolutely delicious, Mrs. Grice."

Mrs. Grice flushed with pleasure. She bent quickly to the tray. A parlour-maid came swiftly forward at her gesture, wheeling a trolley. Beatty got up and waited while the things were cleared. Mrs. Grice hesitated at the door, her face smooth and blank.

"I will ring if we require anything further," Beatty told her.

He smiled as the door closed gently behind Mrs. Grice. The girl was standing by the fireplace, looking down into the flames. She turned as he came up. They acted instinctively, almost automatically, as though controlled by forces and desires beyond themselves. Shaking, profoundly moved, hardly aware of their actions, the couple dissolved into one another's arms. Lips met lips in a blind instinctive reflex. The two, reechoed in the oval mirror, remained crushed together in a long passionate embrace.

27

THE SHOT TOWER

THE atmosphere was becoming thicker. Beatty looked impatiently at his watch. It still wanted twenty minutes to eight, and there was no guarantee that the man would come. But Beatty's carefully worded letter was calculated to bring him. He felt assured of that. If Beardsley were what he suspected him to be—and his conduct in the grounds of Brookwood left no doubt of that—then he must come, if only to secure his own safety.

Beatty glanced around the bleak scene on the South Bank. Already, the outlines of the Shot Tower and the icy Thames beyond were beginning to waver and disappear, though Beatty had stationed himself behind a pile of timber only a hundred feet away.

Beatty had chosen his ground carefully. Contractors were busy with construction work here. In addition to the heaped lumber there were trenches dug; cranes and other machinery. It was an ideal site for the business the young investigator had on hand. He had noticed it some weeks before, and it had come back to him when framing his note to the cemetery Under-Foreman.

He had probably stepped up into the late James Varley's shoes by now, Beatty thought to himself wryly. The beat of horses' hooves and the shuffle of feet came from the roadway beyond. Many labouring people and others were coming home from work, while travellers would be crossing the bridge on their way to the station. A bitter chill came from the river at Beatty's back and he huddled deeper into the thick ulster.

The pistol butt made a gentle pressure inside the pocket of the coat. He had removed it from the holster this time, in case it were needed in a hurry. He had not forgotten the expression on Couchman's face during their encounter on Blackfriars Bridge. Beatty went back again in his mind over the possible sequence of events for this evening. He thought he had covered every eventuality.

He had asked Beardsley to meet him on waste ground some way in front of the Shot Tower, well back from the road which skirted the South Bank but equidistant from the Tower itself. Beatty would have preferred a meeting at the base of the Tower, but, as its name implied, it was in use for the manufacture of shot and lay within private land.

This was the best they could do, and the timber-stack had remained a perfect vantage point to overlook the waste until the onset of the mist. Beatty clicked his tongue in annoyance. He would soon have to move forward from his place of concealment if he were to see when his quarry came to hand. Dotterell was stationed farther down the bank of the Thames, near a roast-chestnut stall on the roadway, an inconspicuous loiterer ready to spring into action on three blasts of the whistle which reposed in Beatty's left-hand coat pocket. He would cut off Beardsley's retreat toward the bridge.

Of course, the man might not be alone; Beatty had not overlooked that. If he had confided in his employers, then they would in turn use him to flush Beatty from his hiding place. Dotterell was an unknown card in this game and might be used to trump any move of their opponents. Beatty consulted his watch again. If the mist had come half an hour later it would have sufficed.

As it was, he would have to move his position within the next ten minutes, if he were not to lose sight of the waste ground altogether. A rough triangle of tangled grassland and stunted blackberry bushes, it was bounded by a wilderness of old huts and contractors' sheds. Ideal for their proposed meeting in clear weather. Beatty wondered if Dotterell were moving down toward him. The whistle would be more difficult to hear in the all-enveloping fog they would shortly be experiencing.

If Beardsley had taken an evening train, there was one which got into Waterloo-road at seven o'clock. This would mean that he could arrive at the meeting place just before eight. Unless he played Beatty's game and hung back while he reconnoitred the land. But the slowly growing mist which had complicated Beatty's plan would also undo Beardsley and any confederates he might have with him, for he would have to go almost to the foot of the Shot Tower because of the worsening visibility.

These speculations were worth very little, Beatty confessed to himself; Beardsley might well have caught a morning train, when he could have inspected the site at his leisure and made any suitable dispositions with his fellow-conspirators. If he were acting alone, then he would follow the procedure outlined in Beatty's note. Beatty shrugged. It was pointless to worry about it further; the next few minutes would decide the matter, one way or the other.

He crept along the base of the timber-stack and moved over cautiously behind a shed whose crazy frame and sagging roof seemed about to topple into nothingness at any moment. A dark shape caught his eye. It flickered across the toe of his boot. Beatty gave an exclamation of disgust, and the great rat, thickly encrusted with black mud from the sewer-pipes and bearing a foul stench with it, jumped on to a heap of tarpaulins and disappeared from view.

Beatty moved behind the sheds and worked his way up toward the road. The mist was a little less thick here, and he could now see the shapes of pedestrians materialising and then disappearing again as they passed along the roadway beyond. Dotterell most certainly would have moved by now. It was five to eight and Beatty would have to take a chance.

He worked back, stepped over a low fence enclosing contractor's material, and got on to the pavement. He went down in the direction in which Dotterell would have been stationed, then turned and slowly retraced his steps. From his new position Beatty could just see to the opposite pavement. A confused rumbling was growing in the mist, farther back toward the bridge.

Beatty stopped near the low wooden picket fence over which he had just stepped. A tall, familiar figure was standing on the edge of the kerb facing him, ready to cross the road toward the Shot Tower. Despite the moleskin cap and the rough pea-jacket, there was no mistaking the erect carriage, the bearded features, and the distinctive scar belonging to Abraham Beardsley.

Beatty felt a tingle of excitement as he looked at Beardsley and glanced casually away. The man had not seen him; indeed, Beatty was only one figure among a number passing and repassing this portion of roadway. But the gas-lamps on the opposite pavement were shining direct on to Beardsley's face, and the private investigator had a clear view.

Beatty's instincts had not served him wrong; here was his man and in a few minutes' time he would know a great deal more about what was going on within the high walls of Brookwood Cemetery. He moved casually away, his fingers on the butt of his revolver. The rumble of wheels had increased now, and a large pantechnicon loomed from the mist, coming from the direction of Waterloo.

Beardsley had stepped out into the roadway. He waited for the pantechnicon to pass, looking this way and that, as though seeking Beatty. The investigator shrank back, aware of the echo of iron-shod wheels which reverberated in the narrow street and which were thrown back by the wall of mist. Beardsley was cut off now by the passing vehicles; they formed a line, Beatty saw, coming up behind the first.

There was a boiling confusion of sound; Beatty heard screams and running feet. Against the whiteness of the mist a silhouette passed in the opposite direction; a brewer's dray loaded with casks, the horses plunging and tossing, being driven like a madman by a figure standing up between the shafts.

Then the vision cut off, as a carter's wagon laden with timber took the foreground. Beatty swore. He pulled out the whistle and gave three urgent blasts, which cut through the swathes of fog. He was already running to the edge of the pavement, waiting impatiently for the last of the vans to pass.

A murmuring cry, composed of many voices, rose in the narrow street. A woman's scream mingled with exclamations of horror. The mist cleared as Beatty crossed into the centre of the street; he elbowed his way through the great crowd of people. He took in swiftly the dray tumbled and askew on the pavement; the police-man quieting the terrified horses; the broken barrels scattered about the road; the stench of ale, sharp and sour in the evening air.

Abraham Beardsley lay, a crushed wreck of a man on the ground where the iron-shod wheels had flung him; one set had passed across his back, breaking the spine; the other had mangled the legs. He must have died instantly. Beatty turned away sick at heart as Dotterell came hopping and staggering from the murk.

Beatty's assistant had never looked more dour. His clothing was dirty and awry and his lips twisted with pain. Beatty helped him back to the opposite pavement. Dotterell's eyes glittered as he looked at his employer.

"I beg your pardon, Mr. Beatty," he said between clenched teeth. "He gave me the slip."

Beatty was so absorbed in the ruin of his plans that he had not looked closely at his assistant; now he gave a hissing cry of sympathy as he took in Dotterell's state. He led him round the barrier and seated him on an adjacent pile of timber. The patter of footsteps went on as more passers-by rushed to the scene of the accident.

"I was just moving up when I heard your whistle," Dotterell went on with difficulty. "There was an almighty crash and then this fellow came hurrying out of the fog."

He looked at Beatty grimly.

"I recognised him at once. The limping man from the lake at Brookwood."

Beatty stared at Dotterell, astonished; his mind was a whirling conflict of thoughts.

"A calm, smiling devil," Dotterell went on. "I closed with him, but he was too quick for me. He caught me across the legs with a leaded cane. I went down, and when I picked myself up he had disappeared into the mist."

"Don't blame yourself," Beatty said.

He had quite recovered his old manner now.

"We are up against some fiendishly clever people. We must get you to a doctor."

Dotterell shook his head.

"It is nothing. Just bruising, but I must rest for a minute or two. I shall be as right as ninepence in the morning. What was the accident?"

Beatty shook his head.

"That was no accident. Our limping friend was undoubtedly driving the dray which has just crushed Beardsley to death. He was certainly followed from Surrey. And just as certainly, I was within a few minutes of learning something more of this bizarre affair. And would have, had not Beardsley been struck down."

Dotterell nodded, his hand massaging his shin.

"Someone could not risk that," he said. "Beardsley must have been watched."

"I am inclined to agree," Beatty said, getting up from the wood-pile and stretching his legs. He glanced over toward the roadway where, beyond the curtain of mist, the crowd was swelling. Two more police officers were pushing their way through.

"The man who passed on the note may have talked. In which case Toby Stevens may be in danger."

He pulled at his ear.

"Though I do not think they will try anything else at Woking for the moment. But an accident in London is a different matter. It happens every day."

He turned back to Dotterell.

"Forgive me, my dear fellow. Here I am in full spate while you are in pain. Wait here while I look for a cab."

"Where does this leave us, Mr. Beatty?" Dotterell asked.

"It appears to be checkmate for the moment," said Beatty. "We could make enquiries for our limping man. But lame characters are not so unusual in London as they would be in a small country town. I fear we shall not get much further there. But we still have Superintendent Bateman. Inspector Munson may try a little gentle pressure, without giving anything away. And, so far as we know, Bateman has not yet heard anything about the two post-mortem results."

He turned to Dotterell.

"There is much to do still, and it is something, after all, to be pitted against such skilled opponents. I will be back in a few minutes, and then we must return to Holborn to formulate fresh plans."

28

IN THE VAULTS

ANGELA MEREDITH smiled. She put her hand gently on Clyde Beatty's arm as he paid off the cab and turned back to her. It was a morning of brilliant sunshine, though still bitingly cold. They walked briskly up the steps to the opulent façade of the City and Suburban Bank. They were evidently expected, because an elderly clerk in sombre black quickly came forward to take Beatty's card, and they were ushered up the staircase to Sir Inigo Walton's private quarters.

A middle-aged man with a bald head and yellow features came out of an office in the first-floor corridor and looked at them sharply. Immaculately dressed in striped trousers and frock-coat, he came toward them, while Miss Meredith made the introduction.

"This is Mr. Connors, one of the Bank directors. Mr. Clyde Beatty has an appointment with Sir Inigo."

Connors shook hands affably with them both and dismissed the clerk.

"Yes, Sir Inigo told me about it. I hope you will be able to assist us, Mr. Beatty. This is a bad business concerning the robberies."

He leaned forward to Beatty confidentially.

"It undermines public confidence in banking altogether, you know."

Beatty nodded. He was studying Connors carefully as they

talked, and his wide brown eyes were taking in the features of the corridor as they walked down it to Connors's office.

"Sir Inigo is at a meeting just now, but he requested me to receive Mr. Beatty," the director told the girl. "My office is here. You will be able to make yourselves comfortable for half an hour or so."

He shot a quick glance at Beatty.

"And I have the necessary papers ready for you to study. Sir Inigo has asked me to give you all the assistance within my power."

"That is very good of him," Beatty drawled.

There was a flicker of amusement in Angela Meredith's eyes as she looked at her companion.

"Mr. Connors is in charge of the Bank's security arrangements," she explained.

They had arrived at Connors's office now, and he opened the door, ushering them forward to the fireplace in the small panelled room which was opulently furnished. Beatty and the girl sank into the big leather armchairs set in front of the rosewood desk while Connors went round to sit at his swivel chair.

"Would you like some refreshment before we begin?" he asked.

Beatty looked at the girl and then across at the Bank director.

"Later, perhaps," he said shortly. "I am anxious to make a start."

"Certainly, certainly, Mr. Beatty."

Connors was shuffling papers he took from a leather folder. "I understood from Miss Meredith that you were brisk and efficient, but I did not realise it meant neglecting the inner man."

He smiled pleasantly at them both.

"As for myself, if I forgo my midmorning chocolate it quite puts out my whole day."

Beatty repressed an inward smile and turned instead to the material Connors had slid across the desk. The latter had uncovered a tray on his blotter and was pouring the drinking chocolate from a hand-painted glazed pot.

"If you'll forgive me, then," he said diffidently, raising the white china cup to his lips. Beatty was already absorbed in the handwritten documents before him. He was making notes on a jotting pad on his knee.

"I see you have deliveries at the same times every week," he said. "That should be changed. There is nothing like fixed routine to attract the attention of thieves."

Connors looked startled; a faint flush started to his cheeks.

"If you think it necessary," he began diplomatically. "But I believe the current crimes concentrate on bullion stored in vaults. And they have all been overnight raids so far, mostly at weekends."

"That is no reason to assume these people will not change their tactics," Beatty returned imperturbably. "If Sir Inigo is to retain my services, then I shall require carte blanche."

"Certainly, certainly," said Connors, a startled expression on his face.

He reached for a silver pencil on the desk in front of him. His eyes sought reassurance from Miss Meredith, found none. He began to scribble furiously on a sheet of paper as Beatty started to pick up other points. The girl watched with ironic amusement. She was enormously impressed with Beatty's manner and expertise; he was on his own, familiar ground now.

It was the first time she had really seen him at work on a problem, and it fascinated her to note the effortless way in which he exposed the weaknesses in the Bank's present security system.

She began to realise for the first time how hollow Connors's own pretensions were. It was obvious, as the question and answer procedure continued, that he was quite unfitted to be in charge of Bank security. But Beatty was far too tactful ever to make him aware of the fact.

Angela Meredith turned her gaze out through the windows to the façades of the buildings opposite and left the two men to their devices. Her mind was pleasantly engaged. Today she wore a pale blue tailored suit, and her eyes reflected the colour scheme in a most fetching manner. Certainly, the effect of the ensemble had not been lost on Beatty. She was aware that his eyes were turned ever and again to her whenever he felt that her attention was directed elsewhere. She sat in a halo of gold from the sun-shimmer at the window, and the watch she wore pinned to the breast of her jacket looked like a pool of molten metal as she moved in the chair.

The door opened abruptly and Sir Inigo Walton marched in. His face wore a worried frown, but his pink features brightened as soon as he caught sight of the girl. He came forward and took both her hands in his own. His iron-grey hair was turned briefly to gold by the sunlight as he moved toward Beatty, who had risen from his chair.

"I have heard much about you from this young lady, Mr. Beatty," he said in clipped tones. "The reality would be hard to live up to."

Beatty smiled, his hand clasped in a crushing grip. Despite his age Sir Inigo was a formidable figure, with the strength of a bull in his erect frame. The hard eyes below the grizzled brows were assessing the young man shrewdly as they all resumed their seats.

"The reality is not exaggerated," said Connors drily. "Mr. Beatty here has just been showing me where our security arrangements are fifty years out of date."

"Oh, come," protested Beatty. "If I am to be of use there is no sense in being anything else but thorough."

Connors shook his head with a wry smile. He pushed his notes across the desk to Sir Inigo.

"My remarks were meant as a compliment, Mr. Beatty. I am most impressed."

"Excellent," Sir Inigo broke in, looking sharply from the girl to Beatty.

He studied the notes in silence for a moment, his brows knotted in concentration. Then he looked up, stabbing a great forefinger at the young investigator.

"This is really first-rate, Mr. Beatty. You have pin-pointed the weaknesses I have had in mind for some time. Have you yet seen the layout of the vaults?"

Beatty shook his head.

"We were just about to go down."

"We may as well all go together," Connors said, standing up behind his desk.

"We have not yet discussed your fees, Mr. Beatty," Sir Inigo said, taking the other's arm. "You will not find us ungenerous."

"I have a standard rate, Sir Inigo," Beatty said crisply. "I will see that my assistant sends your accountant the normal reckoning in due course."

"As you wish," said Sir Inigo, inclining his iron-grey head and standing back to allow Miss Meredith to precede him.

"And now, we will just see where the City and Suburban has gone wrong in protecting the interests of its depositors."

Connors had stayed behind to arrange some papers on his desk. He gave a worried smile and hurried after the others.

Beatty tapped the masonry with a heavy wooden ruler and gave a small exclamation of satisfaction. He gazed round the vault with its heavy steel door, noting its salient features; from time to time he made jottings in his notebook. Sir Inigo and the others stood in a semicircle and watched him in silence.

"The general arrangements seem excellent," said Beatty at length. "However, there are some points which leave a good deal to be desired."

Sir Inigo frowned.

"Standard strong-boxes, my dear sir," he said disarmingly. "Chubb locks and safes of regulation pattern. Limited editions of the main vault keys. Myself, two other directors, the chief cashier . . ."

"I am not criticising that," Beatty interrupted. "If you will just step out into the corridor yonder I will show you what I mean."

Angela Meredith gave a fleeting smile as she passed Beatty. Once again he was aware of the heady perfume of her presence. The others followed him along the corridor and up the steps. The chief cashier, a middle-aged, nervous-looking man named Standish, swung the main vault door to and stood by it. Beatty paused at the head of the steps.

He indicated a small half-moon window of frosted glass, only about eighteen inches high. It was protected by stout iron bars, set into the masonry.

"Where does this lead?"

Connors frowned.

"It gives on to a small alley."

"Exactly," Beatty said.

He was consulting the plan now, following the angles of the building with a blunt forefinger.

"Thieves could work here all night undisturbed."

"But it seems quite secure to me," Sir Inigo protested.

Beatty shook his head.

"Not to the modern screwsman, Sir Inigo. The gang who are

currently breaking City banks with apparent impunity are highly skilled professionals."

He looked thoughtfully at the frosted glass.

"Any competent burglar would cut through that glass in less than fifteen seconds. They use a knife, as star-glaziers do."

"What then?" said Connors.

There was a sceptical edge to his voice, but he could not meet Beatty's eye. The young man smiled.

"Those bars look strong enough, do they not? Yet they can be breached in an astonishingly short time. A jack would soon force them apart. Once started, they can usually be freed from the stonework."

"A jack?"

Sir Inigo's military-looking features wore a baffled expression.

"A special tool developed by cracksmen," Beatty explained. "The jack is placed between the bars, and they are forced apart by a worm worked by a small crank-handle in the middle. Nothing in such a window as the one before us can withstand the pressure."

"But it is such a tiny window," Sir Inigo expostulated. Beatty's face looked resigned.

"I see I have still not made myself clear, gentlemen. The brick wall can be taken apart and sufficient opening made in less than an hour. The wall there is above ground. Or a child could squeeze through the bars and open a door for others to enter."

Sir Inigo pulled at his moustache with thick spatulate fingers.

"You know your business all right, Mr. Beatty," he conceded. "What would you suggest?"

"A grille of hardened steel over that window, together with a strengthening of the brickwork," Beatty said, making another note. Connors smiled.

"They would still have to get into the vaults. They are Chubb locks."

"Chubbs are first-rate," Beatty agreed. "The patent locks cannot be picked, and they are drill-proofed, so impossible to pierce. But there are ways, though I cannot go into details now."

"Well, you had better draw up a schedule of precautions and we will go over them," Sir Inigo said resignedly. "Half an hour with you, sir, is quite an education."

He chuckled heartily and looked at Angela Meredith with mischievous eyes.

"Let us just hope that the alterations will not prove too expensive," Connors put in.

"Better that than lose a fortune in bar-gold," said Beatty.

Sir Inigo coughed. He looked at Connors sharply.

"Quite so, quite so."

He crossed over toward the girl.

"If there is anything else you require, Connors and my chief clerk will be glad to oblige. I really should be getting back up to my office."

"Before you go, Sir Inigo . . ." said Beatty.

The Bank chairman turned, one foot already on the stair.

"Miss Meredith mentioned the other day that Dr. Couchman, who has a connection with this bank, had attended her father. I wondered if that would be the same Dr. Couchman who had a practice in Surrey. He attended my aunt some years ago and was well thought of there."

"He is well thought of here," Sir Inigo smiled. "Though I must confess I do not know him very well myself. He formerly had a practice in London and in fact is the official doctor to the City and Suburban. He runs the rule over the staff and that sort of thing. The connection arose through Connors here. He would be able to tell you if it were the same man."

He nodded affably and was about to withdraw when there came the rapid beat of footsteps on the stair. A top-hatted messenger came down toward them.

"What's this, Peters?" said Sir Inigo sharply. "You know very well the messenger staff are not allowed down here."

"I'm extremely sorry, Sir Inigo," said the man worriedly. "But it's Inspector Bull of Scotland Yard. When I told him you were in the vaults he insisted on coming below here at once."

"Very well, Peters," Sir Inigo said, relaxing his features and dismissing the messenger.

"Just ask him to step down."

He nodded at Beatty.

"As you and he are both engaged on the same business—bank security—it would be as well if you liaised together."

"I know the Inspector well," Beatty told him. "We have had some dealings in the past."

As he finished speaking, heavy footsteps clattered on the steps and the hard weather-beaten face and deep-set green eyes of Inspector Bull appeared at the top of the short flight that led to the vault corridor. He wore a grim expression, and his overcoat was thrown over his arm as though he had arrived in a hurry. The dishevelled appearance of the usually immaculate Inspector had not escaped Beatty.

"I am sorry to intrude in such a precipitate manner," the Scotland Yard man began. "But it is a matter of the utmost urgency."

"Come along down, Inspector," said Sir Inigo. "I believe you know everybody present. This is Mr. Clyde Beatty, who is acting for us in our security arrangements, following our little chat the other day."

The Inspector's expression relaxed slightly. He descended the remaining flight rapidly and shook Beatty's hand warmly.

"We have collaborated previously to our mutual advantage, Sir Inigo. But I have bad news, I'm afraid. There was another raid last night. A big one, not a mile from here."

A deep silence fell in the stuffy atmosphere of the vault. Beatty's sharp eyes were rivetted on the Inspector's face. As though conscious of his appearance, he set down his briefcase and started putting his coat on. Sir Inigo's mouth was fixed in a firm straight line.

"How much?"

The Scotland Yard man shrugged.

"There is no secret. It will all be in this evening's papers. A total of £300,000 in bar-gold from the vaults of the Drovers Bank of Scotland. I thought it best to come to warn you straightaway."

"You have not apprehended the culprits?" Beatty queried.

The Inspector gloomily shook his head.

"I don't mind admitting in this company that we're up against a stone wall. No one saw anything suspicious. It was dead of night, of course, and the City is always deserted after eight P.M."

The Inspector paced up and down the vault corridor as though absorbed with his own thoughts.

"The weight alone should have meant something," he murmured. "This would need heavy vehicles and men for loading."

He turned to Beatty.

"I am delighted that you are on hand to advise Sir Inigo."

"I have already prepared a list of recommendations if you would care to run your eye over them," Beatty told him.

He passed his copy to Inspector Bull, who studied it with care. He grunted and handed it back.

"Capital. I could not have done it better myself. You are in good hands, Sir Inigo."

"What time was this latest theft discovered?" Beatty asked.

"At eight o'clock this morning. The felons had entered by forcing insecure bars on a fanlight."

Beatty exchanged a long ironical glance with Sir Inigo. Connors shifted his feet awkwardly. The girl's blue eyes never left Beatty's face.

"Well, I must get back to the Yard," Bull said crisply.

He gave Beatty a conspiratorial look, as though conscious of the other's thoughts.

"There are a great many more banks which need skilled advice on security, I am afraid."

Sir Inigo coughed discreetly and nodded at Standish, who started to close and lock the great vault door. He led the way back upstairs, the others following in single file. Beatty smiled, putting the sheets of his report in his pocket. He and the girl were the last to quit the corridor. She put her hand on his arm and drew him aside. Her blue eyes searched his face.

"Is there some quiet place where we could talk?"

"We could have lunch together," Beatty said smoothly.

He looked quickly back over his shoulder, but Standish was bent to the vault door, checking the locks. The girl's lips fleetingly brushed the young man's cheek. Beatty had his arm round her shoulders as they went slowly up the stairs.

29

MCMURDO AGAIN

IT was very quiet in the workshop. The only sound was the faint noise made by a bunsen burner, whose bluish flame illuminated one end of the bench; and Dotterell's pen racing squeakily over the paper. Beatty got up wearily from the desk and went over to the fire at their end of the room and poked it into brighter flame. He glanced down into the office below but nothing stirred; a faint mist billowed outside the windows in the Holborn court. It was dusk and the gas-lamps had been lit, sending a feeble yellow light through the murk.

Dotterell stopped writing and looked at his employer with his piercing blue eyes. He sat easily and patiently, waiting for Beatty to continue his spoken thoughts. Beatty showed no sign of doing that so he finally broke the silence.

"So we are not at a standstill?"

Beatty shook his head and turned back to the desk.

"By no means," he said crisply. "I have a number of enquiries afoot. And Inspector Munson's letter confirms my earlier opinion of his abilities and discretion."

He went back to sit down next to Dotterell and smoothed the sheets of blue writing paper he had received from the Surrey detective that morning. He went through it again, swiftly, tracing the paragraphs with his forefinger, searching for the relevant passage.

"Ah, here we are. He has made further investigations regarding Superintendent Bateman. Nothing conclusive has emerged. But he adds that he himself would personally vouch for the man's integrity. I find that significant."

Dotterell crossed a *t* in his report with a flourish.

"How so?"

"It merely reinforces my earlier impressions," Beatty returned. "As you may recall I have already commented that a great many things could be going on at Brookwood without Bateman necessarily being aware of them. And remember, he has a staff of over sixty people under his control. How have your own enquiries in the East End been going?"

Dotterell frowned and shifted his weight in his chair.

"Nothing definite, unfortunately. I have made some contacts in the underworld. There are three limping men who might be possibles. But it takes time . . ."

"Well, well," said Beatty imperturbably. "Time is one thing we have plenty of. But it is certain that we cannot return to Brookwood at present without revealing our hand."

He got up again and resumed his pacing about the silent workshop.

"There is a damnable secret behind that door. But if whoever is directing this business knows that I am still alive, then we have lost the element of surprise."

He went to stand looking down moodily into the consulting room.

"In the meantime I must prepare the material for Sir Inigo's security arrangements. These private banks are damnably slack in that direction."

Dotterell nodded.

"I can have the first draft ready later this evening. Best copperplate, of course. What do you make of these robberies?"

Beatty turned to face his assistant and gave a slow smile.

"A very smart operation. But there are a few points of interest which I fancy Scotland Yard may have overlooked."

He sat down at the desk again and pulled across a map he had been annotating earlier that afternoon. He placed it in front of Dotterell so that he could examine it. Dotterell studied it in silence, his shaggy eyebrows drawn down over his eyes.

"You will notice that every bank involved—I have circled the four there—is in the City. That means the thieves were able to strike at night with the double certainty of deserted streets and premises. All the banks were private concerns. I have discovered from Inspector Bull that in each case their security arrangements were lax."

Dotterell raised his head from the map and stared at him.

"I understood Inspector Bull was in process of gingering them up."

Beatty smiled.

"It all takes time, Dotterell. If you had been at the City and Suburban today . . ."

He broke off and resumed his earlier musings.

"However, the most striking thing from my point of view was that the methods coincided; bar-gold was involved each time; and the banks were within a radius of one mile, spaced out like the spokes of a wheel."

His brown eyes were dancing with animation, and Dotterell looked at Beatty curiously.

"They would need transport," he began. "Bar-gold is extremely heavy to convey. And yet no one has noticed anything unusual . . ."

"Exactly," Beatty broke in. He was no longer able to keep the excitement out of his voice. He leaned forward and tapped the map in front of his assistant.

"Something like a brewer's dray, perhaps? There are many breweries and public houses in the vicinity. The stolen bullion might be hidden among the barrels."

"With the thieves dressed as draymen," Dotterell put in.

His lugubrious features were animated now, as he followed and began to anticipate Beatty's drift.

"We are running on somewhat," Beatty said. "But I am convinced there is something in my line of reasoning."

He bent to the map again.

"Supposing there were a depot here? Somewhere unsuspected, where the bullion was cached until the hue and cry had died down."

Dotterell let out his breath in a hissing sigh. He put a massive finger on the map.

"In the centre here? At the hub of the wheel?"

Beatty stood up.

"It's worth a try. Would that the Brookwood Cemetery business were as readily explainable."

Dotterell smiled wryly.

"It is the difference between town and country," he observed. "Give me bricks and mortar every time."

He broke off and examined his engagement pad.

"You have not forgotten my message about Dr. Rossington?"

Beatty shook his head.

"I am engaged to dine with him tomorrow evening."

He crossed the room and picked up his top-coat, which had been thrown carelessly across a chair.

"In the meantime I think a long walk through the quiet byeways of the City of London is indicated."

Beatty stopped aimlessly by a corner beneath a gas-lamp and steadied himself with a hand against the wall. With his tie pushed awry and his dishevelled clothing, he looked much like any inebriated loafer. A raucous noise came from a gin-shop behind him, and the garish lights of its windows threw a dappled pattern across the mean street.

The young investigator pretended to gather his fuddled wits, but in reality he was searching the façade of the buildings opposite; examining the details of the street; storing information in his memory. He had already reconnoitred three of the banks on the list in his pocket. He was working through the City in ever-narrowing circles.

He waved away two young prostitutes who came enquiringly toward him; one of them could not have been more than fourteen years old. He shivered slightly as they passed on toward the entrance of the gin-shop. He contrasted their lot with that of Miss Angela Meredith. His expression softened a little as her image again flickered into his mind. She was inextricably entangled now with the incidents of Brookwood and, latterly, with the security problems of the City and Suburban Bank.

Beatty swayed convincingly and pushed away from the wall. He set off at a tottering stoop, entering a squalid court, checking the fading signs of the streets and alleys by the flickering uncertain light of the gas-lamps; making an apparently haphazard course through the meandering ways between the tall buildings, but in reality keeping to a carefully predetermined course.

He pulled his coat more tightly about him; though the wind had dropped after dusk, the cold had again descended like a blanket and there was a raw edge to it tonight, as though there were snow somewhere about. Beatty prayed that it would not snow. If it did it might lie for months, and that would put an end to investigations at Brookwood and even to such enquiries as he had undertaken this evening.

He walked on, leaving the lighted area behind, and plunged into a maze of foetid courts and alleys; rubbish and decaying matter was lying inches deep here. There was no one about, and Beatty temporarily abandoned his role of drunkard and walked carefully, giving emphasis to where he placed his feet. He went into a long tunnel, on the walls of which frost sparkled faintly, indicating that in milder weather the stone would weep water.

A brazier glowed toward the end of it; an old woman in rags sat with the ruddy light beating on her face, her shrivelled hands held out to the warmth. She mutely proffered a bag of roasted chestnuts as Beatty came up, the hopelessness of her supplication showing in her eyes. Moved by an obscure impulse of pity, Beatty searched his pockets; he took the bag and quickly dropped the guinea into the woman's outstretched palm, hurrying on before she could realise her good fortune or thank him.

A child was sitting on a heap of sacking two streets farther on, shawl tightly tied about her. Beatty put the chestnuts in her lap before the girl could turn and quickly gained the corner. He wondered idly why the old woman would sell her wares in such a deserted spot. Perhaps because she was too old and feeble to drag herself into a more populated area?

Beatty never ceased to wonder at the strange ways of London's poor; he pitied them with all his heart and tried to alleviate their lot in his own small way whenever possible. He had a deep understanding of the roots of crime; it was only the incorrigible professional criminal he hated; the brutal, the depraved, the corrupter of children.

He sauntered on now, at a more leisurely pace, consulting the street map and the rough sketch plan he carried, when he was certain that no one was near to observe him. For some little while he had been aware of the faint echo of horses' hooves on the setts and the occasional rumble of vehicles passing in the distance. Beatty now came out of a side-road on to a main thoroughfare and followed it in an easterly direction.

A hearse drawn by two black horses in single file, and with nod-ding plumes, passed the end of the street as he gained it. Beatty paused, his eyes searching the gaslit area ahead. A child-mute in black crêpe followed, treading carefully behind the hearse, avoid-ing the places where ice starred the pavement. More muffled hoof-beats sounded. Beatty let the vehicle get ahead of him and followed at a cautious distance.

The road led to a large square backed by tall buildings; some-where near the rumble of a train sounded along the embankment, the hiss of steam and the beat of pistons startlingly clear in the crisp air. Other hoof-beats, other vehicles, were converging on the square. Sparks from the passing engine danced in the night sky, and the houses trembled as the train of carriages straddled the rooftops of the next street.

Beatty stood in an entry of dark shadow and waited. Another hearse and then a third converged like ghostly messengers of woe; the horses snorted and steam from their nostrils reeked beneath the yellow gaslight. They were making for a large and imposing entrance, flanked by high brick pillars. The tall wooden gates were drawn back on either side, and from within the high-walled yard came a bustle of activity.

The approaching vehicles halted for a moment to allow a loaded hearse to pass out the gates and then got in file to process inside. Beatty hung back, his mind heavy with thought; the hearse which had just emerged came toward him, the driver heavily muffled on the box. The huge oak coffin, clearly visible through the glass sides, was banked with artificial flowers. The noise of the vehicle's progress died out along the street.

Beatty waited until the yard entrance was clear and then moved off round the northern perimeter of the square, taking a wide circle which would bring him back up toward the undertaker's establishment. He paused again as there came the noise of hurry-ing footsteps along the far pavement.

There was an imposing brick building next to the yard, whose windows were brightly lit. There was something about it which roused a chord in Beatty's memory. He walked slowly along the edge of the square, making for the entrance to a small court. Once in the shadow of its mouth he paused. The footsteps were nearer now. There was an uneven quality in them which arrested Beatty's attention.

The slightest pause and then a faint slithering noise before the insistent beat of the second foot. Beatty did a strange thing. He did not quite know why. He opened up the front of his coat and eased out his pistol. He transferred it to his overcoat pocket and stood in the entry with his hand on the butt.

The walker on the far pavement had momentarily halted. Then he moved on again. From his new position Beatty could not see the yard entrance direct but only the high brick wall leading to it. On that wall, thrown there by the gaslight, a monstrous shadow crawled.

It flickered forward and presently disappeared, presumably within the yard entrance. So far as Beatty could make out, its owner was a tall, thin man with a distinctive limp. There was a grim smile on Beatty's face as he waited for the echo of the foot-steps to die away.

Then he walked quietly round the edge of the square and back down toward the yard gates. He paused, looking briefly in the entry, but there was nothing except vague shadows, lamp-light, and the hint of stabling and warehouses. Beatty drew near to the lights of the establishment adjoining the yard. He took in the well-cleaned bow-windows, the printed cards, and the flowers.

He stepped back and looked up at the façade. The gaslight shimmered gently on the gold-script lettering: McMURDO AND COMPANY: FUNERAL FURNISHINGS—CENTRAL DEPOT.

30

DANGER IN THE FOG

BEATTY straightened his tie, brushed his clothes, and assumed an alert posture. He was quite transformed from the indolent loafer of a few minutes before when he entered the Central Depot prem-ises of McMurdo and Company. A bell jangled somewhere in the depths of the long room, and a deep-toned clock on a wall-bracket behind the mahogany counter proclaimed that the time was just approaching seven o'clock.

It was quiet in here after the bustle of the yard outside, and Beatty waited patiently, assuming the crushed, defeated air of a man in mourning. He studied the banked wreaths heaped against the counter, swiftly reading the cards. A sickly perfume of flowers filled the air. Beatty saw there were three massive oak coffins on trestles beyond the counter. They had silver handles and silver nameplates.

He looked again at the wreaths and cards. These were obviously funerals of well-placed people, judging by the expensive coffins. And the flowers must have been grown under glass, artificially heated. Beatty bent again and studied the inscriptions on the cards attached to the wreaths more closely. All appeared to have been written by the same hand.

He straightened up as a door opened somewhere in the rear. Soft footfalls approached, and a tall, bald man with a yellow face and sandy eyebrows came gliding down the room. He wore an expression of mingled sympathy and business acumen. Beatty had his story prepared now; he took his cue from the name on the wreaths. The tall man inclined his head. He looked at Beatty with sharp brown eyes.

"Can I help you, sir?"

There was just the right mixture of deference and superiority in his manner. Beatty affected to be ill at ease. He focused his gaze up behind the tall man's shoulder.

"I would really like to see the manager?" he began hesitantly.

The tall man screwed up his face as though the dim gaslight were hurting his eyes.

"I am the manager, sir. Alasdair Vair. Or perhaps you require Mr. McMurdo, the managing director. He does not see anyone without an appointment."

"I would not wish to trouble him," said Beatty earnestly. "I required some information on the funeral arrangements. For Mr. Vickers . . ."

A startling change had come across the bald man's yellow face. He licked his lips and appeared taken aback.

"That is not really within my purview, sir," he began.

"I thought you said you were the manager," Beatty said mildly.

He glanced over toward the coffins and the banked wreaths.

"And I see you have everything in hand. All I require to know is the time of the service and the place of interment. My family and I intend to be present, you see."

The manager's eyes half closed as though Beatty had struck him a physical blow.

"You knew Mr. Vickers, sir?"

"Of course. I should not be enquiring otherwise."

The bald man coughed. He was obviously off balance.

"Quite so. The services will be at Brookwood in Surrey to-morrow."

Beatty turned to look at the coffins. His heart gave a great leap and a number of questions were hovering on his lips. But he controlled his excitement, merely clicking his teeth in annoyance.

"Oh, dear. I did not realise it would be out of town. The eleven o'clock from Waterloo-road, I suppose?"

The manager nodded.

"Yes, sir. All these will be leaving by the same train."

Beatty stared at the coffins again.

"You do seem rather busy," he said sympathetically.

He sighed.

"There are so many deaths at the moment. The hard winter, I suppose?"

The manager inclined his head again.

"There has been an influenza epidemic in the capital of late. That is why we are so pressed. But if you will wait a moment I will fetch Mr. McMurdo."

"I thought you said he would see no one without an appointment," Beatty said mildly.

The bald-headed man flushed.

"Mr. Vickers was an important man, sir. Mr. McMurdo would not wish any discourtesy to the mourners. And he has more information on the matter than I have at my disposal. If you will just wait a moment."

He glided away into the back of the building. In the two minutes he was away Beatty had prepared his story. He was certain he was on to something important now. The facts were all before him, but he had to make sense of them. The name on the façade of another building flickered into Beatty's mind. He had passed it half a dozen streets away. A firm, decisive tread sounded in the shop.

"This is Mr. McMurdo, sir."

Vair smiled at Beatty and glided away. McMurdo was enormous. He towered over the young investigator by more than a foot. He was proportionately broad though his strength was running to fat in early middle-age. He was about forty-five but looked older because his black beard was tinged with grey.

His complexion was red and coarse-grained. His hard grey eyes were lost in rolls of fat, and his silver-flecked hair was close-cropped and lay flat against his skull.

His big hands were well-kept, but Beatty noticed that the nails had been broken. He wore a gold ring on his left hand and an ornamental one with a ruby on his right. He was dressed in a discreet dark suit with a grey silk stock, and a gold watch-chain with seals showed across his ample waistcoat. His breath smelled slightly of spirits as he leaned toward Beatty across the counter.

"You were enquiring about Mr. Vickers's funeral, sir?"

The voice was harsh and commanding, with a lowland Scots accent underneath it somewhere.

"Yes, that is correct," Beatty went on, keeping up his part. "He was a friend of my wife's family. But I am a little put out as I understand the arrangements are for Surrey?"

McMurdo's brows corrugated with puzzlement.

"How so? If Mrs. Vickers is a friend . . ."

"That is just the difficulty," Beatty put in quickly. "She has gone away, you see, which is why I have to come here."

McMurdo fought back his anger with an effort. He was a formidable figure in the gloom of the funeral parlour, his big hands tensed slightly on the surface of the counter.

"Mr. Vickers is a widower," he said ponderously. "I think you must be in error, sir."

Beatty shook his head.

"My wife said McCorqudale were carrying out the arrangements, and she asked me to call here this evening particularly."

McMurdo's face cleared. A faint smile appeared at the corners of his mouth.

"We are at cross purposes, sir. You must be referring to another Mr. Vickers. The premises of McCorqudale are about half a mile from here. First turning on the right across the square and keep going."

He waved vaguely out the window.

"This is McMurdo and Company."

Beatty stepped back and put his hand to his mouth in embarrassment.

"I beg your pardon, sir. A foolish mistake on my part. Please forgive me."

He looked again at the row of coffins under the gold of the gaslight.

"It was fortunate you were here, sir. Otherwise my wife and I would have been on train for Surrey in the morning, attending the wrong funeral."

McMurdo gave a dry chuckle.

"Very like, sir. You'd be surprised at some of the strange mix-ups we get in our profession. No harm done. You'll find Mr. Solomon Sanders of the other firm most cooperative."

"Thank you again," Beatty said.

He looked thoughtfully at the coffins and the massed wreaths. Then he turned on his heel and regained the street. He walked slowly across the square in the direction indicated by McMurdo, though he felt more like skipping with excitement. He sensed the big man's eyes still fixed on him through the window. Beatty quitted the square and walked back the way he had come.

He was prudent enough to visit McCorqudale's premises. As he had suspected they were closed and shuttered. He tried the door-handle in a disappointed manner two or three times in case anyone was watching. Then he walked on, circling round to make sure he was not followed. When he was quite certain, he caught a horse-bus which took him back to the West End, his mind engrossed with schemes.

He had a full schedule for Dotterell in the morning. He looked at his watch. It was still early evening. It was imperative that he visit Scotland Yard tonight. They would require a blank warrant. And he would have to warn Munson. Beatty rubbed his hands together as he alighted in the bustle of Piccadilly. He would be riding the Ghost Train for the second time the following morning.

"Will you not have some more coffee, Clyde?" Angela Meredith urged.

Beatty smilingly shook his head. It was almost midnight. The couple were sitting in the drawing room on the first floor of the girl's St. John's Wood house. A cheerful fire burned in the grate, and the low table at which they sat was covered with sheets of paper bearing the young investigator's pencilled notations.

"It is late, Angela," he said, looking at the tall cased clock which gave out a sonorous ticking. "I would not like to compromise you in the eyes of your housekeeper."

Angela Meredith smiled.

"I am already compromised in her eyes, Clyde. One may as well be hung for a sheep as a lamb."

Beatty looked at her curiously.

"It is strange to hear you talking like that," he said.

The girl flushed. Impulsively, she put out her hands to Beatty across the table. He felt their warmth beneath his own fingers.

"I have changed since I knew you," she whispered.

Her eyes looked very blue and very trusting beneath the dark hair. Beatty felt a rising tide of feeling sweeping over him; he fought to keep it in check. He put one hand up and gently ran it along her jawline.

"It is late," he repeated. "And we have not yet completed the report on Sir Inigo's security arrangements."

Angela Meredith gave a small impatient movement of her shoulders.

"It can wait," she said carelessly.

"It is we who should wait, Angela," Beatty said earnestly. "This business is too important for me to rest until I have brought it to a successful conclusion."

He got up and went over to her side. She moved to make room for him on the low sofa. Beatty cradled her in his arms, her hair warm and perfumed against his face. His left hand felt the firmness of her breasts beneath her thin dress. They sat together for what seemed like a long time. Then the girl stirred and pushed herself away. She poured herself another cup of coffee.

"You were extremely mysterious when you arrived, Clyde."

Beatty nodded. He sat back on the sofa and smiled grimly.

"Perhaps I will have that other cup after all, Angela."

He waited until she had poured the hot black coffee before he went on.

"Something happened tonight. Something that may have inadvertently brought all the ends of the affair into my hand. But as yet I cannot see my way clear. Until then I prefer to say nothing of my suspicions."

The girl watched him quietly over the rim of her cup. She made no observation and he continued after a few moments.

"I am back to Surrey on the Brookwood train in the morning. I shall have Scotland Yard officers with me and a blank warrant. Exactly what we shall find there I do not know."

He leaned forward in his excitement, his brown eyes searching her face.

"By tomorrow, Angela, the mystery of your father's death may be made clear to us."

"He has already been avenged," the girl said simply.

Beatty nodded.

"That may well be. But there are greater villains than Couchman yet unpunished."

Angela Meredith's eyes were troubled as they sought Beatty's own.

"Promise you will take great care."

"I shall have assistance at hand on this occasion," he said. "The last time I was alone. There will be danger, assuredly. But it will be minimised."

He tapped his breast pocket significantly and drained his cup.

"I really must go now."

The girl stood up and they walked to the door. She peered through the gap in the window curtains and shivered.

"The fog is as close as ever tonight. You are sure you would not prefer me to send one of the servants out for a cab?"

Beatty shook his head.

"I shall walk until I find something. The exercise will do me good."

He took up his cane with a smile and tapped the silver head.

"And I have a little measure of brandy here to keep out the cold."

Angela Meredith came into his arms; her tongue was boring into his mouth and his hand sought her breasts, was not repulsed. They were like two young animals fiercely locked together. He pushed her gently away in the end. Their mouths were white with the crushing pressure of the embrace; their eyes looked bruised with unspoken thoughts.

"Come back soon," the girl breathed.

She put her hand up unsteadily to her hair.

"We have much to discuss."

Beatty moved to the door.

"Much to discuss," he repeated. "About our future."

He took the girl's fingers and carried them to his mouth.

"I will let myself out."

He ran lightly down the stairs. Outside, he hardly noticed the cold and the encroaching fog.

Beatty walked down the avenue to its intersection with the major road beyond. The fog was thicker now. He could hardly see across to the other side of the street. With the fog had come an even greater cold that seemed to cling greasily to his skin and clothing. Beatty used the cane as a guide, dragging the ferrule along the edge of the kerb so that he could get advance warning of any low-lying obstructions.

The gas-lamps were few and far between here, and he paused at the corner, waiting until his eyes had adjusted to the pallid whiteness that left the hedges and gardens in deep shadow. The sound of horses' hooves came muffled through the billowing vapour. Beatty stepped out briskly toward the sound. The sooner he found a cab and got back to Chelsea the better. He had to be up early that morning. He continued walking south-west toward Maida Vale.

The grating noise of wheels had stopped. Beatty was closer to the source and could see the dark silhouette of a four-wheeler drawn up at the kerb. There were two horses in the shafts. He was about ten yards away when there came the sudden patter of feet. Three dark forms materialised from the fog, converging on Beatty. The attack was well-planned, but Beatty was not entirely unprepared.

Moreover, he was young, fit, and highly skilled at boxing and single-stick. The tall man with the thick club staggered and grunted as Beatty's cane swung round and caught him across the shoulder. Beatty swiftly backed away to face the rush of the other two. The slim man took the ferrule of the cane on his bowler without faltering, while the third, a thick-set fellow with a beaver-skin cap pulled low over his eyes, seized the opportunity to strike.

Beatty absorbed the glancing blow on his left shoulder and immediately turned aside, but the shock and the numbing sensation which followed warned him the odds were heavily against him in this type of fighting.

He sidestepped the rush from the third man and circled round a pillar-box; there was a brittle click as the sharp rapier point emerged from the ferrule of his cane. Beatty gave a low laugh which seemed to deter the three men. They stood hesitating in a semicircle. Then the man in the bowler gave a sharp command and they came on again, swerving round the pillar-box.

The tall man let out a howl as the cane raked across his shins; Beatty drew blood with his next blow, the sword-point penetrating the biggest man's arm near the elbow. He gave a sobbing cry and drew back. The man in the bowler paused in his headlong progress. He stood away, weighing the chances. Coolly, he put the blackjack in his pocket. He put his hand to his hat.

"Some other time, perhaps," he said politely. He limped off.

The three men melted back into the fog as there came the piercing blast of a police whistle from the next street. The thunder of the cab-wheels died in the mist. Beatty smiled grimly and leaned against the pillar-box. He was taking the first sip from the flask in the cane-head when the thick-moustached constable came panting through the murk.

Beatty acquainted him with the situation in a few terse words. He had already resheathed the sword-point. The constable looked at him concernedly, the moisture glistening on his cape.

"You aren't hurt, guv'nor?"

Beatty shook his head. "Just shaken up. But I'd be greatly obliged if you could find me a cab."

The officer looked disbelievingly at the guinea Beatty had put into his hand.

"You want to get back to Chelsea? Right away."

He went off at a lumbering run, leaving Beatty to finish his brandy.

The Solution

31

INSPECTOR LESTRADE

DOTTERELL looked anxious.

"You are sure you are all right?"

"Of course," Beatty said curtly. "Only slight bruising."

He looked round the milling throng of passengers with unusually sharp eyes.

"There is no point in further concealment then?" said Dotterell.

Beatty shook his head.

"Cunning and dangerous I said and I will repeat it now. They are on to me just as surely as they killed Beardsley and Varley. I recognised your limping friend."

Dotterell's gaunt face set in implacable lines.

"I wish I had been there."

Beatty smiled.

"You may get your wish before long. I am keeping you in reserve. And I am hoping that we may catch them off guard today."

Dotterell strained his eyes as he glanced to and fro among the ever-changing patterns made by the mass of humanity in front of them.

"The Inspector will be here, I trust?"

Beatty nodded.

"It is all arranged. We still have a quarter of an hour before the appointed time. And the train does not leave for more than an hour."

The two men moved farther down the platform, instinctively taking up position in a shadowy corner near a kiosk. It was a day of biting cold and their breath made thick clouds about them, despite the comparative warmth of the station. A thin mist still hung over the metropolis. Beatty hoped it would clear before dark. It might seriously hinder their plans otherwise.

He again ran over in his mind the salient points he had outlined the night before. He had only dared give voice to hinted suspicions; the whole thing was so fantastic that Beatty was afraid the police would not believe him if he indicated the true drift of his conclusions.

His musings were interrupted by the swift beat of footsteps; unlike the aimless tread of the scurrying passengers, they had a definite rhythm and purpose. Two slightly built men in top-coats and bowler hats came briskly toward them. Beatty recognised the dark rat-faced figure of Inspector Lestrade of Scotland Yard. His alert grey eyes were alive with interest as he came forward to shake hands. His brown hair descended in long side-whiskers below the brim of his hard hat.

"Well, Mr. Beatty, here we are on time."

"Inspector, this is my assistant Dotterell."

Lestrade nodded pleasantly. He indicated the dark-haired, broad-faced man at his elbow.

"Sergeant Bassett. A good man in a tight corner. I have three other plain-clothes officers joining the train."

Beatty nodded with satisfaction. His brown eyes were shining with excitement.

"Just so long as they do not declare themselves before we are ready, Lestrade."

The wiry little detective pursed his lips.

"They have their instructions, sir. I have not worked with Mr. Holmes himself for nothing."

Beatty burst out laughing.

"That puts me in my place, eh, Dotterell?"

Lestrade smiled.

"You must admit, sir, he's the doyen of your profession."

"I give you that," Beatty answered quietly. "I am not disputing the crown."

The Scotland Yard men fell into step with Beatty and Dotterell, and they walked down the concourse beneath the smoky fanlights of Waterloo-road Station.

"But what is this all about, Mr. Beatty?" Lestrade said in a puzzled voice. "I must confess our conversation last night whetted my appetite."

"All in good time," Beatty replied. "I suggest we spend the next hour in this refreshment room where we can formulate our plans in more comfort. You brought the warrants?"

Lestrade pursed his lips wryly.

"Blank, as you suggested. And a fine time I had getting them. I hope something is to come of this wild-goose chase."

Beatty put a soothing hand on the little detective's arm as they went through into the steaming warmth of the refreshment room.

"Inspector Munson of the Surrey Constabulary will be meeting us at Brookwood. He treats this business seriously enough."

"Well, well," said Lestrade good-humouredly. "We must just wait on events it seems."

They were ensconced at a corner table of the noisy room before the Inspector again returned to the subject.

"I cannot really see why we are dragging all the way down to Surrey on this famous train of yours, Mr. Beatty. I hope we are to have an explanation before the trip is over."

"I trust that the events of our journey will themselves provide the explanation," said Beatty mysteriously, his alert brown eyes searching the tables about them. Dotterell gave a crooked smile to Sergeant Bassett across the table from him. The Scotland Yard man pursed up his mouth and took a sip from his steaming mug.

"This Dr. Couchman would appear to be a most damnable villain. It seems certain from the autopsy reports that he poisoned two people. And that closes the case if he is dead, as you say he is."

"He is dead enough, all right," said Beatty carelessly. "I saw him break through the Thames ice in his fall from the bridge. Nobody could have survived that temperature and those conditions."

"Well, well," said Lestrade affably. "Poetic justice, Mr. Beatty. It has saved the hangman the price of a rope."

Beatty nodded.

"Our journey today is all part of the same business. I hope to explain everything before we return from Surrey."

Lestrade exchanged a wry glance with Bassett.

"We must just possess ourselves in patience, then."

"You are armed as I requested?" Beatty asked.

Lestrade tapped the breast of his top-coat.

"Bassett and I have a brace of pistols between us. And there is enough muscle available, I fancy, to cow the strongest opposition."

"Let us hope so," said Beatty soberly. "We are up against some desperate characters. They will stop at nothing. As you know, I almost fell victim myself."

Lestrade had a sympathetic look in his eyes as he gazed sombrely at Beatty.

"What do you really expect to find in that graveyard, Mr. Beatty? Ghosts?"

Beatty chuckled.

"Human beings, the same as you and me."

Lestrade smiled too.

"In that case we shall have no difficulty in handling the situation."

"You have not recovered Couchman's body, then?"

The Inspector shook his head.

"We made another attempt yesterday, but the conditions are too severe for dragging operations. The ice has re-formed over the broken area. And who knows where underwater currents may have taken the body. It could be a mile downstream by now."

He shook his head and pursed his lips.

"It may be spring before we have any news. He could be down at the Estuary by then."

"It makes no matter," Beatty said. "Our case is complete without him. Or it will be if we are successful today."

He finished his tea and ordered another. The party sat in almost unbroken silence until it was time to board the train.

"The arrangements are clear?" said Beatty as they quitted the refreshment room for the cold of the platforms.

Sergeant Bassett nodded.

"We part here and board the train separately. No communication during the journey. I am to occupy the compartment next to those containing the coffins. Myself and the plain-clothes men to be within easy call."

"Excellent," Beatty said.

He turned to Inspector Lestrade.

"Dotterell here will be in the carriage forward of the police, assuming there is room. Inspector Lestrade will be nearby, in the same carriage as Dotterell. It is a special with corridors."

"Where will you be?" said Lestrade.

"I shall station myself as far forward as possible," Beatty said. "During the journey I will work my way down to the end of the train. I am the only one on board who knows the people involved. If I see anything suspicious I will pass a message to the Inspector. Similarly, in appropriate circumstances, you will pass a message to me."

He paused and looked round at the three expectant faces in front of him. Steam hissed under the high vaulted roof, and above the pattering footsteps of the passengers who passed and repassed about them came the loud reverberation of wheels and the harsh clanking of pistons.

"We do nothing until after our arrival at Brookwood. Everything depends on our avoiding the suspicion of the criminals. The solution of the mystery lies at the cemetery itself."

He paused and consulted a telegraph form he took from his pocket.

"I am hoping that the London Necropolis Company has been able to make special arrangements for us. We really need a light engine and a carriage."

Lestrade's eyes were blank as he stared at Sergeant Bassett.

"A light engine and carriage? I hardly see . . ."

"We may have need of them," Beatty said crisply. "The special itself returns after the services, taking the mourners and officials back to London. Brookwood is a remote spot. We shall have to wait until after dark before we set things in motion. The train will be long gone."

Beatty exchanged a glance with Dotterell. His assistant's lean face bore a thoughtful look.

"We shall require transport for ourselves and the men whose names you will eventually inscribe on those warrants."

Lestrade gave a short laugh.

"I hope you know what you are doing, Mr. Beatty. Just who is to bear the expense of these facilities?"

"Scotland Yard and ultimately the state, if we are successful," was the young detective's reply. "From friend Munson's carefully worded message, it seems the railway has an engine and carriages which can be sent from a nearby station if need be. It will be easy enough to get a message to the railway authorities if we require a special of our own."

Lestrade looked shrewdly at Beatty as they walked slowly across the echoing vault of Waterloo-road Station.

"You strike a hard bargain, Mr. Beatty. If we are successful tonight, then both the Surrey Constabulary and Scotland Yard will have cause to be grateful to you."

He paused and exchanged a meaningful glance with Sergeant Bassett.

"But if you are wrong and this business ends in failure, then you must bear sole responsibility," he added grimly. "So long as that is understood."

Beatty smiled slowly at Dotterell.

"Clearly, Inspector. I think you will find our little trip interesting—to say the least."

He paused and caught the Scotland Yard man by the arm. He drew him into the shadow of a massive iron girder which came down to platform level at that point.

"And now I think it is time to part. We will take up our positions aboard the train separately. We neither talk nor give any visible sign that we know each other. There may be sharp eyes aboard the train."

He looked at Dotterell.

"Everyone knows what he has to do at Brookwood?"

There were murmurs of assent.

"Good," said Beatty crisply. "In any event we meet at the Church of England Station as arranged. We will then decide on the plan of action."

Beatty strode off briskly and disappeared amid the swirling steam as his companions dispersed and were swiftly lost to view among the teeming throng of passengers.

32

THE SILVER COFFINS

IT wanted but a few minutes to eleven. Beatty consulted his watch and glanced along the platform again. From his corner seat he could see the whole curve of the blanched whiteness that was the Ghost Train. The last coffins were being loaded. There were only two elderly ladies and a strained-looking young man in his compartment.

The station-master, lordly and imposing in his top-hat and frock-coat, was talking earnestly to the representative of the London Necropolis Company on the platform a few yards from where Beatty sat at the window of his compartment. This was the reason he had chosen this vantage point. He was, in fact, only halfway down the train, and he intended to move to the front and work his way back as soon as they had left the station.

The heads of the undertaking concerns were converging on the small group formed by the station-master, the company representative, and an imposing official in gold-braid. Mostly serious middle-aged men in silk hats and frock-coats, they carried bundles of documents and printed lists; they would compare these with the company director who had a clip-board in his gloved hand.

Beatty recognised the burly, bearded figure of McMurdo striding aggressively forward; there was something bull-like about his vigorous stance and almost ferocious energy in the alert set of the head and the brilliance of the eyes. Beatty shrank back and concealed his face in the edge of the braided curtain at the window of the carriage. He waited until the group had dispersed; McMurdo went back to the rear, where the compartments containing the coffins were.

Beatty did not think the funeral director would recognise him, but he could not be too careful at this stage. Today he carried a small black case such as Masons used; it contained a few of the more essential tools Beatty felt might be needed on the present mission. All the instruments were embedded in velvet to prevent them from rattling about; among them was a long-handled jemmy which Beatty felt would be particularly useful.

He had a rough idea of the sequence of events, but anything could upset his calculations. He did not think there would be any problems from the police end; the officers Lestrade had carefully selected were too well trained for that. But a thousand and one things might upset the calculations; Beatty intended to be fully on top of circumstances tonight and he was glad that Dotterell was aboard.

Not only was he a source of great strength and intelligence, but he was used to Beatty's methods of working and would act on his own initiative in accord with Beatty's movements; this was an essential prerequisite in the type of operation in which they were involved.

He leaned forward again and watched the distant figure of McMurdo board the train at the far end. Doors were slamming now, and the station-master was shaking hands with the Necropolis Company representative. He thought wryly of Rossington and the lost dinner. He was engaged to dine with him this evening, and he had been so engrossed in their plans that he had had no time to get a message to him.

Beatty suddenly drew back and hid his face behind the curtain; only his eyes were visible as he scrutinised the man who was limping down the platform toward him. Despite the fact that the train was on the point of departure, there was an air of casualness about him that was belied by the alertness of his features. He was a small man, neatly dressed in a brown overcoat with a fur collar. He wore a brown bowler hat of the same shade as his coat, which gave him a curious aspect.

As he got closer, looking about him as though seeking a friend in one of the carriages, Beatty was certain that all his thoughts and feelings about the case were correct; something welled up in his throat and he momentarily closed his eyes, so strong were his emotions. He opened them again, aware that the other people in the carriage were looking at him. No matter; it merely strengthened the atmosphere of grief that Beatty wished to impress on those about him.

The limping man was almost level with the carriage now; he had drawn back from the edge of the platform in order to allow porters with a trolley to pass. Beatty saw that he had a set white face; there was a mirthless smile on the mouth, which revealed strong pointed teeth. There was a long scar on one cheek, which was so deep it stood out as a whiter gash on the whiteness of the face.

It was a visage which might have been carved out of marble; mirthless and terrible, despite or perhaps because of the rigidity of the smile; under the shadow of the hat-brim the eyes were like those of dead insects. Beatty had seen enough. He was already on his feet, gathering up his case. He slid back the door of the compartment with a muffled apology. He hurried along the corridor; fortunately it was on the side opposite the platform.

He kept pace with the limping man. Whistles were blowing, and there was a low stutter caused by the staccato closing of carriage doors. The man in the bowler hat turned casually and lifted himself up into an open doorway with a lithe, sinuous movement. He moved like an athlete, Beatty felt. He remembered again the agile movements of his adversary in the fog. He moved on, making sure the small man was settling into the carriage.

Then he passed on down the train, walking quickly, putting several carriages between himself and the man with the scar before he felt able to relax. He hunched his face into the collar of his coat in case there might be anyone in the compartments who would recognise him. They appeared to be fairly full here. The train gave a visible shudder, and Beatty lurched slightly. They were moving slowly forward, out of the station. The dirty yellow brick wall slid backward at his elbow.

Beatty noted the wide arch of the station canopy gliding smoothly toward them; beyond it was a thin haze of vapour, through which the tangled skein of metals could be seen. Shadows passed across the windows and the rumble of the wheels grew, mingled with the hiss of steam. Beatty was up near the engine now; he could go no farther and sought a seat in the half-empty compartment in front of him. He would wait a few moments before starting back down the train. He would have to be extremely careful.

He lowered himself into a corner seat, watching the platforms

of Waterloo wheel by under the banner of steam the engine was
throwing back. Porters and gold-braided station staff were standing stiffly to attention. A clergyman in a black broad-brimmed hat
was standing with upraised arm near the platform edge, as though
giving a benediction. The train gave another whistle, the wheels
bit the rails with a rough vibration, and then the Ghost Train was
on the long curve, its white flanks fading and blending with the
mist.

There were two clergymen in the carriage, one with a gold pince-
nez secured by a gold chain. They were talking theological matters
to themselves in droning voices and displaying a great deal of
dogmatic intolerance, Beatty thought. The other persons in the
carriage were a young girl and two middle-aged men; husband and
brother-in-law, the investigator surmised. All wore black, but in
contrast to the animated clerics, the remainder of the company
kept unbroken silence all the while he was there.

Beatty amused himself for a few more minutes in futile specu-
lation on his companions' identity and then buried himself in the
pages of *The Morning Star*, part of his new persona today. The train
rattled on, gathering speed through the suburbs; a dim blanket of
dirty mist hung over the city, visibility outside the windows being
restricted to a few yards. Occasionally the faint silhouette of a
building, a post, or a human being could be seen; the latter waiting
in patient rows at suburban stations for their absent trains.

The engine maintained a fair speed, despite the fog, but a little
later slowed; signals were detonating down the line. They sounded
like a farewell gun-salute for the funeral train, Beatty thought.
Then naphtha flares were burning outside the windows and a
stolid frieze of workmen was glimpsed, wielding pick and shovel.
The train proceeded at a crawl for a while and then shuddered to a
stop.

Beatty finished the paper and put it down on the seat at his
elbow. The two clerics were still engaged in fierce controversy.
Beatty rose, his back to the compartment, a brief smile lighting
his face. He picked up his case and stepped over the two men's feet
with a mumbled apology; he opened the door and closed it behind
him again.

The corridor was empty. The train lurched forward, and Beatty went slowly back down the carriage, scrutinising the compartments carefully. He took his time, taking pains to avoid revealing his own features. He held up one hand to the collar of his coat as though he were cold and surveyed the occupants through his fingers.

He worked back through several carriages like this; he could not see any sign of the three detective officers Lestrade was holding in reserve; that was all to the good. If they were present then they did not betray their profession, which was extremely important today of all days.

In any event they should also have worked their way back toward the rear by now; Beatty wanted them within easy call near the compartments containing the coffins. He had already ascertained that these carriages were not locked. There would be no need normally. He could safely leave all that to Bassett.

The train was proceeding very slowly now; if anything, the fog appeared to be thickening. Any delay on the line would hold up but not seriously dislocate their plans; but it would be important if the fog persisted after dark. That could hamper operations considerably on the ground at Brookwood. Beatty dismissed the possibility with a shrug; there would be time to worry over that later.

He went on down the corridor very cautiously, pausing now and again to look out at the blank white wall of vapour that pressed close to the windows, leaving damp smears on the glass. The train was like a warm and opulent oasis compared with the conditions outside; there was the comforting smell of leather, waxed rosewood, and mahogany; and the perfume of soft upholstery all about him.

He could not see the limping man anywhere among these passengers; he would have to be extremely careful when he got farther down. The man knew him, of course, and he had proved a deadly opponent; Beatty could not afford to take any chances. He was in the buffet car now; small groups of black-clad mourners sipped tea at side-tables in an air of gentle melancholy.

Beatty was amused to see Dotterell sitting at one of the tables in earnest conversation with a Catholic priest; the door was open at that moment, and Beatty could have sworn that they were talking in Greek. Dotterell had seen him; he did not change his position or give any flicker of recognition, but his employer realised that his assistant had his piercing eyes sharply fixed on the mirror at the back of the counter. In it he would be able to see everyone who passed along the corridor.

The train was picking up speed momentarily; the mist had cleared a little and Beatty could see objects at the side of the line. They were out in the country, maintaining a steady pace. Beatty worked his way methodically to the end of the train; one or two people were passing him in the corridor, progressing to and from the buffet car. Beatty's nerves were tingling; this was the moment of greatest danger.

At any moment he might be confronted by someone who knew him, and that would destroy any element of surprise. He stepped against the rail which ran alongside the corridor windows as a big man squeezed by with a mumbled apology; the butt of the pistol felt hard and unyielding against his chest. It was also infinitely reassuring. He stepped back into the middle of the corridor, feeling a similar quiet pressure from the derringer in its special holster on his calf. He was well prepared; but they would need luck as well as weapons against such opponents.

Beatty stiffened; he looked quickly into the compartment opposite and stepped back through its half-open door. Inspector Lestrade was coming down the corridor. He passed Beatty with his face set, eyes blank. Beatty felt satisfied; they had done all they could. He glanced at his watch. There was plenty of time yet. It would take him only a few moments more to reach the cars where the coffins were.

He watched Lestrade disappear down the corridor in the direction of the buffet car. No doubt he was relieving Dotterell and taking a little refreshment at the same time. Beatty stayed where he was, and a few seconds later the tall, gaunt form of Dotterell squeezed past him where he stood at the window.

Beatty waited until his assistant had disappeared from sight and then followed, moving slowly and scrutinising the faces of every person in the compartments he passed without seeming to do so. He could not quite remember the exact place where the limping man had joined the train, and he was worried at his disappearance.

He could, of course, have escaped Beatty's attention in a place like the buffet car, but Beatty did not think so. He was particularly careful in his leisurely examination of the passengers, and he was convinced that he had not yet passed the man. He continued his slow way back down the train with a slightly heightened pulse.

He gave his ticket for examination to the silver-haired and much-braided inspector who accosted him and then moved on, as Beatty replaced the ticket in his notecase. A few moments later he recognised Sergeant Bassett. He was in a half-empty carriage, reading a magazine. There was a seat opposite him on which reposed an overcoat and bowler hat. Beatty guessed that this was where Inspector Lestrade was sitting. He must be almost at the rear of the train.

He passed through into the next car. The air was thick with cigar smoke; sober-looking men with beards, some wearing silk hats, were engaged in animated conversation. It was such a contrast with the rest of the train that Beatty was, for a moment, slightly startled.

Then he realised that these were the last two compartments before those containing the coffins. They were mostly undertakers and their employees in here; hence the jovial atmosphere. Death was an everyday matter to these people; they were professionals, and today was no different from any other. Outside, among the mourners, they would be grave and discreet. Here, in private, they were free to unbutton, joke, and talk shop.

Beatty's dark clothing did not make him seem out of place, and no one took any notice of him. Nevertheless he did not linger, as he might have done in the public part of the train. There might well be someone who could recognise him; McMurdo certainly could. Moreover, the layout of the carriages was different here, in that there was a central gangway with padded seats either side.

Here the professionals lounged at their ease; Beatty noticed flasks open on the table, and there was the pungent reek of spirits sharp above the rich aroma of the cigar smoke. A gale of laughter came from one group as he passed.

"That was the moment he dropped the coffin," said a tall, thin man with burning eyes, his remark evoking a tremendous shout of amusement from those gathered around him. Beatty saw McMurdo's coarse features and gigantic form as he passed this tableau. The director had his head bent, recorking a flask, his white teeth glinting in his beard, as he shared the general mirth.

Beatty was in the next compartment now; this had a rather more decorous air. Beatty surmised that these would be the lesser fry; the employees and undertakers' assistants who were excluded from the more affluent and considerably more free and easy fraternity of their employers.

He drew aside, lowering his face toward the floor as a tall, bald-headed man with yellow features squeezed past him without a glance. Alasdair Vair passed on to the coach occupied by McMurdo and his colleagues. Beatty stopped a moment, surveying the compartment before him; he could not see the small man with the limp. He must have missed him on the train somewhere. It was hardly important at this stage anyway.

He went on down the last coach, trying to look as casual and preoccupied as possible. No one gave a glance at the figure in the dark formal clothes. Most of the men were playing cards or reading; some dozed, their mouths hanging slackly open. They looked an ugly and lugubrious group of people, Beatty thought. Death was ugly, and its attendants had gathered some of its own squalor in their pursuance of the woeful trade.

He stopped at the far door and bent down quickly, ostensibly to fasten his shoe-lace; the train was rattling along at a good pace now and the fog had thinned a little. Beatty estimated that they would be at Brookwood in slightly more than twenty minutes at the rate they were going. He would have to act quickly. He had wasted rather more time than he had intended in working his way down the train.

He glanced at the door in front of him. It was swaying with the movement of the train, and he could see that it was unlocked. He looked quickly round the compartment, saw that no one was watching. He quietly slid the door open a couple of feet, eased himself through, and closed it behind him.

It was darker in here, and Beatty waited for a moment in order to allow his eyes to adjust. There was an overpowering, sickly perfume of flowers. As he moved forward he saw the wreaths and sprays of blooms stacked along the floor and vibrating slowly with the movement of the train. Some of the floral tributes were arranged with their stems in buckets of water, which had slopped over on to the floor.

The coffins were resting on special oak stands set along the sides of the carriage and in rows down the centre, making aisles along which Beatty walked in the semigloom, his eyes passing quickly over the silent ranks of caskets. He carried his case under his arm now; pale oblongs of mist shone in the windows at the sides of the carriage, and the roar of the train intensified as they passed under a bridge.

He reached the end of the aisle and turned back. He swiftly examined the whole of the compartment. What he was looking for was not there. He passed through into the last carriage; there would be nothing beyond that but the guard's van. The next was a replica of the first: the coffins on their stands set out in aisles, more flowers, the same sickly perfume.

It was darker here as some of the window blinds appeared to be drawn. Beatty went down the central aisle, almost instinctively. He quickly examined the serried rows of caskets. He stopped near the end, where the shadow was thickest. The silver handles and nameplates of the oak coffins shimmered softly in the dim light.

Beatty put the case down on the vibrating floor of the compartment; the roar of the wheels was much louder in here, and mist swirled at the window, ripped into tatters by the train's passing. The young man knelt, stooping his head to read the inscriptions on the wreaths banked at the foot of the stand. He made out the name of Vickers in the immaculate copperplate writing. He gave a brief grunt of satisfaction.

He got up and looked at the topmost coffin of the tier. The lid was held with heavy silver clamps, he noticed. He felt a tingle of excitement run through him; that was curious in itself. He went down the coffin lid carefully, oblivious of the roar of the train and the swaying of the compartment, completely absorbed in what he was doing.

He saw there were six heavy screw clamps holding the lid. It would take only a very few moments to release it under such circumstances. Beatty looked swiftly round in the gloom. Then he reached over and turned the head on the heavy screw fitting.

Something came at him out of the shadow. The limping man's eyes were like dead butterflies as he moved to put the wire trace round Beatty's neck.

33

THE LIMPING MAN STRIKES

BEATTY was taken unaware. He moved his hand to his throat, dropping to his knees. The thin wire bit deeply into the back of his hand instead of his neck muscles; the other end was sawing across the collar of the young investigator's overcoat. Even so he felt blinding pain, and blood was dripping down his wrist. Instinctively, he struck out heavily with his right, felt his balled fist strike bone and muscle.

The limping man grunted; he fell back against the rack of coffins at the edge of the aisle, and Beatty had twisted aside, the cheese-cutter with bone handles harmlessly slicing air. He reached for the pistol in his pocket, but the small man came back with astonishing speed and ferocity. Beatty kicked him as he came, his thick-soled boot connecting heavily with his attacker's kneecap.

The eyes half closed momentarily and tears started out the lids, but the fixed expression of the smile did not change; the two men were face to face for a brief second as the limping man clawed at Beatty's throat. The half-drawn pistol discharged itself into the air with a tremendous report.

The detonation, followed by the almost instantaneous flash of flame and smoke, had a deafening and blinding effect; both men reeled away, Beatty's pistol dropping to the floor, the cheese-cutter left hanging on the wooden rack holding the silver-handled coffin. The bullet had gone somewhere up in the roof, and wood chips rained down toward them.

Beatty was up first, kicking at the figure with the blackened features. The limping man had taken the pistol-flash almost in the face; it had momentarily blinded him, and burns from the hot powder pocked his features, which were distorted with pain. But he said nothing, merely reached inside his coat.

Beatty caught his wrist as the knife emerged, and a long silent struggle commenced; both men were well-matched, despite the discrepancy in their sizes. Beatty was well-versed in boxing, wrestling, and single-stick, and he was in hard, fit condition.

But this man was a formidable opponent, despite his diminutive build; he had a steel-wire athleticism and his unleashed strength was testing Beatty to the utmost as they staggered about, sending the tiers of coffins rocking on their supports. Their boots trampled the wreaths and sprays of flowers, and petals and black-edged mourning cards were scattered along the floor.

The most unnerving thing to Beatty was the silence of his opponent and the fixed smile, which remained unchanged throughout the struggle. Blood from Beatty's cut wrist dripped down on to a wreath of lilies as they edged over toward the side of the carriage; the dark stains against the whiteness of the blooms were a symbol which remained in Beatty's mind for long after.

He felt the resurgence of strength in the wiry man's arms; he had fantastic vitality. Despite the blows Beatty had rained on him and the explosion of the pistol, his effectiveness was unimpaired. He wrenched his knife-wrist free and tore himself away; Beatty, off balance, went over backward. They were at the end of the aisle now and Beatty dodged round as the small man lunged at him.

He tugged at one of the silver-handled coffins; it rocked and then came thunderously down, halting the limping man's rush and causing him to jump back against the far end of the coach. Failing a decisive outcome to the struggle, Beatty felt the utmost instinct to disengage and warn his companions on the train; but at the same time it would leave the small man free to alert his own side. Beatty at least had to disable him or put him out of action temporarily if he were to succeed in his objective today.

He picked up a bundle of wreaths and threw them at the fixed smile before him as his opponent came on again; a faint grunting noise came out of the man's mouth, and there was a whiteness about the nostrils. He plucked the wreaths from him and jumped over the sprawled coffin, the knife glinting in the dim, misty light of the coffin-compartment.

The noise of the train effectively masked all sound of their struggle, but Beatty was worried in case someone might come to the compartment; he glanced at the mist whirling past the window. The engine had gathered speed, and they would be at their destination in a few minutes now.

Beatty backed away and got into the middle aisle. He could hear the other man's boots making scraping noises on the floor as he moved swiftly after him. His limp did not seem to handicap him to any extent. Beatty longed for his sword-stick. He ran down to the far end of the coach again. His foot kicked against something. He reached down and picked up his case of instruments.

He swung it as the limping man launched himself in a shallow arc along the aisle at him; it deflected the knife and Beatty heard it clatter somewhere on the floor. He sidestepped quickly and got in a heavy head-blow with the case as his opponent rushed past, unable to stop. He bounced against the end of the carriage and whirled back with tremendous speed.

The limping man paused for a moment, the smile still on his face. There was a thin trickle of blood now, coming from his temple and making a lacework pattern which joined up with the blackness of the powder-smoke. He reached out to the carriage door at his elbow and opened it. He kept his deep-set eyes on Beatty and pushed the heavy door back against the rush of air. Tendrils of fog mingled with dense smoke billowed into the compartment.

His spring was well-timed; Beatty was just a fraction late. He moved slightly too slowly, found powerful hands at his throat. Despite his weight and size he felt himself dragged toward the open door.

He ignored the grip on his throat. With his thick neck muscles he felt confident that it would be a formidable opponent indeed who could induce unconsciousness before he had time to counterattack. He hunched his shoulders as he swayed back and brought the case in his right hand round. It would have been a stunning blow, but the limping man ducked beneath it; the case glanced harmlessly off the wooden side of the carriage.

Beatty was swaying at the door edge now; he lurched to one side, smoke billowing in his face, his opponent clinging doggedly on. Beatty had his shoulders against the woodwork; he lifted the limping man completely clear of the floor as he shook his head. It was the terrier shaking the rat, only the rat had its teeth in the terrier's throat.

The pressure on Beatty was considerable; he felt his senses swimming as he moved forward. The two men were enveloped in smoke and fog as they teetered in the doorway. Then Beatty brought the case round for the last time, felt it connect against flesh and bone. The limping man grunted; Beatty felt the fingers at his throat relax.

He moved forward; his opponent's heels were clear of the floor. Beatty flung himself outward, caught himself by his two hands at the door-frame. The wind of the train's passage plucked at their clothing; vapour and steam boiled about them. Beatty was left with the rictus of the smile. Then he was clear, his senses swiftly returning.

The small man remained poised for an incredibly long segment of time, his body clear-etched against the mist. Then he was gone, tumbling downward among the rumbling wheels. His thin scream was cut off by the rocking vibration of the carriages. Beatty drew back and slammed the door shut. He sank to the floor and closed his eyes; a violent fit of trembling seized him.

When it had passed he got to his feet. Blood was still dripping down his hand. He had not felt the pain until then. He bound a handkerchief round the wound. He kicked the small man's knife under one of the coffin racks and retrieved his pistol. He lifted the fallen coffin back on to a lower shelf, rearranged the flowers and floral tributes as best he could.

Those irretrievably trampled and broken he took and threw out of the window together with the wire trace. He mopped up flecks of blood with his handkerchief, spilled water from the buckets over the floor. When he was certain that all appeared normal, he put his injured hand in his pocket. He walked back down the train and regained his seat without incident.

Fog billowed yellowly about the platform as the Ghost Train drew in to the Church of England Station at Brookwood Cemetery with a shuddering of brakes. Gas-lamps bloomed through the murk despite the early hour, and the raw air held a hint of snow in it. Beatty shrugged more closely into his top-coat as he quitted the carriage. He deliberately walked farther down the platform, away from the compartments containing the coffins.

Already, priests and clergymen were gathering the mourn-ers into groups; more lamps showed through the darkness at the entrance to the shallow flight of steps where cabs for the relatives and hearses for the remains of the departed would be waiting. Beatty walked quickly to the refreshment room, looking neither right nor left.

He knew that McMurdo and Company would be too busy unloading to have time for anything else for some while. The room was almost empty; a bright fire burned in the hearth and a dark girl with a sad face was polishing glasses. Beatty joined the man who stood with his back to the windows, his head bowed over the bar.

"I took the liberty of ordering you a whisky," Inspector Munson said in a low voice.

His grey eyes twinkled as he looked sharply at Beatty, taking in the slight disorder of his dress. His unspoken question hung in the air between them as he noted the young investigator's bandaged hand.

"We are on the right track," said Beatty slowly, his eyes raking the people passing and repassing the buffet windows. "A man tried to murder me on the train when I was attempting to examine the coffins. I had to kill him, I'm afraid."

Munson's mouth opened wide as he gazed at Beatty in astonish-ment.

"Self-defence, I take it?"

"Undoubtedly," Beatty said crisply. "But I do not think we have any cause to mourn him. It was unquestionably the same man who killed friend Beardsley on the South Bank of the Thames the other day. He went off the train during our struggle."

"No matter," Munson continued, lifting his glass. "What are we looking for?"

"McMurdo and Company," Beatty said quickly.

People were beginning to drift into the refreshment room now. He did not wish to be seen engaged in talk with the Inspector.

"Oak coffins with silver fittings," he went on. "We want to know where they go. Inspector Lestrade of Scotland Yard and four other officers are also here."

Munson rubbed his chin with a thick finger and drained his glass.

"This is no time for self-congratulation, Mr. Beatty," he said. "But remind me to take this up with you at a later date."

Beatty smiled.

"What news your end?"

"I have a closed cab outside," Munson went on. "Driven by Toby Stevens. We shall need it if we want to follow those coffins unobserved. I telegraphed you about the railway facilities."

Beatty nodded.

"I think we shall require them. Can you give the necessary instructions?"

"Straightaway," Munson retorted. "The special can be brought to a siding within the cemetery, a little farther down. The Brookwood station-master is discreet. No one else need know."

"Excellent," said Beatty. "With a little luck we should be able to bring this business to a conclusion within the next few hours."

The two men walked to the door of the refreshment room and back on to the platform. The noises of the unloading went on, cloaked by the fog. Beatty felt that it might be made to serve its purpose; he had feared it when he first set out on his journey that day, but it could yet prove an ally.

He turned to Munson, the Inspector's form already indistinct in the white blanket, though he stood only a yard away.

"If you would make the arrangements for the engine, I will meet you at the cab."

Munson disappeared into the mist; Beatty, clutching the instrument case firmly, strode out down the steps to where the indistinct shapes of the waiting vehicles began to compose themselves from out the enveloping whiteness.

34

THE CHAPEL

Toby Stevens's face was creased in a welcoming smile. He got down from the box and came through the mist to take Beatty's hand with obvious warmth.

"Glad to see you back, Mr. Beatty. You can't keep away from Woking, eh?"

Beatty put his hand up to enjoin silence. He drew the cabman forward into the shadow of the vehicle.

"Just step into the cab for a moment if you will, Stevens. This is a matter of the utmost discretion."

Stevens's alert face beneath the iron-grey hair was alive with interest.

"You may rely on me, sir. After you, if you please."

Beatty opened the familiar yellow door and stepped into the interior. The cab-lamps were lit, and the warm rays fell across the opposite seat as Stevens got in facing the young investigator and closed the door behind him. His face was serious as he gazed at Beatty.

"You remember our last conversation a short while ago. About your wife and Dr. Couchman?"

Stevens nodded. His thoughtful eyes never left Beatty's face.

"Well, this is part of the same business that brought me to Couchman's nursing home in the first place. You will be serving the ends of justice if you follow my instructions exactly today. May I count on you?"

Stevens let out a long sigh.

"You may that, sir. What do you want me to do?"

"Stand at our disposal for today and do everything that is asked of you without question. You will be well paid for your trouble."

Stevens made an eloquent movement of his shoulders.

"Payment's the least of it, sir. But can you give me any idea of what is involved?"

Beatty gave a low chuckle.

"That's just it, Stevens. I don't really know myself. But it's an official police matter now. Inspector Munson will be joining us in a few minutes."

Stevens laid his finger alongside his nose in a gesture which Beatty remembered; it was as though he had known Stevens for years.

"You'll want someone followed, I take it?"

"That and other things," Beatty said. "There may be some danger."

Stevens looked steadily at Beatty.

"You'll not find me flinching from that, sir."

Beatty put his hand out and shook the other's.

"Good," he said crisply. "I am afraid that is all I can tell you for the moment. But you will know more later. We must just follow circumstances."

Stevens looked up as there came the brisk sound of boot-nails on the steps outside.

"For the commencement, we shall be following one of the funeral cortèges," Beatty told Stevens. "I want you to keep your eyes open and your senses alert. Let me or Inspector Munson know the moment you see anything unusual or out of the ordinary."

"Right, sir," said Stevens shortly.

He got out the door and held it open for the Inspector as Munson came hurrying from the gloom. The Inspector spoke affably to the cab-driver, and then Beatty beckoned him back into the cab interior.

"Just stay there by the window," he said. "Be ready to follow the cortège of McMurdo and Company. Mr. McMurdo himself is an enormous man with a beard. His manager is a tall, bald man called Alasdair Vair. They must not know they are being followed. The coffins concerned have silver fittings. Unless I am much mistaken there will be few or no mourners following."

Stevens looked at the two men in astonishment.

"Unusual," he muttered.

"Precisely," said Beatty. "Now, just keep watching the station entrance so that we do not miss them."

Stevens nodded. He got up to quit the cab.

"I'll do that best outside, gentlemen."

"Very well," Beatty said. "When they come out we must just follow at a discreet distance. And be prepared to turn down a side-path, if necessary. If you see the cortège making for a known place, let us know and we will reconnoitre on foot."

Stevens put up his hand to his nose again and got out. He shut the door quietly behind him, and the two men in the cab heard his footsteps receding in the mist. Then began a long and melancholy wait. Through the gloom they could see the vague shapes as undertakers' men bearing caskets came down a sloping ramp at the side of the station steps.

Hearses rumbled and grated on the gravel as the processions formed up and horses' hooves pawed the ground. There was intense activity for something like half an hour and then it began to die away. Stevens had parked his cab at the edge of the station entrance so that his vehicle was not in the way of conveyances arriving and leaving.

It was all done very efficiently, and Beatty began to have an inkling of the gigantic scale of the operations at Brookwood. Munson said little and after a few minutes settled back on his seat to smoke his pipe, glancing at Beatty benevolently from time to time. Beatty was conscious now of the lack of lunch; he had not brought any refreshment with him, and he hoped that later they would be able to get something to eat at one of the station buffets.

Stevens was gone a long time. Presently Munson stirred on the seat and moved forward to the window. Beatty took the opportunity to ask him a question.

"Where is the Roman Catholic Station?"

Munson grunted.

"About half a mile away. It is very similar to this one. Did you have any particular reason . . . ?"

"Just idle curiosity," Beatty interrupted him. "It is as well to know these things. We might have cause to go there before the night is out."

Munson looked startled.

"Day, I hope," he said.

He shivered, drawing his overcoat about him.

"You are optimistic, Inspector," Beatty said. "But I fear our friends will not work for our convenience. Nightfall and an empty cemetery will suit them better, I fancy."

Munson grunted again and gave Beatty a long searching look before settling back on the cushions. Another quarter of an hour had passed before he spoke again. He sat up with an abrupt movement and knocked out his pipe against the inside of the door.

"I suppose it is too much to ask exactly why we are here? I must confess I have turned it over in my mind a few times, but something which is evidently crystal-clear to you completely escapes me."

Beatty smiled.

"A little more patience, Inspector. I can assure you our friends from Scotland Yard know no more than you. I must insist on keeping you in the dark for just a little longer."

"I cannot really see the point."

The Surrey detective's voice had an acid edge to it. Beatty looked at him sharply.

"Because my theory is so outrageous and fantastic that no one would believe me if I voiced it aloud. I prefer to make my own mistakes in my own way. If I am proved wrong, then I can apologise to you and Lestrade in private and there's an end of the matter. If I made my suspicions known at this point, it would be difficult to keep the information within a restricted circle. To say nothing of the fact that Lestrade would not have come at all if I had told him what I had in mind."

He broke off as footsteps sounded through the fog.

"But I fancy we shall know soon enough. If you would just possess yourself in patience for a while longer . . ."

Stevens had appeared at the door. He opened it and thrust his head into the dank darkness of the cab.

"The McMurdo party is on the move, sir," he said. "I'll take the cab up a little way and then fall in behind."

Beatty nodded. The two men moved forward instinctively to the window as Stevens ascended to the driving seat of the cab. The wheels grated on the gravel and the horse moved forward, anxious to be off again. Stevens drove in a broad circle and in a few moments pulled in under the shadow of some thickly overgrown trees which bordered the pavement.

None too soon as footsteps sounded from the station forecourt. Straining his eyes through the mist, Beatty made out dark forms carrying the coffins down the ramp. There came the muffled sound of harness creaking; the wheels of vehicles grating against the icebound gravel of the concourse; and the occasional sharp, coughing breath of a horse.

Stevens's face appeared framed in the trap, looking down on his passengers.

"Just about to move off, sir," he hissed.

Beatty's face was flushed with excitement.

"Give them a few seconds but don't let them out of your sight."

Stevens smiled.

"I know the cemetery pretty well, sir," he said. "Don't worry."

He snapped the trap shut. Beatty and Munson remained with their faces pressed against the window. A few moments later they heard the sharp, brittle sound of horses' hooves through the freezing air as the cortège moved off. After a discreet interval their own cab glided in pursuit.

The two men stared at each other, Beatty with mounting interest, the official detective with increasing curiosity, as they followed in the wake of the unseen hearse in front of them. Munson put his pipe back in his wallet. He produced a revolver from the depths of his greatcoat and examined it critically. Then he thrust it back into his pocket.

Beatty had followed his actions with approval. He leaned forward, watching the ghostly outlines of tree-branches slowly passing the window, gauntly outlined against the billowing whiteness.

"I see that you at least take me seriously," he observed.

Munson pursed his lips.

"I have no doubt there is something desperate afoot," he rejoined shortly. "Events have already proved that. It is not knowing exactly our objective . . ."

He drummed with impatient fingers on the leather seat at his side. Beatty put the conversation in another tangent.

"I have not heard the news from Brookwood."

Munson shook his head gloomily.

"There is precious little to tell. My telegraph told you all. I have not alarmed Bateman in any way. I had to approach him regarding the autopsies, of course. I gave him a noncommittal report, and to the best of my knowledge he took it at its face value. I would be willing to swear my entire pension that the Superintendent knows nothing of what is going on within these walls. He seemed more worried at finding replacements for Varley and Beardsley. He thinks the latter was involved in an accident."

Beatty put his head on his hands and stared fixedly at his companion.

"You may well be right. It was an open question, as I remember."

Munson smiled wryly.

"The Superintendent is not the only one lacking information," he observed tartly.

Beatty was about to make some bantering rejoinder when a sudden violent movement of the cab arrested his attention. Stevens had reined the horse in with unwonted abruptness. The trap in the ceiling drew quietly back, and Stevens's head was framed in the opening. Dank mist drifted into the cab interior.

"Can't go any farther, gentlemen. They're unloading now."

He jerked his head off to the right.

"There's an old chapel down there. It's of the Catholic persuasion, but not much used nowadays since they built the big one near the second station."

Munson and Beatty had drawn forward to the window on the side of the vehicle indicated by Stevens. They could see little through the swirling mist except the faint outlines of trees.

"Very well," said Beatty. "We will get down. Back to the station with you. It will be a long wait, I am afraid. We are not expecting anything further of note until after dark."

He paused and looked at Munson, but the Inspector was already getting out the carriage. Beatty followed and the two men stood straining their eyes into the mist. Up ahead of them came the muffled noises they had earlier heard; the sound of wood on wood and footsteps on the gravel.

"The chapel is just off to the right," Stevens said, pointing with his whip. "If you take the side-path you can't miss it."

"Very well," said Beatty. "Make yourself comfortable in the

station refreshment room. If we require your services we will seek you there."

Stevens saluted with his whip, his features grave beneath his iron-grey hair. He wheeled the horse and set off back at a leisurely pace. Beatty joined Munson on the grass, and the two men walked down a narrow alley between sombre yews, half-seen through the vaporous haze that surrounded them. The smell of evergreens, rank and damp, came to their nostrils, and frost crackled beneath their boots as they went on across the turf, avoiding the gravelled path which would have betrayed their presence.

The air was so cold it made breathing painful, and Beatty kept his chin hunched into the collar of his coat. He still carried the case of instruments, and he had his revolver loose in his right-hand pocket. The Inspector was silent, perhaps oppressed by the melancholy of their surroundings and the nature of their errand.

All about them in the great cemetery could be felt the stir of activity—the creak of harness; the rasp of iron-bound wheels on roadways; the tread of feet as coffins were carried to chapels; and even, once, the mumbling of a priest—all faint and blanketed by the fog, but seeming far away.

"To their long rest," Beatty quoted solemnly. He had spoken under his breath, but Inspector Munson paused in his steady pace and muttered, "Eigh?"

"Nothing," said Beatty shortly. "Just fancy."

Munson looked at him shrewdly, his grey eyes wide and guileless.

"Brookwood," he said shortly. "It's got you too, has it? Always affects people the same way."

He shook his head and waved his hand round to indicate the great grey immensity that pressed upon them.

"All these lives cut short. The ceaseless journeys; day in, day out; and the thousands that come to Brookwood and never leave again."

Beatty stared at his companion for a moment and they resumed their steady progress, keeping the path at their right, following its looping course through the trees and bushes.

"Why, Inspector, you're quite a poet."

Munson smiled diffidently, but his eyes were serious beneath his hat-brim.

"Don't tell me it hasn't affected you too, Mr. Beatty. You must have felt it."

"There is certainly something bizarre about the place," Beatty admitted. "But I suspect it is less due to the presence of the dead than the sort of human activity which people like you and me are dedicated to stamping out."

Munson smiled grimly and said no more until their walk was ended. A few minutes more and their stealthy progress was arrested as the faint outlines of a great grey building loomed out of the murk before them. Beatty put his hand to his lips to enjoin silence.

"There, if I am not mistaken, is the Catholic chapel of which Stevens has spoken."

He crouched low behind a monument where Munson joined him. As by an unspoken command both men checked their revolvers.

"Not a sound from now on," Beatty said. "We have some dangerous work before us."

35

CREATURES OF DARKNESS

THE two men crouched, staring into the aching whiteness where the gravelled path was cut off by the encroaching mist. A slight wind was stirring now, sending eddies of vapour wreathing about the gravestones. They were well concealed here by heavy groups of statuary. The windows of the Catholic chapel were dark and blank, the porch and steps moss-grown and neglected. But they were just close enough for Beatty to see that the roof had been partly retiled and was well-kept.

Munson's hand was on Beatty's arm. At the same moment the young investigator heard what the Inspector had already picked up; the faint, slow footsteps of men carrying heavy burdens. A few moments later dim figures appeared from the mist. The orange-blue disc wavering in the vaporous air gradually resolved itself into a lighted lantern. Munson cast a puzzled glance at his companion, noted the glint of excitement in his eyes.

"It is dark inside the chapel, which was why it was chosen," Beatty whispered. "We are dealing with creatures of the darkness."

Munson nodded, but he was far from sure that he understood fully what Beatty was implying. He turned his head again, looking through the crook of a bronze elbow belonging to a sorrowing angel on the group before them.

A huge bearded figure was carrying the lantern. Beatty recognised the saturnine countenance of McMurdo, the funeral director. Behind him came four men, legs slightly bowed under the weight of the coffin they were carrying. The thin form of Alasdair Vair had already hurried past McMurdo and disappeared within the shadowed oak porch. There came the grating of a heavy key in an even heavier lock. Vair came back to the entrance and took the lantern from McMurdo.

The big man went back down the path. Already, other figures were emerging from the mist as the bearers of the first coffin disappeared within the chapel. The two men lay still as death behind the monument, watching the slow procession through the wavering veils of mist.

Beatty counted four coffins with silver handles. He frowned. He had noticed only three at McMurdo's City premises. Perhaps there had been another out of sight, around the corner of the shop. It did not really matter. But it cleared up a small point which had been troubling him. The last coffin was just passing within the porch. There were only three men for this one and they were having some difficulty in negotiating the steps.

The boots of the leading man slipped on the icy stone, and for one moment the coffin tipped, hanging at an awkward angle. Munson and Beatty crouched low as a heavy tread came across the gravel. The burly form of McMurdo was rushing down a small side-path which they had not noticed, fortunately parallel to them and lined with gravestones which concealed them from his sight.

The three men looked up startled, as the formidable figure of the funeral director ran at tremendous speed toward them. His mouth was open and working, but no sound came out. He presented a frightening spectacle. He uttered not a word but put his shoulder beneath the falling coffin and steadied it. The three men lowered it gently to the floor of the porch, getting their breath.

McMurdo put a heavy hand gently on the trembling shoulder of the man who had slipped. His eyes were starting from his head, but his voice was low and controlled as he said, in a deadly tone, "I cannot emphasise enough that you must exercise extreme care."

The man shrank away from his touch as though it had burned him. He turned a blanched face over his shoulder and stammered something in a frightened voice. McMurdo had already turned away, was snapping his fingers at the next man.

"Fetch the others," he commanded.

He went out the porch and looked anxiously up and down the pathway. Then he turned to the third man.

"Get back to the vehicles and see that they are ready to return. We shall be finished here within ten minutes."

The man nodded and ran back down the pathway. The bearers who had earlier gone into the chapel were back. Four of the strongest lifted the casket by the handles and bore it swiftly within the chapel. A glimmer of light showed at the windows as someone carried the lantern past. Then the tall form of Alasdair Vair reappeared.

He said something in a low muffled voice to the funeral director, and the two men went back inside the chapel. The bearers were coming out; in ones and twos they drifted down the pathway until their movements and voices alike were lost in the mist.

McMurdo and Vair were the last to leave, reemerging almost furtively. The director waited impatiently while the other man locked the door. Then he went over to test the iron handle himself. After several exploratory rattles he seemed satisfied.

The two men walked along the path, the echoes of their footsteps dying away at last. Only when they heard the grating rattle as the hearses started off, did Munson and Beatty quit the shelter of the tombs and walk slowly toward the porch.

The two men paused in the shadow of the beamed entrance, listening intently until the last staccato hoof-beat of the retreating hearses had faded in the curtain of mist before they entered. As they had expected the great door was securely locked, though Beatty instinctively tried the handle.

The Inspector looked interrogatively at his companion.

"What now?"

"We must make a check," Beatty said. "Firstly, we must establish whether there is another way into the chapel."

He was out of the porch now, his powerful shoulders hunched in the thick overcoat, striding through the mist, following the building around. The great grey chapel looked almost part of the mist itself, silvery and insubstantial in the pallid light of the early afternoon. Beatty was again conscious of the pangs of hunger; he looked forward to the comfort of the station buffet, but they had much to do before nightfall and he pressed on.

The two men found another door at the far end of the building, shaded by heavy banks of rhododendron. There was no porch and the area was dank and dark, the cobbled walk slippery with moss and lichen. It was a melancholy place here, and Munson looked apprehensively about him, his hand on the butt of the revolver in his overcoat pocket.

The cemetery was a difficult place for a mission such as theirs, and more than once the pair had paused as a figure had come gliding out of the white vapour, only to find themselves confronted by a piece of memorial statuary. Beatty tried the heavy elm door which had probably been used in the past as a convenient means of entry for the officiating priest. Like the main door it was securely locked.

"We must go round," Beatty whispered, moving forward on to the grass. They circled the building, their boots rustling on rank turf, the roots stiff and brittle with frost. Their breath smoked in the raw air, mingling with the mist which pressed in upon them with clammy fingers.

"What do you expect to find?" Munson grunted, his grey eyes darting keenly about him. "Is there any point in getting inside?"

"A great deal if it can be managed without arousing the suspicions of these men," Beatty said in a low voice. "In fact, a way out of the chapel is of considerably more importance than a way in."

And with that enigmatic utterance the Inspector had to be content for the time being. The two men had now almost completed their circuit of the building. Beatty paused as they approached a place where two large windows came down to the ground and looked about him. Visibility extended only a few yards, and the white lacelike veil of the mist pressed rawly on their faces and clothing.

Munson hunched deeply into his thick coat and waited, containing his impatience and curiosity. His empty pipe was in his pocket and he longed for its solace, but it would not have been wise, under the circumstances, to have risked a light at this point. If they were discovered in their purposes all would be lost; Munson realised wryly, almost as soon as the thought was formulated, that he did not understand clearly what their purposes at Brookwood were this day.

He turned back to the building, conscious that Beatty was examining the panes carefully. Beatty breathed on the ice which was frosting the glass, clearing a space through which to look. Munson saw the glimmer of candle-shine within the darkness of the chapel. He put his face to the glass as his companion beckoned him forward.

He saw, after a moment or two, a phantasmal scene swim into his vision; flagstones thick with dust and stamped with the footprints of the visitors; frayed banners hanging from the raftered ceiling; cobwebs and evidence of decay everywhere. Before the chapel altar were ranged, in a clear space on the flags, the four silver-handled coffins on trestles. Candles burned before the altar and provided the sole illumination. Beatty rubbed his hands with satisfaction.

"What do you make of it, Inspector?"

Something of Munson's bewilderment must have showed on his face, for Beatty smiled.

"Why, merely that the coffins have been set out to await the burial service before interment," Munson said.

Beatty's brown eyes held a strange expression as he looked at the Surrey detective.

"Perhaps . . ." he said absently. "We shall know before the day is out, at any rate."

He turned back to the window. To Munson's amazement, he went round the framework, inch by inch. He looked sharply at the Inspector.

"Well, if we are to gain access there is no way but to smash the glass."

"You do not mean to say you intend to break in?" said Munson in astonishment.

Something of his disapproval was betrayed in his raised tone of voice, for Beatty put a hand on his arm. Munson's eyes were bleak as he stared at his companion.

"Without knowing more I cannot sanction this," he said sharply.

There was frustration in Beatty's eyes as he turned.

"Very well, there is no other way of it," he said in a disappointed voice. "We must just wait for nightfall and take our chances."

"Mr. Beatty, if you could just absorb the fact that the official police force is not free to adopt your buccaneering practices, we should make more progress," said Munson.

But there was a glint of amusement in his eyes which belied the coldness in his voice, a fact not lost on the young investigator.

"I should very much like to confide all my hopes and suspicions to you, as you well know," he muttered. "But it would take too long and might, I fear, only confirm some feelings you might entertain as to my sanity. Can you not trust me this bit further?"

Munson shook his head, regret showing in his eyes.

"It would be breaking and entering without a warrant," he said. "I could not sanction it, and if anything goes amiss with this business it is the official force which must suffer."

Beatty made a wry face and stepped back.

"I understand your position, Inspector. We must just both contain our impatience until this evening. We can do no more here."

The two men walked back to the front of the chapel and regained the path. Beatty stood heavy in thought for a moment more, looking at the silver-grey building in front of him, apparently oblivious of the cold and the mist.

"We had best stick to our plan," he said. "You back to the Church of England Station to pass a message to Lestrade, I to the buffet at the Roman Catholic Station and Stevens. I will meet you there in half an hour."

Munson nodded and strode off into the mist, his figure rapidly swallowed in the billowing whiteness. Beatty stood irresolute for a few seconds more, looking regretfully at the locked door of the chapel. Then he too turned away, and the building was left to the mist and the silence.

36

THE DEAD FACE

THE darkness was coming on apace. The short winter's day was almost at an end. Beatty sat moodily at a side-table of the buffet, watching the passengers boarding the coaches of the white-painted train which stood at the platform outside the window. A light wind dispersed the mist, momentarily revealing the busy scene, then obscuring it. Munson was silent opposite, his second whisky untasted before him.

Beatty glanced at the case of instruments on the chair beside him. They would have to move within the next fifteen minutes. Everything depended on their being in the right place in time to catch their opponents.

Beatty had a heavy responsibility, and it was beginning to weigh upon him now that the time for action was near. But he was clear-headed and alert, warmed and refreshed by the food and drink he had consumed in the last hour.

He had been correct. Neither McMurdo nor anyone Beatty had recognised on the train had come near the Roman Catholic Station. With Lestrade and his men, together with Dotterell at the Church of England Station and Stevens available with the cab, they should have every eventuality covered. And the special train Munson had ordered should be in position on the siding by now.

He glanced surreptitiously at his watch, his face heavy with unspoken thought. Munson picked up his glass, looked at him sympathetically over the rim as he drank.

"To success," he said.

Beatty reached for his own glass and the two men drank in silence. Despite the sombre atmosphere—with the black-garbed mourners slowly groping their way through the mist to their carriages; themselves pale and insubstantial phantoms; their bereavements heavy upon them; their own hold on life seeming frail and intangible—the food and spirits Beatty had so recently consumed had totally revived his spirits.

For the rest his youth and natural vigour, combined with the ebullience of his nature, had made him confident of success in the evening's enterprise. Munson noted the sparkle in the brown eyes before him and the strength of the jaw as Beatty turned against the white light which came in at the window; the Roman head denoted courage and resolution. The detective officer savoured the warming spirit and inwardly reflected that Clyde Beatty might have achieved high rank in the regular Force if his inclinations had lain that way.

It was almost dark outside now and a whistle shrilled. A thin plume of steam tore the mist to tatters, and the engine gave a low keening blast in reply. The station staff were lined up on the platform as the engine gave a few preliminary shuddering vibrations. The wheels slipped once or twice, the pistons revolving swiftly, and then steel gripped the rail and the bleached length of the train drew slowly out the platform, blurring and vibrating as the mist eddied around it.

The two men were silent as the rumbling died away; so still was the air outside that they could hear the train draw into the next station at the other side of Brookwood Cemetery. There were only two or three people in the buffet now, and Munson and Beatty sat on for a few moments longer, each heavy with thoughts that they would not—or could not—communicate to the other.

Once again Angela Meredith's face floated unbidden into Beatty's consciousness, like a scarf obscuring one's features on a windy day. He put down his glass with a loud impact on the table, which caused the waitress behind the bar to look at him curiously. He rose to his feet, Munson following his example.

The two men walked over to the door and gained the platform, the raw air like ice upon their faces after the steamy heat of the buffet. Smoke from the locomotive still hung in swathes about the platform, mingled with the streamers of fog, and a red signal-light glowed like a savage eye through the gloom. Then the clatter of the signal-arm reached the two men.

They walked along the platform, heard the buffet door click behind them. Toby Stevens followed casually in their rear, waiting until they were well down the ramp. It was almost dark and there were no other vehicles in the concourse, save for that drawn by Stevens's patient horse, covered by a thick rug and with its head buried in its feedbag.

The two men clambered into the interior of the cab and closed the door. A few seconds later the strong step of Stevens was heard on the metal tread as he ascended to the box. The trap above their heads opened. Stevens's face looked serious as he gazed down at them.

"The same place, gentlemen?"

Beatty nodded.

"The same. And you need not take quite so many precautions this time. But just stop a way short of where you dropped us on the previous occasion."

Toby Stevens put his hand up to the side of his nose in the familiar salute. Munson stirred in the gloom, lighting his pipe with a grunt of satisfaction. The red glow threw his strong features into relief as he puffed contentedly. He shot a glance up at the hatch.

"You saw nothing unusual since you left us?"

Stevens shook his head.

"Just the usual comings and goings at the Church of England Station. I spent the last hour in the buffet here in compliance with your message."

Munson puffed out clouds of fragrant smoke, looking enigmatically at his companion.

"I did not expect anything before dark," Beatty muttered. "You may drive on."

Stevens shut the hatch and the cab lurched off through the ever-growing darkness and the thickening mist.

A profound silence reigned in the cemetery as Beatty and Munson walked stealthily toward the chapel. Their feet made soft crunching noises on the frozen grass; the sheeted forms of angels and seraphs lifted frozen smiles toward the sky as they slid by in the mist. Once the harsh cry of an owl broke the silence; otherwise there was nothing but the faintest indication of their progress across the turf. Nothing but the hammer of the blood in the temples; the steady, slightly heightened pumping of the heart; the rasp of breath in the freezing air.

The two men paused as they came out on to the path facing the great porch; Beatty went quickly to try the heavy door with its iron knocker. He put the faintest pressure on it, careful to make no noise. It was still locked, as he had expected. He went back to Munson. He put his face close to the detective's ear in order to whisper as quietly as possible.

"We must be very careful now. They will be coming soon."

Munson looked at him queryingly, but he only nodded and tapped the pocket which contained his revolver. The two men moved round to the side of the building, almost invisible in the mist, and walked quietly on the grass, making their way to the small door they had quitted a few hours before.

They paused in the shadow of a great marble tomb and listened for a minute or more. The strain of concentration was showing on Beatty's face as he turned to his companion.

"I think we might risk it. But we must be ready to get back into shelter."

They crossed the grass strip and gained the small door. There was something wrong. A muffled exclamation broke from Beatty's lips as he saw that it was ajar. He put his hand on Munson's arm. The Inspector's revolver was already out as they quietly pushed the door back. It went smoothly, on well-oiled hinges. A short, dim passage brought them to a second door, also unlocked. Once beyond it they were within the chapel. As their eyes became accustomed to the feeble light, Beatty stared disbelievingly. Coffins, trestles, and lighted candles: all were gone. Beatty's eyes were wild as he took a step toward Munson.

"We are too late!" he said with a heavy oath. "There is not a second to lose!"

He was already running back to the side-door, oblivious of the noise. Munson hurried after him, his mind turning over a mass of conflicting ideas. They were in the churchyard now.

"Back to the station as fast as Stevens's horse can go!" Beatty said. "Warn Lestrade and get his men to stop any funeral cortège attempting to leave the cemetery."

"Where will you be?" Munson asked.

"I am going down to look at the empty sheds on the other side of the cemetery," Beatty said. "They may have gone that way."

He was down on his knees, searching around. He got up again, smoothing his trousers.

"Be so good as to ask Dotterell to join me there as soon as possible."

"Right!"

Munson hurried off down the path, and a few seconds later Beatty heard the hoof-beats of Stevens's horse receding into the mist. He was already running through the gloom, swerving to avoid gravestones, an angry doubt forming in his mind. He halted after a few yards, examined the ground. There was a changed look on his face as he saw the heavy indentations of boots in the grass. They were impressions such as would have been made by men carrying a heavy burden. He increased his pace, hampered by the mist, but bearing, he hoped, in the right direction.

It was difficult to be certain under such conditions that he was going correctly, and more than once he had to pause to cast about him; the extent and scope of this great city of the dead had never been borne in on him so powerfully, and Beatty felt, despite himself, an oppression descend upon his senses. He seemed to have been contesting with the personality of the cemetery itself ever since he had first visited it at Miss Meredith's behest.

He could not, even at this brief distance in time, quite recall the circumstances; the intervening days had blurred the details in his consciousness. Yet Beatty, as he ran on in the enveloping gloom, the case of instruments heavy in his hand, his revolver a comforting weight in his pocket, had the buoyancy of youth on his side and the burning conviction in his mind that he was at last on the right track.

He slackened speed instinctively as he came out in the area of the cemetery with which he was familiar. For the past few minutes he had seen signs of the party he was seeking: here an extraclear set of prints in the frosty grass; there a broken tree-branch; and once, a deep groove in the turf where the bearers had slipped and a coffin had obviously fallen to the ground.

For the men he was seeking were all avoiding the paths; they cut diametrically across the cemetery, straight over the grass, skirting tombs and statuary, but otherwise ignoring the man-made avenues which it would be more natural to take. This told Beatty two things: that they were making their fastest speed, oblivious of the traces their passage would leave on the softer medium of the turf; and that their burdens were heavy, necessitating the shortest route.

He stopped only once, near the chapel in which Rossington had carried out his autopsies, and checked his revolver, throwing off the safety-catch. Then he was running on across the grass, down toward the blocked-off area of the sheds. He slackened his pace as he drew near, finally coming to a halt by an ancient mausoleum whose spiked railings were rimed with ice and whose convoluted statuary was covered with moss and lichen. He listened intently, but could hear nothing of his quarry. He went forward again, walking on tiptoe, his movements shrouded by the masking and now friendly mist.

Beatty finally made out through the darkness and fog the wavering outlines of the barrier across the path, where he had twice been turned away. To his surprise he found one end of the planking down. His excitement rose. Quite clearly whoever had removed the coffins from the Catholic chapel had passed through. There was nowhere else for them to go down here.

The silence remained unbroken. Beatty was up near the sheds, his hand on the butt of the revolver, his nerves screwed up to the tightest pitch. To his astonishment he found the great barred door standing ajar, the padlocks which had secured it dangling from the hasps. He swallowed quickly and then slipped aside, hardly moving the door in his anxiety to avoid remaining too long against the light.

He waited in the dimness of the workshop, his eyes adjusting to the gloom, aware of a faint subterranean noise up ahead. He worked his way down the long building, all his senses telling him that it was empty. The second door also was standing ajar. Beatty received another surprise then. An oil lantern dimly burned up ahead, illuminating the passageway with its golden yellow light.

There was no sign of the skeletal thing which had almost robbed Beatty of his senses on his previous visit. But the smell of earth and decay was heavy and cloying in his nostrils again. He went forward slowly, his shadow thrown across the baulked timbers of the passage.

He paused at the big iron-bound door, his heart jumping to find that too ajar. Perspiration trickled down his face as he opened it slowly, using the barrel of the revolver for the purpose. Once again there came the sharp creaking which set all his nerves aflame. He could see a golden band of light spilling in; he opened the door only a few inches, just enough to slip through. One swift look showed him that the passageway ahead was empty. The illumination came from another oil lantern hanging from a pillar which supported the roof. There was a brick floor here and the roof was groined.

Beatty glanced around; the place was void of life, but the floor sloped downward and a cool draught blew from somewhere up ahead, setting the wick of the lantern flaring and throwing great jumping shadows of the pillar on the wall. There was an old brown stone sink on one side, and from the tap over it again came the slow monotonous dripping which had so fretted the young investigator's nerves on the previous visit.

He went down the centre of the chamber, keeping behind the pillars. He soon saw that there were three, in the middle of the floor, supporting the ancient roof. Beatty stopped suddenly, his breath hissing in his throat. As he gained the second pillar he could see that there were sheafs of flowers and wreaths jumbled unceremoniously in a heap. Beatty gave a tight, sardonic smile.

He approached the mound cautiously. A scratched and dirty shoe protruded from the heap. He knelt and moved the flowers gently. There was a second lantern hanging from a hook on the third pillar some way down the vaulted chamber from him. It threw a flickering light on the grey hair, stubbled cheeks, and staring eyes of the roughly dressed man beneath the flowers. Once again Beatty put his fingers on the marble-coldness of a dead face.

37

DERRINGER

A HAND emerging from behind the pillar turned down the wick of the lantern. A shadow passed across Beatty as he rose to his feet. A flame split the darkness, and the crack of an explosion reverberated monstrously beneath the arches of the vaulted ceiling.

Something brought chips of stone raining to the floor, pattering about the cellar. With a convulsive reflex action Beatty had rolled behind the pillar. He had his revolver up as the dark figure disappeared behind the far pillar. Beatty fired. His target was the lantern hanging on the hook behind him. At that range his aim was sure; the crash of the glass was followed by the swift extinction of the light. He heard the lantern smash to the floor, and there was a brief flare of flame as the oil spilled on the flags.

By the smoky and uneven light Beatty could see that the third pillar ahead stood up stark and bare. Beyond it was a vague, indefinable area of shadow, where he had earlier glimpsed a haphazard jumble of boxes and crates. If his man had gone in there it would be a difficult and dangerous task to venture after him. If he were behind the far pillar the odds would be more balanced.

In any event Beatty had to force things to a decision; he could not hope to escape with his life otherwise. He would have to cover many yards to the door through which he had entered. The yellow glow from the lantern beyond it was the only illumination in the cellar now that the spilled oil was burning out into stinking and smoky gloom. Even as Beatty watched, the bluish-yellow flames winked and died.

The mingled stench of oil and flowers from the wreaths was acrid in his nostrils. Somewhere up ahead a nailed boot grated on stone. Beatty was standing upright behind the pillar. It was about three feet wide and afforded him good cover. Unfortunately, the same circumstances applied to the far buttress behind which his opponent might be concealed. There was silence now and Beatty did not feel encouraged to make the first overtures; the deadly game would continue in silence until its conclusion one way or another.

He still had the case of instruments. It was lying about a yard away from the heaped wreaths. Beatty reached out a cautious foot to his left and eased the valise toward him. The slithering noise, minute as it was, brought an immediate reaction. The bright flash of flame and the almost simultaneous boom of the explosion made the ears ring.

Beatty had immediately withdrawn his foot, but the shot had been uncannily accurate. The bullet ricochetted from the floor near the case and exploded flower petals in a cascade across the cellar floor. Beatty realised that the faint illumination from the far door behind him was enough to silhouette the pillar behind which he crouched.

But he had seen enough to indicate his opponent's position. The muzzle flash had come from the right-hand side of the far buttress. His man was undoubtedly behind it, and now that Beatty's eyes were becoming accustomed to the lower level of illumination he could see that the nearest crate behind which he might take refuge was three yards beyond.

There would be time enough for Beatty to drop him, even if he retreated, keeping shelter between him and Beatty. His case was near enough now for him to retrieve it in safety. Beatty quietly lowered himself to his knees and lifted it by the handle. He stood up again, keeping his eyes ahead, looking for a change in the dim outline of the pillar's silhouette which would tell him where danger lurked.

His disengaged hand was quietly unsnapping the hasp securing the case, while the case itself was held by the pressure of his body against the pillar. This left his right, pistol-hand free. Beatty felt perspiration running into his eyes, and his nerves were screwed to high pitch. His ears were straining to catch the faintest sound out of the ordinary.

He was also conscious that he was highly vulnerable. If anyone should come in through the far door behind him, it would create an extremely dangerous situation which Beatty could no longer control. But he did not think that would happen. The men who had removed the coffins from the Roman Catholic chapel had been too preoccupied and in too much of a hurry.

It was obvious that they had all gone through the tunnel and into whatever lay beyond this catacomb. The secret of Brookwood was behind the far door. It was a secret which was being desperately defended by the man with the pistol at the third buttress. He was evidently determined to spend his own life—or Beatty's—in the process. Beatty did not underestimate him; he was a formidable opponent and he was beginning to have a good idea as to his identity.

Beatty had the small spanner in his hand now. He put the case down at his feet. The tool seemed to make a tremendous clatter as it landed among the crates. The flare of the pistol and the slap of the report were almost simultaneous. Beatty had already quitted the pillar. He was in against the stonework of the third buttress before wood-splinters from the crates had finished their pattering on the floor.

But he had badly miscalculated in the semidarkness. Despite himself a groan forced itself from his lips as his knuckles struck a protruding cornice on the pillar. Blood started from the broken flesh. The hand, numbed, relaxed its grip on the butt of the pistol, which clattered down and bounced across the cellar.

It lay a good three feet out from the shelter of the stonework. Beatty was already on his knees, desperately tugging at his shoe, as a dark form stepped out from the deeper shadow and came toward him.

Beatty lay back against the pillar now, his injured right hand concealed in the skirt of his coat. His heart was pumping uncomfortably in his throat. He kept his head down as though he were badly injured, but his eyes missed nothing. The faint shadow of the man behind the pillar crawled forward across the floor until it reached the young investigator's body.

The big man looked even more enormous as he towered over Beatty. His face was lost in the darkness, but the faint light coming in from the far door glinted on the barrel of the pistol as he raised it to take aim at the man sprawled at his feet. He took another step nearer, his face coming into focus. The barrel of the pistol and the pin-points of his eyeballs made a glinting triangle of light in the darkness.

The derringer emitted an absurd popping noise as Beatty swiftly brought it up into the firing position. He had no time to aim properly, but it was impossible to miss at that range and the small bullet would do considerable damage under those conditions. The big man stumbled and made a hoarse coughing sound.

He staggered and stepped blindly to one side of Beatty. The young man was up with a rush, but no further effort was required from him. The pistol barrel was descending. It hit the floor with a loud clatter as the muscles of the fingers relaxed. The man with the beard was taking short, jerky steps now, as though he were dancing.

He had his hands out stiffly before him. Beatty got to his own revolver and followed. There was more light in here now. McMurdo's eyes were wide open, but he saw nothing. Dark blood descended from his mouth, spread in a deepening stain across the waistcoat with the handsome gold watch-chain. His marionette-dance ended abruptly as his jerky steps took him to the tumbled pile of wreaths. He went down head-first among the flowers and lay still.

Beatty felt a violent trembling in all his limbs. His mouth was dry and perspiration ran down into his eyes. He stood back against the pillar and tried to control the shuddering. When he was master of himself he went over and turned the funeral director. The face was already set in an unmistakable mask. Beatty got up as a door slammed suddenly.

He forced himself forward, felt vital energy flowing through him again. He held the revolver up as he ran. The far end of the vault ended in a massive iron-faced door. It had a large ring-handle. Beatty had his hand on it when he heard the grating noise of heavy bolts being driven home on the other side.

He could do nothing further here. He had to have the help that only Lestrade and his men could give. Beatty went rapidly back down the arches. He found the spanner lying where he had thrown it, retrieved his case. He put the derringer back in its holster and picked up McMurdo's pistol.

He ran back down the vault and through the far door, not car-ing how much noise he made. It was darker in the passage than he had remembered. He regained the workshop with bursting lungs and paused a moment, putting McMurdo's pistol in a side pocket. He transferred the case to his left hand and put the revolver into his right-hand pocket.

He opened the door of the shed and stepped out into the mist and darkness of Brookwood Cemetery. At the same moment an iron hand was at his throat and he was thrown violently backward.

38

SCOTLAND YARD STEPS IN

DOTTERELL's face looked grim. His eyes were startled as he took in the details of Beatty's features. The grip on Beatty's throat relaxed, and he stumbled and would have fallen had it not been for his assistant's restraining hand. Dotterell's face had regained its usual enigmatic expression as he stepped away.

"You should have announced yourself, Mr. Beatty," he said dourly. "I almost did you an injury."

"Almost," said Beatty wryly, fingering the red mark on his throat where Dotterell's fingernails had rested.

"Did I hear a shot just now?" Dotterell asked.

"You did," Beatty replied, handing his case to his companion. "We must get Lestrade."

The two men started back through the cemetery as Beatty spoke. The mist swirled thickly about them, and it seemed to be increasing. Beatty explained the circumstances in short, clipped sentences. His breath was coming more easily and his hand had stopped bleeding.

"Once again I seem to have missed the core of activity," Dotterell observed in disappointed tones as they came out by the chapel which Superintendent Bateman had put at Beatty's disposal for the autopsies.

Beatty smiled grimly.

"There will be plenty of opportunity before the night is out."

Dotterell looked at him sharply.

"So McMurdo was at the heart of this criminal conspiracy? But I still do not see . . ."

"There is no use in theorising at this point," Beatty interrupted. "There will be time for explanations later."

There came the clatter of hooves, and the black silhouette of a cab drawn by a single horse appeared clear-etched against the blank whiteness of the fog. Beatty chuckled with satisfaction.

"I thought I would hold myself in readiness, gentlemen," Toby Stevens called. "What are your instructions?"

Beatty and Dotterell were already tumbling into the interior of the vehicle.

"The Church of England Station, as hard as you can go," Beatty said.

He turned to Dotterell as Stevens slammed the trap shut.

"Frankly, I am worried that something has miscarried. It was no accident that McMurdo was waiting for me in the tunnel. And why is not Munson back? I sent him for help a long time ago."

The cab was lurching along at an alarming speed now, despite the thickness of the fog. Dotterell looked blankly out of the window, rubbing to clear the pane. The sidelights showed the edge of the pathway and the occasional gravestone whirling by at a dangerously close distance. Dotterell realised that Stevens must know every inch of these grounds; he would need to if they were not to crash to disaster under such conditions.

It was with something like relief that the two men felt the cab suddenly grind to a halt. They got out, found they were at the bottom of the station ramp.

"Wait," Beatty called. "We will be back in a few minutes."

He ran lightly up toward the station entrance, Dotterell following. It was a little clearer here, and Beatty was dismayed to see an empty platform facing him. He hurried down toward the buffet. At the same moment Munson was coming out; the two men almost collided in the doorway. The Surrey detective's face was stern.

"What is happening, Mr. Beatty?" he asked. "I am unable to find Lestrade and his men anywhere. I have been to the main entrance of the cemetery. I was waiting at the buffet hoping to hear from them, but now it is closing."

Beatty looked grimly round the platform.

"I knew something was wrong, Inspector," he rapped. "Where is the light engine, for example?"

"In the siding, I presume," said Munson carelessly. He took out his pipe as he spoke and lit up, the red glow of the burning tobacco making little stippled markings on his face. His attitude told Beatty clearly that in Munson's opinion he should have confided in his colleagues more frankly. Beatty took two steps up the platform. The mist billowed dankly about them. For once he appeared at a loss.

"Things have gone badly awry," he told the Inspector. "The arrangement was that Lestrade and his men should remain here within call when they had finished checking the cemetery entrances. Something must have engaged their attention."

"They were certainly not at the gates," said Munson, puffing at his pipe until it was burning to his satisfaction. "I have checked two of the main entrances and they were firmly closed and locked. It is Bateman's invariable custom at dusk."

Beatty nodded. He turned to Dotterell.

"We must take immediate steps . . ." he began, when Dotterell interrupted him. The tall man had a puzzled expression on his face.

"I saw the Inspector and his men leave here just a few minutes before I met Inspector Munson. I presumed they were checking the entrances. I stayed on for a while and then walked down the ramp. I had just got to the concourse when I met the Inspector coming to fetch me."

"That is correct," Munson verified.

He puffed slowly at his pipe, emphasising his short, clipped sentences.

"Stevens had lost no time in getting me here. I gave Dotterell your message and he hurried off. I then waited for Lestrade to come back."

Beatty rubbed his chin with strong fingers.

"The sequence seems perfectly clear. Something must have happened either just before you arrived at the station or shortly after the police left the premises."

He turned as there came a rattling noise at the door of the

buffet. He went forward to find a tall man with a dark moustache and the fair girl from the buffet locking up. He went back
to Munson.

"You might just ask them if they have seen anything suspicious,"
he whispered. "It will come better from you, as a well-known local
police officer."

Munson nodded curtly and went forward. A mumbled conversation ensued. Dotterell and Beatty waited a little apart, the
raw mist billowing about them. Beatty was conscious of a sour
feeling of failure. Every moment was vital, but he could do little
without the reinforcements Lestrade and his men represented.
Plus the authority of Scotland Yard.

Munson came back. His face looked worried.

"You were right, Mr. Beatty. The girl at the buffet saw what
happened. A man who answers Lestrade's description was given a
message at the buffet door. Lestrade came in and a few moments
later five men in all left the buffet in a group."

Beatty gave a muffled oath.

"By a rough-looking man who delivers messages from Woking
Station!" he said excitedly.

He looked bleakly at Inspector Munson.

"Whose body is lying in a tunnel back at the edge of the cemetery there."

Munson's pipe wobbled in his mouth, but he prevented its falling to the ground. Before he could speak again Beatty went on.

"Inspector Munson, I have never been more deadly serious. We
must find Inspector Lestrade and his officers within the next few
minutes. Someone tried to kill me in the tunnel just now. I had to
shoot him in self-defence. It was McMurdo, the funeral director. If
Lestrade has been lured away by a message delivered by the Woking Station man, it means someone knows we are here. And why
we are here."

Munson's pipe wobbled again. His voice came out in a strangled
grunt.

"Good God!" he said.

The three men were interrupted by the faint blast of a whistle.
It came from their left, where the railway lines disappeared in the
wall of fog. Beatty seized Munson's arm.

"The light engine," he said. "I had thought it was at the siding! Quickly! We haven't a moment to lose."

He turned and ran down the ramp, the others following behind him. The three men tumbled into Toby Stevens's cab.

"To the Roman Catholic Station!" Beatty shouted. "Hurry, man. Drive for your life!"

The pulsating vibrations of the engine reverberated through the foggy air. Beatty ran down the platform with bursting lungs. Quick as he was, Dotterell was quicker. His figure disappeared in the swirling steam up ahead. Their feet beat a rapid tattoo down the icy platform. Munson was only a stride or two behind. Beatty and Dotterell kept in hard condition, but the private investigator was surprised at the Surrey detective's stamina.

They had run several hundred yards already and he seemed as fresh as Beatty. Then Beatty remembered his companion's rugby history and wondered no longer. Beatty swerved to avoid an iron post which loomed out of the mist, warned Munson with a hoarse shout. Signals glowed green through the blanketing fog. The train was already moving.

The dim sheen of oil lamps inside the carriage revealed the startled face of Lestrade. Beatty swore, but Dotterell already had a carriage door open. The train was gathering speed now and Dotterell jumped aboard, holding the door wide for Beatty. Both he and Munson increased their pace. By a desperate effort Beatty caught the door-edge and hauled himself aboard. He had already turned and offered his hand to the Surrey detective. Together, he and Dotterell almost dragged the Inspector in.

Dotterell slammed the door to behind them and sank back against the carriage panelling. The three men fought for breath for a few moments.

"That was close," Dotterell panted, sliding open the carriage door. The sharp features of Inspector Lestrade were already framed in the opening.

"Too close," said Beatty. "Good evening, Inspector. I am afraid we have been taken in by the oldest of tricks."

Lestrade's face was a study. He simply motioned them in, and the three men gratefully slumped into seats in the warmth of the compartment. The only other occupant was Sergeant Bassett, whose face bore the same expression of baffled bewilderment as his chief.

"We must find a way of stopping this train," Beatty muttered to Dotterell.

The gaunt assistant nodded and went out into the corridor. The wheels were beating a steady rhythm now, and fog swirled at the windows. Lestrade sat down opposite Beatty and regarded him grimly.

"Have you gone mad, Mr. Beatty?"

Beatty shook his head, exchanging a wry glance with Munson.

"No, Inspector, but I should like to see the note you were given on the platform earlier this evening. It is a decoy."

Lestrade fished in his overcoat pocket with a startled expression. He drew out a large sheet of paper and passed it over.

"By the way, I don't believe you have been formally introduced," Beatty went on. "This is Inspector Munson of the Surrey Force. Inspector Lestrade of Scotland Yard."

The two men shook hands with wary glances as Beatty studied the note. It was written in a reasonable facsimile of his own handwriting.

Its contents were curt and to the point: "Inspector—A false trail, I am afraid. Return to London forthwith. I will explain later. Beatty."

Beatty smiled grimly and passed the note to Munson. Lestrade looked at the two men opposite with a stony face. The Sergeant wisely kept his own counsel.

"We have both been tricked, Inspector," said Beatty. "Far from being a false trail, it is the warmest I have ever encountered."

Lestrade's face was alive with interest now. Beatty held up the note.

"This was given you by the man Cronk who hangs about Woking Station and delivers messages. His body is now lying in a rough tunnel back at Brookwood Cemetery. He was obviously killed because his usefulness as a spy and courier had expired."

Lestrade gave a curt exclamation. There was a strange expression in his eyes as he glanced at Munson. He was about to open his mouth to begin an angry outburst when Beatty anticipated him.

"This means that someone on the train down recognised me and realised my errand," he said quietly. "We have no time to lose. It is vital to get this engine turned round and headed back to Woking."

He glanced up as the carriage door slid open. The tall, lean form of Dotterell entered.

"It appears that the special is not scheduled to stop until Waterloo," he said. "I shall have to get to the driver."

Lestrade was on his feet. He looked incredulous.

"That means you will have to go outside the carriage," he said sharply. "It is far too dangerous. I will not take the responsibility."

Dotterell smiled crookedly at Beatty.

"You will not have to, Inspector," he said. "Mr. Beatty understands my methods of working."

Beatty nodded. His brown eyes were fixed thoughtfully on the Scotland Yard man.

"There will be no danger the way Dotterell will set about it," he said. "Best leave him be."

Munson smiled as Lestrade gave a resigned shrug. He sat down again.

"I take no responsibility," he repeated emphatically.

"That is quite understood," Beatty answered soothingly. He nodded at Dotterell who quitted the carriage, sliding the door to behind him.

"He will leave the carriage near the point where it joins the engine," Beatty said. "There will be only a few yards to go to warn the driver."

Lestrade appeared unhappy. He crossed his bony hands on his knees and avoided looking at Sergeant Bassett.

"I think it is time we had a full explanation," he said gruffly.

Beatty chuckled. Munson paused in restuffing the bowl of his pipe. His grey eyes looked at Beatty reflectively, but he did not say anything.

"You are quite right, Inspector Lestrade," Beatty said, leaning forward to look the Scotland Yard man full in the face. "You have all been very patient. The reason I kept you in the dark was that I was not at all sure of my facts. I still have not got all the ends in my hands. But there is enough to be going on with."

He paused and looked round the carriage grimly.

"More than enough to bring this bizarre business to its conclusion tonight. But it will have to wait just a few minutes. Just so soon as we are on our way back to Woking. Then I shall feel free to settle. Every yard this engine takes us from Brookwood increases the chances that our men may yet slip through our fingers."

He paused and looked round the intent faces before him.

"We are up against damnably cunning opponents," he said softly. "They have already killed again and again. And but for the gods of chance I myself would be lying dead back in that tunnel while you here would be travelling Londonwards none the wiser."

He broke off as there was a sudden squeal. The four men in the carriage were thrown in all directions as the brakes were violently applied. The other three Scotland Yard officers appeared in the corridor with startled expressions. Lestrade got up and slid the door back.

"There has been a change of plan," he said curtly. "We are going back to Brookwood. Hold yourselves in readiness."

The train had almost stopped now. Beatty let the nearest window down. Acrid fog billowed into the carriage, mingled with smoke. A muffled shout came from below, and heavy footsteps crunched on the ballast at the lineside.

"Mr. Beatty, sir."

"What is it?"

Dotterell appeared below them in the mist. His hat was awry and there was a smudge of coal-dust alongside his nose, but there was a humorous expression dancing in his eyes.

"It seems I have upset the railway schedules," he said. "I had to apply the brake myself, and now the driver threatens me with the processes of the law."

Munson and Lestrade exchanged amused glances.

"We must get back to Woking," Beatty said impatiently.

"The driver refuses to return without an express order in writing from someone in authority. If Inspector Lestrade would come forward . . ."

"Very well," grumbled Lestrade wearily. He jammed his hat on to his head and lowered himself gingerly on to the train running-board from the open door. He looked fiercely at Beatty.

"It is my head on the block, Mr. Beatty. I must have some reasons for these proceedings before we reach Woking."

"You shall have them," said Beatty equably.

The three men watched as the figures of Dotterell and Lestrade disappeared into the mist.

39

BACK TO BROOKWOOD

BEATTY'S thick fingers drummed impatiently on the ledge as his eyes anxiously searched the impenetrable white wall outside the carriage window. The train was stationary still; they seemed to have been marooned in a white cocoon for hours. Munson consulted his watch for the third time. Beatty's lips were thin and tightly compressed.

"Another ten minutes already," he muttered.

Lestrade put a reassuring hand on his shoulder.

"Come, Mr. Beatty, the delay is not all that serious. The driver has had to go back down the line to telegraph the change of plans. After all, we cannot risk an accident . . ."

"You are quite right, Inspector," Beatty said steadily. "I will pass the time instead by telling you what I know about this affair and what I suspect. Beyond that I cannot go, for I have not yet all the ends in my hands."

He looked across at Dotterell and then back to Lestrade.

"Should you not bring your men forward to join us? They may be going against desperate, heavily armed men. I think it only fair."

"By all means," Lestrade said.

At a sign from him Sergeant Bassett got up and left the carriage. When he returned with the other three officers, the carriage was filled with a comfortable blue fug from Munson's pipe. With the newcomers settled, Beatty cast a glance out at the heavy white mass that lay like thick folds of cloth beyond the window.

"If you cast your mind back, Inspector," he began. "Your involvement with this affair began with my reporting Dr. Couchman's death off Blackfriars Bridge. Inspector Munson's began much earlier. Dr. Couchman's death is linked with incidents at Brookwood Cemetery. But both began a great deal earlier still in London."

He looked reflectively at the Scotland Yard officer and from him to the strong red-complexioned face of Sergeant Bassett. There was no sound in the carriage; the only thing that broke the silence was the faint hiss of steam from the engine, two coaches ahead.

"You wondered, as I recall, why I insisted on firearms. I think you will understand a little better when I tell you there have already been three deaths since the funeral train left Waterloo this morning."

Lestrade's eyes narrowed, but he just sat with his hands clasped on his lap, waiting for Beatty to go on.

"A man with a limp tried to throw me off the train on our way down," Beatty continued. "During our struggle he fell to his death. In an underground passage at Brookwood I found the body of the man Cronk. At almost the same instant I was fired at with intent to kill by McMurdo, the managing director of one of the funeral firms engaged in today's interments. I was obliged to kill him to preserve my own life."

Lestrade made a choking noise at this point. Munson had a sudden fit of coughing, and even Dotterell looked off balance. Beatty went hastily on, avoiding Lestrade's shocked face.

"You now see, I hope, why official police methods are impossible in this case. And at the same time why I had to enlist the help of both the London and Surrey Forces."

"Yes, well, never mind that," said Lestrade in a flat voice, clearing his throat. He looked frowningly at Sergeant Bassett.

"What's done is done. We want to know the reason why."

"Inspector Munson's viewpoint exactly," replied Beatty, turning to the man on the seat beside him. "My apologies for keeping you both in the dark so long."

There came a shout from the lineside. Dotterell leaned over and lowered the window. The raw cold of the January air billowed in, bringing fog and coal-smoke with it.

"I have permission to proceed, but there is a fog alert," the driver called up. "There will be a delay of a quarter of an hour to allow an up-express to pass."

"Very well," called Lestrade. "I will make the matter clear to your superiors."

He slammed the window down and turned an enquiring face to Beatty.

"Come, Mr. Beatty," said Munson in a friendly voice. "You have done much so far and carried the burden alone. Now it is time to share it."

Before Beatty could answer, he stabbed with the stem of his pipe at Lestrade and gave him and his officers a brief résumé of events at Brookwood; of Couchman's suspected involvement in the poisoning of Tredegar Meredith and of Varley; his suicide; and of the scheme compounded to bring Beardsley to the Shot Tower.

Lestrade's face had been getting more and more incredulous as the recital proceeded. His face was black as Munson paused in his flow.

"I can see that things are a little more informal in the Surrey Force," he murmured, looking from Munson's bland face wreathed in tobacco smoke to Beatty. Munson smiled and seemed not at all put out.

"I think you would have done the same in my place, Inspector," he said. "Mr. Beatty has been invaluable. And we are a little thin on the ground in Surrey, you know. I could have had my own officers at Brookwood today, but news spreads quickly in small country places."

He looked pointedly at the five police officers sprawled about the carriage. Lestrade shifted his feet.

"Mayhap, mayhap, Inspector," he said awkwardly. "You mentioned something about the man Beardsley. If you suspected how he died, why did you not report it? It has probably gone down as an accident report."

"Very likely," interrupted Beatty. "But we had good reason, after all. I could not involve myself with the South Bank incidents without also revealing that I was still alive. And that would not have suited our plans."

Lestrade did not answer but drew his thin lips sullenly in. It was plain that the breach of protocol upset his sense of exactitude and ideas of duty.

"If it makes you feel any better, Inspector, the man who killed Beardsley with the brewer's dray is lying dead on the track back there," said Munson equably. He went on sucking steadily at his pipe, smiling to himself as he caught Lestrade's sudden intake of breath.

"An eye for an eye," Lestrade murmured, raising his eyebrows to Sergeant Bassett, "Please continue, Mr. Beatty."

"The threads came to my hand in a haphazard manner," Beatty said. "I had been engaged by the late Mr. Meredith's daughter to investigate the circumstances surrounding her father's death. Through her good offices also I was asked by Sir Inigo Walton to prepare a report on the security arrangements at the City and Suburban Bank. You may remember your colleague Inspector Bull is the expert there, Lestrade."

The Scotland Yard man nodded, his eyes heavy beneath his bowler hat. He looked unseeingly at the heavy mantle of fog that obscured the windows. It was bitterly cold in the carriage now, and the oil lamps in their brass holders cast a pale sheen on the rime that frosted the glass.

"Varley had died at McMurdo's East End establishment," Beatty went on. "And I had seen Couchman there. When checking those City bank premises which had been raided and had lost considerable sums of bullion, I came upon McMurdo's main depot right in the centre of the circle. Everything crystallised in my mind. There was the common factor for which I had been searching."

Every eye in the carriage was upon him now. Beatty went on.

"I saw the limping man vanish into the darkness of McMurdo's yard. When I learned from the manager, Alasdair Vair, that the firm was carrying out a number of funerals at Brookwood this morning, the chain was complete."

Lestrade leaned forward, excitement sparking a faint flush on his sallow features.

"You don't mean to say, Mr. Beatty . . ."

"Try not to anticipate, Lestrade," Beatty interrupted calmly. "There were a number of factors which drew my attention to the somewhat unusual circumstances. The funeral of a man named Vickers, for instance. Every card attached to the wreaths and sprays was written in the same hand. When I noticed that they formed part of the tributes for a group of silver-handled coffins, my suspicions became certainty."

"Mr. Vickers did not exist, and the silver-handled coffins could easily be picked out from the masses of others at the cemetery," said Lestrade suddenly.

He shut his mouth with a satisfied snap, like a fish taking a fly.

"Excellent, Lestrade!" said Beatty enthusiastically. "You surpass yourself."

He looked round the carriage, aware that everyone there was hanging on his words. So engrossed were they that they hardly noticed the lurch as the train started to glide forward again.

"I had one big advantage at McMurdo's when I appeared there in my guise as a mourner," Beatty went on. "The limping man knew me, of course. Couchman had seen me, but that did not matter, since he was dead. But McMurdo had never seen me. As I was so suspicious about the activities of his establishment by this time, I raised no objections when his manager volunteered to fetch him. There was nothing about Mr. McMurdo personally to arouse my suspicions. And nothing about me to raise his, I should hope. But I did notice one thing."

Beatty leaned forward and looked with satisfaction at the mist billowing at the window; the train had gathered speed now and they were at last travelling in the right direction.

"Something odd about McMurdo. He was impeccably dressed and well turned out. And his fingernails were well-scrubbed and scrupulously clean as befitted one of his profession. But I noticed that they were badly scarred and broken."

He looked round the carriage with satisfaction in his eyes.

"Does that suggest nothing?"

"Digging in the tunnel!" said Dotterell with an air of quiet satisfaction.

"Precisely," said Beatty. "Here we had a connection between McMurdo's establishment and Brookwood. It was only a short way from that to the tunnel beneath the old sheds which someone was so scrupulously guarding. I took a risk in meeting McMurdo face to face, I admit. But it was a risk well weighed. I was banking on the fact that McMurdo himself with his position to keep up would not have been personally involved with the men who put me in the lake when the attempt was made on my life. I was convinced that McMurdo had not recognised me as Clyde Beatty, private investigator."

Lestrade looked puzzled.

"Then you don't think he could be responsible for this note?" he said, taking it from his pocket again.

Beatty shook his head.

"Not directly."

Lestrade sat silently for a moment, but his mounting excitement became too much for him.

"You are not suggesting that the gold from the London bullion robberies is concealed in the coffins with the silver handles?"

"I am suggesting exactly that!" Beatty retorted. "And admit that if I had told you so at Waterloo-road, you would never have come here."

Admiration fought with resignation in Lestrade's dour features. He put out his hand impulsively.

"Well, if you are right, Mr. Beatty, I for one will rate you greater than Sherlock Holmes!"

Beatty smiled and made a clicking noise with his tongue.

"That is pitching it a little high," he murmured deprecatingly. "But I appreciate the compliment nonetheless."

The train was gathering speed, the engine shovelling angry red sparks over its shoulder, making fiery streamers in the tattered banners of the fog. Beatty glanced out the window.

"We should be there in a few minutes, gentlemen. You told the driver we wanted the Roman Catholic Station? I have asked Toby Stevens to remain there."

The last question was addressed to Dotterell. He nodded without speaking.

"What I cannot understand is why Miss Meredith's father should have been poisoned," said Munson abruptly.

"Perhaps he found out something about Couchman's activities at Brookwood?" suggested Sergeant Bassett, who had been deferentially silent while his superiors were talking.

"Perhaps," said Lestrade cautiously. "We shall learn more when we arrive at Woking. At least the major criminals have met their just deserts."

"On the contrary," said Beatty enigmatically. "The greatest villains have yet to be unmasked."

There came a lurching and a squealing as the brakes were applied. Munson was already at the window. The mist stung their faces with its coldness as it swirled in. Footsteps crunched on the gravel. The guard of the train came into view, his head buried in his greatcoat and scarf.

"The gates are across," he called. "Across and locked."

Beatty turned a puzzled face to Munson.

"What does he mean?"

"The railway entrance to the cemetery is blocked off at night," Munson explained. "There is a metal and wire-mesh barrier which is locked every evening to discourage trespassers. It is usually secured after the London train leaves in the afternoon."

Lestrade's face had resumed its usual dour expression.

"Secured as soon as our engine was away," he muttered. "We have returned just in time. We'd best have a look at it."

His men were already descending to the permanent way, and Beatty and Munson hurriedly followed. It was bitterly cold after the atmosphere of the carriage, and the party followed the guard back a short distance along the line. A red oil lamp glowed like a baleful eye through the murk.

"A good thing you spotted the gate," said Lestrade.

The guard, a burly man with greasy black hair and a thick moustache, chuckled.

"Bless you, sir, we know every inch of the line. We were expecting to find it closed, and I signalled the driver in good time."

The party waited while Beatty and Munson tried the gate. It was in two halves, secured in the centre with an iron chain and padlocks. Beatty came back, his face set.

"We shall waste time if we walk," he said.

He turned to the guard.

"Do you think you can burst through the gate without any risk to the train?"

The guard's face was perturbed.

"No problem at all, sir. But who's going to authorise it?"

"Scotland Yard," said Lestrade. "In writing, if necessary. Break down that gate. We're wasting time."

The guard looked from Lestrade to Munson and then to Beatty, meeting only purposeful, determined faces. He lifted a deferential forefinger to his cap.

"As you say, gentlemen. If you will resume your seats."

He went away at a fast run toward the engine while the party tumbled back aboard the train. Within two minutes they were under way again. There was a slight cracking noise through the fog and then an almost imperceptible lurch as they burst through the gate. Beatty, at the window, glimpsed the barrier reeling drunkenly aside in the mist as they rushed past.

They were on the platform before the train had come to a stop at the Catholic Station. Beatty was already running toward the welcoming form of Toby Stevens.

40

AT THE FIRS

STEVENS was startled at the warmth of Beatty's greeting. The young investigator pumped him by the hand.

"I have never been so glad to see anyone, Stevens. We shall need you and your cab before the evening is out."

"I said I would remain here all night if necessary," Stevens replied, his strong face animated and alert beneath the mane of grey hair. He looked curiously at the Scotland Yard men, noted their purposeful air. His eyes widened as he took in the revolver Sergeant Bassett was checking.

"If there's trouble, I'm your man, gentlemen."

"There will be trouble right enough," Beatty said.

He looked swiftly round the bleak platform, pulling at Lestrade's sleeve.

"Sergeant Bassett had better take two men and get down to the disused section of the cemetery to seal off the tunnel."

"They will need guidance in this fog," Munson said. "I know the place and will take them there."

Beatty nodded.

"That will leave five of us, including Stevens," he told Lestrade.

"That should be enough."

"Enough for what?" said the Scotland Yard man, looking at Beatty shrewdly.

"Why, for the other end of the tunnel."

He turned back to Stevens.

"How is it you managed to remain inside the walls once the cemetery had closed for the night? I understand the Superintendent's arrangements are very strict."

Stevens smiled. He was already leading the way down the platform, the others following. He laid his finger alongside his nose in the old familiar gesture.

"Nothing easier in this fog. Besides, I have a key to the side-gate. I come out regularly, and it saves disturbing the keepers."

With a few curt words to the others Munson strode off with Sergeant Bassett and the men, the glow of his pipe rapidly disappearing in the fog.

"We shall want the side-gate, then," Beatty said. "I am looking for the nearest house."

Stevens paused in opening the cab-door. He ushered Lestrade and the remaining detective constable inside. Dotterell followed.

"You mean The Firs, sir. The big house just outside the cemetery walls. Been let to a wealthy London gentleman for the past two years."

Stevens's voice and remarks were mundane enough, but the effect on Beatty was electric. He executed a dance on the freezing pavement of the concourse to the amazement of his companions.

"I have been incredibly obtuse!" said Beatty, jumping into the cab and slamming the door after him. He looked at Dotterell.

"The big mansion just outside the cemetery wall. Of course! It had to be. It was so simple I could not see it. That is where the tunnel leads! To the cellars of the house beyond the wall. That is why they had to use pit-props, they were burrowing so deep."

There was still some perplexity on Lestrade's face as Beatty went on. Toby Stevens was on the box of the cab now, and the horse's hooves were striking a joyful sound from the flags as it picked its way carefully through the murk to the side-gate of the cemetery.

"They needed a secure base, safe from the hue and cry in London. McMurdo's establishment was merely a temporary resting place. And they could not risk the constant coming and going of people and vehicles at the house itself. What simpler than to store the bullion in the coffins, transfer it from the chapel under cover of darkness and through the workings to the cellars of The Firs!"

He thrust his balled fist into the palm of his hand in his enthusiasm, and even Lestrade was moved to comment. He looked at his turnip watch in the dim glow of the sidelamps.

"They will surely have been thoroughly alarmed by tonight's proceedings. And they will know of McMurdo's death by now."

"No matter," Beatty said. "We shall be in time. They will have too much to load if they intend to fly the coop."

He patted his pocket.

"And we have some very persuasive arguments here."

A deep silence descended on the cab for a few minutes. The vehicle was slowing, and Beatty could see the cemetery wall looming up through the mist outside. Stevens got down and the men in the cab heard the chink of metal on metal as he unlocked the gate. Then they were bowling smoothly along the same metalled road Beatty and Dotterell had traversed the night he had so nearly met his death in the lake. He remembered the setting now.

The bizarre circumstances of their mission and the excitement and strain of the past few hours momentarily overcame him, and Beatty felt his head swim. He leaned back against the cushions and closed his eyes, conscious of the swaying of the cab; the circle of watchful faces in the yellow sheen of the sidelamps; the crisp clacking of the cab-horse's shoes on the iron-hard road surface; the chill bulk of the revolver in his pocket.

When he opened his eyes, himself again, mist swirled at the window and Dotterell's eyes were on his. Beatty forced a smile, aware of his assistant's concern. He thought he would remember this evening for the rest of his life. Something of the same feeling must have descended on the four men in the cab, for no one spoke a word until they were nearing their destination. Stevens opened the hatch above them with a thumping creak that made their already strained nerves jump.

"The Firs is just a few hundred yards ahead, gentlemen," he said softly. "I can see lights."

Beatty nodded.

"We will get down here and proceed on foot," he said.

The party descended and paused while Stevens turned the cab and tethered the horse to a bush.

"You are not obliged to come with us," Lestrade told the driver. "If you do, you must keep behind these officers. I cannot be responsible for your safety."

Toby Stevens's grey eyes twinkled beneath his hat-brim.

"*C'est la guerre,*" he muttered, his grey eyes fixed on Beatty. "I am tired of waiting in the cold, sir."

"Come with us, then," said Beatty. "The more the better."

The group had converged now on a narrow lane which led to the lodge-gates of a large mansion. The lake which Beatty had cause to remember was some way behind them, and the road which led to the distant village wound on. The earth of the rutted lane was bound with ice, and hoar-frost glittered like crystals in the dim light. The mist was thinning and they could see that the iron gates that opened to the house driveway were standing ajar. All was darkness in the lodge, but lights shimmered from the main residence beyond.

Dotterell had lit the special dark-lantern in the cab, and now he directed the pencil-beam toward the ground at Beatty's instruction. The young investigator knelt with a grunt of satisfaction. The iron-rimmed wheels of carriages or carts had made heavy indentations in the ice.

"We are on the right track," he whispered to Lestrade.

The five men walked through the lodge-gates without any trace of concealment. It was a large mansion in extensive grounds which now began to reveal itself. Wings spread to left and right with a stable area in which a cart with two horses in the traces stood. Lestrade and Beatty exchanged long glances.

The front door of the house, within its massive portico, stood ajar, and a thin pencil of yellow light from within pierced the swirling whiteness of the fog. Their footsteps crunched on the frozen gravel as they hurried on toward the entrance. Lestrade's revolver was out, and the yellow light glinted on the barrels of the others' weapons as they followed suit.

"Best leave this to us, Mr. Beatty," Lestrade grunted as they ran quickly up the steps.

Beatty nodded. He was just a pace or two behind, with Dotterell on his right, the latter still carrying the case of instruments. He never forgets anything, Beatty thought to himself grimly. They pushed open the front door and went through in a rush. They were in a once handsome hallway with black- and white-tiled paving. A marble staircase spiralled upward into the gloom of the first floor.

A massive gilt chandelier with thousands of lustres glittered chilly in the ceiling, but no light came from it. It was thick with dust, and grime covered the panelling of the hall. The furniture and fittings were damp and mildewed. Lestrade's keen face looked like a terrier's as he glanced about him this way and that, as though he were hot upon the scent.

"An accommodation address only," he said to the remaining detective.

He turned back to Beatty.

"They certainly do not use this for entertaining."

The light in the hall came from four oil lanterns set upon brackets. Their pale golden light shone on the tumble of coffins and lids with silver fittings on the floor in the centre. The detectives were already busy in the heap.

"Quite empty," said the other officer, whose name was Lowell.

His face bore the same look of suppressed excitement as that worn by Lestrade.

"Spread out and search the house," Lestrade ordered. "Lowell and Stevens take the upper floor. We will search down here. If anyone sees anything suspicious, shout and we will be there."

Lowell gave a curt nod. He and Stevens each took a lantern and ascended to the first floor.

Lestrade went over to shut the big main door and shoot the bolts. He smiled wryly at Beatty.

"I am afraid we are already too late."

"Perhaps," Beatty replied. "But they cannot have gone far. I fancy the cellar will yield more interesting data. But we must just make sure here first."

Before they could proceed further there came a dramatic interruption. The portières of a side room parted, and a large fat man with dundreary whiskers erupted from them. He was quivering with rage, and his huge cheeks, of lardlike consistency, wobbled like jellies. He wore a frock-coat with a green baize apron, and he carried in his hands a clawlike instrument used for opening packing cases.

"What is the meaning of this intrusion?" he cried in a high, shrill falsetto, incongruous in a man of his build.

"It means that the game is up!" Lestrade rapped in official tones. "Scotland Yard. Take us to your master."

The man's face expressed bewilderment and he staggered back, dropping the claw with a heavy clatter upon the floor.

"What do the police want here?" he said, all the bluster gone. "Sir Hector McMurdo will be extremely angry when he learns of this."

Beatty smiled.

"I fancy it will not bother him further," he said. "Who might you be?"

"Balsover," the fat man replied, a worried look settling upon his face. "I am the caretaker here."

"Well then, you are in serious trouble, Balsover," said Lestrade sternly, showing him the pistol in his hand. Balsover's eyes opened wide and he started to tremble.

"Where is your master? Quickly, or I will not be responsible for the consequences."

The caretaker turned white. His voice was quivering as he replied.

"I do not rightly know, sir. I believe they are packing to go abroad. I was told to keep my quarters."

"You do little work here at any event," said Lestrade contemptuously, looking with disgust at the filthy state of the rooms. Beatty and Lestrade had quitted the hall now and were leaving Dotterell to continue the search on the ground floor. The measured footsteps of their companions sounded on the ceilings above their head.

"I swear to you, sir, that I have done nothing wrong," the fat man went on piteously, wringing his hands. He looked imploringly from the Inspector to Beatty.

"We shall see in due course," said Lestrade evenly.

He led the way back into the hall as Lowell appeared at the head of the staircase.

"Nothing up here, sir. I do not know about the wings, of course."

Lestrade went to the bottom of the stairs. He looked blankly at the tumbled coffins with their silver fittings lying in the middle of the hall in the dim light of the lanterns.

"Come down."

Beatty and Lestrade waited at the foot of the stairs while the others descended. Dotterell had rejoined them. His lean face was stern beneath the hard hat.

"Nothing of any consequence," he offered to Beatty's mute question.

Lestrade seized the quivering caretaker by the collar and held the pistol barrel in front of his nose.

"Now, my man," he said mildly. "Kindly show us the cellars. I fancy you know a little more about the activities at The Firs than you have so far cared to divulge."

The caretaker opened a massive oaken door at the end of a passage leading off the main hall. Their footsteps echoed hollowly on the broad stone stair as the party wound its way downward. The oil lamps cast flickering shadows. Lestrade had his revolver drawn, and Beatty was close behind him with Dotterell and the others following on.

They made no effort to conceal their presence, and indeed the noise they were making could have been heard a long distance. As though conscious of this Lestrade grunted back over his shoulder, "I cannot imagine that we shall find anything useful here."

"On the contrary, criminal activity and the proof of their crimes," said Beatty enigmatically. "The men who left here tonight in such disorder cannot have gone far with such heavy loads. We must have good reason for pursuing them and for inscribing their names on the warrants you carry."

He smiled over his shoulder at Dotterell.

"And I fancy friend Munson and his party will not relish being locked away in the tunnel."

Even as he spoke Balsover gave a start and stopped, his fat cheeks wobbling like jelly. The men at the foot of the stair now heard for the first time the faint hammering noise that echoed through the arched cellars. Sharp above it came a low moaning noise that set the hair erect on more than one scalp in the company.

"I will go no farther," the caretaker said, attempting to push back up the stairway. "These are very ancient catacombs, part of an older house. There are legends associated with them. And local people speak of ghosts."

Beatty laughed shortly. It sent an uneasy echo round the pillared chamber in which they found themselves.

"A superstition no doubt fostered by your master," he said. "I fancy there is something more tangible than ghosts involved here."

"Stay here with Balsover," Lestrade ordered Stevens. "He must not get away."

Toby Stevens smiled a slow smile. He held up a massive fist.

"He will not get past me, sir," he said with emphasis.

Beatty took the lantern from the caretaker and shone it around the cellar. There was nothing there but dust and debris; old trunks and decayed furniture. But heavy indentations in the dust showed the passage of many feet.

"Your master has had a busy evening," said Lestrade drily.

He led the way forward again. The party walked for about a hundred yards toward a dark Norman archway. More steps led down. Beatty held up the lantern; the pale yellow light showed a worn flight of steps. The moaning sounded again. The noise was so unexpected and had such pain in it that the men hesitating at the top of the stair were momentarily unnerved. Then Beatty leaped downward, bearing the lantern with him.

Its dancing light illuminated another large cellar, older and more massive than the previous. There was a warmth here and an acridity. Lestrade, hastily following, saw heavy machinery, a table, and chairs. But their attention was for the moment centred on the figure lying where it had crawled to the foot of the steps.

"Thank God!" a husky voice called. "Is that you, McMurdo?"

"I am afraid he had an urgent appointment elsewhere," said Beatty coolly, his pistol barrel dipped toward the recumbent figure on the floor. It was that of a tall man in a dark suit, now dusty and indescribably filthy from the debris of the cellar. One leg was doubled under the other in an awkward manner, and as Lestrade went to lift him the tall man gave a piercing howl of pain.

"Don't move him," said Beatty sharply. "It looks as though his leg is broken."

He put the lantern down on a barrel near the foot of the steps. Dotterell and the detective officer had joined them, and a second lamp cast a strong light on the bizarre scene as the party clustered round. The lamplight glimmered on the grey face of a bald man with sandy eyebrows. The brown eyes were clouded with pain as he glanced uncomprehendingly from one to another of the figures bending over him.

"Well, well," said Beatty pleasantly. "Mr. Alasdair Vair. You would have done better to have remained at your City depot."

The bald man's eyes cleared; anger shone in them as he started to struggle up. Lestrade pushed him back none too gently, waving the revolver in his face.

"You will not be going anywhere. You are under arrest."

A renewed banging noise from the corner of the cellar intruded into the silence. Lestrade turned to the remaining plain-clothes officer.

"You had better let Inspector Munson in."

He looked sternly at the sprawled figure before him. Vair licked his lips. He had a sick expression on his face.

"Scotland Yard," said Lestrade shortly. "Your little charade is over. You'd better tell us all you know. It will make things easier for you."

A stream of obscenities came from the bald man's lips. He was halfway on to his feet, holding to the edge of the steps, his weight on his good leg, when restraining hands brought him gently down. The cellar seemed full of people now as Munson's party entered. The little Surrey detective's pipe glowed evenly between his teeth as he calmly took in the scene.

"Your shot was a good one," he told Beatty. "McMurdo is quite dead."

"Dead?" said Vair.

His lips were trembling and he was an ashy colour. "Mr. McMurdo dead?"

"No more than his deserts," said Munson shortly. "He would have killed Mr. Beatty otherwise."

"We'd better get this man upstairs," Lestrade ordered. "We can talk better there."

He caught Sergeant Bassett by the arm.

"There's a fat caretaker called Balsover above, being detained by Stevens. On no account is he to leave the building."

Bassett drew himself up.

"Right, sir."

The two plain-clothes men had got Vair beneath the shoulders. Broken leg dangling, he was slowly eased up the steps. Lestrade and Beatty now turned to an examination of the cellar.

"What do you make of it?"

Beatty shrugged.

"Vair was in too much of a hurry to leave. He slipped on the steps, fell, and broke his leg. The others left him as a liability."

Lestrade snorted, walking across the cellar with one of the lanterns.

"Honour among thieves, eh? What's this?"

He held the lantern high, frowning at the furnace and the heavy metal moulds.

"A foundry for smelting gold," Beatty told him, his eyes dancing with excitement. His eyes met Dotterell's in quiet satisfaction.

"The Firs has been prepared for these operations for a long time. They had to clear out in a hurry. They had a great deal to carry, which is why I am confident they cannot have gone far."

He followed Lestrade over to the door through which Munson's party had come. The pale lamplight shone on the corpse of McMurdo and the body of Cronk sprawled among the flowers. Even Lestrade's iron nerves were shaken.

"Good Lord!" he said. "What a business. I hope we are able to explain everything satisfactorily."

"We shall be when we catch up with the gold," Beatty said.

He led the way back through into the cellar with the smelting equipment.

"I wondered why they needed the sink in the workings," he told Lestrade. "They would have to wash their hands after their tunnelling operations. It would not do to emerge in the house looking like miners."

He said nothing further in reply to Lestrade's puzzled look but glanced up to the top of the steps where Vair's helpless form was being eased through the archway, watched by Sergeant Bassett.

"We shall have time for explanations afterwards. It is vital now to discover the route by which the gold has gone. We shall need Stevens's local knowledge for that."

They quitted the cellar, easing past the helpless form of Vair. His smouldering eyes sought Beatty's face.

"I have you to thank for this."

Beatty smiled a slow smile.

"That will be something to reflect upon during the long evenings in your cell."

Vair made a strangled noise deep in his throat and lunged at Beatty. He slumped back with a groan of pain as his injured leg touched the ground. Toby Stevens saluted as Beatty and Lestrade came up. He looked reflectively at the fat man sitting on the steps, his head buried in his hands.

"I think he knows more than he admits, sir," he told Lestrade.

The Scotland Yard man nodded. He seemed abstracted and ill at ease; almost irritated at Beatty's casual manner. But the young investigator had carefully thought out the plan of operation by now.

He led the way upstairs into the hall. When the party were all present, Lestrade gave his orders. The two detective constables would remain to attend the prisoners, while the other six would take cab with Stevens. Lestrade looked at the sullen face of Balsover.

"How long since the party left this house? Answer truthfully or it will go worse for you."

Balsover hesitated, but one look at the steely eyes of the detective officers surrounding him was enough.

"About twenty minutes before your arrival," he said.

Lestrade cast a triumphant look at Beatty. He consulted his watch.

"Forty minutes in all. We shall have to hurry."

Beatty nodded.

"'They cannot travel fast with the loads they were transporting."

He caught Toby Stevens by the sleeve and drew him out to the porch. The mist was lifting a little now, and moonlight was beginning to silver the foliage of the surrounding trees. He pointed toward the lodge-gates.

"What is out there?"

"Just the village," Stevens said. "They could only have gone that way."

Beatty had to agree. The party could not have gone in the Woking direction or they would have seen or heard something of them.

"How far is it?"

"About seven miles," Stevens said. "There is a level-crossing where the railway line crosses the road near the village."

"Nothing else?"

Stevens hesitated. Lestrade and Dotterell had joined them on the porch, with the burly forms of Sergeant Bassett and the constable behind.

"There is a lane leads off, but it is muddy and rutted, besides being uphill all the way. I do not think anyone with heavy loads would use it."

"Nevertheless, we must bear it in mind," Beatty said. "Let us know just as soon as we reach it. In the meantime we need to make our best speed."

A few moments later the party had climbed into the cab with yellow door-panels, and Stevens was coaxing the rested horse through the gates of The Firs and along the lonely road at a fast pace.

41

UNMASKED

BEATTY sat on the box next to Stevens and frowningly studied the road. Despite the load the chestnut was maintaining a fine pace, and the hedgerows whirled past at a satisfying speed through the swirling mist. The moon was a little stronger now, but it was obvious that Stevens, apart from being a highly skilled driver, knew every curve and bend of the way. It was, if anything, even colder, and from far off came the harsh shrieking cry of some night bird.

They had been travelling several minutes and there had been no sign or sound of the men they were seeking; but then they could hardly expect that. They had a fair start though the speed of the pursuers would soon begin to decrease the distance between them. There had been no side turns as yet, and hereabouts the road wound steeply downward, between dark woods.

It was a grim and depressing place, and Beatty was glad when, after a little while, the road levelled off and they began climbing upwards again. Stevens slackened the horse to a walk to rest him, and Beatty took the opportunity to get down. He flitted about at the edge of the road, his eyes missing nothing. Once he gave an exclamation and Stevens stopped the cab at his gestured order. Lestrade's sharp features appeared at the window and he joined Beatty at the roadside. The two men knelt, and Beatty pointed to the deep rut cut into the icy turf by an iron-rimmed wheel.

"That was done recently," Beatty said. "And made by a heavily laden vehicle."

He got up, his eyes shining.

"They cannot be all that far ahead."

Lestrade said nothing but jumped back into the cab as Beatty reascended to the box. He pointed to the woodland which came down closely to within a few yards of both sides of the road.

"You are sure there is no place they could turn off into the woods?"

Stevens shook his head. His grey eyes were serious as he looked at his companion.

"They could do, Mr. Beatty," he said dubiously. "But there would be no point. There is nowhere to go. And these woods are a blind-alley."

He pointed with his whip.

"There is steep hillside where the woodland ends."

Beatty shook his head.

"Nevertheless, we must keep a sharp lookout. They might take shelter off the road temporarily to throw us off the scent."

"Are we looking for one vehicle or more than one?"

"One only, I think," said Beatty slowly. "The other material would have been moved long ago."

Toby Stevens focused his grey eyes on Beatty's face and pursed his lips but kept his own counsel. They were slowly going downhill again now, the mist creeping to meet them like an inland sea. Once again the outlines of the bare-branched trees were wavering and insubstantial, and the light of the moon began to fade. Beatty looked anxiously at his watch. Another ten minutes had gone by before he spoke again. This time it was Lestrade banging upon the interior hatch. His sharp face looked up at them from the gloom of the interior.

"We should be seeing something of them before now, Mr. Beatty. Ought we to cast about?"

Beatty clenched his jaw.

"I am certain we are right," he said. "We have only to bear on. In ten minutes more we should be up with them. The heavy ruts in the grass indicate that they cannot move fast. Their greed may prove their undoing."

"Let us hope that you are right," Lestrade said.

The trap snapped shut again and Beatty was left to his own reflections; the sharp beat of the horse's hooves on the flinty road; the creak of harness; the dark surface winding away through the night; the icy cold and the mist, which caught at the throat and made vision difficult.

Fortunately it was intermittent; one moment it would be laid like swathes of filmy lace across the view before them; a few seconds later, as though cleared by an invisible sponge, the way would be evident. Beatty searched long and anxiously the twisting route ahead; he was troubled within though outwardly calm. Lestrade's words weighed more heavily upon him than he cared to admit.

It was a burdensome responsibility he had laid upon himself; the bullion he was so sure was there somewhere ahead of him might be worth an untold amount of money. If he had led Scotland Yard in the wrong direction and the men they sought escaped . . . He made a sharp clicking noise with his teeth so that Stevens eyed him curiously; it did not bear thinking about. He was relieved when a thin wailing whistle from far ahead broke the monotony of the drive.

He looked at his watch again. It was just drawing close to eleven; it seemed more like days than hours since they had come to Woking that afternoon. Stevens had brightened at the railway whistle.

"The station is up yonder just beyond the village," he said. "We have only another mile or two to go."

He broke off and consulted his own watch.

"That will be the midnight goods getting up steam. . . ."

Beatty had the alert look back on his face now, and the uncertainty had dropped away from him. He caught Stevens by the arm.

"Stop the cab a moment," he said urgently.

He was down off the box before the vehicle had stopped. He stooped, putting his ear to the frozen surface of the road, aware of the irritated face of Lestrade at the window. At first he was not certain, but then his conviction grew. He put up a hand to Stevens for silence, bending closer to the road surface. Faint and far away but clear and distinct in the frosty air he could hear the beat of hooves and the low muted rumble of a heavy vehicle.

"They are not more than a mile off!" he announced to Lestrade.

He vaulted back to Stevens's side even as the whip cracked over the chestnut's head.

"And now, Stevens, your best pace, if you please."

The cab lurched and jolted from side to side and the cold air stung Beatty's face as he clung to the box, barely conscious of the grim profile of Toby Stevens bent over the ribbons. They were going downhill in the mist at a dangerous pace; Beatty could see dark tree-roots all about them, and he could hear noises indicative of alarm from within the cab interior.

That would be Lestrade grumbling again; his face relaxed very slightly as he thought of the Inspector's discomfiture. He checked his revolver, holding on with one hand to the icy rail at his side.

His breath came fast and his eyes were raking the dim wood-lands about them, noting every aspect of the broken verges. He was no longer conscious of the biting cold or the numbness of his hand. Stevens bent to his work, his open face set and serious beneath the hard rim of his hat. He handled the reins in masterly fashion, and the strong chestnut was as sure-footed as his master was skilful.

In a very few minutes more they were breasting a long rise, the horse reined back to save his wind. The mist was lifting and the road stretched clear before them. Beatty gave an exultant exclamation as he caught sight of the dark bulk of a heavy waggon drawn by several horses about a quarter of a mile ahead. He rapped on the trap to draw Lestrade's attention.

"Here are our men, I fancy. We shall be upon them in three minutes."

He turned to Stevens.

"You had best stop a little way back. They are violent men and most likely armed."

"I am not afraid of danger, sir," said Stevens with set lips.

"I know that," Beatty replied. "But if shots are exchanged, it will be difficult to look out for the safety of you and your horse."

Stevens's eyes widened as though he had not thought of the latter possibility.

"That's a different matter, Mr. Beatty. The horse is my livelihood. And my friend."

He made an affectionate movement of the reins and drew the chestnut back to a less hectic pace. Beatty could now see that the vehicle ahead of them was on the verge; several men were clustered about it, trying to free its wheels from the icy ruts in the soil of the roadside. There were four horses harnessed to the tall unwieldy van, and the cloaked figure of the driver was cracking the whip vigorously.

There was a concentration of effort as the cab came up and the vehicle suddenly lurched back on to the road. The men who had been shouldering the work at the rear axle dispersed into the interior, and the horses broke into a trot as the equipage started off again. The train whistle sounded from ahead as Lestrade's features appeared in the opening of the trap.

"We are just overtaking them," Beatty whispered. "Stand ready for my signal."

The hatch dropped again and Stevens drew the chestnut back to a walk; the rumbling of the heavy vehicle ahead of them was loud in the ears. It was only a few yards away, the driver hunched incuriously over the reins. Beatty's first feeling was one of disappointment. The feeble light of the moon shone on the monogram V.R. on the side of the big pantechniconlike vehicle.

"It looks like a mail-van," said Stevens dubiously.

Beatty kept his own counsel, but doubt was edging at his mind. He took his hand off the cab rail and put his revolver back in his right-hand pocket, keeping his fingers round the butt. They were level with the other vehicle now, and Beatty hailed the driver of the mail-van. He was a big heavily muffled figure who looked annoyed at being stopped. He was no doubt on his way to catch the train at the station ahead and late already. But he reined in obediently enough and waited for Beatty to get down from the cab.

Boots grated on the icy roadway and the damp smell of the woodlands drifted to the road-edge, thick and cloying, as Beatty walked over to the van. Lestrade, Dotterell, and Bassett were down and stood in a thick cluster midway between Stevens's cab and the large vehicle which towered over Beatty.

"We are looking for a waggon travelling toward the village," said Beatty, staring up at the mail-van driver. "It would have been going fast and within the last half-hour."

The driver nodded his head grimly. He spat reflectively.

"Aye," he said dourly. "Not ten minutes since. A large dray so badly driven it put us in the ditch. I would like to catch up with it."

"That would be it!" Lestrade said exultantly. "We have no time to lose!"

The Scotland Yard man had joined Beatty now, and the latter's brown eyes had a strange look as he stared past Lestrade to the mail-van driver.

"Even so, I must detain you a while further," he said.

For the first time the driver's voice displayed a slight agitation.

"I have no time to waste here," he said sullenly. "I have to catch the train. This is government business."

Beatty said nothing for a moment but looked reflectively at the driver. At his subtle gesture Lestrade stationed himself near the head of the lead horse while the others drew closer. Munson and the constable had also descended from the cab while Stevens remained on the driving seat.

Beatty walked slowly round the rear of the mail-van in the

thinning mist. He found the tall form of Dotterell already before him. His assistant was in process of trying the handle of the heavy doors; he found them locked. He shot Beatty a warning glance. The investigator nodded and walked on, noting every detail of the vehicle as he circled it. He was now up alongside the driver again, who sat impatiently, the whip dangling from his hand, as though eager to be off.

Beatty studied him carefully; he was a middle-aged, florid-faced man with a hard-hat jammed down over his eyes, leaving the upper part of his face in darkness. He wore a heavy caped driving jacket of a bottle-green shade, and his large hands were encased in thick gloves. He appeared to be bearded, but it was difficult to make out his features clearly as his coat collar was turned up above his ears and a thick woollen scarf concealed the lower part of his face.

"Thank you for your assistance," said Beatty mildly.

He pointed away in the direction of the station.

"If you could just direct me to the village I would be obliged."

The driver bent down, his hand extended, when Beatty did an astonishing thing. He jumped up on to the wheel of the van and with two quick, convulsive movements knocked off the driver's hat and dragged the scarf down from the lower part of the jaw. He found himself looking into the distorted features of Sir Inigo Walton.

42

RACE FOR LIFE

Sir Inigo turned a face like yellow clay back over his shoulder. He shouted a hoarse obscenity. The back of his hand came round in a sweeping arc, knocking Beatty to the ground. At the same instant the whip sang over the heads of the horses, cracked about Lestrade's ears. The Scotland Yard man ducked as the lead horse plunged and then the whole equipage thundered forward, Walton standing up on the box, whipping the team on.

By the time Beatty and Lestrade had picked themselves up, the mail-van was careering at a mad pace down the road and already disappearing round the first bend.

"Quickly!" panted Lestrade.

His sallow face was flushed with triumph. There was a momentary tangle of arms and legs in the cab doorway as Dotterell and Sergeant Bassett met head on. The detective constable ran around to the other side and threw open the door for Lestrade and Munson. Toby Stevens was impatiently restraining the chestnut. The thundering rumble of the mail-van echoed back through the mist, magnified by the dark tunnel of trees.

Then Stevens had given the chestnut its head and the cab bounced in pursuit, rocking from side to side as the driver made the whip sing through the air. Beatty felt the icy rail on the cab-top sear his hand as he was wrenched sideways with the force of their motion. Then he had recovered himself, throwing off the safety-catch of his revolver as he peered grimly ahead in the direction which Walton's vehicle had taken.

The remainder of the drive was a blur of impressions to be recollected diversely over the years by all those who took part. The man in front of them must have been driving at maniacal speed, heedless of his own safety or that of the horses, for there was no sign of the vehicle as Stevens rounded the first bend. But the iron-shod wheels were making tremendous noise, and it was clear to Beatty that they must soon pull up and that their quarry was only a bend or so away. It was a miracle that even four horses could have kept up such a pace with the heavy load, and the gradient here was slightly uphill.

Then the cab was rocking round the second S-bend and the men on the box had a clear view of the quarry. Beatty leaned forward and put a shot into the air. The crack was almost immediately lost in the thunder of hooves on the icy road surface, but a bright yellow flame from the muzzle split the semidarkness. This signal was answered almost immediately by the slap of a second shot from the mail-van.

It could not have been Walton for he was lying forward across the backs of the labouring horses, plying the long driving whip; but Beatty felt the bullet whistle past a short distance away and chop twigs from the trees. The shooting was too accurate for comfort and he felt instant apprehension, but one look at Stevens's calm face set his doubts at rest. Their driver would not fail them; Beatty was certain of that.

It would be tragic if through accident or lack of fortitude they lost their men now. Beatty strained his eyes through the mist and gloom to where the heavy van with its four horses was striking bright sparks from the roadway. The shot must have come from inside the vehicle; either the rear-door was open or one of the men inside was firing through a ventilation slot. Whoever it was, he had a firm purchase and a steady platform to give him a better aim than Beatty was able to command.

"Can you get over on to the grass?" Beatty asked, pointing with the hand holding the revolver. Stevens looked dubious but nodded. The next moment he had turned the horse and they were bouncing along the frozen turf that edged the road. Stevens had checked the chestnut's speed, but even so it would be a rough ride for Lestrade and the other passengers.

But the advantage was immediately apparent. Beatty now had the clear silhouette of the mail-van against the white pallor of the road, whereas they themselves were at an oblique angle to the men in the van interior. Moreover, they were in the deep shadow of the thick woodland which came down almost to the road at this point and would make an almost impossible target. Beatty was deeply concerned that the horse should not be hit. Even if the animal were wounded, it would put paid to their chances of overtaking their quarry.

The high fluting sound of the train whistle echoed again, cutting through the rapidly thinning mist. Beatty had the revolver up, looking for the right opportunity. He was loath to shoot to hit someone, though he knew the men in the mail-van would have no compunction in their own case. Beatty instinctively felt that their cause was lost. He was looking instead for some way of stopping the progress of the vehicle which rocked and lurched alarmingly in front of them.

Twice he raised the muzzle and sighted on the swaying rear wheels; two well-placed shots at the right section of the spokes would do it, but nothing would be more difficult at this speed and under these conditions. Beatty lowered the muzzle and looked at

Stevens's set, concentrated face. He was having difficulty in holding the chestnut. All the horse's instinct was to regain the road, but
the driver had to keep his head turned to remain on the verge.

Beatty could hear noisy thuds and tumbling motions from
inside the cab as Dotterell, Lestrade, Munson, and the detectives
were rattled helplessly about, but he had no time to spare for their
plight. Instead, he put the revolver up for the second time and sent
another shot high and wide.

It roused echoes through the woodland and slowly died away;
there was no response from the men inside the van, but the effect
on the driver was only to intensify his efforts. The whip sang angrily
over the horses' heads, and with flying hooves and manes, nostrils
flared and eyes bolting from their heads, they put their shoulders
into the harness and actually forged ahead for something like a
minute.

Sparks cascaded from the frozen surface of the road as the mail-
van drew away, but it was the last shot in the locker and Walton
knew it as well as Beatty. Nothing made of flesh and blood could
keep up that inhuman pace, and slowly, inexorably, Stevens's chestnut was gaining on the flying mail-van. Beatty lowered the pistol
and held on grimly, critically watching the slowly diminishing gap.

The rumble of the train ahead of them was intensifying; it was
already leaving the station. The first houses of the village could
be dimly glimpsed through the vaporous haze, beyond the point
where the level-crossing bisected the silent road. Whatever happened, the consignment would not reach its destination via the
railway, Beatty thought with satisfaction.

Walton was standing up in the shafts now, the road level and
clear before him, the team picking up a little speed on the straight,
easy gradient. A trail of sparks split the darkness, dying as they
drifted to the ground, then reborn as the engine settled into its
stride. Beatty grunted an exhortation to Stevens, but the little cabman had already seen the danger and was trying to increase the
pace.

Walton hoped to reach the level-crossing before the train
passed; with the delay caused by their vehicle having to wait he
might hope to elude Beatty altogether. Or did he hope, in some
way, to board the moving train itself? It might be; no one could

know what seething thoughts occupied the brain of the man belabouring the horses so cruelly.

Beatty could see the engine now, not a hundred yards from the crossing; another shower of sparks cascaded through the air as the locomotive settled to its work. The mail-van was no more than fifty yards from the crossing, still careering on at what seemed a tremendous pace. There were no gates at the crossing so far as Beatty could see.

It was simply a place where the road cut the railway line at right angles; boards being placed between the rails to assist the carriage of vehicles across the metals. A red lantern on an iron post glowed bloodily through the mist.

"We shall never catch them, Mr. Beatty," said Stevens despairingly.

"We must see," said Beatty steadily. "It will be touch and go for them."

He was roused by the noise of the hatch being raised, and Lestrade's dishevelled head appeared in the opening; at any other time the apparition would have been comic, but the occasion was too serious to warrant attention.

"How do we stand?" said the Scotland Yarder grimly.

Beatty pointed ahead.

"We are gaining on them. There, as you see, is the railway crossing. It will be closely run."

Lestrade grunted, squinting down the road.

"Can you get off the verge?" he asked Stevens. "We shall be shaken to pieces."

The driver looked swiftly at Beatty, who nodded. He had the revolver up as Stevens eased the chestnut on to the smoother surface again. Lestrade looked thankfully at the two men on the box and almost dropped backward out of sight. Beatty smiled in the darkness and concentrated all his attention forward to where the swaying mail-van was drawing close to the red eye of the crossing. The flame and steam of the locomotive off to the left seemed equidistant. It looked a suicidal contest with the two vehicles drawing inexorably together.

As if at a signal, the moon, which had previously been veiled, suddenly burst out from behind a bank of cloud. In a moment the scene before Beatty was clear-bleached and silver white; every blade of grass, every twig held in the grip of hoar-frost, sparkled with an artificial glaze.

The cumbersome mass of the swaying mail-van, the frozen breath of the frenzied horses, the detail of the railway crossing, the mass of the engine itself, now so close to the road, seemed as sharp and precisely delineated as an engraving.

For a brief moment the whole scene seemed arrested as though in some timeless limbo. Then the sharp sounds of harness, the rumble of the wheels of vehicles, the crack of whips, and the brittle impact of hooves, suddenly rushed in on Beatty.

He was conscious of the harsh wind on his face; the rough contact of the freezing air; the biting cold of the rail on which his fingers rested. They whirled through the clear shimmering light at what seemed a fantastic speed. The last shreds of mist cleared away before their passage, and there was the lead horse, snorting and terrified with its forefeet upon the metals.

The great bulk of the engine was only a few yards from the crossing now; the ground trembled and shook, and smoke and steam wreathed the slowly turning pistons. Flame and sparks belched from the funnel and descended in slow-trailing arcs.

Stevens was already reining the chestnut in. There would be no time to stop otherwise. His grim face reflected Beatty's own thoughts. The latter suddenly raised his arm and brought his clenched fist down in a resounding blow on the cab roof.

"They will not do it," he said decisively.

Stevens was applying the brake and the cab was shuddering to a stop. Beatty just had time to notice the figure of Walton, standing erect, lashing at the four-horse team. There was something wrong; the mail-van had tilted at a crazy angle.

"She's jammed on the crossing!" said Stevens in a low, intense voice. "He'll break the shafts."

Even as he spoke, the ungainly bulk of the mail-van slewed sideways on to the engine, now only yards away; there was a loud cracking noise, audible to the two men on the cab roof, even above the hissing of steam. The thin scream was lost in the chaos of boiling vapour, fire, and the tumble of the engine's wheels. Stevens brought the cab to a halt a short distance from the crossing as the mail-van shafts snapped.

The body of the driver, his hands still tangled in the reins, was pulled from the box so swiftly that Beatty hardly saw him go. Sir Inigo Walton was dragged to bloody ruin as the terrified horses plunged on to safety beyond the crossing. Their agitated hoof-beats died in the night. Beatty and Stevens watched in awful fascination as the engine loomed over the stranded van. The driver was applying the brakes, and the metallic screaming was added to those of the trapped men inside the vehicle. Lestrade and the others were down on the road now. The Inspector's face was turned up toward Beatty.

"My God, what a business," he said in an unsteady voice.

The rest of his words were lost in the grinding impact of the collision. Sparks showered from the roadway and the heavy mail-van was thrown across the line, the mass slowly leaving the ground as though the laws of gravity had been momentarily suspended. The engine went ploughing on, throwing up baulks of timber, pieces of metal, and the remains of human beings.

43

THE END OF THE LINE

THE men on the road, their will-power temporarily frozen by the spectacle, their ears ringing with the shouts and screams of trapped men and the crashing and splintering of mangled wood-work, stood immobile, unconscious of anything except the great bulk of the engine which swept inexorably on as it completed its work of destruction.

Beatty somehow found himself on the road; he was still stupe-fied by the spectacle and had no recollection of climbing down from the box. Dotterell was running toward the crossing, his iron nerves quite unaffected. Beatty saw him disappear among the steam and tangled wood and metal as he reached the crossing fence where the blood-red lantern hung.

The engine-driver was reversing the engine; it shook itself like some massive animal, cascading timber and metal from its shoulders, as it slowly backed to where Beatty stood. The driver's face, white and shaking, gazed down at Beatty without saying anything. The hiss of steam made conversation difficult, but Lestrade had already pointed down the line, and Munson and the others were following Dotterell.

Lestrade joined Beatty as he ran on across the metals; one shaft of the van, a shattered stump now, remained sticking upright from between the rails and one of the crossing boards. There were drag-marks in the road and blood; much blood. Lestrade looked at Beatty grimly as they ran. The village was not far. Already, there were lights in the upstairs windows of the cottages. Anxious voices sounded in the still, cold air.

The slap of a shot came over the hiss of escaping steam, small and futile in the immensity of the night. It was immediately answered by another. Lestrade raised his eyebrows in surprise, made as though to turn back.

"Best leave it to them," Beatty said. "Dotterell is a first-rate marksman."

"I am surprised there was anyone left alive," said Lestrade, panting a little from his exertions.

"I told you we were dealing with desperate men," Beatty said. "Durable men too."

He made no further comment until they had turned off the road into the trampled confines of a pasture; a small gate of thin palings had been brushed aside as though it did not exist. The two men hurried forward, following the recognisable trail of drag-marks in the stiff and frozen grass. Lestrade glanced curiously at his companion as they walked.

"You recognised the driver?"

"I did," said Beatty grimly.

"Then who?" Lestrade began.

Beatty put his hand on the other's arm.

"You have only to wait a few more moments now. Then you will realise why you would have thought me mad, had I voiced my suspicions when I asked you to accompany me to Woking."

There was a snorting noise from up ahead. Lestrade and Beatty hurried on. Four horses stood shivering and trembling in a corner

of the field. Beatty went to soothe them while Lestrade stood looking down as though struck dumb. Beatty hobbled the lead horse
with a leather harness strap. He came back to stand by Lestrade.

The bloodied remains of the human being who was inextricably tangled in the leather reins and broken shafting was almost
unrecognisable. Beatty turned him gently over, but it was apparent
that life was quite extinct. The once florid and arrogant features
had been almost erased by the fierce passage across the steel-hard
ground.

"Perhaps it is better so," Beatty murmured, almost to himself.

He looked grimly at Lestrade.

"The driver, as you call him, was Sir Inigo Walton, managing
director of the City and Suburban Bank, one of the most respected
private banking firms in the City of London."

Lestrade looked at him, his jaw hanging slack.

"You cannot be serious, Mr. Beatty."

"I was never more serious," Beatty told him.

He looked around, aware for the first time that people were
stealing through the entrance to the quiet field; villagers aroused
from their sleep by the noise and atmosphere of violence. Lestrade
stepped back, bewilderment on his face.

"I do not begin to understand, Mr. Beatty."

"And this is no place for it," Beatty said crisply. "I myself only
fully realised the truth this evening. Undoubtedly, Walton was on
the train down. It must have been he who recognised me and had
the note passed to the station platform recalling you to London."

"There will be a heavy accounting," Lestrade said dolefully.
"And I hope we shall have all the right answers."

Beatty looked at him shrewdly.

"I think the affair is likely to cover you and Inspector Munson
with glory when the full story comes to be told. There will be time
for explanations later. We must get back to the others."

As he finished speaking there was a wavering in the thin fringe
of people who pressed forward at the field entrance. Sergeant Bassett elbowed his way through, his eyes bright. He glanced briefly at
the thing on the ground and then addressed himself to his superior.

"We have them all, sir. Two dead and one badly injured in the
van. We captured four others who attempted to resist arrest."

He lowered his voice and stepped closer to Lestrade.

"Inspector Munson is getting help in. There is a great quantity of bar-gold scattered up and down the track."

Lestrade's eyes widened. He turned to Beatty, his brisk manner returning.

"Stay here and guard this body for a few minutes, Bassett. I'll send someone to relieve you. Mr. Beatty and I must get back to the crossing."

He led the way across the field at a furious pace. As they neared the knot of villagers who huddled shivering at the edge of the road, he put on his official manner.

"Police business!" he called. "Return to your homes. Everything is in hand."

He turned irritably as a middle-aged man in a thick jersey plucked at his sleeve.

"Constable Turner, sir. The village police officer. I shall have to ask for your credentials."

Lestrade smiled at Beatty.

"Inspector Lestrade of Scotland Yard. Here is my warrant card. We shall need your help, Turner. Come along with me."

The constable saluted, realised it looked ridiculous without his helmet, and changed the gesture to a respectful forehead touching. He fell in alongside the Inspector and Beatty as they hurried back to the crossing. Dotterell materialised out of the engine-steam, smiled crookedly at his employer.

"A not unsatisfactory evening, Mr. Beatty."

He wiped a thin trickle of blood from his forehead.

"A slight argument with one of the men in the van," he explained.

"Are you all right?"

Beatty looked concerned. Dotterell nodded.

"I slipped on the track and caught my head on an iron upright. It is nothing."

Beatty walked along from the crossing, picking his way between shattered woodwork and other debris. Lestrade followed, the village constable at his heels. The Scotland Yard man's eyes glanced across at the humped forms under the rough canvas at the lineside. Groans and cries sounded above the hissing of steam. The driver and firemen of the train were arguing with an official in gold-braid.

The moonlight glinted on the barrel of Munson's revolver as the group of newcomers came up. Several men were slumped in a semicircle. Toby Stevens's eyes were gleaming with excitement as he held his pistol steadily upon them. He touched his nose in the gesture Beatty remembered as he caught sight of him.

"What an evening, sir!" he said. "I wouldn't have missed this for anything."

Munson chuckled.

"A pity you weren't a little younger," he told the cab-driver. "I could use a few of your sort in the Surrey Force."

He turned to Lestrade.

"Your men are guarding the gold, but I fear there are a number of bars still scattered over the track. We'd best gather them up before daylight or there'll be the devil to pay."

Lestrade nodded. He went off to instruct the rest of his men, leaving Beatty and Dotterell. Munson hesitated for a moment.

"The three of us can manage all right if you want to follow Lestrade," said Beatty, tapping his overcoat pocket.

Munson smiled and went off through the thin mist, following the others.

Beatty waited until the glow of his pipe had died away and then turned back to survey the scene before him. It was a wild and bizarre spectacle that stayed with him for a long time to come. As far as the eye could see, debris was strewn along the track; the pair of massive iron-shod wheels of the mail-van, upside down and torn bodily from the coachwork, occupied the foreground. Beyond that masses of ironwork had torn up the ballast at the side of the track and was heaped thickly along the lineside. Mingled among it were wooden boxes, crates, and other articles; and here and there, commonplace items of clothing and once, a boot containing a human foot.

Behind them the engine waited, panting steam like a wounded beast, its lamps glowing dimly through the dark. The guard of the mail train had appeared, and his own voice added to the mumble of the other railmen in the background. Beatty's foot kicked

against something as he went forward; he bent down and eased
the dull-looking mass from the ballast. It was icy cold to the touch
and extremely heavy. He lifted it and carried it over to the lantern
Dotterell had put down on a baulk of timber next the line.

The dull yellow of the bar shimmered in the lamplight. Beatty
made out a number incised in the surface. From force of habit he
drew out his notebook and listed it. He put the ingot down on top
of the baulk of timber. Toby Stevens's eyes were wide as he caught
its significance.

"It doesn't look much, sir, does it?" he observed, gesturing
round at the scene of desolation with his pistol barrel.

"A poor return for all this," said Beatty grimly. "But men have
always died for love of gold. There is no reason to believe they will
do otherwise in the future."

He looked across at the sorry group of men who lay twisted
in pain in the pale circle cast by the lamplight. Then he stepped
forward and stopped in front of one man who sat sullen and
silent apart from the others, nursing his shoulder with the blood-
streaked fingers of his right hand. He wore a coarse-fitting grey
smock, belted at the waist, but despite his dishevelled appearance,
the striped trousers and expensive boots which showed beneath
the skirts of the smock denoted that he was no mere hireling.

The bald head and yellow face shone with perspiration in the
lamplight as he raised haunted eyes to Beatty's own.

"Mr. Connors, is it not?" said Beatty pleasantly. "In charge of
security as I remember. Well, your security was not very effective
this evening."

Connors shrugged closer into his smock and turned his burning glance on to the young man standing over him in the gloom
and smoke of that lineside scene of desolation. Beatty remained
indifferent to the bitter curses heaped upon him.

"You'd best save your breath for your police statement," he said.
"Sir Inigo Walton is dead. So is McMurdo, and Vair is in our custody. Tongues will soon be wagging. We have most of the threads
in our hand, but we need the fine detail. It will go easier with you
if you cooperate."

Connors turned away his head with a violent gesture. Beatty
shrugged and stepped over to Dotterell. The latter looked with

grim amusement at the rueful group sprawled under the watchful eye of Toby Stevens.

"They'll talk soon enough when the time comes," he said contemptuously.

His eyes shone with excitement and enthusiasm as they searched Beatty's face.

"This is the best evening's work I can remember, Mr. Beatty. Allow me to congratulate you. How did you . . ."

Beatty felt suddenly very tired. He gestured his assistant back as he felt a sudden sagging of his legs. He steadied himself against an iron upright which now leaned at a bizarre angle at the lineside. His eyes no longer saw the shattered wreckage, the writhing steam; and even the metallic noises made by the locomotive and the excited shouts of the searching men were dim and distant.

"There will be time for that later," he told his assistant. "We still have much to do before the final story can be told. The gold, for instance. They would need help in high places."

He was still standing there, his eyes lost in the complexity of his thoughts, when Lestrade and his men came back and the long process began of transferring the manacled prisoners to medical care aboard the waiting special at Brookwood.

44

EXPLANATIONS

MUNSON leaned forward and tapped out the ash from his pipe in the tray on the dining table. The lunch had been a good one, and the air was thick with smoke now as the men lit up at Miss Meredith's extended permission. It seemed a large gathering in the elegant first-floor dining room of Beatty's Cheyne Walk house. Beatty himself, as befitted the host, sat at the head of the table, with the girl in a position of honour at his right.

Dotterell sat at his left, his lank hair falling over his eyes, their piercing blue softened and kindly today in the mellow atmosphere engendered by the brandy and cigars. Even Lestrade, seated opposite Munson farther down the circular table, had momentarily lost his perennial air of impending disaster. Only Rossington's bearded face, strong and sensual through the fragrant blue smoke of his cigar, seemed discontented; or so it appeared to Beatty. But perhaps it was only baffled curiosity.

A voluptuous blonde girl, lively and vivacious, sat next to Rossington; the doctor's fiancée Rosalind, who had joined the party at Beatty's insistence. They had already toasted Rossington's engagement twice, and at any moment it looked as though the process might be repeated. Mrs. Grice hovered at the end of the table, gracious and efficient, yet never deferential. Now she came forward to Beatty and murmured softly, "I trust everything is to your liking, Mr. Beatty?"

"Just perfect," said Beatty, giving her a glance of approbation; he noted the faint flush which came to her cheeks and checked her as she was about to withdraw.

"Do sit down and join us, Mrs. Grice. I am sure the company will second me in congratulating you on the excellent lunch we have just enjoyed."

There was a murmur of approval, and Mrs. Grice sank into a vacant chair at the end of the table and smilingly accepted the glass of cognac Rossington gallantly poured for her.

"I have no secrets from Mrs. Grice," Beatty explained. "And I am sure she would be interested to know what has kept me from home so often in late weeks."

There was laughter as Rossington observed that there could be no doubt in Mrs. Grice's mind; looking pointedly at his host and Angela Meredith. Beatty glanced round the smiling faces, his brain heavy with thought.

"It is time," he said. "Will you begin, Inspector, or shall I?"

He was addressing Lestrade, and the little officer shook his head.

"It is true Scotland Yard has learned a great deal in the past two weeks. But I feel the honour should go to you. If you had not got on to this business at Brookwood, we should still be no further forward with the bullion robberies."

"Very well, then," Beatty said, looking round to make sure he had their attention. "As the Inspector says, we have learned much from Scotland Yard's activities this last fortnight. And we now have

an almost complete dossier on one of the most diabolical and ingenious schemes for large-scale robbery that I have ever come across.
Large-scale robbery that led to large-scale murder."

There was no sound in the room now apart from the faint
crackling of the fire.

"The seeds of the affair go back a long way," Beatty continued.
"Some years, in fact. Connors's confession makes that perfectly
clear. It began with Sir Inigo Walton, the managing director of
the City and Suburban Bank. He had got through one vast fortune
with his gambling and dissipated life and had been sequestering the
Bank's funds when his own ran out. By the aid of skilful bookkeep-
ing and the assistance of Connors, another unscrupulous scoundrel,
they managed to avoid disaster. But things obviously could not go
on like that. Walton was desperately looking for a way of replacing
the missing funds when an instrument came to his hand."

Beatty paused and caught Munson's eye. The Surrey detective
leaned forward and poured himself fresh coffee from the pot on
the table in front of him.

"An instrument," their host went on, "in the shape of McMurdo,
a funeral director with establishments in the City and the East End.
He too had his problems. He had expensive tastes and a criminal
record. He had a large overdraft with Sir Inigo's bank and there
was some question of calling it in. He made it his business to seek
out Walton privately—we have this from Connors—and the two
men drifted into intimacy. An unholy alliance was formed. This
took a good deal of time, of course, but eventually a criminal conspiracy evolved which culminated in the biggest bullion robberies
London had ever seen."

"With McMurdo and his associates carrying out the robberies on
the instructions of Walton and his confederates," Lestrade put in.

"Precisely," Munson interjected. "Walton, with his inside
knowledge, knowing exactly what bullion was stored and where
from the confidential bulletins supplied by his fellow-bankers."

"But how does Brookwood come in?" Rossington's fiancée
asked; her blonde head glowed like fire in the lamplight and she
had been attentively listening to the narrative, one pink hand resting affectionately on Rossington's arm.

"That was the masterstroke," Beatty explained. "McMurdo and

Vair already had a long connection there, through their funeral business. To make certain of this end they had to have inside help. They recruited the cemetery Foreman and his assistant and paid them well for their cooperation and silence. These seem to be the only men involved on the Brookwood staff. Superintendent Bateman's astonishment may be imagined when he found police swarming all over his grounds."

Beatty smiled at the memory.

"He was innocent then?" said Angela Meredith, keeping her cornflower blue eyes on Beatty's face. The young detective nodded.

"Dr. Couchman was invaluable there. An unscrupulous man, he was already in Walton's confidence. He was the Bank's official physician and had close contacts with Brookwood through his nursing home and private asylum nearby. As can be imagined, there were frequent funerals from his establishment."

"With legacies of the inmates going to the doctor," said Lestrade grimly. "If ever a man deserved death it was he."

"They thus had three trusted allies at Brookwood," Beatty said. "The doctor and the two chief servants, those in charge of the ground staff. Events moved swiftly after that. Walton took a long lease on The Firs, a house outside the cemetery walls. A tunnel was dug from the cellar, coming up inside a large cemetery outbuilding which was kept locked and which was, in any event, the sole domain of the Foreman and the Under-Foreman."

Beatty paused. He was growing hoarse with talking and reached out for a carafe of water at his elbow. Nobody in the room moved; all sat attentively, as though they feared to miss a word.

"The doctor, of course, kept a sharp eye on the situation at the cemetery and particularly on the two underlings there. When a City robbery occurred, the bullion was transferred to a waiting hearse at dead of night and transported openly to McMurdo's funeral establishment.

"There it was packed in the coffins with silver fittings—so that it could be easily kept under surveillance—loaded on to the funeral train at Waterloo, and shipped to Brookwood under cover of the bona fide funerals."

"A masterstroke," said Rossington, banging a big fist on the table. "How much money was involved?"

Lestrade looked grave.

"It may be as much as two million pounds," he observed. "Our enquiries are still continuing."

"There are a number of things I still don't understand," said Rossington.

Beatty smiled. "Patience, friend John. There is a good deal to tell yet."

He waited until the guests had refilled their coffee cups and cognac glasses, before he went on.

"This was the situation then. The bullion, in the special coffins, was left in a deserted chapel. When the funeral train had left Brookwood, the coffins were taken secretly to the outbuildings, and through the tunnel into the cellar of The Firs, the large mansion Sir Inigo had rented just outside the cemetery walls. Later, the coffins were returned to London for reuse, hidden in a sealed carrier's van, while the gold was smelted down in the cellars."

"Smelted down?" said Angela Meredith, her brow creased in puzzlement.

"It had to be," Lestrade interrupted. "All the bars were numbered and registered, of course. And the Bank of England would have known immediately."

"I still do not see . . ." Angela Meredith said, her eyes fixed on the little detective.

"The gold was cast into fresh ingots in the cellars of The Firs," Lestrade continued. "The bars were then renumbered. Piece by piece, they would be transported by private coach, to find their way into the strong-rooms of the City and Suburban Bank."

Beatty nodded, his eyes bright with excitement.

"It was a brilliant scheme. And it almost succeeded. The bullion would replace the depredations of Sir Inigo and his colleagues, of course. And build up another sterling fortune for the criminals."

"What about the numbering?" asked Rossington.

Lestrade's face was heavy and troubled as he answered.

"This would require registration from within the Bank of England. Someone high up is involved, I fear. So far we have not been able to discover the culprit."

"You see, Miss Meredith," Beatty explained to the girl. "The original gold bars could not simply be transferred to the City and Suburban. They were listed as stolen. There had to be fresh bars with legitimate registration numbers. And to do that they had to have inside help at the Bank of England."

He was silent for a moment, his strong fingers drumming on the table surface in front of him. Dotterell looked at Beatty sharply but kept silent, waiting for him to go on. In the event it was Rossington who again voiced a query.

"Surely the tunnel and all the other arrangements at The Firs would be unnecessary?" he ventured. "Why go to all that trouble? Why not simply take the bullion to the house, rather than risk discovery within the cemetery walls?"

Beatty shook his head, smiling.

"You still have not got the point, John. That was the simplicity and the brilliance of it. Imagine the comment such comings and goings at a deserted mansion would have caused. That would have drawn attention to it immediately, which was the last thing they wanted. A few coffins amid dozens of others at Brookwood, on the contrary, would pass unnoticed; and who would have followed closely one cortège in the cemetery grounds among so many? Brookwood, as the world's largest cemetery, was ideal for their purposes. By this method they could store the gold safely until the hue and cry died down and then transfer it, bar by bar, in hand luggage if necessary."

He turned back to the girl.

"This was the situation which obtained when Miss Meredith called me in. From what we have been able to gather from Connors, there were three Bank directors, including Sir Inigo, who were involved in these crimes. Alone among the other directors Mr. Tredegar Meredith was a fearless and enquiring personality. His honesty was above question and Sir Inigo dare not evoke his curiosity. But by mistake some papers came into Mr. Meredith's hands which aroused his suspicions. Being an open and forthright sort of man, he made his doubts known to Sir Inigo. For that reason he had to be removed."

The girl lowered her face toward the table as Beatty went on so that he was unable to read her expression.

"Sir Inigo could not afford to waste time; he perhaps made some heated remarks to his fellow-director. At all events Mr. Meredith wrote him a letter. That also was indiscreet, but it sealed his fate. Walton summoned Dr. Couchman, who called to see his old friend. Unfortunately, Mr. Meredith was suffering from a chill and the doctor prescribed for him. The treatment included arsenic mixed with the sick man's gruel. Miss Meredith found a half-burnt portion of a draft of the letter in the grate of her father's study, which was why she consulted me. Meanwhile, Dr. Couchman, to conceal his crime, had the markers on Mr. Meredith's grave transposed with that of another body, so that if there were a post-mortem it would not reveal anything untoward. He chose, of course, a body whose owner had died of the same complaints as those given on Mr. Meredith's death certificate."

Beatty put his hand out on the table-top to cover the girl's trembling fingers; she cast him a grateful glance.

"I am sorry to evoke painful memories for Miss Meredith," Beatty went on. "But we are gathered here to discuss the truth today. And the truth is sometimes a painful business. What I cannot understand, is why such an odious creature as the doctor should have been such a close friend of your father's."

The girl's eyes had a strange expression as she raised them to Beatty.

"Human nature is past understanding, Clyde," she said gently. "I myself could never understand. But it stemmed, I believe, from some financial help the doctor was able to give my father in much earlier days when they were both young men."

Beatty shrugged and looked about the circle of faces at the table. Mrs. Grice got up and went round quickly with the liqueur tray. Beatty waited until she had resumed her seat.

"Well, let us leave it at that," he said. "As you say, strange friendships do exist. And with charity, we may perhaps assume, difficult to believe though it is, that Dr. Couchman may have once been other than the odious creature he appeared to us. It was a friendship which cost your father dear, nevertheless. With my being called into the case, several other events rapidly transpired. Walton had to be sure that your father had not left any documents or evidence that might incriminate him or the other directors."

"So he had our house broken into and made to look as though it were an ordinary robbery," said Angela Meredith softly.

"Exactly," said Beatty.

Munson's grey eyes were fixed steadily on Beatty. His pipe made a stippled glow on his cheeks as he puffed out clouds of fragrant smoke.

"What about the limping man?" he said. "We may be a little out of touch in Surrey, but I have not yet heard any report from Scotland Yard. Though his lineside death occurred in my area."

Lestrade smiled thinly.

"A diplomatic clogging of the channels, my dear colleague," he said smoothly. "I have received instructions from above that no written reports on this affair are to be sent out until further orders."

Munson shrugged and sank back in his chair.

"However," Lestrade went on, his eyes gleaming, "I am at liberty to disclose within these walls that the man was a Dutchman, a professional assassin called Dorn, who is wanted for murder and theft in half a dozen Continental countries. I should think Mr. Beatty deserves a testimonial for putting a term to his activities."

"Certainly, I have no conscience in the matter," said Beatty carelessly. "The Brookwood tunnel was well guarded and Dorn was undoubtedly the villain who knocked me unconscious. He would have had my life too, if Dotterell here had not stepped in."

There was a murmur round the table as Beatty explained the situation and Dotterell made a deprecating remark as his employer gave him an approving glance. Miss Meredith had given a hissed intake of breath as the recital came to a close, and her fingers tightened in Beatty's.

"My enquiries at Brookwood caused alarm in some quarters," Beatty went on. "Instead of alerting Superintendent Bateman who was, of course, quite unconscious of the undercurrents at Brookwood, Couchman instead had naturally apprised the Foreman Varley of what was afoot. His caution created despondency and alarm, which aroused my suspicions. Varley's silence had to be ensured. He was an unknown risk, and with another big bullion robbery planned Couchman could not afford to take it. He summoned him to London through the medium of Cronk, the man who ran messages at Woking Station, with what result we have seen."

"That still does not explain Beardsley's death at the Shot Tower," Munson put in.

Beatty leaned forward across the dining table.

"The explanation is not very hard to find. And it has been confirmed by Connors. Walton had undoubtedly been kept apprised of the situation by Couchman so he knew that someone called Clyde Fitzgibbon, an obscure doctor, had called for an autopsy. He was undoubtedly also keeping an eye on Miss Meredith through the man Dorn and his criminal associates.

"At what period he became aware that I was Clyde Beatty, private investigator, I do not know. By that time Couchman himself had been removed from the scene, which must have caused a great deal of consternation among Walton's associates. But I think that we must assume that if Miss Meredith had not offered my services to Walton as an expert on bank security, he would at some stage have approached me for help."

The girl's eyes were wide.

"Then I played into his hands? He was keeping an eye on your investigations while pretending to employ you?"

Beatty nodded.

"Do not blame yourself, Miss Meredith. I did not suspect him myself at that moment. Why should I? But a number of things were building up. Firstly, Beardsley, the Under-Foreman at Brookwood, had been given a letter from me by the man Cronk. It is my guess that he habitually opened them.

"Naturally, neither I nor Inspector Munson knew of Cronk's connection with the events at Brookwood. So when Beardsley left on the London train, Cronk would undoubtedly have reported it. The event was unusual in itself in such a small community. A telegram to Dorn in London would have warned him. Which would have given him time to run down our man at the Shot Tower before he could pass on any incriminating information."

"Why do you suppose Beardsley kept the appointment at all?" said Rossington.

"He had no choice," said Beatty briefly. "He knew the jig was up and was concerned with saving his own neck. He was undoubtedly one of the men who helped to place me on the ice and was therefore guilty of attempted murder. At exactly what point Walton realised I was still alive I am not sure. But when Couchman disappeared, Walton must have been thoroughly alarmed. He kept my office and Miss Meredith's house under surveillance. Dorn and his thugs then attempted to kill or cripple me in the fog and so prevent me taking any further part in activities against them. Similarly, Walton was on the funeral train and sent a message to Inspector Lestrade here to return to London. I was in time to prevent that, and so we were able to stop them transferring the stolen bullion from The Firs. Walton already had samples of my handwriting in the security reports and merely copied the style."

"Why did they kill Cronk?" Rossington asked.

Beatty shook his head.

"Because his usefulness had expired. He had delivered messages to two men, both employed at Brookwood, both of whom died under mysterious circumstances. The police would undoubtedly question everyone in the Woking area who could throw any light on the affair, and Cronk, as a sort of public messenger, would naturally be among them. So McMurdo shot him in the tunnel. We know from Connors that Cronk had read the message I had sent to Beardsley before he delivered it. So McMurdo would know that Beardsley was suspected and that someone in London knew a great deal about Brookwood."

"It must have been a great shock to Sir Inigo when he realised you were alive," Angela Meredith said suddenly.

"Undoubtedly," said Beatty, with a grim smile.

"I am still not sure, Clyde, at what point you realised Sir Inigo was behind this business," said Rossington sardonically.

"I claim no special powers," said Beatty modestly. "At an extremely late stage, I fear. I am a very poor detective."

"On the contrary," said Lestrade, a flush suffusing his sallow features. "You have done brilliantly. Sherlock Holmes himself could not have done better!"

Rossington, puffing out cigar smoke furiously, leaned over the table and fixed Beatty with a baffled stare.

"I only wish I had been in at the kill," he murmured. "I have not yet forgiven you for that. But why, in God's name, should out-

wardly distinguished men like Sir Inigo and his fellow-directors of
a great commercial bank do this highly dangerous criminal work
in person?"

Beatty smiled a slow smile. He looked from the intent face of
Angela Meredith at his side round the circle of absorbed faces in
the silent room.

"The explanation, like most extraordinary things, is quite simple. Secrecy. The more people involved in their operations, the
greater the risk. McMurdo and Vair were in charge of the criminal division. They operated with a picked, small band of criminals
with limited knowledge. They also engaged Dorn, the professional
assassin. But when Vair and McMurdo conducted their funerals
to Brookwood they had their ordinary employees with them, for
whom the funeral was a perfectly normal occasion. They returned
to Waterloo on the special train. After dark the other conspira-
tors took over. In short, Walton and his fellow-directors had to be
their own labourers. The same thing applied to the tunnel digging. Safety dictated it should be so. When Walton realised I had
escaped death in the lake, he had no option but to order Dorn,
through McMurdo, into open attack."

Beatty leaned back and toyed with the stem of his cognac glass.

"Where I was fortunate was in the break in the chain of
command. After I had established a link between McMurdo,
Couchman, and Brookwood, I took a risk by appearing in person
before McMurdo. But he had heard of me only by name; the limping man could have identified me, but he was otherwise engaged
in a different part of the premises. McMurdo inadvertently supplied me with the link for which I had been searching, with the
present happy results for our investigation."

The young man was silent for a moment. The group round the
table stirred as though they had been under a spell.

"There are still a few ends, of course," said Munson diffidently.
"The Bank of England, for example . . ."

Lestrade nodded.

"That will take time. But we are working on it."

He shivered suddenly.

"This has been a bizarre business, Mr. Beatty. Glades of Remembrance, eh . . . You were quite right. If you had told me your

suspicions when we met at Waterloo-road, I should have thought you insane."

Beatty smiled round at the group.

"If you had read my monograph, *Basis for Stasis*, my dear Inspector, you would have realised something of our methods. Those of Dotterell and myself, that is."

The gaunt face of Dotterell expanded into a smile as Lestrade frowned and moved in his chair uncomfortably. He rose awkwardly.

"I had best be going. What time is your train, Inspector? Good-bye, Mr. Beatty, and thank you for the excellent lunch. We have much to do at the Yard. And when the weather breaks we must resume dredging for Couchman's body."

Chairs scraped back as the guests rose. Beatty smiled at Dotterell and took his assistant's hand.

"Thank you again," he said. "Fortunately, we have the weekend before us. I will see you at Holborn on Monday."

Dotterell nodded slowly.

"I will wait outside, Inspector," he said to Munson. "Perhaps we could take a cab together?"

Munson nodded. He came forward to clasp Beatty's hand. His grey eyes were clear and steady as he gazed into Beatty's face.

"As Inspector Lestrade said earlier, it has been a memorable occasion. Shall we be seeing you in Woking again?"

Beatty looked from Angela Meredith to the little Surrey detective.

"I am thinking of starting a branch office there," he said drily. "Yes, we shall be down. You might tell Toby Stevens if you see him that I shall be along shortly, when I hope to make more tangible expression of my appreciation."

"Until then," Munson rejoined. "My turn to be host at the White Horse."

Beatty became aware that Dotterell was lingering at his elbow. His gaunt assistant had a strange smile on his face. He drew him aside into a distant part of the room.

"There is only one thing which has been puzzling me, Mr. Beatty," he whispered. "It was something which occurred right at the beginning of the case. And that is why you should have chosen to travel to Woking via Guildford."

Beatty's eyes were dancing with strange lights as he looked keenly at Dotterell.

"Is there nothing gets past you?" he murmured. "Miss Meredith's only surviving relative, an aunt, lives there. I never begin any investigation, however attractive my client may be, without very good reason. I needed something a little stronger than woman's intuition regarding Miss Meredith's suspicions of Dr. Couchman. The aunt supplied them. She was able to tell me that Couchman had once made indecent advances to Miss Meredith when she was a very young girl. She confided only in her aunt but would not let her father be informed. She never trusted Couchman after that."

Dotterell's face was grim. He nodded slowly.

"I ask you," Beatty went on. "What sort of medical man would behave in that manner? It utterly discredited Couchman in my eyes from the beginning and made me resolve to investigate the case with the utmost vigour. And who knows, the unlawful desire of a man of fifty for a girl of fifteen might even have prompted Couchman's friendship with Tredegar Meredith in earlier years. Who can say? As Miss Meredith herself observed, human nature is a strange thing. I had the aunt's story in confidence, and I must request you to keep the same."

Dotterell nodded again. "You may rely on me, Mr. Beatty."

Beatty smiled and put his hand on his assistant's arm.

"I relied on you not to overlook the point. I was not disappointed."

He stood immobile as the tall form of his assistant melted through the far door.

Mrs. Grice had started to clear the table. Only Rossington and his fiancée Rosalind lingered. Angela Meredith and Beatty walked down to the end of the table to join them.

"Will you stay on for a game of cards?" Beatty asked.

Rossington got up and looked at the leafless trees outside the window.

"I think not, Clyde," he said gravely. "We both doubtless have much to do."

His glance was innocent of guile, but one eyelid drooped almost imperceptibly, unnoticed by the two ladies, who were engaged in praising each other's taste in dress.

"But remember," he added. "You are both engaged to dine with us tomorrow evening."

"We will be there," Beatty promised him.

He and Angela Meredith stood silently as Mrs. Grice closed the door behind the last of the visitors. Then they moved, as though by instinct, more closely together.

45

EPILOGUE

THE day was dying outside the windows. The table had long been cleared, and the fire blazed cheerfully in the hearth. They had been quiet for the last half-hour. Angela Meredith leaned forward and looked into the flickering flames. Her breast rose and fell almost imperceptibly, but there was a faint flush on her cheeks that was not entirely due to the warmth or the reflection of the firelight.

Beatty got up abruptly as though the heat of the fire were too much for him. He went to stand near the window looking at a porcelain cabinet as though he had not noticed its contents before. Then he crossed to the mantelpiece. Shadows fled before him as he turned up one of the gas-jets. The girl moved as if the sudden light had startled her. Her eyes studied Beatty's face anxiously. She was the first to break the silence.

"I am more grateful than I can ever convey, Clyde," she began. "I mean, what you have done for me and the memory of my father . . ."

"It was little enough," Beatty said casually, turning back toward the window.

Angela Meredith bit her lip.

"On the contrary, it was everything," she said.

She got up too and went to stand near him. There was a tension in her body, and her hands, unconsciously, were clenching and unclenching as they had on that seemingly long-ago occasion when she had first come to Beatty's Holborn office.

"I have not yet received your account."

Beatty made a slight gesture with his shoulder as though he

were irritated. She could not see his face, which was reflected merely as a pale oval in the window glass.

"There will be time enough for that," he said carelessly.

Angela Meredith's face lightened.

"Will there?" she said in a tone so low that Beatty could not have heard it. At least he gave no sign of doing so. Instead, he moved closer to the window, pulling back the thick red curtain to give himself a clearer view.

"By God, it is snowing at last," he said. "At least it will be warmer after this."

Now it was the girl's turn to be irritated. But she said nothing further, merely moved to stand beside him, looking out over the tree-tops to the dusky Embankment where the heavy white flakes whirled against the paler background of the icy Thames. She smiled faintly.

"Will there, Clyde?" she said again.

Beatty frowned. He turned his gaze from the window.

"Will there what?"

The question was a genuine one.

"Be time enough," she said softly.

Beatty smiled.

"You know there will, Angela."

He put his arm round her and they were suddenly fused together. He could feel her body trembling through the fur-trimmed pelisse.

"Not in front of the window," she breathed.

"Of course not," said Beatty absently, recollecting himself. He turned to the curtains, was suddenly arrested. There was something about the curious, rigid pose of his body that caught her attention.

"What is it, Clyde?"

"There!" said Beatty, his voice ringing out loud and clear. She followed his stiffly pointing finger. The gas-lamps bloomed along the Embankment now, giving an unearthly beauty to the drifting flakes of snow. Against them, clear-cut like silhouettes in a child's scrapbook, were the profiles of two men. Even Angela Meredith could not mistake them.

They were walking quickly along the Embankment in the direction of Chelsea Bridge, a chain of sparks from the thickly smoking pipe of the first man dancing through the lamplight. The lean, angular figure in the thick ulster was surmounted by a flapped deerstalker cap.

The hawklike face with its keen, alert expression was clearly seen under the street lamp now. The first man passed on, leaving a more portly figure labouring protestingly in the rear. The second man had a thick moustache and carried a shabby-looking medical bag.

Beatty's voice echoed through the silent room.

"There goes the world's greatest private consulting detective!"

He drew the girl close to him, and they stood there at the window until the two rapidly receding figures had faded in the dusk.

MORE NEW TITLES FROM VALANCOURT BOOKS

MICHAEL ARLEN	Hell! said the Duchess
FRANK BAKER	The Birds
CHARLES BEAUMONT	The Hunger and Other Stories
DAVID BENEDICTUS	The Fourth of June
SIR CHARLES BIRKIN	The Smell of Evil
JOHN BLACKBURN	A Scent of New-Mown Hay
	Nothing But the Night
	Bury Him Darkly
THOMAS BLACKBURN	The Feast of the Wolf
JOHN BRAINE	Room at the Top
	The Vodi
BASIL COPPER	The Great White Space
BARRY ENGLAND	Figures in a Landscape
RONALD FRASER	Flower Phantoms
STEPHEN GILBERT	Ratman's Notebooks
STEPHEN GREGORY	The Cormorant
THOMAS HINDE	The Day the Call Came
CLAUDE HOUGHTON	I Am Jonathan Scrivener
GERALD KERSH	Nightshade and Damnations
FRANCIS KING	An Air That Kills
C.H.B. KITCHIN	Ten Pollitt Place
HILDA LEWIS	The Witch and the Priest
MICHAEL McDOWELL	The Amulet
OLIVER ONIONS	The Hand of Kornelius Voyt
J.B. PRIESTLEY	Benighted
	The Other Place
PIERS PAUL READ	Monk Dawson
FORREST REID	Following Darkness
ANDREW SINCLAIR	The Raker
	The Facts in the Case of E.A. Poe
DAVID STOREY	Radcliffe
RUSSELL THORNDIKE	The Master of the Macabre
JOHN WAIN	Hurry on Down
	The Smaller Sky
KEITH WATERHOUSE	There is a Happy Land
	Billy Liar
COLIN WILSON	Ritual in the Dark
	Man Without a Shadow
	The Philosopher's Stone
	The God of the Labyrinth

Printed in February 2023
by Rotomail Italia S.p.A., Vignate (MI) - Italy